Marika

Other Novels by Darwin Porter

Butterflies in Heat

Marika

DARWIN PORTER

ARBOR HOUSE
New York

To Stanley Haggart

Prologue

The elephant-brown Rolls-Royce pulled up on the field at New York's Kennedy Airport, two motorcycle policemen flanking it like sentinels, to meet the plane from Zurich. The slight drizzle of early morning had given way to a heavy downpour in this dreary, gray day in late November.

In the back of the car, Marika sat quietly, smoking a long cigarette, her thoughts as clouded as the afternoon. Earlier this morning, she'd been tempted to flee New York altogether. To hell with the celebration tonight.

On an impulse, she'd cabled her young cousin the money to fly here. The girl had been writing to her faithfully since she was eight years old, pouring out impassioned letters for more than a decade, her fantasies so similar to her own at that age. Marika rarely felt a responsibility for others, but she'd convinced herself she had to prevent the girl from making the same mistakes she had made. When the letter arrived detailing the anguish of a broken love affair, Marika was so touched by her desperation that she'd hastily agreed to let her come to America.

But now she wasn't so sure. It had been longer than she could remember since anyone had intruded upon her privacy. After sending the cable, she'd begun to fear the invasion. What would it be like living with someone else in the apartment after all these years?

Marika's heart beat faster as she watched the girl run toward her car through the rain. As her cousin's face came into view, Marika gasped in astonishment.

Heidi Schulz was a young Marika!

Her mouth was fuller, more girlish, but her eyes were just as luminous. Even when running, her manner was assured. She commanded attention.

With a rush of emotion, Marika enclosed Heidi in her arms. She'd dreamed about this moment for years, but had been too afraid to bring it about. She held onto the girl so long and so desperately she was suddenly aware that her nails were digging into her young cousin's back. Marika quickly withdrew, adjusting her hair.

"I don't believe it's really you," Heidi said, in a slightly husky voice. Her English was good, but she still spoke with an accent.

"I'm not a phantom after all," Marika said. "Despite what some critics say." Slowly she drank in the image of the girl: her pale skin, white-blonde hair, and ice-blue eyes. It was intoxicating. She became aware that she was staring too intently, and paused to reach for another cigarette.

"You're very real!" Heidi said. She was staring at Marika with the same intensity.

"You look amazingly like me when I was your age," Marika said. "Maybe you're more me now than I am."

"You talk funny," Heidi said, reaching for Marika's gloved hand and pressing it against her cheek. "No one will ever replace you."

A wry smile crossed Marika's lips, as Heidi's statement registered. "I think I used that exact line on someone once."

At Customs, Heidi's passport was stamped with more than the usual dispatch.

"It's incredible the attention we're getting," Heidi said. "You must be the most important person in New York."

"Only for today," Marika said bitterly crushing out her cigarette. "I don't usually get this kind of treatment. But the mayor has officially proclaimed this horrible, ugly Tuesday *my* day."

After Customs, Heidi settled back into the car again, but suddenly the door opened and a flashbulb went off. Marika's hands instinctively rose to cover her face, but it was too late. She'd been snapped in an unguarded moment.

"You silly man!" she shouted at the photographer. "The world's greatest photographers have taken my picture. Is it so important to your ego to have your own stupid little picture?"

The man's face was surly. "I get paid!" he said. "That's reason enough. I'm not going to frame it and put it over my bed—if that's what you mean."

"Get out of my sight!" she yelled.

Her driver pulled the photographer back. The door shut, she put her hand to her face, knowing already what the picture would look like on tomorrow's front page. "I want to be remembered for what I was," she said, almost in a whisper. "Not for what I've become."

On the way into New York, Marika tried to calm down. If she couldn't get a tight hold on her nerves, she'd be in no shape to face the crowd at the Waldorf-Astoria tonight. They'd be taking pictures there, all right. She knew the photographers were no longer interested in depicting her as the world's most beautiful woman. More as a living fossil, she thought bitterly.

Sinking deep into her seat, she clutched her thoughts tighter around her, occasionally looking into Heidi's eyes, finding them as impenetrable as her own—and filled with just as much impatience. Heidi, it was clear, was desperate to begin the act of living. Her letters reflected a gargantuan appetite for experience, an electric energy. Marika herself began to feel the tingle of excitement. Nothing had moved her to tears or laughter in years.

"Vienna's so dead compared to New York," Heidi said.

"How can you say that?" Marika asked. "We haven't even reached New York."

"But I can just *feel* it," Heidi answered.

Marika turned to look at her. "Yes," she said, "you're right. Long ago Vienna could have contained you. In my day, it could have. But not now." She reached for the girl's hand again.

"I'm here," Heidi said. "I'll forget all about Vienna and that dreadful Otto."

"The best way to get rid of an old love," Marika said, "is to burn him out with a new one."

"I know." The way Heidi said those words sent a sudden chill

· 3 ·

through Marika. Heidi seemed far older than her years.

"What do you want to do in New York?" Marika asked.

Heidi turned in her seat to face Marika. "Be just like you. Live the kind of life you did."

Marika raised her head, astonished. "That's impossible," she said. "My life was dictated by the times. Those times are now vague memories—and very painful ones. The old lessons still hold true. The only trouble is, I never learned mine well."

"But you're famous!" Heidi said, her eyes lighting up. "Everything about you seems enchanting. I know . . . about the . . . the bad things, too."

Marika was startled, not by the words, but by the way the girl's eyes sparkled at her. Yes, she was excited now, trying to allure, but once that was accomplished, those eyes would become cold and distant again.

"You've had such a glamorous life," Heidi went on, growing even more enthusiastic.

"That's not true!" Marika replied sharply. "I've been the victim of every lie and distortion imaginable. My dreams have become so deformed, I no longer recognize them." She moistened her lips with the tip of her ancient tongue. In the shadows of the afternoon, her mouth had a savagery to it, her crimson lip-sheen glowed. She stared straight at Heidi. "No one told me when I was your age that much of what we want, or think we want, is only to be dreamed. Not experienced or fulfilled."

But Heidi was no longer listening. She was almost bouncing in her seat, her eyes eagerly searching for something in the industrial landscape to hold her interest. All she heard was the voice inside herself. Marika sighed.

At the approach to the city, neon lights picked up Marika's shimmering silvery blonde hair and danced across the lines of her tired face, making her features translucent, almost ethereal. The chauffeur had flicked off the windshield wipers, but the mist made him turn them on again.

"I can't wait to meet all your friends," Heidi said.

"My friends are few," Marika answered. "They've drifted away or died. I live alone. A very quiet life."

"We'll change all that," Heidi said calmly. "We've got to open you up again."

Marika's eyes were only now becoming accustomed to Heidi's startling resemblance. She was beautiful. A pure beauty. Marika could see glimpses of her own distorted face in the car mirror. She wanted to go back. To exchange places with this young girl. To do it all again—but differently.

"I imagine you know all sorts of exciting people," Heidi said. "You're just not admitting it."

"I know people," Marika replied flatly. The girl's spirit was like something alive that could be caught in one's hand. For one brief moment, Marika found herself eager for the changes Heidi had promised to bring about in her life. She needed someone to take charge. She herself was thoroughly drained, bereft of ideas about how to live.

"If you have so few friends," Heidi said, "what do you do for excitement?"

At first Marika was tempted to brush off the question. Excitement, indeed! But she decided to answer it honestly. "I love to watch the morning sun come up. It casts rays through a panel of stained glass in my bedroom. I can sit there for hours, just drinking my coffee and watching the patterns reflected on the carpet." She noticed the overwhelming boredom creeping over Heidi's face. "When you've had everything, you go back to the simple things."

The rain lashed the car, and Marika feared she'd never be able to control Heidi. It was clear the girl would only believe what she wanted to, and it would be hard to shake her out of her stubbornness.

As the car approached Marika's penthouse apartment on Park Avenue, the traffic got thicker.

"I'll never go back to Vienna," Heidi said. "I just love it here already. So many people, so much happening. I can understand why you decided to settle in New York after all the places you've been."

"I came to New York because I had pain," Marika said. "And I didn't want to be reminded of it. New York is totally indifferent to pain, its own and everybody else's."

A doorman let Marika out of the car, shielding her with a large black umbrella, then escorted her to the entrance to the building. There she stood regally, waiting for him to rescue Heidi.

Heidi, too, stood for a moment, breathing in the cold, damp air of the sidewalk and looking at the ordinary people passing by. The fragrance of Marika's perfume still lingered in the car and some of it had even permeated Heidi's clothing.

A middle-aged man and woman stopped under the canopy of the apartment house to protect themselves from the driving rain. Seeing Marika, the woman nudged her husband. "Look, it's *her.*"

Marika turned quickly and headed for the elevator.

* * *

In the privacy of her dressing room, Marika began the long, tedious task of preparing herself for her long-awaited personal appearance. Standing before a full-length, three-way mirror, she looked dejectedly at her nude figure.

Her weight had shriveled to ninety pounds and she was now a frail, pathetic old woman. Her sagging breasts seemed without nipples, her skin, white as a turnip, was furrowed with creases. Her calves drooped below her skinny thighs, accentuating her knobby knees.

No one had seen her fully nude in decades except her doctor, a woman. A bitter smile crossed her face. This was the figure that once was one of the most celebrated on earth. What if her admirers knew what she really looked like? She ran her hands across her withered skin before slipping into an aqua dressing gown. She'd work the same miracle she always had before facing her public tonight. It had to be special this time.

At her gilt dressing table, she sat before a large mirror lit by tiers of strong, cruel lights. She wiped her face clean of her light afternoon makeup, then stared long and hard at the reflection in the glass. It made her heartsick. How cruel of life to steal her youth.

She looked at the slight rolls of flesh that once had been flawless skin held up by youthful muscles. The flesh over her eyelids seemed accentuated, and under those once-luminous eyes shadows were furrowed with the weariness of years. Her eyes glazed with defeat and hopelessness.

Suddenly, she sucked in air, deep, to the bottom of her lungs, summoning her inner forces. As her shoulders rose, so did her breasts. Gently she raised her head, jutting her chin out. She would defy her age! With a strong rhythm, she began to massage her cheeks with a continuous, soothing movement. Her fingers dipped into a jar of special face cream, the secret formula of which had once been given to her by her grandmother in Vienna. From other jars, she began her shading, warmly accentuating the prominent cheekbones, touching the high points with blushing pink. Her eyes deftly shaded, she reached into a little silver box and removed and inserted blue contact lenses, then pencilled her high, arched brows. That was better, she thought.

Reaching toward her wig stands, she removed a blonde creation made from the hair of an eight-year-old girl in a Swedish village. It had the same lustrous glow that had won her such rapturous admiration decades ago, and fitting it snugly, she admired how it flowed and moved gracefully at the slightest shift of her head.

There was a knock at her door, and Heidi came into her dressing room. Clad in a see-through gown, she moved toward the shower room. "I'd better get ready, too," she said, seeing Marika. "My, so much equipment—even a sauna bath."

"One has to look one's best," Marika replied in a faint voice. She hardly knew what she was saying. All her shocked attention was on Heidi as she slipped off her gown. Her figure in the glory of young womanhood contrasted painfully with what Marika had witnessed in her own mirror.

Sitting down in front of her mirror again, Marika tried to continue with her makeup, but the sound of the running shower water distracted her. It was opening her up. She was beginning to flow with it. The fierce isolation that had gripped her heart had started to weaken ever so slightly.

For years, wandering alone in the apartment or disguised on the streets of New York, Marika had looked hard, but seen nothing. Days would go by without her speaking to a soul, or even talking out loud to herself. Thinking was impossible, too. Too hard on her. Every time she allowed herself to think, a floodgate of memories opened up, like that running shower water.

She'd find herself drifting dangerously back . . . remembering . . . living it all over again.

She dug her long nails into the soft flesh of her arm. "Hold yourself together," she whispered into the pedestal mirror her mother had left her long ago, when the century was just beginning. Seeing herself in that mirror gave her renewed strength. Her mind was destroyed, her body wrecked, but her heart was still fierce. It still beat undiminished.

Regardless of what her enemies said, she had triumphed in the world, scoring victory after victory in all her many reincarnations. She'd also known defeat. The despair of wandering without friends or love in foreign lands. But she'd endured. She was, in the end, a survivor. A hawk. But she'd caged herself, and you don't cage hawks. She'd deceived herself into thinking she wanted to remain in that cage forever, but the presence of Heidi, a perfect re-creation of her own image, was doing something to her now, upsetting the steely reserve of decades.

Marika was getting up. The sound of running water drew her closer and closer to the door of the shower. She didn't know what was happening, but somehow she felt the girl in that shower was part of her, a living part, and she had a perfect right to connect herself with a *real* person. She'd spent years receiving many forms of rejuvenation, including injections from the cells of the foetus of a lamb, but the injection she needed now had to come not from needles but from Heidi.

Marika's lips moved, as if mouthing the words to one of her old songs. She wanted to say something—to warn her body against what she was about to do—but her body had taken control of her mind. It moved of its own free will.

A terrible white light burned in the room. The brightness made her blind to everything else but the foggy shower door.

Violently, she threw it open. The girl gasped as she turned off the faucet. Heidi's skin was like a white snow-flower. Her wide eyes filled with fright, but Marika's own eyes mesmerized her, told her not to be afraid. Her hands were on Heidi. Bewildered, confused, near tears, the girl at first resisted, pulled back, but the dry old hands were fondling the young, wet breasts now. Marika felt them as if they were her own.

For years, while singing in cabarets, Marika had stuck out her tongue in a pretended sexuality. Then, her tongue had known only the air. Now it met flesh, it danced and loved its way down Heidi's chin to her breasts. So many delightful nerve ends. So much life!

With her hands she traced the contour of the wet body. She wanted to get closer and closer until she could taste the girl's breath. She had to feel that breath inside her.

Heidi would take her back into the world again. The young woman could make it happen a second time for Marika. This was not the end of life, but the beginning. She could do it again . . . through Heidi.

Her lips were on Heidi's, not kissing, but biting, chewing on the stunned girl's mouth. She almost wanted to bring blood from those lips, but didn't dare. In a foggy, distant time . . . was it pre-war Warsaw? . . . the great Madame Modrzejewska had sucked at her own warm, young mouth. She hadn't understood at the time that the old actress had not sought sex or love. She wanted life.

Marika thrilled at the beat of Heidi's heart. It was strong and durable. It would endure, like hers.

More memories. Another old woman. But why was she thinking of her now? Marika ran her fingers across Heidi's tense stomach, yet the image of the old crone persisted, her face became clearer. With a shock, she realized it was the grasping, loathsome Contessa. That woman . . . *no* . . .

At Marika's hesitancy, Heidi suddenly broke away. Clutching a towel, her face a mask of horror, she rushed from the dressing room. Desperate to stop her, Marika ran after her, stumbling and nearly falling on her dressing table. In the pedestal mirror, she encountered her own image. She was like a vampire! She held her hands up to the mirror. Those hands didn't want to caress, but devour. She quickly covered her face, blotting out the image in the mirror.

Voices were calling, distant but familiar faces appearing before vanishing again into their graves.

They were . . . oh, no! . . . why had Friedrich left her? . . . Julian? . . . the night, hard and cold . . . she wanted only velvety darkness . . . a wasteland out there . . . vast in all its depravity . . . romance, a moon all silver and bright . . . why did Heidi go? . . . like all the rest . . . people always leaving her . . . the image in the mirror growing dimmer . . . a sound . . . the rustle of a long-ago dress . . . hands reaching down . . . a fountain . . . goldfish.

A chill descended across the dressing room as the vapor left from the shower evaporated. Now the mirror presented a new image. Marika was no more. She'd become Heidi. But then . . .

"No!" Marika shouted.

But it was too late. The features of youth faded, and in their place, those clutching hands reached down for her again. The hands belonged to the Contessa. With a sickening blow, the truth hit Marika. She'd come full circle in life. She herself had become the Contessa.

Slowly and helplessly she watched the features of the Contessa in the mirror obliterate her own. Those hands were reaching out from the mirror, summoning her back. She was being pulled into the mirror. Though she feared what lay beyond, the fight was out of her.

All the ghosts of yesterday were marching tonight.

Book One

1913-1918

Chapter 1

In the silk-filtered dusk of her bedroom, Marika Kreisler's face, in soft focus, appeared older than her thirteen years. "I'm a woman," she whispered to her gilt mirror on its pedestal stand.

The mirror was the only real possession she'd brought with her from Berlin to the spa at Baden-Baden where Papa was on a three-month vacation from the Hussars. With a girl's sense of wonder, she tried to conjure up the lovely, perfumed ladies who'd powdered their noses in the mirror before her, but as Marika gazed at her own face she felt the mirror had never seen beauty such as hers. She was radiant.

Her soft, blonde hair sat in tight curls on her head. Her finely chiseled bone structure, her brow, her cheeks, her chin, everything was perfect except for a slight chubbiness in the cheeks.

She smiled, her mouth leaning toward severity with a disturbing line. Her eyes, with their long lashes, picked up the pale, ice-blue light of her room and stared straight into the mirror without compromise. When she closed them, it was like lowering a veil.

On her dressing table rested a bottle of perfume Papa had given her. She sniffed at it with a delicate nose—"the kind made for smelling perfume," a boyfriend had whispered to her the first time he'd kissed it.

She exuded sensuality.

Her afternoon walk outside the Bad-Hotel zum Hirsch that day had disappointed her. She'd gazed at white horses, their manes blowing in the wind, pulling carriages along the roadway beside the Oos River, but somehow Baden-Baden was not what she had expected it to be. An old driver, idling his horses and waiting for a paying customer, had told her, "Baden-Baden is sad now. I remember a better day. You could look up and see Napoleon III, Queen Victoria, even Bismarck riding by."

She'd passed the Spielbank, although its doors were locked. Even so, she could imagine the plush velvet, the frescoes, the gilt, and the crystal chandeliers, and somehow this decor seemed reflected in her bedroom mirror. In that same mirror, she was no longer clad in a drab, white schoolgirl dress, but in a dazzling pink gown with ostrich feathers. Even though she was completely alone, her bedroom seemed filled with men. All of them stared at her as she floated by on her white cloud.

* * *

In the rich, fat spring of 1913, Europe was in its global ascendancy. It was a world of kaisers, tsars, kings, and emperors, of plumed helmets and crimson sashes, a world at the zenith of its power and wealth. But the Age of Imperialism was nearing its end. It simply waited for the spark that would change the map of the world for all time. The Iron Chancellor had predicted it would begin over "some damned foolish thing in the Balkans," and already the grand alliances were being made, an encircled Imperial Germany, Austria-Hungary, and Italy on the one side, the formidable Triple Entente of France, England and Imperial Russia on the other.

Known to millions as "the Kaiser," Wilhelm II with his upturned moustache was a crowned megalomaniac ruling Germany "by the grace of God." The upper crust, though aware of the Kaiser's infantile arrogance and vanity, preferred not to rebel. Instead, they idled away their long, drawn-out days at such fashionable spas as Baden-Baden. Some were reading a book, *The*

Great Illusion, whose author claimed that war had become impossible.

* * *

Marika did not read such books, nor did she care about war. She was much more interested in romantic novels.

There were still two hours before dinner, so she looked at herself one final time in the mirror, then left her room, descending the steps to the patio. There she perched beside a fountain, teasing a goldfish with a straw.

Suddenly, the rustle of a woman's dress caused her to turn around. Startled, Marika just had time to glimpse the hem of a midnight-blue gown before losing her balance and nearly falling into the fountain. Hands reached for her, clutching.

"Don't be afraid," the woman said reassuringly, lifting Marika up, her German colored by a lilting Italian accent. "I won't hurt you. My name is the Contessa Villoresi de Loche."

"My name is Marika," she replied, standing up to curtsy. The late afternoon sun shone in her eyes.

The Contessa's heavily veiled face remained in shadow, but as she moved closer to Marika, it became clearer, her dyed black hair accentuating her facial lines, making them appear harsher than they were, though she tried to conceal them with makeup. But behind the facade was a strong suggestion of a once-great beauty. Grandeur, a certain regal bearing, had replaced that faded beauty now.

"I always stay in my room until this time," the Contessa said. "Baden-Baden is bathed in a golden light then. It's kind to old women." She gently touched Marika's hair.

Marika stepped back.

"The cold March sun just leaps down on you," the Contessa said. "It sets your beautiful blonde hair on fire."

"Thank you," said Marika. She was not used to such compliments.

The Contessa stood silently, as the sun sank lower. "I used to be young and pretty, too." Her voice was forlorn, as if speaking not to Marika but to someone she once knew. She looked down. "The other night when you came into the dining room, I saw myself as I used to be. Once everybody turned *my* way."

"I'm sorry," Marika said, feeling uncomfortable, yet at the same time reassured that the woman was not going to harm her. The Contessa's voice was kind, and her veil couldn't conceal a sorrow that hung over her.

"You seem alone," the Contessa said in a clearer tone. "I hope I'm not being too personal, but your parents are never with you."

"My Papa's very busy," Marika said. "Mother is dead. Are you lonely, too?"

The Contessa hesitated a moment. "No one's ever asked me that. To anyone else, I'd deny it. But you can lie only to grown-ups —never to a child." Leaning down, she whispered, "Very lonely. You must promise not to reveal my secret."

"I promise," Marika said proudly. "No one's ever told me a secret before."

"I'm glad to be the first," the Contessa said. "Perhaps you'll have tea with me? We'll share more secrets."

* * *

Young men stood smoking cigarettes along the path that led to the Schwarzwald tearoom, their smoke mingling with the sweet, lingering perfume of the early spring flowers and foliage that covered the grounds. Elegantly dressed ladies passed by, so fair they reminded Marika of goddesses. It was enchanting.

The Contessa had reserved a table for them in a darkened rear salon against a bank of flowers, and from the front room, the sounds of violin music drifted back.

Smiling, a waiter approached them, and just as he was pouring tea for Marika, a distinguished gentleman stopped at their table, his hair and moustache white, a black frock coat draped around his shoulders over a pearl-gray vest and dark gray trousers. "My dear Contessa," he said, "I had no idea you were in Baden-Baden." He bowed as he kissed her hand.

"I'm here for the cure," she said. She smiled at him, then turned to Marika. "Count Dabrowsky, Marika Kreisler."

Marika got up from the table, curtsying before the gentleman.

"A most charming young lady," the Count said.

"Thank you," she replied demurely.

"Unless you're having tea with friends," the Contessa said, "would you be so kind as to join us?"

"An honor." In moments the waiter had arrived with a Louis

· 16 ·

XVI chair upholstered in silk damask. The Count sat down with authority, as the waiter took his coat.

"How is life in Warsaw these days?" the Contessa asked.

"Very bad," he replied. "I've just returned from there. My wife died. Scarlet fever."

"My deepest sympathy," the Contessa said. "She was your third, wasn't she? And so young."

"Yes," he said sadly. "Only sixteen, practically a child." His eyes drifted to Marika.

She could not believe what she'd heard. The Count looked old enough to be her Papa's father. How could he have married a girl so close to Marika's own age?

"You must be absolutely lost without her," the Contessa said.

"I am," he answered. "I can't sleep at night. Poland is too melancholy in March. That's why I'm here."

The Contessa placed her cup in its saucer. "We cannot allow your loneliness to continue much longer," she said firmly. "A man must have companionship, particularly at a time like this. Tomorrow I absolutely insist you join Marika and me for a ride in the Black Forest. I'll even break a firm rule and get up in the morning."

"I'd be delighted," he said, smiling at the Contessa. But quickly his eyes turned to Marika again.

She faced him squarely, unblinkingly. Only children blushed, she decided. Mature women, such as the Contessa, looked men straight in the eye.

Late the following morning, Count Dabrowsky sat on a purple Victorian sofa in the hotel, sipping Polish vodka. Marika could feel his eyes piercing through her. He took in her hair, her face, her legs, her dress. The way he was always looking at her made her feel funny. What did he want?

"What does your father do, young lady?" the Count asked.

"He is a hussar," she replied politely.

"That's nice," he said.

The stillness of the morning drifted over the room. Marika sensed the Count's loneliness, but his aloofness made talking to him nearly impossible. All he wanted to do, it seemed, was stare at her.

The appearance of the Contessa was a relief. Her black, curled hair had been freshly retouched, and, if anything, she was even more heavily made up than yesterday, the rouge on her cheeks so thick it made them look like peonies in full bloom. A great gray hat with two purple-dyed egret plumes crowned her head, and she'd draped a red and black cape around her stooped shoulders.

"How lovely you look today, Contessa," the Count said, rising from the sofa. His eyes drifted from the Contessa to Marika. "How lovely both of my lady companions look. I'm the proudest man in Baden-Baden." It thrilled Marika to have such a mature, sophisticated man refer to her as a lady, not a child.

The Count walked over to the reception desk to arrange a carriage. Anxiously, Marika turned to the Contessa. "Papa isn't awake yet. I need his permission to go on a trip."

The Contessa patted her arm soothingly. "We can't let the Count wait all morning. Let's keep our adventure a secret. It's important for women to have secrets, not to share everything with men."

"I understand," Marika said, though still not quite at ease. "I like secrets."

As their carriage passed along the promenade, the Count pointed out people to Marika. "Look there. Everybody in Baden-Baden is overweight. The richer a German gets, the more food he eats and beer he drinks. It is as though the body becomes an investment!"

"That's why everybody is ailing," the Contessa agreed. "Here, they call it 'the burdens of bowel and belly.'"

"But you're not fat," Marika protested, turning to the Count. "Neither is Papa."

"Ah, now that is because I take care of myself," the Count replied. "My last wife told me I had the physique of a forty-year-old."

"If that," the Contessa added.

At an open-air café with a beautiful view, Marika was treated to goose-liver pâté from Strasbourg and allowed to have all the cream cakes she wanted. She reveled in the attention being paid her, though when the Count trapped food in his extravagant whiskers, she was tempted to giggle. Observing a German family with two large boys and an equally large daughter pass by, the Count wiped his whiskers with his napkin and, turning to Marika, said, "You should be with companions your own age. Not sitting here talking to grown-ups."

"I don't know anybody my own age," Marika replied.

The Contessa interrupted her. "What Marika means is that she finds companions her own age dull. They're too limited to hold her interest."

"I see," the Count said.

Marika feared something was going on which she didn't understand.

Suddenly, it was late afternoon and Marika realized with a shock that Papa must be frantic over her absence. Back at the hotel, she stared in panic at the slightly drunk, unshaven man standing in the lobby, talking to two officers of the police. "Papa," she cried out, running up to him.

"May I ask where you've been?" he said with biting anger. "My own daughter?"

The coldness in his voice sent a chill through her. "I meant to leave a note," she stammered. "I went riding with friends."

"With friends?" he asked in astonishment. He turned solemnly to the police. "I suspected kidnappers," he said apologetically. "What else was a father to think? She's so young."

"Perfectly understandable, Herr Kreisler," one of the police officers murmured. He looked sternly at Marika. "We'll leave you to discipline your daughter." The click of heeled boots on the marble floor resounded through the hotel.

Instead of facing her father, Marika stared out a great bay window, where an old man sat drinking beer. Behind her Friedrich Kreisler stood looking down at her blonde head. For a moment he might have been tempted to reach down and stroke her hair, telling her he was glad she was safe. But he wasn't that kind of man.

In his fifties, Friedrich often passed for a man twenty years younger. He walked with his strong, straight nose held high, jutting out above a shaggy moustache, and his hair, though receding a bit at the temples, remained silky and blond and a source of pride. He looked at the world through pale blue eyes that seemed never to have been innocent or amused.

He'd always wanted to be a thick powerhouse of a man with a bold, muscled physique, but such had not been his fate. Instead, his body stood tall and lean, almost like a piece of Renaissance sculpture. Once when they were bathing, a fellow hussar had told him his body was "beautiful." Friedrich had struck the man in the mouth.

Finally, he managed to speak to Marika. "I have neglected you shamefully, allowing you to do as you please," he said. "Beginning this morning you're going on a strict schedule. We are returning to Berlin."

"It will be good to get back home," Marika said.

"No," he said, "not home. I'm putting you in a school."

Dismayed, Marika felt her eyes fill with tears. "But I don't want to go to school," she protested. "I want to be with you."

"It's out of the question," Friedrich said with finality. "There's another reason as well. I've had a sudden . . ." He paused, as if the words were painful to him. "A sudden financial reversal." His voice was merely a whisper. "I'm going to have to sell our house in Berlin. Because of what has happened to me, I want a school that will train you in the practical side of life. You're no longer the daughter of a rich man."

The news was too sudden for her to handle. People just didn't have money one day, then not have it the next. "But . . ."

"You're going to school," he said. "That is that!" He always seemed embarrassed when having conversations with women, even his own daughter. "As for me," he added, "I'm planning a tour of duty in Hungary."

They were interrupted by the appearance of the Contessa, who emerged through the dusty public parlor, a frown creasing her brow. Suddenly, she spotted them and her face grew animated and bright, almost compensating for its lines of fatigue. "My dear Mr. Kreisler," she said, "I've not had the pleasure of an introduction, although I know your daughter."

Marika ran to her side, reaching for her hand. "Papa, this is my friend," she said, praying for him to approve. "She's a Contessa."

Friedrich looked sternly at the aging, overdressed woman. Apparently, he'd seen too many like her at Baden-Baden, and had always avoided contact with them.

"I am the Contessa Villoresi de Loche."

"I see," he said. "You seem to know who I am. Friedrich Kreisler."

"Indeed I do," the Contessa said, smiling. "Your daughter and I have become good friends. My dear companion, Count Dabrowsky, invited us for a ride. I'm sure Marika explained."

"Yes," he said hesitantly. "Count Dabrowsky? I know of him."

Marika nervously clutched the Contessa's hand. "We're leaving Baden-Baden. Papa is going back to Berlin. I must go to a school."

"A school?" the Contessa asked. "That's understandable. But what a pity." She turned to Friedrich. "I was just getting to know Marika well. Now I see the pleasure may be denied me." She reached down to caress Marika's hand. "Since I may soon be saying good-bye to Marika, why don't both of you join me for dinner tonight?"

Friedrich glanced at his gold watch. "That is very kind of you, but I really can't. I've been up all night, and I need the rest."

"Soldiers such as yourself recover quite rapidly," the Contessa said, a flirtatious challenge in her voice.

He stared at her for a long moment.

"Even the Count is returning to Warsaw," the Contessa said. "I fear I'll be left all alone at Baden-Baden. It is still too damp to return to my villa in Rome."

"You have a villa there?" Friedrich asked tentatively.

"Yes," she said, "but I really prefer to live on my estate in the Tuscan hills. It's good for a retreat. I grow restless, though."

"Why, in heaven's name?" Friedrich asked.

"Florence is such a dull city," she said. "I need to be surrounded by more life."

Friedrich bowed from the waist and reached to kiss the Contessa's hand. "I was thinking," he said. "If I retire for the rest of the afternoon, I should be in fine form for this evening's dinner. Would you kindly overlook my appearance right now?"

"I hardly noticed," the Contessa said. "You hussars cut such striking figures."

"A compliment, madame, for which I'm in your debt."

The Contessa smoothed Marika's hair. "Get some rest, darling," she said. "That was a very bumpy ride back into town."

After the Contessa had gone, Marika turned to her Papa. "Please don't be angry with me."

He glared at her. "Why didn't you tell me you knew such important people? I had no idea you were acquainted with Count

Dabrowsky. And this rich woman, the Contessa. In my present circumstances, it's necessary to have good connections." He turned on his heels. "I can't understand why such people want to befriend a little girl."

Marika held her head high. "They don't consider me a little girl. To the Count and the Contessa, I'm a young lady."

Friedrich smiled. "I'm going to bed now. We'll meet at dinner." As an afterthought, he added, "You stay out of trouble."

* * *

That was the last time Marika had dinner with the Contessa and Friedrich because from that night on, she found herself excluded from their invitations. Both the Contessa and Friedrich called themselves night people, and their late engagements came when it was time for Marika to go to bed.

As the spring green deepened in the gardens of Baden-Baden, Marika heard no more talk of school or of returning to Berlin. The Contessa had taken her Papa away from her, and she couldn't compete.

Each day now she sat near the entrance to the hotel, hoping somebody her own age would check in. But no one did. Sometimes she'd sit for more than an hour, watching the clock in the lobby in despair, until one day papers arrived for her father, a special pouch from Berlin. Marika's brow tingled with excitement. Maybe it was from the Kaiser himself! "I'm his daughter," she said, proudly asserting herself. "I'll take them to him." Although she'd been told never to enter a room without knocking, she forgot the instruction in her enthusiasm and, rushing to their rooms, she turned the knob on the door to Papa's private chambers and hurried inside.

Standing for a moment in the shadows of the suite, she noticed that though the shutters were closed, and only the faintest light came in, the rays of the sun were just enough to cause a trembling effect on the velvet-covered furniture. An overturned wine bottle lay on the table and flies buzzed around half-filled glasses.

Like the flickering light, Marika's head was unclear. A noise came from her Papa's bedroom. The sound of his heavy breathing drowned out the buzzing of the flies. Was he having a heart attack? Perhaps he was still drunk. She'd have to wake him up. The papers . . . maybe war had been declared!

"Papa," she called out, her fright growing. "It's from Berlin. You must get up." She paused at the doorway to his room, her eyes adjusting to the light.

"What the hell!" came Friedrich's muffled reply. "Who's there?" He was on the bed with someone, mounting someone, but at the sound of Marika's voice, he collapsed, causing a scream of outrage from the woman beneath. Marika knew at once it was the Contessa. Sliding off her, Friedrich stood up by the bed, then ran forward to shut the bedroom door while the woman frantically reached for a sheet to cover her nude body.

Marika froze. The thought passed through her mind that her naked father looked like one of those rampaging bulls she'd seen in the fields, and then a slap sent her sprawling onto the carpet of the parlor. Too shocked to feel the pain, she let the room whirl around her. She crouched on the floor, dazed, stunned, afraid to move. Looking up, she saw her Papa standing over her, hastily tying a satin dressing gown around his middle.

"Get out!" he shouted at her. "How dare you enter my private quarters without knocking!"

Picking herself up from the floor, Marika rushed for the door, not wanting him to strike her again. "Forgive me," she cried out. "I didn't mean anything wrong." She slammed the door behind her, wanting walls, doors, anything, between her and her Papa.

Safe in her own room, Marika raged against the Contessa. She'd introduced the woman to her Papa. The Contessa had betrayed her. She'd been deliberately taking advantage of him. Marika'd heard how men were weak and could be turned into playtoys by clever women. The air in the room suffocated her. She had to get out. But there was no place for her to go. How could she face Papa after she'd seen him like that? Did all men look like him without their clothes? Throughout the rest of the afternoon and into the early evening she lay there on her bed. The more she thought of the encounter in Papa's suite, the more her romantic hopes and dreams faded. She'd wanted to fall in love one day with a dashing Hussar, the kind she'd read about in books. But not if they looked like Papa. Not if they rode you the way a bull did a cow. Why didn't any of the books tell you about that? The books she'd read had been fantasies, lies to trick foolish girls.

She squeezed her arms about her in a tight embrace, almost as

· 23 ·

if defending her body against an invasion. The throbbing sound of her heart grew louder. Then the tension broke. She began sobbing loudly and didn't care whether the people in the next room heard her or not.

* * *

Marika wasn't surprised when Friedrich told her he was marrying the Contessa. On the day of the wedding, she woke in a deep depression and stayed all day in her room, dreading the hour of five o'clock when she would have to descend the stairs. The hotel seemed like a tomb. She wanted to avoid the wedding, but she knew that Papa would make her attend, so when it was no longer possible to delay, Marika dressed in her favorite white chiffon, on which the Contessa had gotten a seamstress to sew a deep hem of red fox, and slowly walked to the ballroom.

As she approached, she felt a chill at the sound of the violin music. The wedding was underway. At the front of the room, she saw the Contessa standing regally, in pale blue organza, under a headdress of bird-of-paradise feathers, a large purple flower obscuring her wrinkled throat. Soon, the vows were exchanged in front of a dwarfish priest hidden behind a large black moustache, and then Marika closed her eyes tightly as her father presented the Contessa with a ring once worn by Marika's mother, Lotte. It was done.

As the guests showered the couple with flower petals, Marika trailed her Papa and the Contessa into the reception room, too miserable to notice the grand buffet dominated by a punch bowl containing strawberries floating in champagne. The Contessa crossed to it right away, however, and delightedly twirled the stem of a glass. "My favorite drink," she said, bending down to kiss Marika on both cheeks.

Marika did not respond. She wanted to cry.

Friedrich came up to his new wife. "Darling," she said, reaching to kiss him, but Friedrich stepped back from her embrace. "Now that you're Frau Kreisler," he said, softly, but firmly, "it won't be necessary to wear the headdress."

The Contessa looked startled. Eagerly she sought out the eyes of the other guests to see if they were listening. "You don't like it?" she asked weakly.

"Feathers are best left for birds, or perhaps cannibals in the

African jungles." He cut a piece of the wedding cake and handed it to her. With trembling hands, the Contessa reached for it, nearly dropping it.

"The wedding cake is all the adornment our marriage needs." He turned and left the room.

The Contessa searched Marika's face for understanding, but Marika was already leaving the ballroom, heading for the garden. There, wandering by herself, she enjoyed the spring flowers and tried to still the numbing anguish churning within her.

She was dying slowly, she feared, and it was because she was too young to live. Her life was a prison . . . and she'd wait quietly for the right hour to make her escape.

* * *

Berlin was alive in the spring morning. Windows were opened wide, and lilies filled the air with a sweet fragrance. Coming back home again brought a resurgence of life to Marika.

Baden-Baden was trapped in the past. Berlin was aggressive, restless, modern. Everybody seemed supremely confident, from the porter at the train station to the police officer directing traffic on a corner of Unter den Linden. On the way into town, Marika watched in fascination as smoke poured from factories making armaments and weapons.

They passed notorious dance halls and Papa fulminated against the changing morality. "They're filled with nothing but con artists and pickpockets," he lamented. "Berlin is nothing but a web of intrigue these days—corruption and deviation. This must change. I personally heard the Chief of Staff say that in the coming war, the German people will be called upon to make great sacrifices."

From underneath their house, Friedrich's dogs surged to greet Marika, hurling themselves at her in a frenzied scramble. She wanted to rest and spend the day alone, but the Contessa had other plans.

"It's important that you be photographed," she said to Marika. "Such beauty as yours must be captured on film. I was shocked to find that not one photograph of you exists anywhere. We must do this right away."

At the photographer's studio, a faded sign read, "COURT PHOTOGRAPHER. AWARDS FROM RULING SOVEREIGNS AND PRINCES." Marika was amused to find that the photographer, Hermann

Goetz, was only five feet three, and as they entered, he stood to greet them, his bald head glistening in the light of the studio, exclaiming "Such a lovely girl," at the sight of her. Marika felt as nervous in front of him as she did visiting her doctor, and the flash blinded her, but something magical had happened. In all her life nothing had ever thrilled her as much as having her picture taken.

"Now there you'll be for all time," the Contessa said, "looking as beautiful as you are today. Even if you grow old, like me, you'll have this picture to prove how lovely you once looked."

When they returned that afternoon, they were giggling and chatting, Marika laden down with packages of clothing charged to Friedrich, the Contessa laughing so hard at some joke the chauffeur had told her that tears rimmed her eyes. She'd been like a young woman again on their shopping spree. The tilt of her head, the wave of her hands, the lightness of her walk had convinced Marika that the Contessa had found the man of her dreams in Friedrich.

But Friedrich himself was waiting for them in full-dress uniform when they arrived, and at the sight of her Papa's stern face, Marika almost dropped one of her packages. He always dressed in full uniform when he was going to discipline her.

Sensing something wrong, the Contessa stopped laughing, and a silence fell over the hallway. "I much admire your carriage, my dear," she said at last. "It's one of the finest equipages in Berlin. And I've ridden with kings."

More silence. Arms folded, Friedrich said, "Ladies, would you please come with me to my study?"

Seated at his desk, he turned around in his chair to confront them. An expression unexpectedly pathetic came over Marika's face. "What is it, Papa?"

He cleared his throat, glancing furtively at the Contessa. "Up to now we've been on one long vacation. Or, most recently, honeymoon." He said the last word with a certain amount of embarrassment. The Contessa smiled and sought his eyes, but failed to make contact with them.

"We've never had a chance to discuss our affairs," Friedrich continued. "The way families should." Suddenly, he picked up a pile of bills, letting them cascade to the floor, forming a hill at his feet. Marika stared in amazement at her father. Only a matter of the gravest concern would make him create such disorder in his own study.

"Bills! Bills!" he said, his voice rising. "Nothing but bills these days. More arrive each morning. Many of the bills are the fourth and fifth notices, and the threats are no longer polite."

The Contessa sat up straight in her chair, then, tentatively got up, heading for the mantelpiece. Her eyes wandered around the room, taking in the blackening portraits, the yellowing quarterlies, and the leather-bound books. In the fading light, Marika had a hard time seeing her Papa's face or that of the Contessa.

Finally, the Contessa asked, "Why don't you pay them?"

Surely, Marika thought, the question sounded more provocative than the Contessa had really meant. Marika knew her Papa had no money, and the Contessa was a rich woman. Didn't the Contessa know he couldn't pay his bills?

The Contessa's question momentarily shocked Friedrich. Instant anger flashed across his face, but he tried to subdue it. "I intend to," he said, frowning at the Contessa. His voice had a nervous quiver Marika had not known before. "I intend to pay all the bills, including the bill you ran up at Baden-Baden this past winter. The hotel director was kind enough to send it today, along with the charges for our wedding reception."

"Yes," the Contessa replied. "I knew it would be coming soon."

"In fact, several of your bills from Baden-Baden have arrived addressed to me," he said. "Some date back more than three years." He stared at her with a long, searching look. "Why didn't you pay them or have your banker do it for you?"

At the mantelpiece, the Contessa aimlessly lifted a gold-framed portrait. She held it up to the light, deliberately stalling. "It is not possible for me to pay," she said. "I'm such an innocent about finances. Somehow money just slips through my fingers. My father never taught me about business. He always believed a woman should find a man to take care of financial affairs for her."

"Indeed," Friedrich said, "and you've found such a man. But, my dear, you must go through the formalities of turning over your money to me so I can manage it for you."

The Contessa gently placed the portrait back on the mantel. She kept her back to Friedrich. Finally, she spoke, her voice strangled. "I have no money."

Friedrich gave her a startled look, then slumped back in his seat. His alarm sent shudders through Marika. She could not believe the Contessa was telling the truth. Twice her Papa tried to say something, but each time the effort appeared too much. Marika wanted to reach out to him and offer him some comfort, but she was afraid. Tears came to her eyes. She felt the desperate hurt coming from him. In a matter of minutes his hopes and dreams of a comfortable life had ended.

Weakly, he stood. "You are without funds?" he asked the Contessa. The tone of his voice almost beseeched her to admit she was telling a lie.

"It's true," she repeated vacantly.

Friedrich turned red. "But you own villas in Tuscany and Rome."

The Contessa faced him squarely. *"Owned,"* she said. "My family hasn't actually owned the land since the 1890's. But we did once." Beneath the red paint on her mouth, her lips seemed drained of all color. "We still think of it as ours."

Friedrich walked to the long draperies and, pulling them back, looked out at his garden and the dogs racing to their dinner. In words so soft Marika hardly heard, he said, "I'm penniless."

"What!" The Contessa covered her face with her open palm.

"I'm about to lose even this house," he said. Though speaking to the Contessa, his voice seemed far away.

Marika was in agony, her every breath an effort. She prayed for a heart attack, anything to rid her of this pain.

The Contessa began to make her way to the door. Unlike this morning, her step was slow, almost a limp, the slump-shouldered walk of a defeated old woman. "I feel right now like a thousand needles are pricking my flesh." She fingered her neck. "My throat is parched. I thought when I met you, my troubles were over. That I'd be able to live out my days in peace and dignity with a good man." She gazed blankly back at Friedrich's shoulder. "Now I see they have only begun."

"The vanity of women always amazes me," Friedrich said.

"Exactly what do you mean?" the Contessa asked.

"My dear lady," he said, sucking in a deep breath. "Do you think a man like me would have married you if I didn't think you had money?" With these words, he brushed past her and slammed the study door behind him.

Marika thought the Contessa was going to faint. The old woman raised her hand to the shut the door, as if wanting to strike it. "How dare he say such a thing! To think I married beneath me. He's a Prussian swine, deceiving me like he did. I thought he was a gentleman. But he's no more than a fortune-hunter preying on elderly ladies!"

The Contessa's insults infuriated Marika and she quickly crossed the study. "How can you say that about Papa?" she demanded. "He might have tricked you. But you tricked him, too. You're both to blame!"

The Contessa's tears turned into a hollow laugh. "It's unpleasant to admit, but what you say is true. Why pretend with you? Friedrich and I were both play-acting. I did think he was wealthy, and he's right about one thing. I was vain enough to think he wanted me for myself. Even though I know how foolish a thought that was."

Marika was sobbing. "I'll never marry for money," she said. "Only for love."

A stillness came over the Contessa. She stood like a woman who had seen her life filled with nothing but disappointments. Already, however, she seemed to be withstanding it, gearing herself to move in a different direction. "You'll marry for love, you say." Her eyes zeroed in on Marika, the tired muscles of her sagging face tightening. "That remains to be seen."

* * *

Dinner was served that night, but neither Marika nor the Contessa could bring herself to eat. The Contessa sat at the table, her face in deep melancholy, the thought of confronting Friedrich again obviously weighing heavily upon her. Marika stood at the window, staring out at the familiar landscape. She feared she would have to leave home soon. But where would she be sent?

Two days passed, and still Friedrich had not returned. Marika suspected he was never coming back, that he'd already gone on his tour of duty, but just when she'd lost all hope, the front door banged shut and Friedrich barged into the parlor. He faced the Contessa, totally ignoring Marika, his face unshaven, his clothes looking as they'd been slept in. "You're a bitch," he shouted at the Contessa.

"Please," she said, after a long pause. "Conduct yourself like a gentleman, at least in front of your daughter. You've been drinking and aren't fit to have a conversation."

"I'll do what I damn please," he said. "It's my home!"

"No, it isn't," she said softly. "You told us yourself. It belongs to your creditors."

Marika wanted to leave the room, but felt trapped. She sank deeper into the sofa.

"I've been staying with my sister Brigitte," he said. "I should have talked to her before I married you. Your reputation is known, it seems. The discoveries I've made about you are vile."

"I'm sorry if my life offends you," the Contessa said.

"Offends!" he screamed. "Hardly the word. You are the most notorious woman in Europe!"

The Contessa glanced at Marika, then got up from her chair and walked slowly around the room, almost as if wandering in a void. "I think you give me too much credit," she said finally. "The competition is too keen."

"When I married you, I didn't realize the extent of your depravity," he said.

The Contessa backed away.

Suddenly, Marika wanted to protect the Contessa. She jumped up, confronting her Papa. "Please do not speak to her that way. You can't blame her for not having money. You have no money either!"

At first he looked at her as if he would slap her, the way he did that afternoon in Baden-Baden, but he brought himself under control. He turned his attention to the Contessa. "I have found out, madame, that when your youth was gone, and you could no longer operate successfully as a strumpet, you turned to another profession. Matchmaker."

"There's nothing wrong with that," the Contessa said. "It is an old and perfectly respectable profession."

"No, madame, not so respectable," he charged. "You arrange for poor young girls to become the brides of aging, perverted men! Now I understand your interest in Marika. You're getting her ready for that Polish pig, Count Dabrowsky."

Marika bit her lip at the sound of her father's words. Everything was happening so fast. A needle-sharp pain stabbed her chest, and tears welled in her eyes. Instinctively she'd feared the Contessa on their first meeting, and now she knew her original intuition had been right. She did indeed have something to fear from the woman. Glaring at the Contessa, Marika could only feel she'd been betrayed. And she'd naïvely felt her new stepmother was interested in her as a friend.

Her back rigid, the Contessa said nothing.

"A form of concubinage," Friedrich went on, his fists clenched. "That's how you've survived. On the blood of virgins."

"That's melodramatic twaddle!" the Contessa said. "I'm not listening to it anymore."

"I'm leaving you," he said. "I'm signing up for my tour of duty now. It will take me away from Berlin for many years."

"I'll sue you," the Contessa said. "You can't leave me penniless. I'm your wife!"

"As I told you," he said, "I have no money. I'm leaving you to face your creditors—and mine. From what Brigitte has told me, you've spent most of your life running from bill collectors. You have far more experience at it than I do." He turned and strode to the door, only to be stopped by the sound of a muffled cry.

Dizzily, Marika was heading toward him. "But Papa, what about me?"

"Brigitte's arranged for a school for you to attend," he said. "It's in Bohemia. In exchange for domestic duties, you'll be given free room and board with classroom instruction."

"But when will I see you again?" she asked, paralyzed with fear.

He looked at her for a long moment, his face a blank. "Right now," he said, "I don't really care." Turning and stumbling once, he drunkenly began to climb the marble steps.

In desperation, Marika faced the Contessa. "What will happen to me?"

"In the morning," the Contessa said, gliding past her, "everything will be clear. I never make decisions after three o'clock in the afternoon."

Alone in the parlor, Marika sat in darkness. She waited for something, she didn't know what. Crying didn't help. She'd done enough of that. She was in a state of shock, not about the Contessa being penniless, but about what people had to do to survive. Her Papa and the Contessa! Danger was all around her. Would she have to sell herself, too, in order to obtain food and lodging? Didn't that make you a slave, a prostitute?

She lay on the sofa, watching the shadows in the room intently. Somehow they seemed more ominous than ever, and for the first time she was growing afraid of the dark.

The very people she'd depended on for protection were weak and helpless, too, and needed protection just as much as anybody else. How could her Papa look after her and provide for her when he couldn't even take care of his own needs? In his uniform, Papa had seemed superhuman. Now she knew differently. She'd seen the spark in his eyes go out, his face become bruised and disfigured by the humiliation of his oncoming bankruptcy. To her Papa, money and power were everything. She dreaded to think what the lack of them would do to him.

The Contessa's defeat was even harder for her to think about. Without youth and beauty, who would want her? The sadness of growing old swept over Marika. She could not help but feel that the shine on her hair, the gleam on her skin would last forever. But she knew better. In time, your body became broken, your spirit tarnished.

She remembered Papa taking one of his hunting dogs out into the field one day. There, while Marika shuddered, he had fired a bullet through the helpless dog's head. Later, when she had challenged him, he'd told her, "He was no longer good for the chase. When a dog's too old to serve his purpose, he should be shot. People, too."

At two the next morning, Marika still couldn't sleep. Although she pitied the Contessa, she could understand why Friedrich was deserting her. But she couldn't comprehend how he could so callously abandon his own daughter.

Without meaning to, she found herself in the middle of the night walking slowly to his room, turning the knob of the massive door, and going in without bothering to knock. Memories of walking in on him in Baden-Baden came back to her. She feared his brutality, but she dreaded even more the loneliness and uncertainty of life in Bohemia.

Friedrich was asleep. She shook him, trying to arouse him from his drunken stupor. His eyes opened wide, and at first he didn't seem to know her, then suddenly he roared, "What in hell are you doing in here? At this time of night?"

"I'm not going to let you leave me like this," Marika said, confronting him. Though her voice was firm, her knees were shaking. "I won't allow it."

"*You* won't allow it!" Friedrich said, raising his voice. "I don't believe what I'm hearing." Turning over in bed, he reached for his dressing robe, and slipped out from under the eiderdown.

"I'm your daughter," she said. "You can't just abandon me, like the Contessa."

"I'll do as I goddamn please," he said, taking a glass of water. "It was because of you that I got involved with that loathsome creature." He turned to her, his steely eyes filled with hatred, frightening her. "I'm going to make you pay for *that* mistake, young lady." He lowered his voice, each word coming out iron-hard. "It's disgusting to me. Making love to a woman for her money. It makes me a common prostitute. Except that I was doing it for my own daughter—for your future, you ungrateful little bitch."

"I don't believe that," she said. She felt dizzy. The room was spinning around her. She'd never been so reckless with her Papa before, but she'd never had so much to lose, either. "You've never done anything for me. It was always for yourself. Your liquor. Your fancy uniforms. Your women."

"You sound exactly like your mother," he said. He walked to the French doors draped in black velvet. "You are like your mother in so many ways."

Marika stared defiantly, her chin jutting out. "I was told she was wonderful and very beautiful. I'm pleased to be like her."

"She was not wonderful," he said. He pulled at the draperies, as if to rip them from their sockets. "She was a bitch like you. A bitch just like the Contessa. But unlike the Contessa, your mother was at least young."

"So were you, Papa."

"Don't remind me of age," he said. "You'll face getting old soon enough, and you'll like it even less than I do." He slumped in a winged armchair, his heels digging into the carpet. "I've failed!" he shouted. "Nothing I ever wanted in life has happened. And now I know it's not going to happen. Don't you see that? Are you completely stupid?"

"I'm not stupid," Marika said. She almost felt sorry for the embittered man before her. "You're like all the other Berliners. Everything you've ever wanted has to do with money or power." She paused, as if catching her breath. "Not me! I want love."

"I've never been in love and don't ever plan to be," he said matter-of-factly. "I'm not some romantic little schoolgirl like you."

"Do you think only schoolgirls fall in love?"

"I know so," he said. "Enough of them have foolishly loved me. You're insane if you plan to look for love in life. Use yourself, use your beauty, whatever, to marry a rich man when you're older. Not now! Not some swine, like that count. But a top-ranking member of the Reserve Officer Corps."

"Never!"

"When I return," he said, ignoring her protest, "I may even arrange such a marriage for you. Yes, I can use you, when you're a little older. You can help advance my career."

"That makes you just like the Contessa," she hissed. "You're no better than she is."

"We're both trying to live," he said. "To survive. That's something you wouldn't know anything about. Everybody's done your thinking for you. At the school in Bohemia, you'll learn how the rest of the world lives. You'll grow up! Making you grow up will be my biggest contribution to you."

In tears, Marika ran from the room.

In the early hours of the morning, she found herself wandering through her Papa's gardens. These were the playfields of her childhood. She'd spent many lovely hours here, always alone. In the background stood Friedrich's house, a relic from another century, baroque and outdated like Friedrich and the Contessa.

No flowers grew in the garden. Friedrich didn't believe in them. Instead, neat, clipped bushes in perfect geometric shapes lined gravel paths leading to stone stairways and a terrace encircled by a balustrade. In the center of the terrace loomed a mythological figure, its pose ceremonial, its gesture frozen in time.

An empty landscape, just like the life stretching before her. Her wandering in the garden had been just a preview of the wandering that remained in her future. But regardless of where she went, what she did, she was fiercely determined about one thing: she would be a schoolgirl no more!

* * *

At the railway station in Berlin, Marika, weak and trembling, stumbled on the stairs. A tug by Friedrich, and she was on her way again. On the platform, he reached for her. "You'll be in good hands at the school. It's very strict and very religious. It'll make a fine woman out of you."

Marika tried to hold back her tears.

"I want you to obey your instructors and make me proud of you one day."

"You'll write, Papa?" she asked hesitantly. "You promise?"

"I'll write," he said vacantly, looking away.

She grabbed his hand, but he gently withdrew it, and instead kissed her lightly on the cheek. "God bless you." His fingers tightened on her arm, and then he was gone.

Marika stood on the platform, saying nothing, unable to move. Then the conductor signaled her aboard. Inside, the compartments were full, the windows raised, and the thick fumes of cigar smoke permeating the air made her feel faint. Fingering her hair, she found it sticky with perspiration.

The spring fields passed in review, as Marika looked out the window. Her eyes traveled back up the tracks to the imperial city she'd left behind, but Berlin was no longer visible. A hollow feeling came over her, as if her body were empty, floating in space. At last she drifted into sleep.

When she woke with a start, it was totally dark and her eyes had a hard time coming into focus. The smell of an oddly familiar perfume made her nostrils twitch, and then, gradually, through the dimness of the compartment, the shimmer of a midnight-blue gown came into view. Slowly Marika's eyes traveled upward to the face of the Contessa. Smiling serenely, she was smoking a cigar.

"You?" Marika said, sitting up in fright. "But . . . what are you doing on this train?"

"You have youth and beauty, my dear," the Contessa said. "I have discrimination and wisdom. God rarely chooses to bring these combinations together in one person." She paused. "As a team, we can make it."

· 35 ·

Chapter 2

A ticket-taker moved slowly through the compartments. Marika started to hand him her ticket, but the Contessa reached over, caressing Marika's fingers gently. "I have our tickets," she said softly, handing the conductor two envelopes. She quickly slipped Marika's own ticket inside her bag.

"But I don't understand," Marika said, feeling she'd totally lost control. "Papa . . ."

"Your dear Papa is going on a long tour of duty," the Contessa said. "He will not be back for years. I've investigated the school in Bohemia where you're being sent."

"You have?" Marika asked, wishing her Papa had told her what to do if she ever encountered the Contessa again.

"It's a strict religious order," the Contessa went on, removing her hat carefully. "The girls work like slaves. You've been assigned to do laundry. All day long you'll stand over hot pots, ruining your skin with horrible-smelling soap."

"I couldn't do that," Marika said. "I don't know how to work."

"Exactly, my dear," the Contessa said. "It wouldn't be at all suitable. Besides, I suspect you're not aware of one crucial fact. Girls at his school are in training to be nuns."

"Nuns!" Marika was stunned.

"Your nature is far too romantic to be a nun . . . ever."

Marika sank back in her seat, bitterly resentful of what Friedrich was trying to do to her. How could he?

"Fortunately, I have saved the situation," the Contessa said, with a little smile. "You can trust me. We're going to Warsaw instead."

"But that's in Poland," Marika said, almost in protest. She knew nothing of Poland—the very sound of the word was uninviting.

"Of course," the Contessa said. "Count Dabrowsky, I'm sure you will recall, is Polish."

"The Count?" Marika asked lamely. "I don't like him very much. He looks at me in a funny way."

"He's a wonderful man," the Contessa said, reaching across again to caress Marika's hand. "But it takes time to get to know him. I got in touch with him as soon as I heard what Friedrich was planning to do to you. Out of the goodness of his heart, he invited us for a summer vacation. You'll learn to adore him. He's very wealthy, you know."

"I don't care how rich he is," Marika said.

"You've always had everything provided for you," the Contessa said. "But that was when you were a young girl. You've become a young woman now. A young woman without the protection of a man has a hard time of it in this God's world."

"But Papa . . ." Marika almost wanted to cry. "I thought he was going to send me some money."

"I fear he needs what little he has for himself," the Contessa told her. "Surely you wouldn't want to take anything from him, not when he's having so much financial trouble."

"I guess not," Marika said hesitantly.

"Of course not. You're on your own, my dear," the Contessa said. "Except you're lucky. You have me to protect you. And the Count."

Marika closed her eyes, listening not to the Contessa's words but to the sound of the train. It was impossible to think. She'd let the Contessa do that for her. Whatever lay in store for her in Warsaw had to be better than the school in Bohemia.

At the Austrian frontier at Oderberg, a customs official tried to guide Marika and the Contessa into a train bound for Vienna.

"But we're going to Kraków," the Contessa said firmly.

"Forgive me," the conductor answered, "but I couldn't believe such fine ladies as you would want to go to Kraków. Poland is so sad." He elaborately guided Marika and the Contessa to the Kraków-bound train, his face still full of surprise. "I can usually tell where somebody is going just by looking at them," he said apologetically.

* * *

Nose to the window, Marika took in the monotony of the Great Plain of Europe. Part of her had been left forever behind in Berlin. Instinctively she knew she could never go back to that life again. Everything had changed.

The thought of the upcoming adventure did not totally displease her. At least it might free her of the lonely bedrooms she'd occupied in Berlin and at Baden-Baden, when living with her Papa. Maybe she wouldn't have to go to school either. She'd meant her vow not to be a schoolgirl anymore.

But if not a schoolgirl, then what? She was determined not to let the Contessa know she was afraid, but in the back of her mind, she suspected the Contessa was taking her to Warsaw to become the Count's little girl, maybe even his new wife. The idea was abhorrent beyond her imagination.

Perhaps Papa had slandered the Contessa without justification. Maybe what he said wasn't true. Brigitte had always been madly jealous of anyone Friedrich was close to. His sister could have made up those lies about the Contessa. At any rate, Marika would see it through. If they forced her into anything she couldn't stand, she'd simply escape. She wouldn't be a prisoner, after all.

Right now anything, even a life in Warsaw with the Count, sounded better than being a nun.

The Contessa's too-black hair and her excessive makeup caused several of the plain-faced women in the train to look disapprovingly at her, but she kept her head held high, her back erect. If someone stared too long or too contemptuously, the Contessa returned the stare with such power the passenger usually walked on in embarrassment. No words passed between Marika and the Contessa.

In Kraków Marika listened to the sound of her own heart beating, as she waited on the platform for the Contessa to get the luggage. Swarming passengers speaking a strange tongue crowded the platform. Aided by a porter, she climbed a wide, steep stairway that ascended to the street and stood on the busy pavement, helplessly gazing into the eyes of Kraków peasants. Their clothes were turkey-red or the color of coffee with milk. Jews in sinister black came out of alleyways, disappearing again into their back-street doors.

The Contessa spoke to the porter in Polish, seeming completely at home on this foreign soil. Seated in an ancient omnibus, they rattled to town, pulling up at last in front of the Grand Hotel where servants stood in rows, bowing as Marika walked down a long, red-carpeted hallway lit by crystal chandeliers.

In their high-ceilinged room, the Contessa took off her hat and announced: "We're meeting friends of mine for a late supper. It's a romance I arranged. A May-December love which I always find the most enduring."

"You mean the man is older?" Marika asked.

"Usually," the Contessa replied, checking to see that the bed was clean. "In this case, the man is no more than twenty-five."

"And the lady?"

"You're too young to have to worry," the Contessa said. "But a lady never gives her age. The ages of all my clients, male and female, are secret."

"What do I care about age?" Marika asked, noting a black beetle running across the floor. "I'm only thirteen."

"True, but it's important even now to conceal any record of your age," the Contessa said. "Records could be dangerous years from now, when snoopers try to determine your exact age. No one knows when I was born." She checked her makeup in a gilt-framed mirror. "Therefore, I can be any age I choose. Or any age I think I can get away with."

At first Marika was tempted to kill the beetle, but changing her mind she scooped it up and tossed it out the window. "Why are you always arranging marriages between people of such different ages? I think you should help Romeo meet Juliet. Not imprison some poor young man with an old hag."

The Contessa slammed down her bag on the table. "Listen to me and listen well," she said, looking impatiently at Marika. "When one is young, one must be with old lovers of means. That is the only way one can afford virile lovers when one is old oneself." She sighed. "I wasted my youth pursuing handsome beaus. Had I married a wealthy old man when I was your age, I wouldn't be penniless the way I am today."

Marika eyed the plushness of their suite. "If you have no money, how can we afford such an expensive hotel?"

"Count Dabrowsky can afford it."

At dinner that night, an old, moustachioed headwaiter directed Marika and the Contessa to a large table in the corner laden with white linen and crystal. The borscht was good and Marika ate heartily, devouring the poppyseed rolls.

"I'm letting you indulge yourself tonight," the Contessa warned, "but once we reach Warsaw, it's back to your diet. We both need to watch our weight."

It was not until the main course that the Contessa's late-arriving friends appeared in the dining room: an elderly woman in a purple gown, followed by a handsome, olive-skinned young man in a well-tailored blue suit. After introductions, the young man, named Mario, sat opposite Marika, and immediately his intense black eyes met hers with a coquetry that seemed almost girlish. Marika blushed. She blushed again when she caught Madame von Meyerinck staring first at Mario, then at her, then at Mario again. Abruptly, Mario jumped, and, casting a swift, rueful look at Madame von Meyerinck, reached to rub his shin.

Declining all offers of food, Madame von Meyerinck said to the Contessa, "I was surprised when you wrote me you were coming through Kraków."

"I tried to reach you in Vienna," the Contessa replied.

"I wish I were there," Madame von Meyerinck said. "But my first husband owned property here, and I'm having difficulty with it."

"I can't stand the food here," Mario protested. "Poles live on potatoes and roots."

The Contessa took his heavily ringed hand firmly in hers, like a stern grandmother. "When I discovered you on the streets of Rome, you were surviving on nothing. Starving like a rat in a church. Your ribs showed. Now, you're a gourmet!"

Mario slammed a fork against his empty plate. He called for the waiter to bring wine. "I can hardly tolerate the wine either," he said. "It is bad for my complexion. I need to be in the Roman sun."

"Mario even hates Austrian food," Madame von Meyerinck said in desperation. "Surely you agree, Contessa, it is the finest in the world."

"Naturally," the Contessa said unconvincingly.

"Your poor mama would turn over in her grave," Mario said, throwing his hands into the air in exasperation with the Contessa. "You have insulted our homeland. You've been so long in Prussia you're becoming like one of them."

Throughout the exchange between Mario and the Contessa, Madame von Meyerinck kept her eyes fastened on Marika. Her look was skeptical. Concentrating on her fish, Marika pretended not to notice.

"Your new 'discovery' is very beautiful," Madame von Meyerinck said to the Contessa. "And," she added sardonically, "her beauty has not escaped Mario's attention, I see."

Marika resented being talked about as if she weren't there.

"Now, *cara*," Mario said, kissing her gently on the nose, "you know I have eyes only for you."

"A likely story," Madame von Meyerinck said, gently pushing Mario away. She turned slightly to the Contessa, but made sure she did not take her eyes off Marika. "I caught Mario only three weeks ago in the arms of the Baroness in Vienna."

"That's not true," Mario shouted. "He was only showing me the proper way for a gentleman to remove his trousers. You like me to have good manners."

"Excuse me," Marika interrupted. "I thought Madame mentioned a Baroness. You said 'he.'"

"Ah." The Contessa laughed. "You are so pure!"

"In time," she added reassuringly to Marika, "you will learn of such things. The ways of love are many."

"I'm sure you've tried all of them," Mario said, laughing. The Contessa's face turned to stone. Marika had never seen her that angry. "Mario, my dear, you will always be the little boy who urinated against the great statues and fountains of Rome. Those who cannot create art at least can water it."

Madame von Meyerinck burst into laughter, her heavy bosom shaking. "Pardon me," Mario said, rising from the table. "I will not be laughed at by women."

"Darling," Madame von Meyerinck called after him.

Mario headed for the door.

"Let him go," the Contessa said, restraining Madame von Meyerinck. "You run after him, cater to him too much anyway. You must not let him think he has power over you. After all, he's only a peasant boy who refused to work in the fields."

"I'm so jealous," Madame von Meyerinck said. Her voice was slightly tear-choked. "I give parties at which I suspect Mario has been to bed with every woman and probably many of the men, too."

"Madame," Marika said. "Such talk! It is strange."

The Contessa touched Madame von Meyerinck's arm. "Marika is very young. An innocent."

"Innocent!" Madame von Meyerinck said. "My divine Contessa, you've never brought around an innocent in your life. By the time you unleash one of your discoveries on us, you've trained him or her to take everything and give us almost nothing in return."

"That's not true," the Contessa said, bristling at the remark. "I deliver only the finest."

"When the Contessa is through with you," Madame von Meyerinck said to Marika, "you'll be as light-fingered as Mario. Only the other day I caught him trying on my jewelry."

"He wasn't going to steal it," the Contessa objected. "He merely likes to dress the role of the lady on occasion."

Marika stood up, arching her shoulders. "Madame," she said, "I've never taken anything from anybody—and I don't plan to learn how."

"Forgive me," Madame von Meyerinck said with a wink. "I didn't know you were so sensitive."

Excusing herself, Marika hurried from the dining room, her tears blinding her. The woman was a barbarian. Her talk was cheap and vulgar, like the prostitutes of the street. Yet the Contessa had claimed that Madame von Meyerinck was a great lady of wealth in Vienna.

In the corridor a hand reached out for Marika. A sudden blur appeared before her face, and then the sweet-wine taste of Mario's breath was on her mouth. "I knew you'd follow me if I pretended to be angry and left," he whispered into her ear. His hand cupped one of her breasts. "I could tell you wanted me."

At first paralyzed with fear, Marika regained her strength and broke away. She turned and ran down the corridor. It was like an empty void, taking her deeper and deeper into a world she knew nothing about.

* * *

Poland was a conquered, partitioned nation, ruled over in triumph by the Russian colossus. In the summer before the Great War, Warsaw was a hub of intrigue and espionage, as socialists, anarchists, monarchists, and communists—all watched carefully by the secret police—jockeyed for position.

Across the border in East Prussia, mothers nervously gave their *kinder* nightmares by describing the savage rape and pillage that followed in the wake of the infamous cavalry charge of yelling Cossacks. So the tale went; millions of oxlike mujiks—ready to die for Mother Russia—stood poised to march across Poland to rip the very heart out of Germany.

By night express from Kraków, Marika headed for Warsaw.

* * *

On the train platform in Warsaw, the Count waited with two servants for Marika and the Contessa. A porter with a frosty nose banged on the steamed-up window of Marika's compartment.

"Don't worry," the Contessa said. "The Count will take care of everything. We don't need to cope with porters anymore."

In a weakly-lit corridor in the station, Marika carefully evaluated the Count, noting that his jaw and shoulders sloped more heavily than she'd remembered. In his own Russian-occupied country, he looked much less flamboyant than at Baden-Baden— and very old.

He took her hand and looked deeply into her eyes, hazy from lack of sleep on the train. The Contessa talked rapidly to him in Polish, but he seemed to be only half-listening, most of his attention focused on Marika. With infinite care, he led her past noisy cabmen and carriages and, completely lost, she followed blindly.

Soon, the Count's driver pulled into a large courtyard on a street of tall town houses, and at the top of a stone staircase, a servant in a crimson dress opened the door. "We'll talk later," the Count assured Marika. "But first, you need rest from your long journey."

Marika had nothing to talk with the Count about. She hoped there would always be other people around—what would she do alone with the man?

She surveyed the blue wallpaper and white enamel in her large, spotless bedchamber. Was this going to be her new home? For how long? She threw herself on the ornate brass bed, but she couldn't fall asleep. Even though the weather was warm outside, the house was cold—and made all the more so by the presence of the Count. When he looked at her, his eyes seemed to penetrate right through her skin. And his hands were cold, like those of a man who'd been out in the snow.

Sounds from below floated up to her room. There was a knock on her door, and whispers, but she didn't answer it. She closed her eyes, feigning fatigue in case a servant should enter. Maybe whoever it was would go away. Without knowing it, she drifted into a deep, coma-like sleep.

It seemed like only moments later when a servant came into her bedroom and, pulling back the draperies, laughed cheerfully, "Time to get up." The early morning sunlight beamed into her room and startled, Marika sat up, rubbing her eyes.

"You slept for most of yesterday, plus an entire night," the woman said. "A very good rest indeed, miss."

Marika couldn't believe it. She dressed and, slowly, walked down the steps to the dining room, as cold and sparsely furnished as the rest of the house.

The Count and the Contessa greeted her. Marika smiled faintly, her eyes on a portrait hanging in back of the Count. "Was that your Papa?" she asked the Count.

"No, that is Mickiewicz," the Count said patiently, as if she were a child in school. "The greatest poet of Poland. I'm sure you weren't allowed to study him in Prussian schools. But if you're going to live in my country, you should know his work as part of your education. This afternoon I'll read to you some of his best poems."

"Perhaps you'll translate them for me," Marika said.

The Count smiled and nodded his approval. "Tonight we'll have dinner with my sister. She lives here but has been away on a trip. Of course, she's anxious to meet both of you."

The Contessa seemed disappointed at the news.

Moments later, a large woman in a gray dress entered the room, her long brown hair worn closely wound around her head, her movements like a large sheepdog. In her hand she carried a set of keys on a metal ring.

"This is Aunt Nadya," the Count said.

The woman bowed before them.

"She's Russian, but has agreed to work for me if I put her in charge of all household affairs," the Count said. "I wish you'd been here for Easter. She made the finest *kulich* I've ever tasted. The servants ground almond flour for hours!"

Aunt Nadya's eyes were dark and mysterious. She said something in Polish, to which the Contessa bowed her head slightly. "She said she'd be pleased to do anything to make our stay here pleasant," the Contessa informed Marika.

"Thank you, Aunt Nadya."

After the Russian woman had left the dining room, the Count whispered to Marika. "You wouldn't believe it to look at those chunky Slavic features, but rumor has it that gypsy blood flows through Aunt Nadya. That's why she prefers to live outside her own country. Even her own people don't want her."

Marika hardly listened. She was thinking that she must send a letter to her Papa. She didn't have his address, but perhaps she could write it and give it to the Contessa. The Contessa probably knew someone who could deliver it.

"I want to show you ladies some of Warsaw today," the Count said. "That is, what's left of it."

"What do you mean, sir?" Marika asked.

"What's left after the Russians carted off our treasures to St. Petersburg," he answered.

For the next few hours, the Count proudly toured them around the city, but it was in the Saxon Garden that Marika saw what she thought was the most beautiful sight of all. At the end of a broad avenue, she came to a stop at a large stone fountain shaped like a vase, and in the background the gilded domes and white towers of the new Russian Cathedral rose glistening like something out of the exotic East. It was as if she'd been swept away on a magic Byzantine carpet. When the bells sounded, the noise was like a gong, assaulting the brain with its clamor.

But the Count angrily turned his back on the Cathedral, refusing even to look at it. He would have nothing to do with the Russians.

Back at the town house, the Count told Marika, "Tomorrow I have a treat for you. We are going to the theater . . . just the two of us." She thanked him but shuddered at the prospect. As she turned to go to her room, she remembered what the Contessa had told her. "You are in Poland now, and you must learn their customs. You kiss the host on both cheeks."

Marika kissed the Count lightly on both of his sagging cheeks, trying to avoid his moustache. On her last kiss, he held her close, the sound of his heavy breathing as numbing to her brain as the gong of the Russian Cathedral.

* * *

Madame Dalecka, the Count's sister, was even older than her brother. She sat there at dinner that night, her high cheekbones chalk-white, her face bearing no sign of makeup. The effect was ghostly. What struck Marika most, though, were the wide black ribbons around her wrists. "Those are beautiful bands," she said. "Are they Polish bracelets?"

Madame Dalecka stared at her, then in halting German spoke sternly. "An ironic name for them, Fräulein. These 'bracelets' hide hideous scars. They were made by chains I wore when I was marched in a prison convoy to Siberia."

Marika gasped.

The Count gently touched her hand. "My sister has not always accepted our Russian masters as stoically as I have."

"Even though life has given me rank and wealth," Madame Dalecka said, "I cannot eat, drink, and be merry while Poland suffers." She turned her attention to the Contessa. "Don't you agree?"

"I know little of international politics," the Contessa said flatly. "I never discuss the subject."

Madame Dalecka carefully placed her fork on her plate. Full of fury, her eyes focused sharply on the Contessa. "I'm not discussing international politics. I'm talking about the suffering of my people."

"Perhaps the Contessa is right," the Count interjected. "It's wrong to discuss such matters at the table."

A silence fell over the room. Marika found it embarrassing. She

· 46 ·

felt that Madame Dalecka strongly resented the presence of her and the Contessa in the household.

"You and the Fräulein should not waste all your time in Warsaw," Madame Dalecka said finally, this time in a more consoling voice. "There isn't much to do here. I spend my days in charity work."

"My sister has founded an institution for the blind," the Count said, "and a school of peasant embroidery."

"As I was saying," Madame Dalecka continued, "Warsaw is dull under the Russians. However, I'd suggest you go to Zakopane. It's a health resort about a six-hour journey by train from Kraków. You can rent a large wooden villa there."

"I don't plan to be in your country long," Marika interrupted. She held her chin high.

"I see," Madame Dalecka said. "That is good, as I fear there is too much misery for a Prussian child like you to enjoy herself."

The Count and the Contessa remained silent even when Aunt Nadya entered the room with dessert.

"My sister may have a point," the Count said, looking at Marika and smiling. "I will take you and the Contessa to Zakopane. After all, I don't want such charming guests to get bored."

"But you've traveled too much," Madame Dalecka protested. "Besides, it is too soon after the death of your last wife. I do not think one should travel for two years after losing a loved one, unless forced to do so by the government." She held up the black bands around her wrists.

"At my age," the Count said, "I cannot afford to wait for such long periods of time. I must take all from life that I can possibly get—and take it now!"

"Absolutely right," the Contessa agreed.

Their comments seemed to have an unpleasant effect on Madame Dalecka. Rising shakily, her face, if possible, even whiter than before, she stood and excused herself. "I won't be taking dessert tonight." Abruptly, she departed.

Marika turned to the Count, "I hope she's not angry with us."

"If she is," the Count said, "she'll have to live with her anger. This is my house. Your new home."

Marika rose and curtsied. "I don't think I want dessert either." She turned and walked from the cold dining room into the hallway, up a great paneled staircase, and into a gallery at the top. Pictures of the Dabrowsky family filled the walls. She tried to imagine her portrait hanging there with the rest. "But it doesn't belong there," she whispered to herself. "I don't belong here."

Early the next morning, Marika woke, slipped downstairs, avoiding the servants, and closed the front door softly behind her. Alone on the streets of Warsaw, she could breathe again. The people and the buildings were foreign to her, but she needed this time away from the Count and the Contessa. For days now she'd been filled with a sense of foreboding about what was going to happen to her. At least for a few hours she could escape that fear.

She walked and walked, and slowly the city began to change. She came to an ancient square, the Stare Miasto, the old town. Tall fourteenth- and fifteenth-century merchants' homes, crumbling and forbidding, looked down at her. Jews swarmed through the tenements. Large, hand-painted boards advertised various merchandise. Marika was astonished. Instead of being ashamed of their Jewishness, these people were actually calling attention to it. Her hand clutching tightly at her collar, she walked among them, uncomfortably aware of her white dress and her blonde hair glistening in the sun. She felt more Prussian than ever. The Jewish merchants who tried to sell her their wares seemed to know she was Prussian, too, and treated her like a rich German. One of the Jews spoke to her in her native language, dangling a gold necklace in front of her. Repulsed by his yellowing teeth and beard, she loudly turned him down, speaking German in her most halting manner, like her Papa. He laughed at her—everyone seemed to be laughing at her. The buildings leaned crazily and seemed to close her in. In a panic, she ran back up one of the dark streets and desperately boarded a tram. She didn't know where it was going, only that she must escape the Jews.

But she'd made a mistake. Outside the tram window all she could see was miles and miles of the Jewish Ghetto, buildings squalid with neglect and faces that seemed to leer down at her, making her shield her eyes in her white-gloved hands. The tram was her ark of safety, and she trembled every time it stopped. Eyes tightly closed, she vowed not to open them again until the Ghetto was far behind her.

At a nudge from the conductor, she sat up in her seat. Only five people were left on the tram. They carried flowers to the great cemetery of Warsaw. Warily stepping off the tram, she realized she was lost, but she had carefully written the address of the Count's town house on a slip of paper. With the spending money the Contessa had given her on the train, she decided to take a horse and buggy and, handing the driver the address, she realized her day alone had been so frightening it now made the Dabrowsky household a safe haven by comparison. The driver couldn't read, but showed the slip of paper to a policeman, who directed them on their way.

Settling back in the little cab, Marika felt very grown-up. She wished her Papa could see her now. Perhaps he'd have more respect for her. Without his help, she'd moved into a new and different life for herself. A part of her still feared the day when she'd have to see him again, as she was sure he would condemn her, but she'd console him, telling him she'd gone off with the Contessa for his sake. The Count was a man of wealth. When Marika got to know him better, she'd ask him for financial help for Friedrich.

The clock struck five in the afternoon as she returned home. And, stepping from the buggy, she gave all of her money to the driver, who seemed very pleased. Waiting in the cold, dark parlor was the Contessa, smoking a cigar, veiled in purple. The scented darkness of the room blended with her perfume.

"Good afternoon," Marika said, guiltily, and excusing herself headed up the stairs to her room.

"My darling," the Contessa said, "please come in here. I'd like a word with you."

Entering the parlor again, Marika softly asked, searching her mind for some lie to make up about her disappearance, "What is it?"

The Contessa looked at her face for a long time. Then, leaning down to put out her cigar, she said, "I saw some blind children playing today at Madame Dalecka's school." She glanced up again. "I remember their gay laughter, the way the sun made their golden hair shine. Their faces were radiant."

Marika smiled in embarrassment. "I'm sorry the children are blind, but what do they have to do with me?"

The Contessa laid a hand on her right arm, as if suffering from

· 49 ·

an arthritic pain. "It occurred to me that you were like them."

"But I can see."

"No," the Contessa said, "not in the way I mean. For years now you've been running and playing in the sunshine without really seeing the world as it is."

"What are you trying to say?" Marika closed her eyes and rubbed her brow. A migraine headache seemed near.

"As I told you on the train," the Contessa continued, "you're a young woman. As such, you must shoulder certain responsibilities, instead of running off early in the morning without even informing a servant where you are going."

"I'm sorry," Marika said. "I didn't mean to. It just happened."

"Yes," the Contessa said. "Yes." She rose slowly and walked to the window, the fading light casting a pallor on her face. Her heavy makeup was the only vibrant color in the dark room.

A door creaked and Marika turned in fright. But it was only a young maid hurrying to the kitchen at the back of the house.

"Excuse me," Marika said to the Contessa, "I must hurry if I'm to join the Count for the theater tonight."

Climbing the stairs, she felt justified for walking out so abruptly. She was determined not to be some little puppet whose strings could be pulled by the Contessa. Wandering on her own that morning, she'd come to realize that the Contessa needed her more than she needed the Contessa. It was clear the Count had eyes only for Marika. When she made an observation, no matter how trivial, he seemed utterly fascinated. He cooed, he exclaimed over her. He was polite to the Contessa, but it was obviously veiled, as if he merely tolerated her. The knowledge not only made Marika more secure in her dealings with the Contessa; it made her feel more like a real woman, and not some child play-acting at womanhood.

On the way to the theater that night, the Count did not ask Marika where she'd spent the day. His only words were, "It is dangerous for a young girl to be in Warsaw alone."

Marika sensed he was angry, but she didn't really care. She had little desire to please the man at this point. Approaching the theater, dazzled by the gilded décor of the open carriages, she forgot all about his sullen mood.

Getting out of their own equipage, Marika was convinced she

was the center of all attention. Head held high, she wore little beads of perspiration on her forehead like the gems in a tiara. All around, elegant men and women greeted the Count. A tall man in a cape even bowed in front of Marika and kissed her hand. "I pale in the presence of such beauty," he said.

Cheeks turning red, she feared the man would detect her embarrassment, but he didn't seem to. As best she could, she tried to appear used to having men bow before her, kiss her hand, and compliment her beauty.

Seated in the Count's private box, she rested her beaded purse on the railing and surveyed the sea of faces below through mother-of-pearl opera glasses, the ladies dressed in the ostrich feathers and beaded gowns she'd envied so in the boutiques of Baden-Baden, many of the men in uniform, sparkling with braid and medals. Heads turned and nodded to the Count, treating him with great respect. For the first time she was aware of the privilege of being the companion of a special person. Even though she didn't like the Count very much, the idea of his having rank thrilled her.

She wondered if the light coming from the brilliant crystal chandeliers overhead was picking up the brightness in her own eyes. Seated on red velvet, in a gilt chair, she decided this was the world in which she belonged.

The curtain went up on a play, *Warszawianka*, by the Polish poet, Stanislaw Wyspianski, starring the very old, very grand actress, Madame Modrzejewska. "We grew up together," the Count whispered to Marika. "She was such a great beauty when she was young. She later married a Count like myself."

Marika compared herself to Madame Modrzejewska, watching the way she walked and talked. The play was in Polish, and Marika didn't understand a word of it, yet the spell the elderly woman created on the stage intrigued her. Before the final scene ended, she had the audience openly sobbing and sniffling. Even the Count was wiping his eyes. Marika was amazed that any woman could reduce an entire audience to tears.

As the curtain descended, roses showered the stage, and Madame Modrzejewska took repeated bows. At each new bow, Marika found herself resenting the woman more and more. A woman of her age shouldn't be appearing in public. A younger, prettier actress should be up there taking those bows. It wasn't hard for

Marika to imagine herself up there. Surely the audience would be enthralled by her beauty. She pictured herself basking in the spotlight, surrounded by flowers, the audience on its feet.

In the middle of the applause, Marika suddenly reached for the Count's arm. "I don't think I told you," she said, "but I'm an actress, too." She blurted the words out as if they were true.

"I had no idea," the Count said, his eyes still on Madame Modrzejewska.

"Not just an actress," she said, more emphatically, "a *great* actress. I made my debut two years ago on the Berlin stage."

"How did it go?" the Count asked, now concentrating fully on Marika.

"I walked on the stage," Marika told him, her face flushed. "It was deserted. Everything was bathed in red. A murmur went up from the audience. I could see only shadows in the distance. I think a woman had fainted. You see . . ." She paused for dramatic effect. "I was entirely nude. The part called for it."

The Count stared at her, then closed his eyes, sinking back into his chair. She imagined he was trying to conjure up what it must have been like, seeing her in the nude. "One so sweet," he said, finally, "one so beautiful. It must have been a heavenly dream."

"It was."

The lights in the theater went on. Marika stood up regally, discreetly eying the crowd below, dreaming that she was a queen appearing before her subjects. The Count's eyes were on her and many men looked up. The women appeared slightly contemptuous, perhaps because she was young and out with a man old enough to be her grandfather, but it was the look of the men that told Marika she could make any one of them forget Madame Modrzejewska forever.

Through the milling crowd backstage, the Count directed Marika to Madame Modrzejewska's dressing room, where an enthusiastic group of fans waited to give her congratulations. Magic permeated the air. She was able to suspend her jealousy of Madame Modrzejewska and enjoy the moment.

By the time the Count actually presented her to the aging actress, Marika was weeping from excitement. But Madame Modrzejewska mistook Marika's tears. "My darling," she said to her in Polish.

The Count quickly explained that Marika spoke only German.

"My darling," the actress said again, this time in fluent German. "To have one so young and beautiful moved to tears is a great joy to me." She swept Marika into her arms, hugging her close against her ample bosom. Marika was shocked at the sweaty smell of the actress, and was greatly relieved to be released again.

Madame Modrzejewska's body was all cushions and curves, but her hollow-cheeked, colorless face betrayed her age. She turned to the Count, affectionately rubbing her ringed fingers against his moustache. "Like me, you go on forever," she said. Smiling at Marika, she added, "Once I was the one he pursued. But after I turned sixteen I was too old for him."

"Now, Helena," the Count said, "you know that isn't true. By the time you were sixteen, you were pursuing another count far richer than myself."

Marika watched the thinning crowd in the dressing room disappear slowly, leaving just the Count and herself with Madame Modrzejewska. She dreaded having to leave. If she had her wish, she'd stay backstage in the world of the theater forever.

"Please excuse me," Madame Modrzejewska said to the Count, "I've got to get out of these stiff clothes."

"Perhaps you'll join us for supper," the Count said, kissing her hand.

"I'd like that very much," she replied, "but I've made other plans. Let the little girl stay awhile. My wardrobe lady is sick tonight, and I need help."

"Very well," the Count said. "I must tell friends good-bye."

Alone with Madame Modrzejewska, Marika helped her unlace her corset and was shocked at the woman's flabby flesh and sagging bosom. Through eyes shaped like a cat's, Madame Modrzejewska watched Marika closely. "The stage, my dear," she said, "is for the illusion. That is where the magic is created. When I'm not performing, I become the rather ordinary physical woman you see before you."

Marika turned from the woman's body to the autographed pictures of some of the royal families of Europe that surrounded Madame Modrzejewska's dressing table. Dominating them all was a huge, very formal portrait of the Tsar, Tsarina, and Tsarevitch. Autographed photographs of some of the great artists of Europe filled Fabergé frames. "I want to be an actress, too," Marika said. She paused.

"Go on, say it," Madame Modrzejewska commanded. She stared at Marika down a straight, almost Hebraic nose.

"But I don't want the illusion to end . . . ever. I want to be performing always, both on and off the stage."

In front of the mirror, Madame Modrzejewska added clouds of white *poudre-de-riz* to her already colorless face. Her eyes shone through the pallor, blue as star sapphires. "That is a decision every actress has to make for herself. For me, it isn't worth it. Besides, I married a wealthy count, and don't have to pretend to be glamorous day and night. With me, acting is a hobby. I don't depend on it for my livelihood."

Marika dried her eyes. "Did you marry for money?" she asked tentatively.

"Of course, I did," the actress said. She ran her fingers through her reddish-blonde mop. "Doesn't everybody who has a chance?"

"I always planned to marry for love," Marika said, fingering the dress the actress had worn on the stage.

"You talk like an eleven-year-old," Madame Modrzejewska said, "even though you must be all of thirteen. By the time you're sixteen, you will have buried those silly dreams. Then you can get on with the business of living in the real world."

"You talk like someone else I know," Marika said. "A Contessa."

"Listen to her, then," Madame Modrzejewska said. "She's giving you sound advice."

"But I know nothing of sex," Marika blurted out, looking uncomprehendingly at the actress. "That is what terrifies me."

"With Count Dabrowsky," she said, "you're in good hands. He knows little about sex, either, and his demands are so infantile they're almost childlike, as childlike as his last bride."

Without thinking, Marika flew, sobbing, into the woman's arms. Rubbing Marika's smooth hair, the actress cradled her in her breasts. "Don't be afraid, little one," she said. "Old men are vile and disgusting creatures. We must let them have their way with our bodies, then we can be free of them for another week, or another month. It's not too much of a price to pay for the good life, as repugnant as we may find their feeble attempts at sex."

Marika broke away, embarrassed for having cried in front of the woman. "I never had a mother," she said hesitantly. "No one to tell me anything."

"That's just as well," Madame Modrzejewska said. "Nothing my own mother ever told me was of any use. All her information was wrong. Even if you had a mother, I don't think she could have adequately prepared you for the Count. That you'll have to discover for yourself."

Marika looked away, staring at the woman's wardrobe. She longed to try on one of her hats in front of the mirror. "Do you think I should let him . . . ?"

"Only if he marries you," Madame Modrzejewska cautioned. "It won't be easy on you, I know that. But you should get involved with him. He'll be dead in a year or two, and you'll be the Countess Dabrowsky. Then you can live your own life as you please."

Marika turned to face the actress again. The woman's look was tender, compassionate. "If you really think so," she said. "He's not very handsome. And certainly not young and dashing. I once thought I'd marry a hussar, like my Papa."

"You'll know many handsome young men in your life," Madame Modrzejewska said. She shrugged her shoulders and resumed work on her white face. "But all in good time." When she was through, she turned quickly and lifted Marika's chin. Pulling her close, she kissed her deeply, passionately on the mouth, sucking her lips.

The wetness of the woman's tongue shocked Marika. She'd never been kissed like that before. Backing away, she was tempted to rub the wetness from her mouth, but did not dare to.

"Don't be afraid," Madame Modrzejewska said. "That was my way of paying homage to youth. I presume you wanted to be up there on the stage tonight, receiving the roses and applause." She sighed. "As for me, I wanted to change positions with you. To have your youth and beauty." She stood up, and her body sagged more heavily than ever. "Now I've got to get dressed. I have to meet a very young and very boring lover for dinner tonight. It seems that Madame Modrzejewska has to instruct every eighteen-year-old in Warsaw how to make love."

Still trembling from the kiss, Marika stayed clear of the woman.

"One more bit of advice," she said. "Don't ever go to bed with a Russian. They are the roughest lovers in Europe. No finesse whatsoever. An Italian, a Frenchman, even a Prussian has an edge over a Russian." She laughed heartily, her breasts bobbing up and down. Hugging Marika closely once more, she released her.

At the door Marika's hand was shaking as she reached for a brass knob. "I really admire you." She looked back. "As an actress."

Madame Modrzejewska reached for a bouquet of roses, and, choosing carefully, picked a large yellow one and handed it to Marika. "The color of your hair," she said.

"Thank you," Marika replied, accepting the rose.

"Just invite me to the wedding," the actress said.

"We'll see," Marika answered faintly, at the thought of it.

In the street outside, the night air was brisk and bracing, and, standing beside his carriage, Count Dabrowsky waited patiently with a blanket. For a second, Marika wanted to run into the night, to take her chances alone, regardless of the consequences. But another force within her compelled her to walk toward the Count. She took his extended arm. Impulsively, she giggled like a school-girl which seemed to please and excite the Count. Up to now she'd been trying to act the lady in his presence, but suddenly she sensed that he preferred the girl.

"I will perform for him," she vowed to herself, placing the yellow rose in her lap.

* * *

The next few days passed slowly for Marika, and the empty feeling she'd had in Baden-Baden returned. She felt smothered in the company of the older people around her, but though she longed for some friends of her own age, she never went out on her own again. Sometimes the Count would invite her out, but more often she stayed at home. Madame Dalecka never joined in any of their evenings, preferring the privacy of her bedroom.

Afternoon tea alone with the Contessa became a ritual. One Sunday Marika sensed a new excitement on the Contessa's face. Breathing heavily, her cheeks flushed, she almost spilled her tea when she poured it. "A marvelous piece of good fortune came your way today," she said.

"Papa!" Marika said, sliding her chair closer to the Contessa. "You've heard from him?"

"To hell with your Papa!" the Contessa said, her face growing stern and hard. "Chances are you'll never hear from him again. Don't you know that? He's deserted you! Stop being blind—like Madame Dalecka's schoolchildren."

Marika froze at the Contessa's words, then, with sudden force, stood up, only to be hit by a wave of dizziness. Angrily, she threw herself onto the sofa, and for a long while lay there, silent, cradling her head in her arms. Finally sitting up, she looked crossly at the Contessa. "I don't believe you," she said. "You're just trying to hurt me."

"That's ridiculous," the Contessa replied. "Why would I want to hurt you—I, of all people, who has been the one most concerned with your welfare."

Marika placed a hand on her breasts, stroking them gently. There seemed to be a reawakening inside her. At first the Contessa's words had made her feel sad and defeated. But in the past few days Marika had felt a new side of herself struggling to be heard. Sometimes this new side would come like a voice in the middle of the night, waking her up, talking to her in a dream. She found herself wishing she'd said something different that previous day, taken a stronger position, made her own wishes better known. This new side of her was getting tired of being the pawn of everybody—the Contessa, her Papa, Count Dabrowsky.

Even though it had filled her with fear, the act of being out on her own that day in the Ghetto had been good for her. It had only whetted her appetite even more for the day she would control her own actions and be responsible for her own decisions. But, as Madame Modrzejewska had warned, to get into that position would take some doing.

Getting up from the sofa, Marika stood as tall as she could to face the Contessa. "What's this marvelous piece of good fortune?"

The Contessa looked at her strangely for a moment, as if sensing something about Marika she'd never noticed before. "The Count has asked my permission to take you as his bride."

The room whirled around Marika again.

"What's the matter, child?" the Contessa asked, reaching out for her.

Marika steadied herself, her heart pounding. "Why didn't he ask me?"

"Because I'm your legal guardian," the Contessa said softly.

Marika glared at the Contessa. "Don't ever call me a child again. You promised!"

"Indeed I did," the Contessa said. "I'm sorry I forgot for a moment in my enthusiasm. I hope that in return for my promise, you'll stop acting like one. Grow up, Marika!"

Her words cut into Marika, as no others ever had. She said nothing for a long time. "I don't want to be blind anymore." Her voice was barely audible. "I've always wanted to believe things are better than they are. But that has caused me pain." She paused. "I want to ask you something."

The Contessa picked up her cigar from a nearby ashtray and sat down in a winged armchair. "Feel free."

"Don't lie to me," Marika said, raising her voice. "Is what you told me in Kraków completely true? You have no money—nothing. Is that right?"

The Contessa opened her eyes wide. "That is a very realistic appraisal of our situation."

"I will get no help from Papa," Marika went on, her breath coming in gasps. "Whether we eat and have a place to sleep depends a great deal on my accepting the Count's proposal. Is everything right so far?"

The Contessa uttered a slight cry. "It's true." Her voice choked. "I'm helpless. My resources, even my clients, have dried up." She looked up at Marika. *Everything* depends on you." Reaching for her handkerchief, she started to cry.

Marika took the handkerchief from her, dropping it on the floor. "If we're being truthful," she said, "it isn't necessary to pretend to cry. I think you're beyond tears at this point." The other side of Marika, the one struggling to get out, seemed to be speaking for her.

The Contessa stopped crying at once. "All right," she said, straightening, "what's your decision?"

"I will make it tonight when I see the Count," Marika said. Leaving the room quickly, she headed for the stairway, the polished wood creaking under her footsteps. On an impulse, she turned and ran back. Her eyes met the Contessa's. "Remember," Marika cautioned, "it will be *my* decision."

That night, the Count escorted Marika into the large hallway of a celebrated restaurant, where an old man with the eyes of a crow directed them to a private room. "I've made arrangements for us to dine alone tonight," the Count said. "I'll join you in a moment."

Standing by herself in the salon, Marika trembled. Then she tried to breathe deeper. Because she knew a woman like the Contessa, did the Count think she was more experienced than she really was?

Two large paintings dominated the room—one of an Arab muse in a seraglio motif, the other of a Rubens-like lady, all cherubic pink. Her large bosom seemed to spill out of the portrait. Marika found herself feeling her own breasts, noting how small they were in comparison.

She took an upholstered seat under a rickety chandelier and beside a white marble fireplace, the mantel of which bore a gold clock mounted with Cupids. Across the room a maroon brocaded drapery hung, held back by a frayed golden tassel. It was like a stage curtain, pulled back to reveal a table set with crystal and silver, all softly lit by candles.

Marika noticed a musty, unfamiliar smell and wondered what really took place here. It did not look like any restaurant she'd ever seen.

Entering the room, the Count announced, "I've ordered champagne."

"That's good," Marika said.

"And a very big supper."

"But I really shouldn't eat too much," Marika said. "The Contessa said I'll get fat."

"Nonsense," the Count replied. "If you're worried about your figure, don't be. It's just right. A young girl should be what the Viennese call a *mollig*—that is, not fat, but not a rail either." He took a chair immediately next to Marika.

She got up, pretending to look at the paintings more closely. "This restaurant's like a hotel."

"Perhaps," the Count said. "It's very old. Founded many years ago by a friend of mine, Prince Otto, a dashing young man I knew in my youth."

"He's no longer here?" Marika asked.

"No," the Count said sadly. "Otto and another man were in love with the same girl. The other man was killed in an accident one day. Instead of taking the girl and being happy, Otto had to display one final act of vengeance. He saddled a race horse and jumped over the coffin of his former rival, right in the middle of the burial service. The brother of the deceased challenged him to a duel. Otto was shot. He died a day later."

"What happened to the girl?" Marika asked.

The Count smiled. "She was just about your age. With both of her lovers dead, she married me. My first wife."

"I don't understand the world of men," Marika said, sitting down again next to the Count. She stayed very still, keeping her eyes on the open door, wishing a servant would enter to break the sudden silence in the room.

"My dear," the Count said, taking her hand. At first she was tempted to jerk it back, but she closed her eyes instead and sat up straight in the chair.

The Count's fingers were feeling the softness of her arm, testing it as if it were a piece of flesh on the meat counter. "The Contessa has informed me you are in love with me."

Marika gasped, but said nothing. She remained sitting with her eyes closed.

"At first I couldn't believe it," he said. "One so sweet and beautiful wanting a man of my years." He cleared his throat and coughed slightly. "I turned the matter over in my mind many times. My present decision is not to question such good fortune. Rather, I'll just accept it, the way we accept a glass of beer, a glowing fire, a warm bed."

Marika grew dizzy at these words, imagining his nose and leering eyes, though her own remained closed. His hand on her arm was cold and clammy, and for a second she felt she couldn't stand being shut up a moment longer in this musty room with this man. Yet she remained glued to her chair.

The Count eased to the floor and buried his head in her lap, clinging to her legs. Her arms remained limp by her side, but she opened her eyes.

"I'm so lucky," the Count sobbed. "The Contessa assures me you are a virgin. I would have you no other way." He looked up at her.

She turned from the sight of his pathetic face.

"To me has fallen the good fortune to introduce you to the mystery of life," he said.

Marika gently pushed the Count away and slowly, gracefully, eased out of the chair. Her knees shaking, she walked toward the table. Her long hair had come undone and fell across her shoulders. She pretended she was Madame Modrzejewska, giving a performance, the Count the only member of her audience. Turning around, she looked back at him. "I don't want you to speak so intimately with me," she said.

"But . . ." A look of bewilderment crossed his face.

She paused for a long moment, her features a mask. Facing him, she stood with her clear eyes wide open. He moved toward her. From his pocket he took a tiny velvet box, pressing it into her hand. "Please open it," he said. "It belonged to my mother."

Accepting the box, she slowly raised the lid. A large ruby ring rested on a piece of red satin. "It's very pretty," she said.

"But aren't you going to try it on?" he asked.

She reached for his moustache, catching it between her thumb and index finger, and pulled it so that his lips parted slightly. Smiling sweetly, she closed her eyes tightly and kissed him quickly on the mouth.

Fingers at his lips, he seemed to savor the kiss.

"After dinner," she said, seating herself at the table, "I'll see if it fits."

Chapter 3

The monuments of Europe stood firmly in the summer of 1913. They seemed incapable of faltering. As an observer put it, "They were built for eternity."

In Vienna, Eugene Brieux presented a drama about syphilis. Every night, women in the audience fainted, requiring medical attention.

In the same audience sat men in uniform, representing the heterogeneous nationalities of the Hapsburg monarchy, their thoughts impenetrable. Some critics suggested that Austria was preparing for war. Others considered such prophets of gloom irresponsible. "Serbia wouldn't dare!"

Up in the mountains of the High Tatra, the idle wealthy of Central Europe journeyed to breathe the fresh, clean air, to enjoy the final summer before the lights went out in Europe, like the sun setting on the Tatra peaks in a fiery red glow.

That summer was the coldest, wettest, darkest ever recorded in Poland. In their third week at Zakopane, Count Dabrowsky and the Contessa could recall nothing to equal its gloom. For Marika, each day was the same. Covered in gray clouds, the Tatra Mountains seemed to move in on her like a prison.

In the privacy of her bedroom, she gazed lovingly at her reflection in her pedestal mirror, seeing the image of a young princess there. It was easy to dream she was in Zakopane to marry her Prince Charming.

From a catalogue she'd found in her Papa's study, she'd cut out figures of hussars in various dashing uniforms—crimson was her favorite—and pasted them on cardboard. Now they became her suitors, each one beseeching her to marry him. But she would take her own good time making up her mind, she decided. Sometimes she pretended to dance with them, closing her eyes and giggling as she heard the secrets they whispered in her ear.

Eventually she grew bored with her toys, however, and went to stand at the window, looking out at the greenish-gray fir trees and the bleak, constant clouds. Their wooden villa had no heat, being strictly a summer house, and day after day Marika shivered in her winter clothes, even though it was late June.

Her failure to speak any language other than German entrapped her all the more, and the Count had told her they could speak even that only when they were alone, or with the Contessa. "My people resent the German tongue," he said. "I speak Russian, too, but never in the presence of my people."

In desperation one day Marika asked the Count if she could learn Polish. He smiled at her, greatly pleased. "Finally! I'm delighted to see you taking an interest in things Polish. I know just the thing. There's a young tutor nearby who speaks not only Polish, but Russian, German, and English as well. When they want to be, Poles are very adept at languages. Actually," he leaned over to whisper, "he's not a real Pole. He's a Jew."

"A Jew!" The painful memory of the Ghetto returned.

"Yes, but that's all right. In a few days, I'll arrange for your lessons to begin," the Count said.

"I don't know . . ."

"What's the matter, my beauty?" he asked.

"It's nothing," Marika stammered. "It's only . . . Polish is so hard . . ."

"I'm sure you'll be a good pupil," the Count said, standing at the door. "After all, we'll be exchanging our marriage vows in Polish."

* * *

The weather continued to worsen. One Sunday, the Count was gone all day, and in the early afternoon the porter in charge of the summer villas arrived, looking sad and droopy in his sheepskin coat.

"What's the matter?" she asked.

"It is God," the little man said. "He has taken our summer from us." He crossed himself. "The priest gave a sermon this morning and warned us to make our peace with God."

Marika wrinkled her brow and shook her head at the porter's fragmented German. "I don't understand," she said.

"The priest . . . he told us," the man went on. He lowered his voice to exchange a confidential whisper. "God is getting ready to unleash the flood waters again. Your Count Dabrowsky was at the services."

Marika was surprised, but dismissed the porter as a religious fanatic. She mentioned the conversation to the Contessa that afternoon at tea, and snorted, "Zakopane is filled with superstitious peasants." She poured far more milk into her tea than she'd meant to.

"Do not say that ever again, my dear," the Contessa warned her, a look of alarm on her face.

"But why not?" Marika asked. "Surely *you* don't believe such silliness?"

The Contessa took Marika's hand. "Naturally, I don't," she said firmly. Then, under her breath, she whispered, "But Count Dabrowsky does."

Marika drew a sharp breath, then slowly let it out into the stale air of the room. "He must be insane, thinking all of us are going to drown."

The Contessa frowned bitterly. "He's at the stables right now," she said, "getting ready for tomorrow. He's heard of a carpenter up in the mountains who's building an ark. He plans to take us there in the morning."

"For heaven's sake, why?" Marika asked, totally exasperated.

The Contessa closed her eyes, as if the words were too painful to her. "He's going to try to secure passage for us on the ark. Aunt Nadya, too." She paused. "Just in case."

Marika shivered in the damp air. "I can't believe this is happening. The whole world seems crazy."

"The Count isn't completely convinced of the flood," the Contessa said. "But he doesn't want to take chances. We must go along with him, and not challenge his plan in any way. No man wants to appear the fool in front of women."

Marika got up and walked around the room, the wood floor creaking under her feet. "This is the most horrid summer anyone can remember," she said. "But I doubt if it's a sign that God is going to destroy us. There must be some other reason."

"Be more tolerant, Marika," the Contessa said, pouring herself some more strong tea. "When you're old, as Count Dabrowsky is —as I am—you're more willing to believe stories of impending doom."

"I should think the opposite would be true," Marika said. "Isn't it easier to convince a child of a fairy tale?"

"That's true," the Contessa said in a patient, weary voice. "But for an old person, things change. It's your own impending doom you fear. The fear often comes late at night. It gnaws at you. If you can find something in the physical world to focus on, it helps."

Marika nodded and licked her lips. The strong tea made her feel sick to her stomach. "I don't know what he has to worry about," she said. "He seems very healthy."

The Contessa's eyes sought hers and stared intently. "Are you nervous about marrying him?" she asked abruptly.

"Yes," Marika said sharply. Until now she'd resisted involving herself in any discussion about her upcoming marriage, but more and more she resented the fact she'd agreed to it in the first place. "You know I'm nervous."

The Contessa put down her cup of tea with regal authority. "Have you ever considered he might also be nervous about marrying you?"

Marika did not answer the question. Her contempt for the Count bubbled inside her mind. She wanted to tell the Contessa that Count Dabrowsky had had a lot of experience marrying young girls. She didn't know what marriage to an elderly man meant, but, in Marika's mind, Count Dabrowsky was the world's expert on teenage virgin brides.

Instead of pursuing the matter, Marika looked out the window at some women passing by. Their heads were covered by handkerchiefs of bright orange, and the sleeves of their dresses were scarlet, making them the only vibrant colors on the otherwise gray landscape. But the women's faces were dull.

· 65 ·

In contrast, the young men behind them strutted and preened. Handsome, their legs strong and shapely, their trousers tight-fitting, they put shameful images in Marika's mind.

The Contessa walked up beside Marika. "I've had at least four Polish lovers in my life. They're built like stallions. All my lovers could have satisfied Catherine the Great."

The skin of the young men passing by was as white as the thick, blanket-like material of their trousers, and their cheeks a healthy red. Marika found herself contrasting the robust mountain look of these young men with the wrinkled, leathery skin of the Count. She wanted to meet them, to go where they were going. How she wished she could share secrets with them and talk to them. But what could she say to them without knowing Polish?

"Come," the Contessa said, interrupting Marika's thoughts. "I've arranged for you to have a fitting for your wedding gown."

"For all I know," Marika said, "the Count is planning to marry me on the ark."

* * *

The next morning, Count Dabrowsky helped Marika into a long, narrow wagon without springs, and she found herself seated on a wooden bench, facing the Count and the Contessa. His face locked in bitter determination, the Count had said little at breakfast that morning. When she thought he wasn't looking, Marika shot quick glances at him. Was this the man who was going to be her husband?

The ride into the mountains was awful. The bumpy roads tossed Marika against the wagon's basket-work sides and rain poured in through holes in the canvas curtains covering the arched hoops overhead. Marika feared a terrible cold as a result of this excursion, and silently sat shivering in her wet cape.

For a brief moment, the wagon stopped at a tiny shrine with a white-marble Madonna and wilted flowers. Count Dabrowsky got down and crossed himself, standing in the mud in front of the shrine. "Last year a bobsleigh party turned over here," he said. "Two fine ladies were killed on the spot."

Slightly ill, Marika felt a new disaster was at hand.

In the distance, a gray stone building stood anchored into a mountainside, and the Count crossed himself again. "My dear sister spent five years there," he said, "after Siberia. It's for consumptives."

Marika rubbed her perspiring forehead. Maybe she was coming down with a fever instead.

The wagon creaked and rocked its way along a valley road until it came to a rocky gorge. There, the smell of burnt wood permeated the air, and even though rain was pouring down, the women peasants worked the black earth. Five shepherd's huts stood in the mountain glade and the sound of hammering echoed through the gorge.

Looking down at the muddy waters running along the road, Marika found herself believing for a moment that God was indeed going to unleash flood waters. Under a thatched roof a large man with a bulging stomach chiseled an enormous plank, and on a separate bench his son hammered the ends of two wooden poles together. The framework of a small ark lay clearly visible, like the skeleton of a whale, its ribs protruding upward. Stacks of logs had been piled high to dry.

As they became aware of the presence of the Count, the men stopped working, and, coming forward, the large man bowed awkwardly before the Count, his sheepskin coat riding up to reveal a hairy barrel chest. The young man covered his rotten teeth with his hand. Marika felt like a fool and avoided their eyes.

The Count talked a long while to the man, on one occasion raising his voice and swinging his arm in the air in a defiant gesture. "He's just trying to get the shepherd to lower his fare," the Contessa said. "The shepherd has already promised to take the people of the village with him."

"Do you mean the Count is actually going to buy tickets?" Marika asked, dumbfounded.

"That has already been decided," the Contessa said. "They are merely haggling over the tariff."

Turning her back on the men, Marika wandered over to the shepherd's hut. The way she felt right now, she wouldn't get on that ark with Count Dabrowsky even if it did mean drowning in flood waters. She walked up a muddy trail to the top of the hill, and held her face up to the sky and let the rain pepper down on her long eyelashes. Oh God, if only all this were over! Turning around, she noticed she'd attracted a string of little children in ragged sheepskin clothing, who stared at her curiously. One by one, they held out their dirty hands to her and Marika tried to conjure up what she looked like in the eyes of those children. Did they see her as a great lady, a person of rank and wealth?

The Contessa was calling for her.

Swirling her cape around, Marika descended the hill, the little, mud-splattered children running along behind. The Contessa chased them away. "It's settled," she said to Marika. "He's secured passage for us."

"Good!" Marika answered sarcastically. "When do we sail?"

There was a great deal she still did not understand about the world. If she did something foolish, she was severely reprimanded, but if a grown man did something foolish, he seemed to get away with it—not only get away with it, but have all the women go along with the pretense, afraid to voice an objection. The Count had taken Marika and the Contessa into the mountains to secure passage on an ark that wasn't even ready—in case God flooded the world! She'd never been involved in such madness before. The Contessa had made it clear that women must always suffer such schemes to make the men feel good.

"Damn," Marika said to herself. That made all women just as much servants as Aunt Nadya. It was a question of who had power. Marika realized that if she married Count Dabrowsky, and he died in a few years as Madame Modrzejewska had predicted, then it would be she who had the power. The idea warmed her slightly, even though she abhorred what she would have to do to get herself in that position.

On the way back, the Count sat beside her on the wooden bench, his cold hand enclosing one of hers, making her wish she'd worn gloves. "We must proceed immediately with our wedding plans," he said.

Marika swallowed a lump in her throat.

"If the flood should come," the Count continued, "I want to face it as your husband."

Marika smiled into his eyes, but said nothing. Her cape of black serge was cold and completely wet now, and more rain than ever blew in through the holes in the canvas curtains.

The roar of the water, the jolt and clatter of the wagon on the stones—everything seemed to sound the words, "Countess Dabrowsky, Countess Dabrowsky, Countess Dabrowsky."

* * *

The rain let up for Marika's wedding, but the sun did not come out. Under leaden-gray skies, Marika stood still as the Contessa fitted her headdress.

"It's made of apple blossoms and rosemary," the Contessa said. "I know it's a superstition, but it's supposed to ensure a happy married life."

"I feel like a peasant," Marika said bitterly, running her hands along the blouse embroidered with beads and the full white lace skirt. The Contessa had braided her hair tightly that morning so that the headdress would fit, but to Marika, the braids were like cords of bondage. Ever since the Contessa had freed her hair of ribbons for her photograph in Berlin, Marika had liked the idea of her blonde hair flowing freely.

As they stood under a thatched shelter in front of their wooden villa, an old cleaning woman passed by, her head covered with a black kerchief. At the sight of Marika, she stopped and turned her face to them. It seemed burnt, scarred by life.

The Contessa touched Marika's hand gently. "There but for the grace of God go I," she whispered. "That is why we must make sacrifices in life—to keep us from becoming like that poor old hag."

Marika sought out the woman's eyes. They were both staring at her with contempt. Or was it envy? Maybe both. In Baden-Baden Marika had fantasized about running off with a handsome, dashing Hussar, but she realized that to this old cleaning woman, nothing in her whole life would be as exciting as wearing a bridal headdress and waiting for Count Dabrowsky to take her to church. The thought made her upcoming marriage a little more endurable.

With a toss of her head, the old cleaning woman made her way up the road.

Wrapping her cape tighter against the gray of the day, the Contessa muttered impatiently, "I wish those kidnappers would get here!"

"What?" Marika asked, not certain she'd understood.

"You mean no one's told you? It's an old Polish custom," the Contessa explained. "The Count is supposed to kidnap you on horseback and take you to church."

Wonderful, thought Marika sarcastically.

Suddenly, the sound of horses caused her to jump, and there, galloping toward her from the stables, were three young men. The Count was trailing on a white stallion, riding like an accomplished horseman, tall and erect in the saddle, dressed as much like a dandy as the younger men. She had never seen him outfitted so elaborately, with his embroidered waistcoat, ornamented belt, and hat decorated with peacock feathers.

Reaching down, he tried to swoop Marika into his arms, but nearly toppled from his mount. One of the young men quickly jumped down and lifted Marika into the Count's saddle. A slight drizzle began as the Count trotted up the muddy road to the church. Marika was horrified to see stains on her white lace.

The Count held her tightly. "You are such a vision of loveliness this morning," he said. "You were like a dream standing there."

"Thank you," she answered curtly, her embarrassment too strong for her to make any other response.

"Soon you'll be mine," he whispered.

Marika shuddered, both at the uneven gait of the horse and at what the words "be mine" meant. Her attempts to get the Contessa to explain more about marriage had been to no avail.

Soon they came to the little wooden church. "We'll have to wait for the Contessa to catch up," the Count said. "She's following in a carriage."

Eased gently from the white stallion, Marika stood on the muddy ground in front of an old cemetery. She saw tall iron crosses rising in a grove of plum trees and poplars, and rose trees running wild over the elaborately carved stone tombs.

In front of the church, older men smoked ancestral pipes.

For the first time Marika realized that her wedding to the Count was the big social event of the summer in Zakopane. Passing the good-looking young men of the village, she took in their maroon sheepskin coats and their scarlet and pink clothing, but mostly she looked into their eager faces. She suspected that the only girls they were used to were the plump peasant girls of the village, and that she must be an exotic attraction to these men.

Any one of them, she imagined, would be a more exciting candidate to introduce her to what the Count had called the "mystery of life."

Inside, the church had been decorated with sprays of hawthorn, and a priest in a scarlet cape embroidered with gold leaves waited. Marika had been rehearsed in her Polish wedding vows, the only words of the language she knew, but as the wedding proceeded, she dreaded the moment when she had to speak out loud. For one brief instant of panic, she completely forgot what she was going to say. But on cue the sounds came quickly to her lips. She tried to speak the words so low no one could hear, but a bridesmaid standing nearby snickered. Marika suspected she was being laughed at because her Polish accent was so bad. Or was it because she'd said something completely different from what she'd intended? In any case, the Count didn't seem to notice. At the end of the ceremony, he kissed her hand.

It was over. Marika had understood nothing of the commitment she'd made. She knew only that she was now the Countess Dabrowsky.

Tears formed in her new husband's gray eyes.

Enveloped in the smell of French perfume, the Contessa was at Marika's side, hugging and kissing her on both cheeks. "You'll never regret this decision," she whispered. "You've made me the happiest woman in the world. I feel like your mother." She stood back, holding Marika at arm's length. "Now you and I are both countesses."

Back at the villa, it was time for merrymaking. A kind of hysteria swept the crowd as it descended en masse on Marika and the Count. Body arched, she stepped back in fright, reaching for the Count's hand. "Pray to God, what is happening?"

"Run with me!" he shouted, pulling her across the creaky wooden floor of the cavernous room, the other guests in pursuit. It was like a stampede. Marika thought the world had gone mad. Running and shouting, the wedding party chased them until, seeing the Count had become winded, they formed a laughing circle around the pair. Marika looked into the childlike guilelessness of their faces and suddenly felt a wave of weariness sweep over her. She felt she was the only grown-up at the party.

"We're being held for ransom," the Count told her, as the

guests flapped about Marika like flags in the wind. "Oh, please!" she said to no one in particular. She was about to cry. "I don't understand anything. Nobody explains." The Count kept shouting something in Polish at the guests, and pretending to break through the circle of bodies, until, at the clang of a bell, the Contessa appeared, followed by a retinue of servants with trays of food and bottles of vodka.

"We're free," the Count yelled into Marika's ear. "The Contessa has met the ransom demands."

Swept onto the floor, Marika felt the touch of a hand on her arm. "Just follow me," a voice said softly in German. "We're going to do the polonaise."

She found herself staring into the eyes of the most beautiful young man she'd ever seen. His eyes were a liquid brown, fringed by long eyelashes and beautifully arched brows, both of the same shiny black as the ringlets on his head. He was tall and olive-skinned and dressed in a sleeveless coat that hung like a hussar's, held together by a bright-pink ribbon bow. Slowly he led her into the dance until, flushed and laughing, the Count cut in.

"Here I am, to reclaim the bride. Ah, I see you've met. Good, good. This is your new tutor, my dear. Julian Viertel."

With a lurch, Marika's heart started pounding, and a sudden excitement lifted the sadness from her. Through blood-red lips, Julian murmured, "It is an honor. What a lovely pupil I'll have."

"Yes. Well, there will be no lessons for the Countess today," the Count continued. "At least not from you." He laughed loudly at his own joke.

With a smile, Julian faded into the crowd. The Count bowed before Marika, and the dance continued, Marika's head in a whirl. All her thoughts were of Julian. The Count was surely wrong about his being a Jew. Jews were ugly, yet this young man possessed a beauty almost the equal of her own. The prospect of his being her tutor, of being alone with him, made her spirits soar. The dance was solemn, but she could not keep a joyful skip out of her steps. A mysterious electricity seemed to run through her. Her arm was linked with the Count's, but she felt free. She could not care less about life's rules or conventions. Oh, this young man would make everything bearable!

The Count was tiring quickly, and most of the dancers were

slowing down and heading for the vodka, but out of the crowd two dancers emerged with more dignity and elegance than the rest. Moving to the center of the floor, the girl, tall and lean, prettier than the other girls of the village, danced in a red dress with a pink hat. She danced as if she'd never been taught anything else from birth. Opposite her, the male dancer looked deeply into her eyes. It was Julian.

Marika's breathing was growing difficult. She needed more air. Excusing herself from the Count, she sought out the Contessa. "May I have some vodka?" she asked.

"Of course you can," the Contessa said. "You're a woman now."

"Not quite," Marika added. She ran to a wooden platform over-looking a rushing torrent, and was alone at last. Swallowing the foul-tasting liquid, she nearly gagged, and, furiously, threw the rest of the contents of her glass down the steep hill. Was this what the mysterious vodka tasted like? she asked herself. Was this what she had had to wait till she was grown up to taste? A frown crossed her brow. She wondered if all adult pleasures were as disappoint-ing as vodka.

Her eyes turned back to the dance floor inside. Julian and his young girl were still performing in front of the other guests. Com-ing toward her, the Count carried his own drink.

She looked again at the craggy mountain before her, bare and jagged, bleak as her life now seemed. A pain welled up inside her, and she fought it, but it wouldn't go away. The tears she'd tried to hold back for so long now consumed her.

The Count's fingers were on her chin, forcing her to look up into his eyes. "Those are tears of happiness, my lovely," he said, spilling some of his drink on her already stained frock as he pulled her close. The smell of the vodka she'd so disliked seemed to rush overpoweringly from the Count's breath. His moustache covered her lips, his tongue invaded her mouth. She tried to close her lips, but he bit down hard, and the shock and pain caused her to open her mouth again.

Moving back slowly, and only an inch from her lips, he whis-pered, "From now on, you'll close no more doors to me."

* * *

That night in the master bedroom, Marika's eyes scanned the marriage bed. The household servants had decorated it with richly embroidered hangings and fine lacework, but to her it seemed like a coffin. Putting on her dressing gown, she slipped under the covers. The eiderdown seemed damp.

With as little noise as possible, the Count crept into the room. He'd been drinking vodka heavily all evening, and his blouse was open at the chest, revealing a patch of gray hair. "My lovely," he said in a slurred voice.

Marika did not reply. Arms folded across her breasts, she tried to sink into the horsehair mattress.

He looked at her gravely. "It will take me a moment to remove my garments," he said. "Then I will lay my hands on you, the first man to know your body." He coughed. "Remain where you are until I return."

Marika lay listening to the rain beating heavily against the windowpanes, and the wind blowing tempestuously outside. She thought of the weather, the room, anything to divert her mind. Behind a screened-off curtain came the unmistakable sounds of the Count relieving his bowels. Her livid face sank into the goosefeather pillow, trying to blot out the noise.

Moments later, a feeble voice murmured at her side. "Turn over, my angel," the Count said. "I want to see you, and I want you to see me."

Slowly Marika turned over. At the sight of the Count's nude body, she gasped in fright. Somehow the Count could cut a striking figure in his clothes, as if he were in a stage drama, but out of them he was pathetic, his body totally unlike that of her Papa's, the only man she'd ever seen nude before. She stared at his thin, gray face, his open mouth, his caved-in chest. Brown liver spots covered his body, and his sex was shrunken into a large nest of snowy hair. She'd thought all men were like her father, or like the "stallions" the Contessa claimed as lovers. She closed her eyes in disgust.

"I want to undress you," the Count said softly.

"All right," she replied, in a voice barely a whisper. But she was determined to keep her eyes closed. It might make what was going to happen easier. He quickly slipped off her white lace gown, and she was nude in front of him. She shivered at the dampness of the room and the coldness of his fingers tracing patterns across the milky whiteness of her skin. She moaned faintly, like a person asleep but beset by an ugly dream. The bed creaking, the Count climbed in beside her. Kissing her neck, her shoulders, his moist mouth moved to her tiny breasts, and then to her stomach and the insides of her thighs. His tongue darted in and out and she jumped.

"Now, now, my lovely," he said, breathing heavily, gently pulling at her fuzzy pubic hair with his teeth.

Her own teeth clenched, she tried to keep from crying, but it was impossible. Stuffing her fingers into her mouth, she muffled her sobs, as he kissed and massaged and caressed. His fingers probed into her until she cried out. She tried to sit up, but he forced her to lie back on the pillow.

At last it was over, and the Count collapsed on a pillow next to her. He leaned close to her ear. "In the morning," he whispered, "you will do for me what I did for you."

Leaping from the bed, Marika ran behind the screen, and opening the chamber-pot, vomited, her insides seeming to pour out of her. When she was through, she rushed to the window for some fresh air, but it was bolted.

"Come back to bed, my lovely," the Count called to her.

She wrapped her robe tightly around her body and slowly returned. At the bedside, she turned down the lamp and avoided looking into the Count's face.

"Don't tremble," he said. "I heard what was happening to you. I will go easy with you in the morning. It is always this way with my pets. Their little stomachs rebel at first. But then, as with many things in life, they get used to it. Pretty soon they're doing it without my having to lead them."

Wiping her eyes, Marika went back to bed, but stayed as far from the Count as she could as he dozed, off and on. Once or twice he groped for her, but she managed to avoid his reach. Sometime in the middle of the night he stirred again, and said, "I need more vodka."

Turning up the lamp, she went to a cabinet at the end of the bedroom and poured him a large drink. He sat up and took three gulps from it, then feebly set it down on the nightstand. "I remember my first honeymoon," he said. "It was in 1859. I was a great cavalry man in those days." He chuckled, almost to himself. "I still am, as you could see today when I kidnapped you to take you to church." As the lamp burned dry, he began to drone on endlessly about his past glories and those of Poland. The objects in the room danced and flickered in the yellow glare of the lamp, and Marika felt a terrible thirst coming over her. Vodka was the only liquid in the room, and she couldn't stand the smell of it. She felt her throat closing, furring up, her forehead beading with perspiration. Her hands rubbed the lower part of her stomach. She could no longer keep her eyes shut, even when the Count fell into a sleep as sound as a baby's. Her body felt as hot as a rock resting on red coals.

And still the wind howled outside.

* * *

Aunt Nadya remained at Marika's bedside through two days of fever, and on the third day, it broke. So weak she could hardly lift her lids, Marika gazed into the soft gray eyes of Aunt Nadya and smiled faintly. The woman reached for her hand, pressing it against her full lips and kissing it.

When Aunt Nadya released her hand, Marika rubbed the side of the woman's face, seeing her clearly for the first time. Her cheeks sagged and the features were plain, but to Marika it was the most sensitive and subtle face in the world. Aunt Nadya's whole reason for existing seemed to be to bring comfort to others.

At lunchtime that day, the Contessa entered the room, bringing with her the smell of new perfume and a bouquet of early summer flowers. She was dressed in a décolleté gown of white, simple and charming, more for nighttime Baden-Baden than daytime Zakopane. A transformation seemed to have come over her. She appeared more youthful and vibrant than Marika had ever known her, even in the few days when Friedrich had made her happy. "My darling," she said, kissing Marika on both cheeks, "I thought you'd never recover. Of course, I was hovering outside your door if you needed me."

"I feel much better," Marika said slowly, "but I have no energy." She tried to sit up in the bed. "Please bring me my mirror."

"Vanity, my dear," the Contessa said, smiling. "We all suffer from that a bit. But it's a sign your condition has improved." She fetched the mirror, and Marika looked at the emaciated, drawn reflection in shock. Her color seemed to have faded; her eyes were much larger than usual. "Where is the Count?" she asked abruptly.

The Contessa sighed. "He's gone into the mountains for the day. He's not as convinced as he was that God is going to destroy the world. He's conferred with other priests who seem to feel the Zakopane father overstated the case." Her face turned sour, as a thought seemed to strike her. "He's not very happy with you, I fear."

A lump rose in Marika's throat. "I'm not very happy with him either," she said. "He's disgusting!"

"I know, I know," the Contessa said, sitting down beside Marika and reaching for her hand. "But at least we'll be provided for for the rest of our lives. I can't tell you what a burden has been lifted from my shoulders. I think I'm even beginning to enjoy Zakopane, something I thought was not possible." Shuddering at the dampness, she reached for her silk wrap, the color of a pigeon's breast. "What a relief not to have to concern myself anymore with bill collectors."

The memory of Marika's wedding night returned with a violence. "I don't think I can face the Count again."

The Contessa rose to her feet, her chin jutting out. "I'm sure you'll be able to." At the door she called down the hallway to Aunt Nadya. She returned to the bedside. "I've ordered some tea. We must get you well."

"But I don't ever want to get well," Marika protested, turning over and burying herself in her goose-feather pillow.

"My darling," the Contessa said, "eventually you must get well and be the wife to the Count that he desires."

"I can't, I can't," Marika blurted out into the pillow. "He wants me to . . ."

"I know, my dear," the Contessa said, stroking her hair. "Don't say it. I know of such things only too well."

By teatime Marika had calmed down, soothed by the presence of Aunt Nadya. Without the old woman ever doing or saying anything, it was clear she regarded the Contessa with contempt.

The Contessa slowly sipped her tea. "Each day your tutor has come to see you," she said.

Marika's eyes opened wide. "You mean Julian?"

"Yes," the Contessa said, raising an eyebrow. "I did not know you knew his name."

"I danced with him at my wedding." Marika settled back onto her pillow.

Gently, almost caressingly, the Contessa said, "He is ready to begin your lessons in Polish. But, of course, I told him you were not well."

Marika hesitated for a moment, her feelings confused. "It is important that I learn Polish," she said finally. "The Count expects it of me."

The Contessa walked over to the other side of the bed, running her fingers over its post. She looked down at Marika with a smile. "Language is just one of the things he expects from you, Countess Dabrowsky. I suggest you do not disappoint him for too long."

After the Contessa had gone, Marika sought comfort in Aunt Nadya's face. It was sad and gray. Even though she could not understand the German Marika and the Contessa had spoken, the old woman seemed to know.

* * *

Monday was the brightest morning in days, and when Marika awoke, the Count's grandfather clock said half past ten. She had not fallen asleep until dawn. The Count himself stood by her bedside, very formal, making no mention of their wedding night, merely expressed sadness at her illness. "What unfortunate timing," he said.

Putting on a pair of wireless spectacles, he sat down and began to read the poetry of Michiewicz to her, first in Polish, then in a rough German translation which she was sure destroyed all of the words' beauty and subtlety. Eyes closed, Marika tried to concentrate on them anyway. Once the Count reached for her hand, but it was a nervous contact, a false intimacy. She could not bring herself to fully accept that this stranger reading by her bedside was her husband.

Kissing her gently on her fingertips, he soon departed. The question of when they would resume sleeping together never came up, much to her relief.

After a light lunch of cold beets and pork, Julian arrived to begin her first lesson in Polish. He, too, kissed her fingertips, lingering a little. The touch of his lips made her tingle. She was worried about her appearance, fearing she did not look attractive to him.

"I'm sorry to hear you've not been well," he said. "I came to see you every day."

"Thank you," she said. "The Contessa told me. But I'm fine now. I'll soon be up." She turned away. Looking at him made her nervous. "Please sit down."

"We'll have only a short lesson today," he said. "We will go slowly at first."

With flashing eyes, she turned to him. "No, it's all right." He looked at her, and for a long time no words passed from his lips. Awkwardly he reached for his textbook.

"I've been lying here day after day," she said, listening to the water outside. "The sounds are of gurgling and hissing. Sometimes a 'szch.' Not unlike Polish, don't you think?"

"I agree," he said. "The tongue of our country is strange. Your wedding, for example. That's a *wesele.*" He leaned close enough for her to smell him. He smelled of the outdoors, a strong, masculine, earthy aroma. "To begin with," he said, looking at her through half-closed eyes. "In German there are three pronouns, of course. The first, *er,* serves all masculine nouns. *Sie* serves for all feminine ones. But Polish is different. There are two masculine pronouns, one just for men or male animals. But there is only one for the woman and all feminine nouns."

"I'm disappointed," Marika said. "I understand the Poles are very chivalrous. But that seems very rude of them, to make women share a pronoun with a . . ." Her eyes focused on the lamp beside her bed. "With a lamp." Raising her brows, she confronted Julian. "Unless you agree that women are like property and should be treated as such."

"I don't agree at all," he said emphatically. "To me, a woman is God's most beautiful creation. She is to be worshipped."

"Worshipped?" Marika asked in surprise. "That sounds very much like church."

"A different kind of religion," he said, laughing, flashing his white teeth.

She wanted to change the subject. "Are you sorry you came to Zakopane—I mean, the weather's so bad?"

"Not at all," he said proudly. "I always go swimming in the

morning, regardless of how cold it is. I'm a firm believer in lots of exercise. It's good for the body. Swimming leaves me feeling fine."

"I'm afraid of water," she said.

"Why?" he asked.

Face flushed, she hesitated before answering. "I don't know . . . I suppose because Papa doesn't believe that girls should swim."

At first Julian said nothing, his eyes fastened on her. Then, straightening up in his stiff chair, he replied, "I don't see why not. Knowing how to swim could save your life—maybe that of someone else. Perhaps my language lessons might also include some swimming instruction."

Marika reached for a glass of water beside her bed and quickly drank from it, almost choking, but it did little to relieve the sudden parched feeling in her throat. The idea of appearing in bathing dress with him shocked her, yet at the same time she felt a curious thrill running through her. "I don't think it will be possible," she managed to say.

He took the water glass from her hand, his fingers gently touching hers again. "I mean, when you're well."

"Maybe," she said faintly, her eyes wide with bewilderment.

A rap at the door, and the Contessa was in the room. "That's enough for today, Mr. Viertel." She smiled. "We wouldn't want to tire the Countess too much, would we?"

"We would only want to tire her in the pursuit of knowledge," he said, rising swiftly and bowing at the waist. "Then the fatigue will have been worth it."

"Very nicely put," the Contessa said, holding out her hand for Julian to kiss.

When both Julian and the Contessa had gone, Marika got out of her bed on her own. Though a little weak, she was no longer sick. Unbolting the window, she went out to stand on her balcony and took in deep breaths of the fresh air. It smelled like Julian.

"Maybe there will be a summer after all," she said.

* * *

In two weeks the Count still had not returned to the marriage bed. Each time he saw Marika, she informed him her condition had not improved. Finally, a business venture took him to Kraków for many days, and when he came to her room to say good-bye, she softly wished him a safe trip in Polish. Tears came to the old man's eyes as he kissed her hand in farewell.

Each afternoon at two when Julian arrived, Marika's condition seemed to improve dramatically. Skipping lunch each day, she spent the time preparing herself and making sure that her natural beauty was indeed returning. With pleasure, she noted her blonde hair becoming lustrous again, and the creamy peach color returning to her complexion.

With the Count away from Zakopane, the Contessa spent less and less time at their villa. And Marika suspected that when she went riding her white stallions, her interest was not solely in the four-legged variety. As the Contessa confided to Marika one morning, "Polish boys are so different from the men of Prussia. Everybody there, including Friedrich, cares only for young girls, but here, youth is more susceptible to the charms of a mature lady."

On the third day after the Count's departure, the sun shone for the first time in days when Julian arrived for her lesson. Seeing no one at the villa other than Aunt Nadya, he told Marika: "It's a shame to waste such a beautiful day. You should go riding with me into the mountains. I'll teach you the Polish names of the trees and the flowers."

Marika readily agreed. Afraid to ride on a horse by herself, she sat in front of Julian on his saddle. Unlike the Count, he had no trouble lifting her into his mount. The wind in her hair, the sun in her eyes, Marika tried to remember a moment in her life when she had been as happy as she was right now. She could think of none. The slight pressure of Julian's arms seemed to envelop her, offering protection from anything bad that could happen.

In a narrow gorge by a stream of running water, Julian brought the horse to a stop. Dismounting, he held out his arms to her. She glided off the stallion and into his embrace. For a brief moment, he held her, releasing her only to tie up the horse.

"I'm going to have a swim," he announced when he'd joined her again. "I didn't have time this morning. Would you care to go into the water with me?"

Face flushed, she declined.

He quickly removed his clothing behind a large rock, while she spread a blanket on the moist ground and set out the sausage and bread she'd brought along. Only when he ran out from behind the rock and had his back to her did she dare look. He was completely naked. The sight shocked, yet strangely excited her. Watching him wade into the water, she waved at him and he turned and waved back to her. "Come on in," he shouted. "You'll love it."

"No," she yelled, "it's much too cold."

Submerging himself again, he renewed his strokes with vigor, then, after swimming a few minutes, seemed to tire. Floating on the surface, he raised himself in the water and started splashing toward the bank. He emerged dripping wet, and stood completely exposed at the edge of the water.

Even though the afternoon sun shone directly in her face, she could not take her eyes off him. Until this moment she'd thought that only women had beautiful bodies. Peeking at Julian, she realized that God had not been as discriminating as that. His wet skin covered with droplets, Julian stood uncertainly, obviously not sure of what to do next. Finally, moving with grace across the rocks, he put on his trousers, then slowly walked over to her, drying his wet hair with his shirt.

From her perch on the blanket, she glanced up at his body, the flush of her cheeks rapidly turning into a burn. His brown eyes twinkled, and his red lips curled into a smile. "May I join you?"

She nodded that he could. He gently eased onto the blanket beside her. For days she'd wanted to reach out and touch him. Now her hands began moving through his wet hair, shaping the strands into ringlets, but she was still too embarrassed to look at him.

Putting his fingers under her chin, he lifted her face to look into his eyes. The Count had done the same thing on her wedding day, but the feeling was different somehow. Julian took her hand and placed it at the back of his neck, then, easing closer, he drew her to him, kissing her gently at first, then with more force. In her ear he whispered, "I love you, Countess."

His hand moved slowly under her dress, and she did not stop it. She welcomed the pressure of his weight resting on her. All at once tears filled her eyes. He kissed them away. "I'm afraid," she said softly.

"I know," he replied, just as softly. "But you don't have to be. Not with me."

That seemed to be enough to keep her from trembling. She kept her eyes closed as he removed her clothing, helping him when she could, but grateful that he was doing most of the work. His movements seemed to mesmerize her. She would have done anything he asked. She felt his lips at her throat, and a hardness pressing against her bare skin. "I've never known a . . ." she said, not able to complete her statement. "Not that way."

"But you're married," he said. His surprise faded quickly.

"Please, go easy," she asked.

"I will," he promised. He found his way to her.

At the first entry, spears of pain shot through her body. She cried out until he muffled her sobbing with his mouth. Her whole body broke out in perspiration and she was soon as wet as he was. Opening herself to him, she pressed her body tightly against his. The nerve fibers within her seemed to scream out, as if they had a life all their own, unconnected with her upper parts, but after a while, she didn't mind the pain as much. "I'm doing it for Julian," she kept repeating to herself. Maybe she said the words out loud. She really didn't know. All she knew was that he wanted her.

She was crying, but Julian seemed to be crying, too. His rhythm increasing, he thrust deeper inside her, hurting more. Had he forgotten his promise to go easy on her? It didn't matter now.

Her breathing had been matching his, but now he began sucking the air into his lungs and moaning louder than before. With one deep plunge, he cried out, collapsing on top of her.

She held him tightly, not wanting him to go. Even when she felt the hardness of him grow soft, she clung to him. His lips were on her breasts, and he seemed to listen to the pounding of her heart.

A flock of birds flew over. At the sound, he pulled away from her, but soon he was back at her side.

"I've made you a woman now," he whispered.

She knew it was true.

* * *

The following day Marika's lessons stretched on until after sunset. From her balcony they watched peasants bringing in the cows from the field. Reaching out, she found Julian's hand waiting to enclose hers.

"The evening star shines almost with a violence tonight," he said.

She held his hand tighter. "I wish right now my life could come to a standstill. That I wouldn't have to go forward or backward. That the Count wasn't returning from Kraków." Her voice became choked. "That we'd never grow old. That we could stand here just as we are and watch the peasants bring in the cows."

He chucked her under the chin. "What you're saying, my little one, is that you don't want to live." Brushing his lips against her ear, he whispered, "We'd be dead."

Later that evening, Aunt Nadya presided at dinner like a chaperone. Marika had invited Julian to stay since the Contessa had not been seen since morning. Although Julian exchanged a few polite comments with Aunt Nadya in Polish, he was forced to speak German because of Marika, and she found it exciting to exchange intimate conversations with him in the presence of Aunt Nadya.

"I love you," Marika said to Julian, "and I know absolutely nothing about you. Your parents, what about them?" She eagerly searched his face for any sign of embarrassment. There was none. Would he admit to being a Jew?

"Poor souls," he said, "they are both gone now." He sipped his milk, as his eyes wandered to the balcony.

"Were they . . ." She hesitated. "Persecuted?" She dangled her fork in mid-air.

"Not at all," he said emphatically. "Of course, my mother had a hard time of it in the early days. She was born very poor in the ghetto of Warsaw. But everybody in the family loved each other. Mother married well, a bourgeois from Riga. He had a large dry-goods store there, and we lived the good life." He smiled at her. "We could even afford a summer cottage on the coast. There we grew bright flowers and painted our picket fence pink and green. Can you imagine such colors?"

"It's hard to," she said. Her face was now no more than a foot from Julian's. In the fading light, his features were becoming indistinct, but his voice indicated no strain about talking of the past.

In total shadow, Aunt Nadya sat like a sentinel at the other end of the table. Marika wondered how closely the old servant was observing her. Finally, Aunt Nadya stirred to light the kerosene lamps.

"Papa always believed strongly in education," Julian said.

"That's the main reason I know all these languages. I studied for years in Kraków, but I spent all my summers at Zakopane, so that's why I'm here." He was silent for a moment. "Both my parents are dead now."

"Were they killed?" Marika asked.

He threw a curious look at her. "They both died of old age," he replied. "I was born late, you see. Mother thought she could never have a child, but one day I came along."

For a long while Marika didn't know how to ask what she wanted to. "You're part Polish?" she asked finally. "Part Latvian?"

By the soft light of the lamp Aunt Nadya had placed on the dinner table, he moved closer to her. A recognition of what she was after came into his face. "My mother was a Jewess. Is that what you mean?"

"The Count told me," she said quickly, her voice cracking. "But I couldn't believe it."

Reaching out, he enclosed her wrist tightly in a circle of fingers. "Why can't you believe it?" he shouted at her. She'd never seen him angry before. "Because Jews are ugly," he said, "and I'm handsome? Can't a Jew be beautiful, Countess Dabrowsky? Or is beauty a monopoly held only by blonde, blue-eyed Prussian girls?" He rose swiftly, overturning his milk, then walked at once to the front door and threw it open. After a long, searching look at Marika, he left, slamming the door behind him.

The rush of fresh, night air sent shivers across Marika. Stunned, she sat helplessly watching the milk run over the side of the table. Aunt Nadya stood up. But she made no move in any direction. Silence filled the room, as a pain welled inside Marika. She couldn't let Julian go. Without him, she'd have nothing.

Pushing her plate away, she stood up and rushed to the door Julian had slammed. She raced blindly down the road after him. When she found him, she'd beg him to forgive her. But the night was dark and there was no sign of him. She stumbled and almost fell. Finally, she stopped running and started crying.

From behind a hut, arms reached out for her. By the smell of his clothing, she knew at once who it was.

"I felt you'd come after me," he said, holding her close and kissing her swiftly, repeatedly on her lips. "That you'd love me even if you knew."

She clung to him, more urgently than she had, even when she was having sex with him. "Whatever you are," she whispered in his ear, "I want to be, too."

Chapter 4

The Warsaw winter stretched on cold and gray, as Marika assumed her position as the new mistress of the Dabrowsky household. Some of the staff resented her at first, but she soon dealt with that. Her personal maid, Judith, had grown up on a farm and, excited at the idea of serving a real Countess, had been stunned to find that Marika was even younger than herself.

It was on Marika's fourth day in the house, while Judith was gently rubbing her back, that Marika told her first lie. She claimed she had been a German princess before her marriage to the Count. At once she knew the girl believed her. Slowly, but skillfully, Marika embroidered her story, and the more she exaggerated and lied, the more exciting and thrilling it became for her. By the time Judith had toweled her dry, Marika was telling of her seduction by the Kaiser!

Word spread quickly through the household, and by the end of the fifth day, the staff began treating her with respect, even awe. That night Marika lay awake, conjuring up new and better stories about her past.

A routine quickly established itself. The Count habitually left her bed at six o'clock in the morning, but Marika slept until nine, when Aunt Nadya would arrive with her breakfast tray of sticky sweet rolls, hot chocolate, and strawberry preserves. Waking her up, the old Russian gypsy would say, "I kiss your hands."

Over breakfast Aunt Nadya would go through the pretense of consulting Marika about the running of the house. Marika would give her opinions, knowing all the time the old woman would do as she pleased. No one, not even the Count, questioned the decisions of Aunt Nadya.

As a permanent resident of the Dabrowsky household, the Contessa was in her glory. In Warsaw she had no creditors to plague her—they'd all been left behind in Vienna, Rome, Florence, Baden-Baden, and Berlin. The Count took care of the expenses, and although she complained to Marika that he didn't give her enough to spend, nevertheless she never seemed to actually run short of money. Most of her evenings were spent at the Opera Café or at the theater, and whenever possible she joined the Dabrowsky household for dinner—at which Marika reigned as the new mistress, a position Madame Dalecka had very reluctantly relinquished. Neither the Count nor Madame Dalecka had much to talk about on these occasions, so the Contessa would fill the silences with stories about Reinhardt, Gordon Craig, and Stanislavski.

Marika longed to see the performances the Contessa described. She beseeched the Count to take her to the theater when Madame Modrzejewska returned to appear in a play at the Rozmaitisci, but the Count said he wasn't feeling well, and, kindly, the Contessa obtained a copy of the script for Marika. Every morning in the silence of the Count's study, she'd slip away and carefully memorize the lines. The Contessa had brought her a picture of Madame Modrzejewska in the gown she wore in the play, and Marika had Judith duplicate the dress. Soon she would be ready for her premiere performance.

One gray winter's afternoon, after Julian had left word at the house that he'd had to cancel her language lesson, she knew it was time. Nervously she approached the floor-length, oval mirror in the Count's study. She imagined the curtain rising, hundreds of men and women in the audience out there staring at her.

Beads of perspiration fell from her forehead, as she began. Scene by scene, she went through the drama. By the third act she had worked herself up to a proper state of madness, as dictated by the role. She clasped her hands on her bosom, tugged at her hair, and made wild, almond eyes in the mirror, her voice high and strained.

Suddenly, in the background, she was aware of a snicker, then a giggle. In the mirror she saw the faces of maids, their hands at their mouths as if suppressing laughter. In spite of their presence, her lines came out at a frenzied pitch. She would blot out their smug faces! No great actress would let a group of silly maids break up her biggest scene.

As the chorus of snickers went on, Marika grew even more determined. Her beautiful face froze in a defiance that distorted it. She'd see to it that these maids were fired, every last one of them. They couldn't appreciate talent.

Her voice rose to a tremolo, then fell off. So great was the anguish inside her that she could no longer utter a sound. Her hand shot into the air, her fingers reaching out, as if desperately searching for a sound. Silence. Tears flowing, lips trembling, hands shaking, she turned to face the maids. Impulsively she picked up an inkwell from the Count's desk, hurling it at the laughing girls. The black ink splattered the walls, some of it staining their white uniforms. Screaming, the maids turned and ran.

"My darling," came the voice of the Contessa. She'd entered the study through another door without Marika hearing her. "I caught some of your performance. Remember, there will be other actors on the stage, too."

* * *

Promptly at nine o'clock in the evening, the Count insisted on retiring to bed with Marika. Those hours, before he fell asleep at midnight or one o'clock, were long and dreary, and with just the sound of his heavy, labored breathing to keep her company, Marika spent her time dreaming of Julian.

The only way she could get through her day was knowing she'd see Julian at his small apartment at two o'clock in the afternoon. Because she had made such quick progress in learning Polish and Russian, the Count had allowed Julian to return with them from Zakopane, and found living quarters for the tutor in another part of the city. At first the Count had insisted on Julian giving Marika lessons at his own town house only. But because she was so eager to learn Russian, the Count had considered it better to let her study outside after all, since Madame Dalecka refused to allow one word of Russian to be spoken in the house.

Julian not only taught her Polish and Russian, but history, mathematics—even English. To her, English was the most treasured subject of all. None of the Dabrowsky household, including the Contessa, could speak a word of it. It became Marika's secret language of communication with Julian. Every night after dinner, Marika would retire to the Count's study and spend the hour or two before bedtime composing long love letters in English to Julian, filled with phrases copied from romantically florid English plays. When the Count asked her what she was writing, she said it was her homework. "I have to be prepared for my next lesson."

"You are a good student," the Count said. "Usually education is about the last thing a woman needs."

"Then why do you insist I study so hard?" she asked.

"Because I will not always be with you," the Count answered. "You will have to make decisions one day on your own."

In the afternoons Julian would read her love letters through less clouded vision. He'd smile and kiss her on the eyelids. Then he'd correct her mistakes in grammar.

That disappointed her greatly. "But I poured out my heart in those letters," Marika said one day. "Must you always be Herr Professor?"

"I'm not *always* your tutor, now am I?" he asked, his eyes twinkling.

"No, not all the time," she replied petulantly. That was the signal for Julian to make love to her. At first his love-making was new and thrilling, but she'd grown used to it. As she read more and more of the romantic novels to which she was addicted, she began to feel there was more to love-making than her almost daily experiences with Julian. Once she'd tried to make love to him in the way the Count preferred.

Julian pushed her away. "That's disgusting!" he said. "The mongrels on the street tongue each other. Do you want to be a bitch in heat?"

In tears Marika had fled his apartment, preferring to walk nearly two miles to the Dabrowsky house, but the following afternoon, she was back with Julian. He'd taken her in his arms at once and made love to her. It was still the same kind of love, for his pleasure only. She'd tried to hold him close, wanting him to stay in her longer, but his own release had been quickly reached and he was fast to get up and put his trousers back on.

Marika was left lying on the bed, still out of her clothing. Even so, he started her lessons. "The Count must continue to be impressed with the progress you are making," he said as an explanation. "Otherwise, I can't stay on in Warsaw as your tutor."

She was sad when she had to leave Julian in the dusk of Warsaw. It was her favorite time of day, and she resented not being able to share the mood of the city with her lover. Once she determined to ask Julian how he spent his evenings away from her, but with a sudden apprehension she decided she dared not.

Back at the Dabrowsky household, her own evenings had become a predictable ritual. The Count wanted her sexually only once a week, on Saturday night. His prediction had been right. At first her stomach had rebelled when he insisted she make love to him, but he was a patient man. He kept insisting, and she kept trying, and eventually they'd worked out a compromise. The experience continued to be distasteful to her, but it never lasted very long.

Before Saturday-night sex, she was allowed to drink the vodka she'd initially disliked. Since December, she had begun to acquire more of a taste for it—at least with her head swimming, she did not find it as humiliating or repugnant when the Count demanded sex from her. All she had to do was close her eyes tightly, imagining it was Julian.

Once a month the Count invited the Contessa and Marika to the Opera Café, and on one particular evening, the Contessa dressed more flamboyantly than ever. Draping a scarlet feather boa about her shoulders, and resting a pastiche of bird plumes and fake summer flowers on her head, she examined herself carefully in front of the mirror, all the while insisting that Marika wear only a simple black dress. "But I feel like I'm in mourning," she protested, "and that the Count is already dead."

"Don't worry about it, my dear," the Contessa assured her. "When you're young, you don't need to wear scarlet, plumes, and flowers. Your natural beauty is sufficient." She sighed. "It's only when you're old that you must do everything possible to take attention from your face."

In spite of the black dress, the maître d'hôtel at the Opera Café knew who the real Countess was. He bowed very low in front of Marika. The Contessa received merely a polite nod, even though she was a more frequent patron. "We are so honored," he said to Marika.

As she walked across the salon, Marika could feel eyes following her progress, awakening memories of her first visit to a dining room in Baden-Baden. Much to the Count's displeasure, she'd worn her long yellow hair loose tonight, instead of in the tightly wound coils that the Count usually preferred.

For some reason, the maître d'hôtel was detaining the Contessa at the entrance, and the sound of her angry defiance could be heard throughout the room. Marika suspected the Contessa had been running up a big bill at the café, and the Count had not been paying it.

At their table a bottle of champagne in a bucket of ice awaited them, along with a nosegay of artificial flowers, their petals so delicate they looked real. Marika hadn't had champagne since her wedding day. "A toast," the Count said, when the Contessa joined the table. "To my hasty return to Warsaw."

Champagne glass at her lip, Marika started. "But where are you going?"

"I have urgent business in Kraków," he said, patting Marika on the cheek. "I can't take you with me this time." He turned to the Contessa. "I know how difficult it is for a wife to be without her husband, but you must promise to take good care of her."

"I will," the Contessa said, smiling knowingly. "But you must not be gone long. It will break Marika's heart."

Marika was overjoyed at the news, though she tried to conceal her pleasure. The Count's leaving meant she could spend all her days with Julian and as much of the night as she dared. She knew, of course, she'd have to be careful, because Madame Dalecka would be hungry to learn of the slightest indiscretion. But think of the bliss!

After finishing a second bottle of champagne, the Count's face grew sad, and slightly drunkenly he leaned over to Marika. The expression on his face made her uneasy.

"What is it?" she asked.

"In many ways you are so grown-up," the Count said, "but I fear all you know is what Herr Viertel teaches you from books. I even found a copy of Shakespeare's love sonnets in our bedroom."

"It's important I know languages," Marika said nervously. "You said so yourself back in Zakopane."

"Of course," he said impatiently. "But you do not know what is happening. This is a lull before the storm."

"I don't understand," Marika said, alarmed.

"As you know," the Count went on, "I haven't been able to sleep for the past few weeks. That feeling I had back in Zakopane —about some impending doom—has returned. I realize I must have seemed foolish to you ladies, going up in the mountains to book passage on an ark."

Marika grew increasingly more nervous. Did the Count know she was in love with Julian?

"Now I think my anxiety is more justified," the Count said, setting down his glass. "There is going to be a great war in Europe. Wherever I go these days, there is nothing but talk of it."

Marika breathed a sigh of relief. It wasn't Julian that concerned the Count. But then a new fear occurred to her. "You mean Prussia will fight Poland and Russia?" she asked. Her thoughts were of both Friedrich and Julian. Would they oppose each other in battle?

"We've lived so long under the Russian heel," the Count said. "At least we know what they are like, and I've been able to come to some sort of accommodation with them. But I suspect we may soon feel the Prussian heel as well, before the coming war is over." He reached for Marika's hand. "I'm certain of only one thing. Whatever happens, poor Poland will be the victim."

It was snowing when Marika left the café with the Count and Contessa. Normally, Marika approached a snowstorm longing for roaring fires and the taste of winter soups. But tonight Warsaw was strangely deserted. The whiteness of the city seemed ready to engulf her.

* * *

In England political leaders issued statements promising "no commitment," but privately they negotiated with the French, working out the maneuvers for when the fighting began. Codes and ciphers were prepared. The French were informed that Germany had to violate Belgium's neutrality before Britain would enter the war. Meanwhile, new German railway constructions converged ominously at Aachen and the frontier of Belgium.

In Russia the General Staff was worried that its country's railways would be inadequate to transport 800,000 men quickly to the frontier of East Prussia.

When told of Berlin's steamrolling military build-up, Tsar Nicholas looked blankly across his gardens at the setting afternoon sun. "The will of God will prevail," he said vacantly.

As blizzards and snow fell on Europe through its long winter, the air grew heavier with an even greater storm.

* * *

On the third night after the Count's departure for Kraków, Marika refused to leave Julian at the end of her lessons. "I want to spend the whole night with you," she said.

"You're talking like a lovesick child," he said, smiling to soften the impact of his words. "Madame Dalecka will suspect something if you stay out late. I think the Contessa already knows about us."

"The Contessa can hardly afford to tell bad stories about me to the Count," Marika said. "She has me to thank for her daily bread."

Julian patted his pockets in search of something. "I'm going out tonight," he said finally. "I can't take you with me."

Marika turned angrily on him. "I bet you have another girl friend."

"All right, damn it," he said. "If you must know, I'm having supper in the ghetto with my aunt and uncle. They feed me. You don't think I can afford to eat on the little bit of money your Count gives me."

She was stunned. "Come to think of it, I never have seen you cooking anything."

"You're observant," he said sarcastically. Picking up a pillow, he tossed it at the sofa where he had made love to her only an hour ago. "To you, Your Majesty, food is something a cook prepares in the kitchen and a maid serves on a tray, or a great French chef creates in a café."

Tears came to Marika's eyes. "I've been selfish," she admitted hesitantly. "I should have brought you something from the house. We have plenty of food."

He threw his body against the sofa, hugging the pillow to his chest. "Perhaps you should go to the ghetto and have a meal with us. It's about time you learned what being a Jew means."

She wanted to resist, but Julian, the fever of his new idea upon him, insisted. He was determined now to take her back to the ghetto where she'd wandered alone before. Borrowing her energy from him, Marika walked down the narrow streets she'd all too recently viewed in horror. A heavy drizzle was melting the snow piled up against the doors, and under a large black umbrella Marika tried to keep up with Julian without getting wet. Bareheaded, he hurried in front of her.

Though it still frightened her, the ghetto now became enthralling to Marika, as long as she was with Julian. The people who inhabited it seemed to be listening to some ancient code of law. They wanted to be together, to be Jews.

Ushered into a crowded, extremely ugly little apartment on the fourth floor, Marika found herself being introduced to Esther, Julian's aunt, a small woman with gray hair tied in a bun at the back of her head. Before taking Marika's hand, she wiped hers on a long, white apron.

A dim, exposed light overhead provided the only illumination in the kitchen, and Marika found the entire atmosphere utterly depressing.

"Julian speaks of nothing but you," Esther said. "He certainly tells us how beautiful you are. We know Julian has a lot of fantasies —always had, ever since he was a boy—but this time I can see with my own eyes he is telling the truth."

Marika smiled in embarrassment. "Thank you," she said. The smell of the room was beginning to make her feel ill.

Julian's uncle, Simon, came into the kitchen, tall and erect, his snow-white beard framing an elongated face crowned by a skullcap. He was wearing a black kaftan. "My, my," he said to Marika, "what a pretty one. It's sheer *chutzpah* for a Jew to bring a blonde Countess to our humble home."

At first too startled to reply, Marika searched Julian's eyes. He turned from her quickly, heading for the living room. "Nadine," he called.

"I don't understand *chutzpah,*" Marika said.

Simon looked at Marika skeptically. "You don't know *chutzpah?*" he asked. "I must reprimand Julian for not teaching you your lessons properly. *Chutzpah* means gall, daring. You know?"

Marika blushed. "I have only just learned Polish," she said. "I haven't had time to study Yiddish." The sound of Julian's laughter drifted back, his voice blending with that of a girl.

Simon scratched his ear. "Julian thinks he is so smart. But he isn't. My own grandfather spoke twelve languages. He traveled all over Europe and Asia. He knew everything."

"I'll be happy to learn four languages," Marika said curtly, "the ones Julian knows."

Much later, at dinner, Marika sat between two young girls. Julian's cousin, Nadine, on her right, had suffered a spine injury at birth and it gave her the appearance of a hunchback. A slim girl, her eyes darted quickly at a companion's face when she suspected he or she wasn't looking. Sophie, on her other side, was just the opposite. A girl from the neighborhood, it was evident that she resented Marika's presence in the household, and throughout dinner she pointedly refused to direct any remarks to Marika. Her words seemed only for Julian, and the way Sophie flirted caused Marika to suspect the red-haired girl was in love with him. Apparently, Julian had failed to mention that he was Marika's lover.

"You must eat," Esther said to Marika. "You are like your hair, too pale. My cooking's good. I always put good things in the pot, so how can any dish come out bad?"

Marika didn't answer.

"We're glad Julian has a job in Warsaw," Esther went on. "With his own people, not the grand madames of Kraków. Julian can't meet the right kind of girl in Kraków."

Sophie giggled.

Marika's face became cold and rigid. Getting up, she politely excused herself. "I'm afraid I'm not feeling well. Julian, please take me home. I'm sorry."

After a quick slurp, Julian got up. "Do we have to go now? I was just starting to enjoy myself for the first time today."

In the front hallway, Marika turned to look at Julian, wiping the soup from his mouth onto his sleeve. "I see," she said coldly. "You haven't enjoyed yourself all day with me. My hair's not red, and I'm not voluptuous like Sophie. Why don't you go back to her?"

Out the door, down the hallway and stairs, and into the wet street Marika ran, nearly slipping on the cobblestones. Chasing after her, Julian caught up and grabbed her roughly by her shoulder, spinning her around to face him.

"You little fool!" he shouted in the rain. "You can't find your way home alone."

"You're not a Jew!" she screamed back at him. "You're not like them."

"I always knew you didn't accept me as a Jew," he said. "But it doesn't matter." He clutched her arm. "Come along."

In the cold winter rain, she held tightly to his hand as he led her back out of the ghetto. He said nothing, and she had nothing to say to him.

Julian walked with her until they were one block from the Dabrowsky house, then he kissed her lightly on the cheek and told her he'd see her tomorrow. The statement was matter-of-fact, holding out only the vaguest of promises. It matched her own feelings.

From the age of four, Marika had been fed stories about Jews by her wet-nurse. In great and gory detail, she'd been told how Jews ritualistically murdered Christian children, and she'd quivered at the descriptions of lecherous Jewish men desiring beautiful, flaxen-haired, blue-eyed Prussian girls.

Hurrying the last block home, Marika remained firmly convinced Julian wasn't a *real* Jew. How could he be? He'd probably been adopted by a Jewish family. He was a Gentile, just like Marika. Deep down, she really knew.

Running up to the door, she found the Contessa herself waiting for her. "You're late," she charged. "I was very worried. So," she added ominously, "was Madame Dalecka."

"My lessons were extra long today," Marika said, brushing past her.

"I'm sure they were."

The Contessa followed her into her bedroom, and as Marika removed her dress, said, "I must talk to you. You seem to be avoiding me these days."

Marika did not want to face the Contessa. She turned to the large window instead and, pulling back the draperies, looked out at the slate roofs lit by moonlight. A heavy wind was blowing. She felt weak. "I'm not avoiding you," she managed to say. "I've been busy."

"My darling," the Contessa said, walking up behind her, placing her hand on Marika's shoulder. Marika pulled away. "When I suggested you'd know many young men in your life, I didn't mean you should start having an affair with one while still on your honeymoon with the Count."

Marika spun around. "You know?"

"Of course I know," the Contessa said. "I knew that first day you went off horseback riding with him in the mountains. I've got an investment in you, and it's important I protect it. It's important you honor it, too."

"I'm not anyone's investment," Marika said bitterly. "I don't look at life that way. I love Julian."

The Contessa arched her spine. "No one says you can't be in love." In exasperation, she pressed her fist against her cheek. "Just don't be a fool about it, especially over a poor Jew tutor." She paused. "Of course, I admit he's attractive."

A slow, deep flush flowed to Marika's forehead. It was embarrassing to be forced to share her secret life with someone other than Julian.

The Contessa wrapped her shawl around her, as if to ward off a chill. "If you're going to have an affair, you must do it with more discretion. Why, I once managed to have both of my lovers in the same hotel in Rome, and neither found out about the other. But that takes some finesse."

Marika removed her camisole from the closet nervously, untying one of its ribbons. "What do you want me to do?"

Thrusting her hands in the pockets of her dress, the Contessa circled the floor. The lines in her drawn face seemed deeply imbedded. "Make up better excuses," she said. "If you must see your young man, as you did tonight, then we should pretend to go out together, perhaps to the theater."

"Very well," Marika agreed, pleased.

"At dinner this evening, Madame Dalecka was asking many questions about you," the Contessa said. "Also about the wisdom of having a young girl take private lessons in a young boy's apartment, unchaperoned."

"You think she knows?" Marika asked, her hand tightening on the camisole.

"I think she suspects," the Contessa said. "There's a difference."

Marika was astonished at the conversation she was having, and even more so that the Contessa was letting her continue with her affair. "I'll do whatever you want, providing I don't have to give Julian up."

"Thank you," the Contessa said. "I think you should give up Herr Viertel, but I know you won't. My task at this point is to see that you don't do anything foolish. One wrong step could cause our house of cards to come tumbling down."

Marika stood with her gaze directed at the floor. "I'm really quite sleepy now," she said, "and I must get some rest." Tears danced in her eyes. "Thanks for helping me," she said, almost like breathing a small whisper.

"I'm aiding both of us," the Contessa said. At the door, she put her hand on the knob, but paused a moment. Turning, she frowned at Marika. "I haven't told you this before, and I'm not completely sure, but there's something else you ought to know." She paused again. "I think the Count's in some sort of trouble. I fear it's financial."

Slipping into bed, Marika asked, "What makes you think so?"

"These mysterious business trips to Kraków," she said. "That's where most of his holdings are. He goes there in panic and returns depressed. I gather he has just this house in Warsaw, and nothing else, except the little summer place in the hills."

Marika sat up in bed.

"My bill at the Opera Café," the Contessa continued, "is a case in point. He agreed to pay it, but still hasn't done so. Right now I can't even show my face there."

"But the Count's wealthy," Marika said. "You told me so yourself."

"I thought so," the Contessa said. "But I may have been wrong. I also thought Friedrich was rich. I've been disappointed so many times."

Marika bid the Contessa good night and drifted into a deep, troubled sleep that lasted for a few hours only. She woke again at two and for the rest of the night lay still, her mind teeming, until the morning sun shone.

* * *

The next two months passed slowly for Marika, but one day, after she'd finished her lessons, Julian handed her a letter. Her heart leaped.

"You should have given it to me right away," she scolded him.

"I didn't want to distract you from your lessons," he said, but she brushed him away.

She'd written her Papa at least two dozen times, from both Zakopane and Warsaw, each time giving the letters to the Contessa to mail for her, but Marika had come to suspect the Contessa of simply tearing up her letters. The last one she'd mailed herself, addressing it to Brigitte, who was certain to know of Friedrich's whereabouts. To keep her mail away from prying eyes at the Dabrowsky household, she'd asked Friedrich to write her secretly at Julian's apartment.

Eagerly she tore open the envelope.

MY DEAR DAUGHTER,

At last I know where you are. As I have been traveling, Brigitte was late in getting me my mail, which consists mostly of tired old bills these days anyway. The campaign goes well, though I'm anxious to return to Berlin. However, I'd suggest strongly to the Contessa that she never set foot inside Germany again. If she does, I'll have her arrested for kidnapping. Before she left Berlin, she charged many things, including gowns and jewelry, to me, while pretending to be my wife. Therefore, she's also wanted for fraud. It was wise for her to flee and seek Russian protection in Poland. But I'll never forgive you for disobeying my instructions and going with her. Obviously the two of you were planning this for some time behind my back. As for your so-called marriage, I do not acknowledge it. Count Dabrowsky is not your husband. Instead of granting him a marriage license, I'd charge him with child molestation! I urge you to get in touch with Brigitte and plan to leave Warsaw. Otherwise, because of the Count's influence with the Russians, I'm powerless to do anything to save you. The suggestion is ludicrous that the Count might help me financially. Like the Polish swine he is, I'm sure he'd only laugh in your face. It is with a heavy heart that I write farewell.

Your loving father,
Friedrich.

Even before she finished reading the letter, Marika knew she couldn't leave Warsaw. She loved Julian too much.

"Bad news?" Julian asked.

"It's from Papa," she said. "A letter of congratulations on my marriage."

* * *

By late spring Marika had become profoundly disappointed with her new life as a Polish countess. It had quickly become routine. Her husband, at seventy-five, grew more boring by the month, and even her seventeen-year-old lover offered less and less excitement.

The Count had become so obsessed with talk of war that he often failed to preside at the dinner table, his conversations with friends at the Opera Café stretching on till past midnight.

Even when he came home earlier, at ten or eleven, Marika feigned sleep to avoid his attentions. Not that she'd had much to worry about from him. In the last several weeks, he'd showed no interest at all in her body.

One night in late June, he arrived paler than ever, his hands trembling, as the Contessa and Marika were in the middle of an embroidery lesson.

"Archduke Ferdinand has been assassinated at Sarajevo," the Count said. "His wife was killed, too."

"Oh my God!" The Contessa's face became ghostly pale. Long moments passed before she finally spoke. "I fear our old way of life is gone forever."

Silently, the Count headed for the liquor cabinet.

Marika continued to concentrate on her embroidery. She'd never heard of the Archduke, and politics bored her.

Over dinner that night, the drunken Count continued his monologue. "Europe, as we've known it, will no longer exist. We'll kill each other off. Some new power—perhaps from the West—will come to dominate the world. It could be America."

"Surely not," the Contessa said, interrupting her eating. "I hear they are barbarians."

"Kingdoms, monarchies will be no more," the Count said. "America could well move in and conquer us." He reached for Marika's hand.

She offered it reluctantly.

"In my dear wife's lifetime," he said to the Contessa, "she may come under American enslavement."

The prospect stunned Marika as she slowly, but politely, withdrew her hand. Even though she could converse in English, she'd never thought of talking to an American. For her, learning English meant one day going to London.

In the following days, Julian, too, talked of little else but the coming war. Before or after her instruction in the winter, he'd made love to her at least once a day. But now she often received a quick peck on her mouth, nothing else. Instead, he'd suggest walks through Warsaw—she suspected it was to avoid spending so much time alone with her in his apartment.

One afternoon, when she asked to rest, he sat with her on a bench in the warm sun. "Somehow the sun seems bigger in Warsaw than it was in Berlin," she said. "It's white here, the sky much paler."

"I fear the sky will soon be dark with Prussian smoke," he said, looking at the clouds on the horizon.

"I'm so torn between things," Marika said. "When the Count talks of 'the enemy,' I know he means my people. He means Papa. I can't accept the Prussians as enemies. If a war comes, I don't know who I want to win."

Julian's lips grew twisted. "You little fool," he said angrily. "You know nothing of war. Nobody will win. We may even be killed, at least I will. I'm young. They'll send me to the front lines."

The trees, the sky, everything around Marika seemed peaceful, but she wanted to explode inside at his words. "I never thought about that."

"Think about it!" Nervously he rose from the bench. He turned to her, his face frightened and uglier than she'd ever seen it. "I want to skip lessons for a few days. I have to tend to some business."

Her hands reached up to him, but some inner force pulled her back. She didn't think she could reach him in his present mood, even through her touch. Running to catch up with him, she asked, "Are you going home? I could go back to your apartment with you. The Count said he'll be very late tonight."

"No," he replied, walking so fast she could hardly keep up with him. "I'm going to have dinner with Esther and Simon."

"Will Sophie be there?" she asked, not really wanting to hear the answer.

"I guess," he said nonchalantly. Suddenly, he stopped, turning to face her. "You don't own me, you know. The Count hires me as your tutor. That is all. This love you say you have for me, it's so possessive." His voice was now so loud that an old man passing by turned to stare. "I'm smothering!"

Through her clouded eyes she saw only the back of his blue shirt hurrying up the street. It clung to his body with perspiration, just as her white dress clung to her. In the heat of the street she stumbled along, unable to tell where she was going. Her mind could not formulate thoughts. She couldn't comprehend what had happened between Julian and her.

In the pit of her stomach, a ball of nausea formed, and at first she feared she was going to vomit, right on the street. She ran behind a tree and gagged, wishing desperately that she could vomit—anything to rid herself of the knot strangling her insides.

Later, in her bed, Marika felt better as Aunt Nadya rubbed her feverish forehead with a cold, damp cloth. Looking deeply into the woman's eyes, Marika wished she could be a child again. After waiting for years to be grown-up, she decided she didn't like the adult world at all. She wanted to be back with Friedrich. Reaching out, she touched Aunt Nadya's hand.

The old woman took Marika's hand in hers, pressing it against her cheek. "You're pregnant, Countess," she said.

* * *

Outrage in the wake of Sarajevo swept Austria. Slavic agitation in the Empire, it was agreed, had to be brought under control. The secret societies agitating for independence had to be stamped out. But how?

On July 5, a fateful decision was made. The Kaiser notified Vienna that its Empire could count on Germany's "faithful support" in whatever punitive action she might take against Serbia, providing that action brought her into conflict with Imperial Russia.

* * *

That afternoon Marika asked the Contessa to leave the house with her for tea. Always glad to go on an outing, the Contessa readily agreed. It was not until they reached a small tearoom in a remote part of Warsaw that Marika felt she could talk freely. "I've been nauseous for weeks, and I thought I was gaining weight. But Aunt Nadya has told me I'm going to have a child."

"Sweet God," the Contessa said, "It's Julian's!"

"Yes," Marika said, holding back her tears. "I don't know what to do."

"That's always the way," the Contessa said, sighing and laying her gloves on the table. "Everybody, it seems, knows how to get children, but no one knows what to do once one gets them."

"I don't want to hear a lecture," Marika said. "I haven't seen Julian for a long time. We had a fight. I just pretend to go for my lessons every day."

In a doubting, absent voice, the Contessa said, "It looks to me as if you're going to end up without a husband or a lover."

Marika drew back into a silent hostility, but then her blue eyes flashed with light and she sat up suddenly. "I could return to Berlin to stay with my Aunt Brigitte."

The Contessa stared at Marika, wincing at the mention of Berlin, then shrank back a little, as if it were too painful to look her in the eye. "That may be your only alternative, if the Count dismisses us from his household." Her eyes darted across the café, in a flare of impotent anger. "If you go, I'll be out, too. Madame Dalecka can hardly stand me as it is, though I do everything I can to befriend her."

"She's jealous," Marika said.

"Of course she is. She wants her own son, not you, to inherit the Count's estate. That is, if there is an estate."

Through emotionless eyes Marika settled back to look at the patrons in the café. Several of them looked back at her. They were all dull working people, in blacks and grays, and the Contessa's spring green created a lot of attention. For a long while, neither woman knew what to say to the other.

Remaining perfectly still and stiff, the Contessa finally said, through clenched teeth, "I have a plan. At the moment only three people know this secret—you, me, and Aunt Nadya. A little money that I've been saving up will buy the silence of that old gypsy."

"But I trust her," Marika protested.

"Trust no one," the Contessa said. "Not even yourself."

As she talked, the Contessa's face became more animated, her vision crystalizing. "In Zakopane I refused to answer your clinical questions about sex. I thought you'd find out in your own way. Now I must get clinical. Has the Count ever actually penetrated you . . . I mean, the way Julian surely has?"

Marika slammed down her cup with the terror of a destructive child. "No, the Count does not like it that way."

"I had surmised as much," the Contessa said. Slowly she began to pull on her gloves. "Tonight you must use all your womanly charms to seduce the Count."

"But I can't . . ."

"My dear," the Contessa said, "many women have had far less to work with than the Count. I know you can do it."

"You mean . . ." she asked hesitantly. "If I do it, he might think Julian's child is his?"

"Yes, old men are that foolish and vain," the Contessa said. "Of course, it is humanly possible for a seventy-five-year-old man to father a child. Women have tricked men for centuries. You'll be part of a time-honored tradition."

* * *

That night Marika lay awake as the Count joined her in bed. He'd been drinking vodka heavily, and Marika feared her task would be even more difficult.

With trepidation she reached for his dry, withered hand. He seemed surprised, but pleased. Softly, she requested, "Raise your shirt."

In the dim light of the room, his belly was exposed. The sight embarrassed her. The Count wasn't fat, yet folds of useless skin covered his belly. Unlike Julian's beautiful brown sex, that of the Count's was yellow and shriveled and seemingly unused, a worthless part of him.

Hesitantly she moved over his body. The Count looked down at her through glazed eyes. She tried to lock both the smell and the sight of him out of her mind. He let out a gasp as her lips enclosed the tiny head of his cock, pulling it into her mouth and gently biting down in hopes of stirring it to life. She was working hard now, feeling her own sweat falling from her brow.

For a moment, she allowed herself to look up into the Count's eyes and saw they were full of pride. Then she forced herself back to her work, gagging repeatedly, as she always did. She worked frantically, fearing she wouldn't succeed, but the Count's pride must have taken over. Slowly, she felt a slight hardening and lengthening inside her mouth, and quickly removing her mouth from him, she moved her face closer to his. So far she had proceeded as the Contessa had instructed her. She mounted him.

Moving rhythmically, as she did with Julian, she felt the Count inside her, and, keeping her eyes tightly closed, she imagined that the body beneath her was that of a young, beautiful man. She felt him respond. Soon he held her even closer to him, matching his rhythm with hers, breathing so heavily and in such gasps she feared at first he was going to have a heart attack. For five minutes, then ten, she continued to mount him until she thought she'd faint. But then he held her even tighter. Biting her neck, he slumped back. He was finished, and she could feel the almost instant death of his cock inside her.

As she ran behind the screen to wash herself, the only sound was of the Count crying. It was like a baby.

* * *

On July 23, Austria delivered an ultimatum to Serbia. The demands were harsh and called for a response within forty-eight hours. Serbia accepted most of the demands, but rejected the stipulation that Austrian officials move on Serbian soil to investigate the assassination of the Archduke and his wife.

In Berlin, the overjoyed Kaiser announced that the Serbian note "dissipated every cause for war," but Austria would not be appeased so easily. On July 28, Austria declared war on Serbia, and the next day bombarded Belgrade.

The Tsar immediately mobilized his troops along the Austrian frontier. On July 31 Germany issued an ultimatum to Russia to demobilize within twelve hours, and when the deadline for the ultimatum expired without an answer from the Tsar, the German ambassador in St. Petersburg was notified to declare war at five o'clock in the afternoon. The Kaiser ordered general mobilization.

France stood by Russia. England wanted neutrality, but when German troops wantonly marched through Belgium, England declared war.

By August 5, the five major powers of Europe were locked in deadly combat.

In Berlin General Helmuth von Moltke wrote of "the struggle that will decide the course of history for the next hundred years."

* * *

In the next few weeks Marika corseted herself tightly, determined to keep the news of her pregnancy a secret for as long as she could. When she'd had sex with him, the Count hadn't seemed to notice anything unusual about her belly, and after that night he'd had no more relations with her.

He had little time to pay attention to her anyway, for he'd proved more of a prophet about the war than about the return of the Great Flood. Now Marika knew it was too late for her to make plans to return to Berlin. Gleefully, the Count predicted disaster for Russia. "A big mistake is being made," he said. "The Russians are abandoning the saber in favor of those new firearms. Sabers, not silly innovations, win wars!"

Nevertheless, mobilized by the Tsar, Russian troops advanced against East Prussia, and as the summer waned, frivolity was in the very air of Warsaw. Each night the Count invited Marika and the Contessa to a party or ball and Marika danced with the tall, handsome officers of Imperial Russia. These men, not Julian or the Count, were the princes of her girlhood dreams.

Even though she was aware that the world as she'd known it would soon be coming to an end, Marika threw herself with abandon into this social life. For her it was a dance of death, in spite of the life growing and stirring within her. The flourish of a violin could always send a note of high expectation racing through her. She'd find herself running to reach the dance floor. There, the white gloves, the sparkling uniforms, and the diamond brooches blotted out the sound of battle.

Only when swaying to the rhythm of an orchestra could she forget her oncoming doom. The muscles of her neck strained as she threw back her head, and her laughter rang out, attracting the attention of all around her. She knew the verdict of every man there: she was the most beautiful woman at any ball.

One night she danced with twenty-five men. There could have been more, but the Count demanded that she return home with him and the Contessa rather early. The next night she was back again, the red of her cheeks the only color in a complexion which was rapidly taking on the pallor of porcelain. Her satin gowns always matched her face. One officer, holding her close, smelling her subtle perfume, murmured in her ear that she had "the grace of a swan." She listened as his breathing grew heavier.

By late September, Marika's face began to mature, acquiring a piercing, brutal beauty, and her laughter took on a hollow ring. Sometimes, as she whirled around the floor, she would grow suddenly faint and the lights in the lamps at the Warsaw ball would seem to flicker and grow dim.

Far beyond the beautiful sound of the orchestra and the sway and movement of the graceful dancers, a shadow spread across her life. Once, in the middle of a dip, her hand desperately reached out, her mouth gasped for fresh air. Her partner quickly whisked her outside, and there, her cheek pressed against his breast, she could breathe, but only for a moment. The fresh air soon faded as she felt his mouth smothering her own.

As autumn and the war wore on, the frivolity that marked the earlier months dissipated almost entirely. The balls were sadder, somehow, the dances uninspired. Fewer people attended and even the number of musicians dwindled, their notes gone sour. At the last ball of the year, the room began to whirl around Marika, as it had done before, but this time it was different. The movement began slowly at first, and then started to gain in momentum, causing her to gasp and stumble out to the balustraded terrace, alone this time.

Outside, the damp Warsaw night kissed her eyelids and the violins still played in the background, even though morning was coming on. She shivered in the cold, but remained standing on the terrace, as the first rays of dawn appeared in the sky. Her dashing hussars, her dreams of wealth and glory, her hopes for a stage career—everything seemed to be fading with the night.

She jumped, as her unborn child kicked her.

* * *

· 108 ·

Marika still left the Dabrowsky household each afternoon, claiming she was going to her lessons, but she hadn't seen Julian since that hot summer day he'd left her. She'd walked by his apartment several times, hoping for a glimpse of him, but there was never a sign of life; the curtains were always drawn. She kept waiting for him to get in touch with her to apologize, and if he did, she planned to let him know she was pregnant with his child. Surely he would insist she leave the Count and run away with him. Perhaps they would go to the little summer cottage at Latvia he'd told her about. There, Julian could become her new husband, the father of her child.

One afternoon, Aunt Nadya took Marika downstairs for her bath, the old gypsy wearing a gold necklace she'd been given by the Contessa. The central bath was located off the landing on the second floor, and family members had an afternoon reserved just for themselves.

Marika paused, rubbing her hands gently over the growth inside her, as sunlight came in through the two narrow stained glass windows depicting a pair of nearly nude women with urns. Beside her, Aunt Nadya moved to the corner of the bath, checking the ceiling-high ceramic stove, colored in two tones of green, that stood on giant legs of polished copper.

"But we really didn't need the heat," Marika protested. "It's just too hot in here."

"We must not let you or your child catch cold," Aunt Nadya said.

Stepping out of her dress, Marika longed for a full-length mirror so she could examine her figure more closely, but there was none. Aunt Nadya came to unlace her corset, and casting a careful eye over her, asked, "The Count hasn't seen you nude lately?"

"No," Marika replied demurely.

Aunt Nadya remained silent.

As steam filled the room and water splashed around her, Marika could feel the gentle, careful hands of Aunt Nadya scrubbing her back and belly, the perfumed soap scenting the air.

"Your skin is without flaw," Aunt Nadya said. "Never have I seen skin so beautiful. I feel you're going to make the world's most beautiful child."

The thought both thrilled and frightened Marika. She wanted

to have her child, it was her link to Julian, her only link at this point, but if the Count found out who the real father was . . . maybe it would be best if it died within her.

"Your waist," Aunt Nadya said, "it is really amazing. I can enclose it in my two hands. But your stomach, it is growing bigger by the day." The old woman's rough hands were on her small breasts. "They are not the breasts of a woman. At your age, my breasts were very large. My mother would not let me go by myself through the fields. The older boys were always after me."

Marika sat up in the water. She wondered if Julian liked large breasts on a woman, like those of Sophie.

"When you were lying back in the tub," Aunt Nadya said, "your breasts flattened against your body, you looked like a young boy."

"When my breasts fill up with milk, they will be big, won't they?" Marika asked.

Before Aunt Nadya could answer, the figure of Madame Dalecka loomed like a wraith through the steamy room. Marika had not heard her come in. Standing in back of Aunt Nadya, she focused her eyes on Marika's belly, and touched the old woman on the shoulder, as if to brush her aside. "The Count has returned," she said. "He's asking for you. I'll help the *little mother* finish her bath."

Marika shrank into the bath water, covering her tiny breasts with her hands. Everything was happening so fast. What was she to do? With a sigh, Aunt Nadya heaved her body up and quietly left the room.

"Why didn't you tell me you were pregnant?" Madame Dalecka demanded.

"I . . ." Marika didn't know what to say. She cringed at the woman's long fingers massaging her belly, as if to confirm the fact of her pregnancy.

"Until this moment," Madame Dalecka said, "I thought my son was the only male heir in the Dabrowsky family. As you know, he's away at war. Now I see there is at least the possibility of another male heir. I didn't know my brother at his age could father a child." With a suspicious glare, she rose from her kneeling position beside the tub. Reaching for a towel, she dried her hands, then let it drop to the floor. It seemed an act of defiance.

"I'll go immediately and congratulate my brother," Madame Dalecka said, walking to the door and firmly slamming it shut behind her. The sound sent shivers to Marika's heart.

At six that evening, Marika received a summons to the Count's study. For a long time, she stood in silence facing the back of his neck, fearing a screaming denunciation, the kind Friedrich used to give her. But then she realized the Count was a completely different type of man.

"This is going to be a brief interview," he said, coldly and formally. "Not my own wife, but my sister has told me the news."

"I'm sorry," she stammered. Her hands hung motionless by her side.

"I've always considered womanhood the most sacred thing in life," he said softly, drawing out his words. He turned around and faced her, his skin pallid as the floating belly of a fish. "I've always prided myself on bringing true ladies into this household." He fixed his gaze on her.

She trembled.

"Now I see I've become senile," he said, coughing slightly. "I've married a prostitute! I know the child isn't mine. Your chicanery didn't work."

Her head lolled to one side, almost as if she were going to faint at the accusation, and something inside her seemed ready to burst. "I'll leave," she said, "this very night."

"That would be my greatest wish," he said. "An even greater wish would be that I had never met you, but I fear that isn't the case. You're a clever girl. You've forced me to keep you on in this household."

"I don't understand."

"I can't turn you out," he said. He shifted uncomfortably in his seat. Each movement seemed a major effort. "You and I must not let the world know that child isn't mine." He paused, swallowing a lump in his throat. "That I'm not quite the man I used to be."

The situation was now clear to her. He was much more concerned with his vanity than her unfaithfulness.

"I know who the father is," the Count said in a soft but bitter voice. "It's Herr Viertel. I also know you've not been taking lessons from him. You have lied. You haven't seen him in months."

Her head spun. "How long have you known this?" She felt nauseous at the stuffy smell of the room.

"For some time," the Count said, his words like those of a dying man, echoing through a tunnel. He rose swiftly, smiling sardonically to himself. "I've had an interview with Herr Viertel at his apartment. That was some time ago. I pointed out the vulnerability of his position in Warsaw. I also told him of my powerful connections with the Russians. Despite Madame Dalecka's protests, I get on extremely well with our conquerors."

"You threatened Julian," she charged.

"You might say that," the Count replied. "I told him he had to give you up, but slowly, not a sudden break. Too swift a change in his attitude might make you suspicious."

The room whirled around Marika. "You mean, his indifference . . . "

"He wasn't indifferent at all," the Count said, looking her right in the eye. "When I visited him at his apartment, and confronted him with what I knew, he broke down and cried like a little lovesick boy."

She was silent for a moment, trying to understand the implications of his words. Julian did love her! He'd only pretended not to, and had deliberately started that argument with her on the summer day he'd left her. All the time he hadn't wanted to leave her at all. An overwhelming tenderness for Julian came over her, and she felt she could no longer stand still and endure the torture of the Count's study. A clock struck. Her time was running out.

Exhausted and weary, the Count sat down again. "I'm going to allow you to stay in this household. I'll pretend the child is mine, though I'll see to it that he doesn't inherit property. As for you, I don't want you in my bed or even in my presence anymore. I'm assigning you to one of the rooms on the top floor, with Aunt Nadya."

Her eyes looked around the Count's study, but she saw nothing but darkness. "May I go now?" she asked.

"You're dismissed," he said, slumping over into his chair and shutting his eyes. All life seemed drained from him.

Hurrying from the study, she paused briefly in the hallway to get her wrap. And then she ran out the front door. She must get to Julian. Racing down the street, she nearly bumped into three drunken Russian soldiers, and, trembling, stepped back into a doorway until they were gone. The lamp-lit streets stretched endlessly before her, and a bitter wind, sweeping down the avenue, seemed to whistle in her ear. Her heels hit heavily against the pavement, but after a few blocks her steps grew lighter. The panic consuming her was sweet now, sweet with the knowledge that she'd soon be in her lover's arms. She knew Julian would make everything right again.

Racing up the steps to Julian's apartment, she inserted the key he'd given her into the lock. Inside, the apartment was dark, the air filled with the smell of cabbage cooking.

"Julian," she called out.

A rustle from the bed, and someone was reaching for the light. In the sudden glare Marika found herself staring into the face of Sophie. With a gasp, Sophie drew the covers around her shoulders, concealing her breasts. "What are you doing here?" Sophie demanded. "Get out!"

"But . . . Julian," Marika stammered. Motionless, she stood with her head bent, one hand clasped to her breast. Her mouth moved, as she tried to speak again, but no words came out.

"He's gone," Sophie said, her voice forlorn. She held her covers up around her neck, as if needing protection from this invader. "They came for him."

Marika moved her head slightly, looking into the dark corners of the room, expecting Julian to appear at any moment. "Who came for him?"

"The Russians," Sophie said bitterly. "Several weeks ago. We know who sent them. Your precious Count Dabrowsky."

"It can't be true," Marika said. She stepped back from the bed, her shoes squeaking.

"It's true," Sophie said. "Julian is at the front right now. He'll probably be killed." Her gaze fixed on Marika's blue eyes. "Killed by the Prussians."

Blackness welled around Marika.

"Your Count came here one day," Sophie said. "There was a violent confrontation. He accused Julian of having an affair with

· 113 ·

you. Julian denied it. He said he wasn't even your tutor anymore." She coughed, choking on her tears. "In the next few days Julian was not so mysteriously conscripted."

Slowly Marika backed toward the door, the squeak of her shoes seeming to mock her. "He can't be gone," Marika said. "I'm going to have his child."

A deathly stillness came over the room, until the bubbling of a pot caused Sophie to slip out of bed and race to the kitchen. Lifting the lid from the pot, she stepped back and looked at Marika. "So am I."

The strong cabbage smell brought back memories of the apartment in the ghetto. "Oh, God," said Marika in a terrified whisper.

Sophie came toward her. "I'm going to have his *real* child. That's why he married me before he went to the war."

For one brief second Marika wanted to open the door and jump down the steps, killing the child within her and herself, too. Her hands sweated, her whole body seemed to be pricked by splinters. "You are Julian's wife?" Her own words seemed to bounce back from the walls, exploding within her ears.

Sophie's eyes shrank in their frowning sockets, and her small mouth hung open like a stupid child's in a petulant, defiant expression. Her red hair wasn't lustrous, like Marika's, but brittle and thinning, receding back from her shiny forehead. In the harsh light of the apartment, Sophie was so unappealing, so unattractive, Marika couldn't believe that Julian could ever have wanted to make love to her.

Through her thin nightgown, Sophie's breasts were clearly prominent. Marika couldn't take her eyes off them. Thoughts of Julian's child suckling at those breasts were unbearable. Even worse was the picture of Julian loving those breasts himself, the way he'd loved Marika's. Slowly, she spoke, "I'm sorry to have come in like this. I never will again."

"You certainly won't," Sophie said firmly, moving toward her in a slow, cow-like way. "You're dead as far as Julian is concerned. He never loved you. He loved *me*. Didn't you know he made love to you just to hold onto his position as your tutor? He hated your pasty whiteness."

"No!" Marika screamed. "I won't hear it. He turned to you because he felt he couldn't have me." Blindly, she stumbled out the door, rushing down the steps into the dark street.

For hours she wandered in the streets of Warsaw, paying no attention to time or where she was going. There was no place for her to go. Abruptly, two men appeared out of the gloom and halted her. *"Stoi!"* They were Russian soldiers.

Marika's knees quivered as she tried to make out what they were saying, but they spoke too rapidly. She thought they wanted to see her papers, but as she started to reply, a sudden weight hit her legs from behind, tripping her. Brutally, one of the soldiers locked his arm around her throat and dragged her into an alley, then shoved her to the ground. She tried to scream, but the other soldier's heavy body fell on top of her, pinning her down. His vodka breath was like that of the Count's.

She wiggled and squirmed, trying to break free, but the soldier's big hands gripped her shoulders and bit into her neck, deliberately trying to hurt her, it seemed. The ground was cold and damp, and rocks pressed into her back.

The man's elbow cut off her windpipe and Marika started choking. Frantically, she tried to get free, and thrusting upward, she felt her right hand connect with the soldier's Adam's apple. He jumped back in pain, then a gloved hand slammed into her face. Blackness momentarily confused her, then the taste of her own blood was in her mouth. "God, God!" she cried out in a voice hardly audible to herself. She knew she was going to die!

The other soldier fell on top of her, grabbing one wrist in a vise-like grip and pinning her other arm behind her. Closing her eyes, she let her head spin crazily. Her nose was still bleeding, and over her the man grunted drunkenly, crushing the breath from her body. Rough hands seemed to come from all directions. Her blouse was being ripped from her back. The soldier's ugly rasping resounded in her ears as, with one savage jerk, the rest of her clothing was removed from her body.

Marika whimpered, begging the man to stop, but then she realized she was speaking in German. She tried to speak to them in Russian, but she'd completely forgotten the words to say.

The hand locked harder around her neck, and then suddenly the soldier was pushing his trousers down to his knees, plunging brutally into her. She screamed. The pain was unbearable. His attack hurt, really hurt, a racking, searing, splitting pain. Her body bucked and tightened. She wanted to get away from the pain, but there was no escape. She dreaded each new lunge more than the one before.

The soldier was holding her by her hips, slamming in and out of her, while the other man's fingers tightened around her wrists. Her attacker seemed to be growing bigger and harder inside her. Then he shrieked out, reared back, and collapsed on top of her.

When he finally pulled out of her, she felt a vast wave of relief.

But then the other soldier's hand was on her, feeling her pregnant belly, kneading it. It seemed to excite him. It was the one she'd hit in the windpipe, and she feared how he'd punish her. The other man held her wrists now, while her new attacker jerked her legs as far apart as he could. She was almost too weak to resist anymore. Then he ripped into her, digging his fingernails into her skin. Numb, dazed, cold sweat beading her forehead, she was in such pain she couldn't utter a sound. Tears began to stream from her eyes and she no longer minded the taste of her own blood.

Much drunker than her first attacker, the second soldier took forever, and she knew when he'd finished, he would murder her —and Julian's child growing within her.

She started to feel sick to her stomach. Something was tearing loose inside her. A wave of heat seemed to surge through her stomach. Every nerve and muscle tensed under assault.

She passed out.

* * *

For Marika, all sense of time and space disappeared. She felt the tremors inside her womb, her child, Julian's child, wanting to get out, but she was afraid to release it.

She didn't dare open her eyes, but she knew where she was. Somehow, she had mysteriously traveled back to the Count's house. The rustle of a dress, the odor of a freshly starched uniform, told her Aunt Nadya was nearby. Desperately she reached out for the old woman's hand, clutching at her, not to hurt her but to assure herself that Aunt Nadya was actually there.

Her long, slender fingers reached back to touch her own stomach, massaging it, seeking to dull the unbearable pain. Her sheets were soaked with perspiration.

She didn't want to think about the pain. Certainly not about the baby inside her. She wanted to recall a happier day in Berlin, the vision of her own luminous loveliness dressed all in white at a birthday party. The other girls resented her because she was more beautiful than they were. They were surrounding her . . . talking to her . . . their voices were Russian! Aunt Nadya rubbed her brow with a wet towel.

The pain eased slightly and Julian's beautiful face appeared before her. Suddenly the image dimmed and flickered, and the rough peasant features of a Russian soldier took its place. Marika cried out and opened her eyes, but shut them quickly, as violet-colored waves washed across her eyelids. "Julian," she called out in a plaintive voice. But her lover didn't answer. He could not hear her, only the guns of war.

Her hands stopped massaging her stomach for a moment, and as if with a life of their own traveled to her breasts, filled with milk now. The tremors inside were still strong.

"I can't have a child," she whispered to Aunt Nadya. "It'll kill me. I'm a child myself."

Her own baby stirred within her, as if he had heard her. She screamed as he kicked her. Was he punishing her for not bringing him into the world? "My boy," she shouted, "he's alive!"

"Of course," Aunt Nadya said. "But how do you know it's a boy?"

"I just know," she said. "Julian would have wanted a boy." The room was almost black. It was a kind of womb, she thought. But people could walk into this womb and hurt you. The womb in which her unborn baby lived was far safer. It was filled with warmth and darkness. "Kick, my little one," she said. "But I won't let you out."

"The doctor is coming," Aunt Nadya said, trying to reassure Marika.

But the announcement didn't settle her. She feared the doctor. He had secret ways of forcing her to give up her baby. Soon she felt new hands on her body. Marika smiled. All of a sudden, she wasn't afraid. A state of dreamy paralysis consumed her. Perhaps she'd stay awake long enough to release the child after all. Her hands tightened on her stomach. She couldn't give in to sleep, to death. Her blood ran cold, and her mind lay trapped in a foggy gray. She imagined she heard the heartbeat of her own son, growing louder and louder, like a savage drum. If that heart didn't stop beating so furiously, Marika feared the boy would explode within her.

Voices were over her, but she couldn't really understand what they were saying. They grew louder, as the pounding inside her increased. A long groan escaped from her lips, turning into a howl of pain.

Her legs were weighing her down, as if huge rocks were tied to them. She bit down on her tongue until Aunt Nadya forced her fingers into her mouth and took the crunch of Marika's teeth herself. Spasms swept over her body, but she didn't cry out again. She was safe in knowing it would soon be over.

"Push! Push!" the doctor shouted. He sounded angry at her. "Men are dying right now. They need my attention."

With all her remaining strength, Marika pushed. Her bones cracked, but she wanted the child out now.

She was holding her body together now by the sheer power of her own will, pushing, and pushing hard, though she feared it would rob her of her last breath. A giant hand seemed to be choking her heart, but still she pushed. She bit her lips so fiercely she brought blood, and the pressure swelled within her until she felt her eardrums were about to burst. Still, she pushed.

The doctor rested his knee on her stomach and pressed down. She screamed in pain.

"Push! Push!" he shouted.

"The head," Aunt Nadya cried out with joy, "it's showing."

Her womb stirred and dilated. She clutched her stomach. The baby was a demon. It was sapping her own life. He would leave her, as Julian had done.

Tasting her own blood, she pushed harder.

"Look, doctor," Aunt Nadya said.

Flashes of lightning crossed Marika's eyelids. Ice water seemed to run through her veins. Claws dug into her flesh, ripping her son from her, and the ice turned to fire, burning her alive. Her bones were cracking again. She was bleeding to death.

Suddenly a floating weightlessness came over her as she felt a huge slippery mass delivered from her body. She was adrift in space. God had delivered her from all pain.

"It's a boy," Aunt Nadya said.

"The baby is dead," the doctor said solemnly.

At these words, Marika breathed deeply, realizing she was still alive, still on this earth. But her work was over. She could drift into sleep—and hope she'd never emerge.

* * *

In Germany, the Kaiser boasted to his troops, "You'll be home before the leaves have fallen from the trees." But such was not to be the case.

After steamrolling through Belgium, the German armies moved into northern France, but there at the Marne, the rallying French checked their too-rapid advance. The Germans now faced a two-front war, the French on the west, the Russian hordes moving upon them from the east.

The German attempt to take the Channel ports also failed, and the British quickly retaliated by setting up a blockade against their enemy. Many Germans now faced starvation, and the war quickly came to a stalemate, as one huge army hurled itself against another. To gain a few square yards of land, thousands of lives were sacrificed.

From the North Sea to the Swiss frontier, trenches zigzagged for three hundred miles.

* * *

Days went by before Marika woke up, fully coherent, to find Aunt Nadya combing her hair. She reached for the old woman and kissed her on the mouth, desperately needing the woman to fondle her, to bathe her in love.

"Your breasts are hard with milk," Aunt Nadya said. "Too much milk for a young girl. I must tie up your breasts. There is no child to suckle them."

That night Marika could not sleep. Her bedroom seemed a cell, and that she'd survived a rape and a stillbirth filled her with no sense of triumph. On her bed, every part of her body still throbbed with pain. She no longer felt human—but rather a distorted shell of her former beauty. Ulcers, she feared, would appear on her breasts, ruining them forever. But what did it matter? Julian would be her last lover. There would be no more men to caress her breasts.

Humiliation and impotent rage filled her mind. She didn't want to know how or in what condition she'd arrived back in the Dabrowsky household. Her only comfort was that the Count no longer visited her.

As she drifted into another long Warsaw winter, Marika thought she'd come to the end of her life. "I'll never be free again," she whispered.

During the endless, sleepless nights, her mind dwelled more and more on suicide. It seemed the only way out. There was nothing left in life for her. Maybe the Count was right. Europe was destroying itself and perhaps she should throw herself on the funeral pyre, putting an end to her own misery.

An overwhelming hatred and disgust for herself overcame her. She couldn't stand to look at her reflection in the pedestal mirror beside her bed, for she didn't want to see what had become of her face. She knew there had been major changes.

Aunt Nadya told her so one day: "It's not the face of a pretty girl anymore. You've gone through a woman's suffering. You have a woman's face. No one will ever question that again."

All her dreams about a glorious life, about sweeping across Europe in white gowns and ostrich feathers with handsome young men falling at her feet, seemed so silly now. She knew that her upcoming death would be no more significant than crushing an insect. It would be a miserable, anonymous death. The war would surely wipe out her birth records. No one would ever know that Marika Kreisler had ever existed.

She lay quietly in the bed waiting for Aunt Nadya to arrive with the morning tray of food. Marika didn't want to eat, but she wanted her company. This morning it was the Contessa who brought the tea, however. Her face was older, sadder. No longer flamboyantly attired, she was dressed simply in black, almost like Madame Dalecka.

"You have spoiled everything for us," the Contessa began bitterly. "Life was going to be so easy, until your schoolgirl idea of romance got in the way."

"If that's all you have to say to me after all that's happened," Marika said, "then please go."

She waved her hand through the air as if to brush aside Marika's request. "Do you know that almost every day I have to prevail upon the Count to let us remain in this household," she said, reaching for Marika's wrist.

Marika withdrew it. "Who wants to stay here?"

"Where would you go?" the Contessa asked, wearily sitting down in a chair reserved for Aunt Nadya. "You saw what happened to you the last time you wandered alone on the streets of Warsaw."

Marika turned over in bed so that her back was to the Contessa, trying to shut out the memory of the rape. Sometimes she could go for a whole day without thinking about it. The very presence of the Contessa was more than she could tolerate, however. "Get out!" she screamed, sitting up in bed in a rage. "Don't ever come into my room again!"

The Contessa slowly rose to her feet. "I can see there's no talking to you. I came here with a plan to try to get you back into the Count's good graces."

"I don't want to be back in his good graces," Marika said, crying now. "I don't want to see him again . . . ever."

"Very well," the Contessa replied. She paused long enough at the door to reach into the pocket of her dress and place an envelope addressed "To Countess Dabrowsky" on the foot of the bed. Then she left.

Marika reached for the envelope and quickly tore it open. The note read:

> Julian died in battle, but not until he wrote me he hated you. You and your Prussian guns killed him! His child lives within me, and I will give birth to it soon. I'm glad your child died. Julian wrote he hoped it would.
>
> Mrs. Julian Viertel.

Marika stared at the empty chair in which the Contessa had been sitting.

When Aunt Nadya discovered Marika at three o'clock that day, she was still staring at the four legs of the chair in the shadows of the afternoon.

* * *

Along the entire Western Front, battle lines swayed back and forth by no more than ten miles. Armed with bayonets and hand grenades, infantrymen went over the top again and again, only to be downed by machine guns.

In the gloom of Warsaw, Marika seemed to lapse into a coma, weeks building into months. She'd lost all sense of day and night. Sometimes she'd come to, but memories would drift to the front of her brain and make her retreat quickly into a dreamy trance.

Once Aunt Nadya caught her with her face against the wall, her moans filling the room. At night she usually muffled her cries in her pillow, but on this day she cried out, not caring who heard her. Aunt Nadya carried the painfully bewildered Marika back to bed and tucked her in, but Marika's fear remained strong, with the feeling that she'd come back from a long voyage. But where had she been?

Throughout her exile, one part of her wanted to stay alive—the side that believed in miracles—but a much more forceful part of her desired only to sink into a state of forgetfulness, to shut out the world altogether.

One morning she woke up to find her body covered with perspiration, and the brass chandelier overhead seemed to be spinning. The entire room spun with it, and though she shut her eyes as tightly as she could, the room gained in speed, like a merry-go-round out of control.

"Make it stop!" she called out. "Somebody, stop it!" Her plea was heard. Sleep came to her, hours and hours of sleep, and when she woke up she wondered what time it was. That surprised her, as she hadn't cared about time for weeks.

The draperies had been pulled in the dark room, and a pot of tea rested on her night table, with some dry bread and butter. She wanted to remove the top of her skull and pull out the nerve endings that were giving her such a blinding headache.

Catching a whiff of gas, burnt bread, and coffee, she shivered in the cold, not from the room, but from something inside that chilled her. She feared the privacy of her chamber had been invaded by someone other than Aunt Nadya. Was it the Count?

"My little one," came a familiar voice from the far corner. "I thought you were going to sleep forever like Sleeping Beauty."

It was Aunt Nadya, after all.

Marika sat up in bed. "You're dressed, babushka and all. Are you leaving?"

At Marika's bedside, the head of Aunt Nadya seemed even larger, her red nose protruding. The dim light of the room and the shadows it made on Aunt Nadya's face caused her to look like a witch. "Yes," she said finally, "and I'm taking you with me."

"But why?" Marika asked.

Aunt Nadya rubbed Marika's hand. "You'll die if you continue to stay shut up in this room. The war will go on forever, I know that now. But spring is here. I've got permission from the Count to take you to his summer place."

Marika closed her eyes. At first she didn't want to go, but the more she thought about it, the more promising it looked. Any place right now seemed better than the Dabrowsky household.

The long, low country house to which Aunt Nadya took Marika was primitive, but at least she was away from the oppressive feeling of Warsaw at war. As the weeks dragged on, the quietness and the good, clean air helped restore her body, though her spirit still sagged. She'd sit alone on the porch, listening to Aunt Nadya prepare dinner, singing an old Russian folk song that had no more tune than a toothless mumble. Every afternoon she ate rye bread and honey and drank tea poured from a samovar. Tall lime trees led to the untidy kitchen garden and orchard, and there she wandered among the apple trees, trying to forget Julian.

One afternoon the Contessa paid a surprise visit. "I haven't been here sooner," she said, "because the road is the worst ever. Nothing but black, slippery mud all the way. My carriage lurched and plunged. I thought at any moment we were going to be overturned."

Over tea, the Contessa continued with her bad news. "The war is going terribly," she said. "Russia is losing. People are predicting the Prussians will occupy Warsaw before the first autumn leaf falls. Already there are some who are fleeing."

Marika could not care who won the war at this point. The war had already taken her lover and, in a way, her child. For her, the worst was over. But Aunt Nadya was visibly shaken by the Contessa's news. "I must go back to my country," she said. "I can't stay on here. I'll not be ruled by the Prussians."

Ignoring Aunt Nadya, Marika timidly asked the Contessa, "How is the Count?"

"My worst suspicions about him have been confirmed," the

Contessa said. "He's even selling the family furniture. Either he is completely penniless, or else he's liquidating everything in case the Germans come. The Count fears he'll be arrested as a war criminal, because of his collaboration with the Russians. I think he's been turning in so-called disloyal Polish friends of his to the Russians. If the Germans don't shoot him, the 'liberated' Poles will."

"Does Madame Dalecka know this?" Marika asked. "She hates Russians."

"I think she suspects," the Contessa said. "But she dismisses such stories about the Count as slanderous. Do you know what that dreadful woman has done? She has moved her blind children into the house!" the Contessa went on. "The place is a madhouse. That's why I'm welcoming these few days in the country."

As Marika listened to the Contessa, she felt a sudden note of alarm. Excusing herself abruptly, she ran to her bedroom and removed Friedrich's letter from between the pages of a book. Hurrying back, she showed it to the Contessa.

"My God," the Contessa said, "this is terrible. I thought I had nothing to fear if the Germans took over. Now I see that Friedrich will have me arrested." She rose from her chair so swiftly she upset her teacup. "I've got to return to Warsaw tonight. I must go into hiding."

"I'm sorry," Marika said, her eyes downcast.

"Sorry!" the Contessa shouted. "You let Friedrich know of my whereabouts. My dear, you've tightened the noose around my neck." Mumbling to herself, she headed for the door.

Marika swallowed a cry of pain, and it seemed to explode in her stomach.

* * *

In one week Aunt Nadya's fears about a German takeover had become so strong that, begging and pleading, she convinced Marika to take her back to Warsaw. By the time they reached the outskirts, panic was in the air. The Russians had begun blowing up the bridges over the Vistula, but everyone knew the Prussians would find a way in.

Startled, Marika saw that the gypsy had stopped their carriage at the railway station. "But aren't you going back to the Count's house with me?"

"No, my little one," Aunt Nadya said. "They told me a train's leaving for Russia. I belong with my people now. Aunt Nadya arrived in Warsaw with just a few possessions. I'll leave with just a little bundle."

"But . . ."

Aunt Nadya put her hand over Marika's mouth to hush her. "Good-bye, my lovely little pet. Go with God." She kissed Marika on the cheek, then, crying, she squeezed Marika's hand once more and rushed into the station.

Marika stood bewildered for a moment, then ran into the station after her. "Aunt Nadya!" But the milling, frightened crowd had swallowed her whole. All the women looked like Aunt Nadya. Forlornly, Marika walked back outside again, only to find that someone had made off with the carriages and her luggage.

Madame Dalecka greeted her at the front door of the Count's house, and promptly barred her way. "The Count's gone," she said adamantly. "To Russia. The Count gave me this house and all the rest of his land as a school for my children, since my building was commandeered by the army. You might as well leave. As you can see, there is nothing for you here."

"Where's the Contessa?" Marika asked.

"She returned unexpectedly from the country," Madame Dalecka said. "But she's run off, too. In great fear." The woman's back stiffened. "You're on your own now, *Countess.*"

In a rage, Marika pushed her aside and forced her way in. "Yes!" she said. "I *am* the Countess, and while I am here, I am *still* the Countess. I have every intention of leaving, but I plan to collect my possessions first." She stormed up the stairs and began throwing her things together, making sure not to forget the pedestal mirror her mother had given her. Going through her clothes, she tried to decide what to take with her, but suddenly she found herself sitting on the bed, starting to cry. Yes, she was leaving— but where was she to go?

As the distant sounds of bombing grew closer, it quickly became apparent that there was nowhere she could go. The Prussians would soon be on them and the best thing she could do, Marika realized, was to sit tight and wait. Slowly, she wandered downstairs. Madame Dalecka had herded her schoolchildren into the cellar, and their crying only made Marika's tension more unbearable. She entered the parlor. Everything of value had been removed—even the tiles in the ceramic stove were missing. In a sorry pile in the corner, a grand piano lay disemboweled, its former elegance now a welter of disconnected pieces.

Suddenly, with a great bursting crash, the house shook to its very foundations and a roaring burst of bullets shattered the windows in the parlor. Marika fell on the floor, screaming, but the cries of the blind children drowned her out. When she dared raise her head, she stared at her own image in the broken mirror, framed in gilt. The sight of a hollow-eyed and sunken-cheeked woman at twilight made her gasp. "It's not me!" But she knew it was. She'd become the woman in the mirror.

Through the afternoon and long into the night, the shooting continued, the sound of the bullets haphazardly hitting the facade of the Dabrowsky town house and mixing with the thunder of a heavy rainstorm.

On the floor, softly weeping at the madness of the world, Marika spent the longest night of her life.

* * *

By morning the shooting had stopped and Warsaw was deadly still. Even Madame Dalecka's schoolchildren had quieted down.

Madame Dalecka herself came up at noon. "As long as you're still here, you'd better make yourself useful. I must go out to find food for the children. They are starving, and they don't understand. You stay here and watch them."

With a black look, she swept out the door—and never returned. All afternoon, Marika waited, trembling, the sound of the children crying in the cellar shredding her nerves, but still no Madame Dalecka. Finally, the sound of footsteps outside broke her reverie, but the footsteps were wrong—heavy, clumsy. Loud pounding sounded on the front door, and with a crash the glass panes of the windows shattered over the floor.

Still slumped on the floor, Marika summoned her final courage. All night she'd been tempted to cut herself with the jagged piece of glass in which she'd seen her reflection. She wouldn't be raped again!

The soldiers were in the parlor now. She reached out for the mirror, but at the sound of their voices, she stopped. They were Prussians! She was safe. Getting up weakly, she ran up to one of them. "I'm Prussian, too," she cried out. "My father is Friedrich Kreisler. There are blind children in the basement. Don't shoot!"

She fainted.

When Marika came to again, she lay in a strange room that smelled of chemicals. In the shadows stood a tall familiar figure in a dark suit. Slowly, he came toward her, walking with a limp, as if he had a wooden leg. Her heart pounded louder and louder, the nearer he came. Then she could look into his eyes.

It was Friedrich.

Chapter 5

The train ride back to Berlin stretched out endlessly, and to all Marika's questions, Friedrich gave only curt replies. "I'm working as a citizen for the government. I was among the first of the German civilians to arrive in Warsaw. The colonel who rescued you once served under me. Fortunately, he knew how to contact me."

He wouldn't speak of how he lost his leg in battle, but she could tell he still hadn't adjusted to his new wooden one. Every time he got up to go to the rear of the compartment, she'd look away, but not before she'd seen him wince in pain. She pretended not to notice, because she knew how he loathed sympathy, especially from women.

Sitting down opposite her, he said, "Dabrowsky escaped. He left no assets whatsoever. He got rid of everything. If the Contessa thought she was going to make either you or her wealthy by arranging a marriage to Dabrowsky, she was very wrong—the same way she was with me."

"The whole thing was a nightmare."

"Dabrowsky was a collaborator with the Russians," Friedrich said. "He's near the top of our enemy list in Poland."

Outside the window in a clearing, Marika stared wide-eyed at a prisoner-of-war camp. "Am I going to get a divorce from him in Berlin?" she asked.

"Certainly not!" Friedrich said in a loud voice, lowering it as two officers in uniform passed by. "You'll tell no one of your pretend marriage to the despicable swine. Besides, I don't call child molestation marriage."

Marika settled uncomfortably back into her seat. She wanted to ask yet another question, but feared Friedrich's anger.

As if reading her thoughts, Friedrich said, lighting a cigar and biting down hard on it, "As for that monstrous and alleged Contessa, she, too, has eluded us. But not for long. I'm bringing kidnap charges against her—and I have had my marriage to her officially changed. It was never legal to begin with."

Marika raised her face to him, her look a mixture of doubt and interrogation. "Very well," she said, "we'll just wipe out our past. From now on, neither of our marriages existed. The Contessa was right about one thing. She said if you didn't like the past you'd lived, you could always make up a better one for yourself."

He glared at her for a long moment, visibly restraining himself. "I see being in the company of a so-called Polish aristocrat has put acid on your tongue. You're not a girl but a woman who speaks her mind." His voice was sarcastic. "Thank God you're not asking me to call you 'Countess.'"

"It wasn't the Count who made me a woman," she said softly.

"Whoever it was," he said, taking a puff from his cigar and looking out at the barren landscape, "I prefer not to discuss it."

She remained silent as the slow-moving train approached the outskirts of Berlin. The excitement she'd remembered in the Imperial City was gone, for it was now as dull and gray-looking as Warsaw. Berlin seemed sunk in gloom and despair, although the Kaiser still assured his people they were winning the war and the struggle would soon be over.

But all the landmarks were alien to her, as alien as the defeated Papa sitting across from her. She closed her eyes and tried to remember a happier day when she'd seen Friedrich in his perfectly tailored hussar uniform riding high on a white horse in a parade down Unter den Linden. As the train pulled into the station, she tried to keep her mind on that image, on what Friedrich was, not on what he'd become. But it was hard.

In the carriage, Marika sat up straight and adjusted her white dress. "Do we have to live with Aunt Brigitte? I don't think I like her. She never seemed to be too friendly when we visited her before the war."

"We have no choice," Friedrich said, staring at the driver. "It is the only home we have now."

Brigitte Kreisler's apartment was dark and stuffy, with monumental oak furniture. Heavy velvet draperies kept out the late afternoon sun and the air was stale.

After a long wait, Marika stood up as Brigitte approached wearing a floor-length black dress of rustling silk, her auburn hair piled high on her head. Her face was lean and statuesque, and made up like the Contessa's, and under heavily arched brows rested piercing, almond-shaped, green eyes. Her mouth was a slightly larger version of Marika's own wide lips.

"Forgive me," Brigitte said, smiling to reveal the whitest teeth ever. It had been three years since Marika had last seen Brigitte, and she was stunned to see how she looked. She imagined what she might look like when she got old. "I was having afternoon tea," Brigitte continued. "You know my habits by now. I've entertained all my life, but I prefer tea alone these days. I've got all these memories to sort out, and tea time is my only chance."

"For you, my dear Brigitte," Friedrich said, "we will gladly wait." He reached to kiss her hand. "Your hospitality these past few months has made all the difference."

Her nails were long and painted with a dull polish, her hands perfectly shaped, with long, slender fingers. Unlike her lined face, Brigitte's hands were young. Unconsciously Marika found herself examining her own fingers, wondering if they'd grow long like Brigitte's.

After Friedrich kissed her hand, Brigitte threw back her head and laughed. It was theatrical, rehearsed, as if she were projecting to the back row of a theater. Once, Brigitte had been an actress on the Berlin stage. "You've never had enough patience to wait one minute without exploding. After all, I know you better than anyone in the world, better than mother did, bless her."

Marika stood tall and proud in front of her aunt, wondering when she was going to pay her some attention.

"Now let me take a good look at our Polish countess," Brigitte said.

Marika raised her chin defiantly. "I'm not a Polish countess anymore," she said politely but firmly.

"Friedrich told me everything on the telephone," Brigitte said. She bent down to kiss Marika on both cheeks, then accepted Friedrich's outstretched hand as he guided her to the parlor and eased her into a black horsehair armchair.

"Unfortunately," Friedrich said, "I'll not be able to join you ladies tonight. I must report to headquarters." He leaned down to kiss Brigitte good-bye.

For a moment the theatrical mask she'd assumed disappeared. Her features softened, and a look of care and sympathy came into her face. "Do be careful, darling Friedrich. You are all the family I've got left now."

Marika stood in bewilderment. Didn't Brigitte consider her family?

"You be careful yourself," Friedrich said, kissing Brigitte again, this time lightly on the lips. "These political activities of yours— you know they're dangerous."

"Yes, dear Friedrich," Brigitte said, almost lightly. "But theater owners stopped offering me parts. I have to attract attention in *some* way."

Friedrich turned to Marika. "You'll be in good hands here," he said. "I want you to obey Brigitte's every command."

Marika grabbed his hand. "You are coming back?" she asked.

He gently disengaged his hand. "I never know these days." He kissed her lightly on the cheek, his fingers tightened on her arm, and then he quietly limped out of the parlor.

Marika stood looking at his back, saying nothing.

Finally, Brigitte coughed. "What do you want to do now that you're in Berlin?"

Marika hesitated. "I hope you don't think I'm silly, and terribly foolish, but . . . ever since I saw Madame Modrzejewska in Warsaw, I've wanted to be an actress."

Brigitte's green eyes sparkled. "That's an ambition I can understand. I found facing live audiences the most stimulating thing in my life. It does bring out the best in us." Her voice became a husky whisper. "You must have confidence in yourself if you want to be an actress."

"I do have confidence," Marika said somewhat unconvincingly.

Brigitte looked at her. "Very well, then. Before we have a light supper, I'll give you a short drama lesson." She rose from her chair. "Do you know how to bow? Not curtsy, bow."

"No," Marika said, feeling ashamed.

At the door to the hallway, Brigitte turned. Raising her arms, she lifted her hands with their long fingers so that they glided gracefully through the air. Then her whole body seemed to fall forward, as if she were worshipping an imaginary audience, and at the last moment her neck arched up and her head shot back. She ended her bow in a low, graceful swoop, disappearing behind the fringed portiere of the parlor door.

Later that night, the gaslight in Brigitte's parlor glowed softly as, from the end of the hallway, busy sounds emerged from the kitchen. Marika paused outside the door. The past three hours had been spent alone in her new bedroom, thinking and listening to the scratching of tree branches against the closed shutters.

"Is that you, my dear?" came the voice of Brigitte from the parlor.

"Yes," Marika replied.

The sound of Brigitte's voice was like a musical instrument. Her words seemed to dance on the air.

She went in and saw Brigitte lounging on a horsehair sofa, her pose so artfully arranged that Marika suspected she might have staged it. Her crossed legs dangled delicately at the edge of the sofa, her body lay curled like a kitten along the contours of the cushions. Bent fingers gently touched the edge of her hair. Her head was upright, her elbow lodged in the curve of a pillow.

With her free hand, Brigitte traced the outline of her white satin dress across her still-flat stomach and fingered the collar of white-fox fur. "I hope you don't mind," she said, "but I always insist on dressing for dinner, even when no one is here, which is most of the time."

"I don't mind," Marika said, feeling awkward and plain in her simple, pale-hued dress which had long ago lost its freshness. "I think you look very handsome."

"I'll consider that a compliment," Brigitte said. "Although I haven't quite gotten used to the word 'handsome.' " Her shrill laughter sounded slightly malicious. "I still prefer 'pretty.' "

"I'm sorry," Marika stammered.

"Don't be," Brigitte said soothingly. "I fear my pretty days are behind me." She leaned her head back against the horsehair. "I was just lying here thinking about my darling Friedrich."

"You must have many memories of him," Marika said.

"Yes, I do," she said. "He was a mean boy at times, as he'll admit himself. But then he could delight and thrill me, as few brothers rarely can." She paused, as if looking around the room for something. "I remember one summer Sunday when both of us went to spend the day at Potsdam."

Marika sat down in one of the dark oak chairs by a tea table.

"I was blonde then," Brigitte went on. "Just as blonde as Friedrich. We both were dressed in white. Only the sunshine was more dazzling. Friedrich held my hand." She smiled at Marika. "I don't think there was a more stunning couple in all of Prussia. Everybody thought we were lovers."

Marika rested her feet firmly on the floor. "I always wanted Papa to take me to the Tiergarten," she said. "But he was always busy."

Slowly Brigitte glided from the sofa, her gracefulness of movement contrasting with Marika's awkwardness. "I've been mulling over something you said. You are so young, and I have a responsibility to you. Just from what I've seen of you—the way you move, the way you talk—I think it's wrong for me to encourage you to pursue a career in the theater. For that, you need flair. Otherwise, it could lead to heartbreak."

"But I need encouragement," Marika pleaded. "I can learn. Surely someone encouraged you to become an actress."

"No one did," Brigitte said sadly. "Your grandparents considered me a scandal. I had to struggle every step of the way by myself. Even Friedrich was against it." Hand at her throat, she looked up at a glittering portrait that hung over the sofa. It had been painted when she was young. "But then I had a talent worth cultivating."

The parlor was even darker than before. Marika bit her lip and stood looking unblinkingly at her aunt.

"I'm sure Friedrich told you I'm a lady who speaks her mind,"

Brigitte said. "I didn't mean to offend you, but a theatrical career for you seems out of the question."

Marika remained still. In the mirror behind Brigitte, she studied her own stricken face.

As if to soften the impact of her words, Brigitte made as if to reach out to Marika, but her hand froze in the air, eventually finding its way to her ear. "You should find a new husband—not lead the lonely life I've led as an actress."

"But I don't want a husband, ever again," Marika said.

Brigitte laughed, then walked to the doorway, pausing to look back. "One thing I've learned. Acting talent is born in the soul of the artist. It cannot be taught."

"You don't know my abilities," Marika blurted at her. "I *will* become a famous actress one day."

Like some strange, noble bird of prey, Brigitte stood firmly, asserting the rightness of her position. "You don't believe that statement anymore than I do." She turned and her footsteps faded down the hall.

Marika's eyes stared vacantly as she slowly sat down in her chair.

* * *

The next night Marika walked past the door to Brigitte's boudoir, and, on an impulse, stopped and looked in. It was a fantasy room, decorated with satin and crystal, the kind of room an actress should have, nothing like the dreary maid's chamber Marika had been assigned. Draped across a velvet-covered wing chair in front of the fireplace was the white satin gown Brigitte had worn the previous evening, the white-fox boa trailing off the side.

Silently, Marika tiptoed into her aunt's bedroom and, in one lightning move, placed a tail of the white-fox boa in the fire. She stood back, mesmerized, watching its sparkle and listening to its hiss as it burned. Soon, flames raced up the boa to the white satin dress itself and it was only at the sound of footsteps downstairs that Marika snapped out of her trance. Quickly, she hurried to her bedroom, shutting the door securely behind her.

"Fire! Fire!" The maid's terrified screams echoed through the apartment, and with a smile Marika threw open her door again and raced down the steps, sparing not a glance to the burning room.

On the sidewalk in front of the house she shivered in the late night air as Brigitte arrived home, astonished at the firemen and equipment surrounding the house. "The blaze was caught in time," one of the firemen told them. "Only the one room was damaged."

Later that night, Marika walked slowly through the smoke-filled hallway, stopping only to stare into Brigitte's bedroom. It was wet, gray, and bleak, and a permanent haze of sepulchral gloom seemed to have settled over it. Marika felt a small glow of satisfaction in her belly.

* * *

Two weeks later Brigitte unexpectedly invited Marika to the theater. As she sat in the carriage, Marika pressed her forehead against the window and tried not to look at her. She'd never seen her aunt look more beautiful, with her white floor-length fur and her weightless grace, but it was that very beauty that disturbed Marika. She, too, wanted to dress up in furs and wear white satin and silk, but compared to Brigitte's, her white dress looked like a nurse's uniform. In the presence of such glamour, Marika felt sterile, colorless. She knew she'd lost weight.

Brigitte stared Marika straight in the eye. "Before you can be an actress, you must see great acting. One of my favorites is performing tonight."

Marika passed her hand slowly over her hair, her thoughts bitter at Brigitte's words. "I don't know why you are bothering. You made it very clear you think I have no flair for the theater."

Brigitte gave a short laugh, as her face faded into the dimness of the night. "That first night I was just testing you. You must learn to expect such things. If you abandon your ambition after one tiny little rejection from me, how will you be able to stand up to all the rejection the world will invariably heap upon you as an actress?" Leaning over, Brigitte gently touched Marika's arm.

"I see," Marika said, but she didn't really. Almost unconsciously withdrawing from Brigitte's touch, she sat out the rest of the ride in silence.

At the theater, all the excitement of that night with the Count in Warsaw came back: the bustle of carriages, the murmuring of couples—and tonight Richard Strauss was directing the orchestra! With a shimmering aura, Brigitte moved through the milling crowd outside the theater, beautiful, unapproachable, Marika trailing behind, feeling like a servant girl. But for some reason several couples seemed to be turning away from them, deliberately showing their stiff backs to Brigitte.

At first Marika didn't understand. Was it because Brigitte was more flamboyantly attired than the other women and they were jealous? Most of them were in drab black, decidedly ordinary, not like the ladies of Baden-Baden. Or was it because Brigitte wore makeup, and most of the women seemed satisfied with only powder?

At the entrance to their upstairs box, a short, fat man with bulging eyes came up to Brigitte, nervously licking his lips, and identified himself as the manager of the theater. His face seemed as powdered as the women's downstairs. "My dear Miss Kreisler," he said in a high-pitched voice, "I'm afraid your box will not be available tonight. It's been taken." He paused. "By a member of the Kaiser's personal household."

Brigitte stepped back to appraise the manager more carefully. "But it belongs to me," she said loudly, attracting the attention of passersby. "I demand it!"

"I regret your demand cannot be met," the manager said firmly. "Please leave without creating more of a disturbance."

"I most certainly will create a disturbance," Brigitte said, her green eyes sparkling. "Such a disturbance that Strauss will not be able to conduct. This is outrageous!"

The manager was trying to talk in a natural manner, but he could not. Obviously losing control, he squeaked, "Then I fear it will be a matter for the police."

Throughout this exchange, Marika stood motionless, the eyes of the spectators seeming to bore into her. But her embarrassment and bewilderment quickly turned to fear. She tugged at Brigitte's fur. "Let's leave this place," she said. "I don't want to stay."

Her aunt, however, jerked back from the tug, and, facing the manager again, demanded, "And what have I done?"

The manager, sweating profusely, leaned over and whispered confidentially to Brigitte. "Your article, madame. It has made you persona non grata at this theater. We can't afford to incur the hostility of His Majesty."

"Few people can stand the truth," Brigitte said. "Certainly no one like you." Her eyes slanted with fury. "You not only have the appearance of a fattened little goose, you have the mind of one!" Turning on her heel, she stamped out of the theater, the other box-holders stepping back and making a wide path for her, as if she were contaminated.

Marika had no choice but to follow. She didn't understand anything that was happening. She dared not look anybody in the face. Her temples were throbbing, her cheeks a red blush of shame. Reaching the bottom of the carpeted steps, Marika approached Brigitte. "What article did he mean? I have a right to know."

"I don't have time to explain now," Brigitte said, casting a disdainful look over her shoulder and, summoning her carriage, she stood in front of the theater. She had just started to climb in when a boy ran out of a back alley. With one quick movement, he hurled a rotten tomato, which hit her on the side of her cheek, bursting into little pieces and splattering her white fur.

Brigitte froze on the first rung of the carriage steps, as pedestrians stopped to look at her. In the flickering gaslight of the theater lamps, Brigitte stood majestically, holding her swanlike neck high. She seemed to defy anyone else to attack her.

No one did.

She turned and got inside the carriage.

This second shock was too much for Marika. The very air seemed filled with danger. Why was Brigitte so unpopular? "Surely you can tell me now," she said to Brigitte when she sat down beside her in the carriage. "Why would a little boy want to ruin your pretty fur?"

"It was all planned," Brigitte said. "My enemies know I always attend opening-night performances. This isn't the first attack on me. The little boy was merely being used. The police are of no help to me. It's useless to go to them. Our country is being taken over by the swine."

"Who are they?" Marika asked pointedly.

"The Jews and the Marxists, of course," Brigitte said. "Who else?"

Marika shuddered, then breathed deeply of the night air. Brigitte certainly didn't look like the wide-eyed political zealots Marika had seen on the streets of Berlin.

"I'm the president of the Anti-Semitic League," Brigitte continued. "That's what caused the hostility against me tonight at the theater. I wrote an article criticizing the Kaiser for not recognizing the danger of the Jews and Marxists. I accused them of working against the war effort. If Germany loses, the Jews and the Marxists will try to take over the country, abolishing the monarchy." She called to the driver to go even faster. "Instead of being thanked for pointing out the danger to the Kaiser, I'm kicked out of a public theater."

The sound of the horses' shoes hitting the cobblestones resounded in Marika's head, as the lights from beer saloons and busy restaurants glared in at her. The carriage turned down a dark, deserted street, and in the shadows of the night, Marika saw an old woman pulling a little boy along with her. She held him by the ear, and he was screaming, as if anticipating the punishment that surely awaited him.

Marika closed her pale blue eyes. She identified with that little boy.

Three hours later, Brigitte sat in her favorite horsehair chair silently finishing her fourth drink. Her tomato-splattered white fur still encased her. Marika had asked if she could remove the soiled coat, but Brigitte hadn't answered, so Marika had simply sat nearby, respectfully pretending to read by the gas lamp on the tea table. The tension in the air made it hard for her to concentrate, however.

Suddenly, Brigitte slammed her drink down on the marble-topped table. Startled, Marika looked up and saw Brigitte staring at her venomously, as if she were blaming Marika for the night's incident. "I have something to tell you," Brigitte said in a chilly, biting voice. The parlor seemed to become unnaturally quiet. "I've wanted to tell you this for a long time . . . I was there the day you were born."

"You!" Marika said. She stood up and walked over to the window, pulling back the draperies and looking out at the street below. "I . . ." She couldn't speak.

Brigitte stabbed the air with her cigarette. "Yes, I witnessed the whole event."

"Excuse me, I have to go," Marika said, stealing across the room, fearing what Brigitte was going to say.

"Wait!" Brigitte called out. "It's important that you know. Friedrich summoned me late one afternoon. I found him weeping in the garden. He asked me to take charge."

"I want to go to my room," Marika said, wiping her perspiring forehead.

"Not until I dismiss you," Brigitte said. "When I walked into your mother's bedroom, I saw her fingers massaging her stomach. The pain must have been unbearable to her."

Unconsciously Marika reached for her own stomach. She seemed to be experiencing Lotte's pain, then the pain of her own stillbirth.

"At one point," Brigitte said, "Lotte cried out. I can still hear her voice."

"Wasn't there a doctor?" Marika asked. Tears were forming.

"Yes," Brigitte said. "The doctor was shouting at Lotte. Hours and hours passed. Then right before daybreak, your head began to show."

Marika felt sick at her stomach. She had to leave, yet was too paralyzed to do so.

Brigitte moved through the parlor as if she were back on stage. Her green eyes were luminous and her white teeth bit down on her lower lip. "You finally came out of Lotte's womb. It was already morning. I looked at Lotte. Then I screamed. Lotte's eyes were running with blood. She was dead!" Brigitte seized the edge of her chair, as if she were going to fall. "Then your own scream pierced the room."

"Please!" Marika cried out. She couldn't stand hearing any more.

"Before you go," Brigitte said, forcefully restraining Marika from leaving the room. "I must tell you the point of my story. I must tell you who Lotte really was."

"What do you mean?" Marika asked.

"Your mother," Brigitte said slowly, deliberately dragging out her words, "was the daughter of Gabrielle Schulz."

"Who is that?"

"Only the richest woman in Vienna."

"My grandmother?"

"Yes," Brigitte said.

"I didn't know I had a grandmother," Marika said, not able to comprehend everything. "Papa told me both my grandmothers were dead."

"Friedrich deliberately kept it from you, my dear. You see, Lotte Schulz was a Jewess."

"A Jewess!" Marika said, hand at her mouth. "My mother! My grandmother!"

"And *you* also."

At the window Marika could see only blackness, matching the emptiness inside her.

"Friedrich's marrying a Jewess caused a serious split between us," Brigitte said. "I consented to go to his house only once during the course of his marriage. That was to watch Lotte die giving birth to you."

"I just can't believe all this," Marika said, even though she knew it was true. She was breathing deeply.

"Friedrich married Lotte for her money—for no other reason," Brigitte said. "However, the old bitch in Vienna outwitted him. Gabrielle Schulz disinherited Lotte after her wedding."

"I don't want to hear any more, *please*," Marika said, tears at her eyes.

"Your secret is safe with me," Brigitte said, reaching for her hand.

Marika withdrew it.

"As president of the Anti-Semitic League, I'm not anxious to call attention to the fact my brother married a Jewess. I'm not anxious to have my colleagues know I am as of this moment sheltering a Jewess."

"I'm not," Marika cried. "I'm Friedrich's daughter. I'm Prussian."

"We judge cases like this by the mother," Brigitte spat. "It's important to know you were created in the Jew-belly of a woman."

"I wish my Papa were here," Marika whispered, and hurried from the room.

Alone at last, Marika looked at herself in the pedestal mirror Lotte had given her. "A Jewess," she said softly, but out loud. "It can't be true. Brigitte is telling a lie." Her eyes were languorous. Black circles encased them, but they were blue. Pale ice-blue. Wasn't that proof she wasn't a Jewess?

She knew from having seen them on the streets and in the shops that Jews were brown-skinned, with dark, kinky hair, hook noses, and eyes black as coal. Once she'd seen a rabbi with a long, gray beard. She didn't look like one of his people.

Friedrich always proclaimed loudly that Jews were unclean— that you could smell them. If he felt that, how could he have married one, even if her mother did have money? It was hypocrisy.

Pounding her fist on her vanity table, Marika cried out, "I'm not a Jew! I'm not! I'm not! I'll never be a Jew!" She bit her mouth to hold back the tears, then, lips drawn in bitter determination, she looked at her blonde hair and blue eyes again. They could fool anybody. She was Prussian. She looked Prussian. Even the Jews of the Warsaw Ghetto thought she was Prussian.

The sudden memory of Julian raced through her mind. She stopped whimpering. He was a Jew. He was beautiful. Thinking of him made it less painful at the moment to accept her own Jewishness. If he were alive today, if he knew her origin, he might have stayed with her and not turned to Sophie.

"I'm one of you," Marika said to a Julian in space, and began weeping bitterly. She'd never lost anyone before Julian, and she had no idea how empty it was speaking to someone when he's gone to his grave. Throughout the long night, only the shadows in the room listened to her.

* * *

In the months ahead, all talk of theater and future ambitions ended as Brigitte and Friedrich concentrated completely on the war effort. Nightly their concern was of the stalemate on the Western Front. Brigitte abandoned the wearing of makeup and joined the Red Cross, and as a result arrived home late every evening, constantly complaining of being "bone-weary." Daily she urged Marika as well "to do something for Germany. All you do now is stay home and boil turnips." Finally, Marika joined the Red Cross, too.

In the winter of 1916 Friedrich's secret work caused him to be transferred to German-occupied Lille, France, and within two months Brigitte had arranged their transfer to Lille so they could be near Friedrich. At the station, Friedrich kissed Brigitte before Marika. Marika was shocked at her Papa's appearance. His thinning hair had greatly receded, almost as if it were falling out, and he no longer had a youthful, robust look. His face was pinched and beginning to wrinkle, and his spirit seemed just as pinched as his face.

Arriving at a little French house, Friedrich told Marika and Brigitte that the residence had been commandeered by the German army for his use. "The French lady who lived here died two weeks ago," he said. "She objected to living in the cellar. She caught pneumonia down there."

Shown to her small top-floor bedroom, Marika was shocked by the callous way her Papa had reported the death of the former owner of this house. Had he forced her to live in the cellar?

The next morning Brigitte woke Marika up at five o'clock and told her they had to report to the Red Cross station early. Friedrich was still asleep.

"I'll take him some tea," Marika said. "He probably has to get up, too."

"No," Brigitte said, taking the pot from Marika. "I'll see to it." She was gone for a long time in Friedrich's room and, on her return, seemed to be hastily putting on her wrap. "We must leave at once."

The Red Cross hospital was a converted school outside of town, and when they arrived, Marika saw orderlies lugging in heavy jugs of water and pouring it into huge vats on wood-burning stoves in the steamy school cafeteria. Apparently, the supply of running water had been cut off.

At the entrance to one of the classrooms, Marika felt nauseous at the smell in the air and at the sight of doctors without surgical masks performing emergency operations on four men strapped to long tables. She knew she was about to see the blood she'd dreaded.

Marika's hand reached for Brigitte's, but her aunt ignored it. "Don't be weak," she said sharply. "The men expect you to be strong. You have to do it." She paused. "For Germany."

Into this world of the dazed and maimed, Marika wandered, her spirit feeling just as shattered as theirs, but their real suffering made her squeamishness look silly. Many of the men lay with limbs shattered, and some legs had gangrened. The body of one young soldier she tended was covered with putrid sores. An old French nun showed her how to wash the wounded and change a dressing. Another man had lost both his arms, and Marika was asked to spoon-feed him. For a while, she tried to look into the eyes of the man, to make some human contact and let him know she cared about his suffering, but her penetrating look was met with an uncomprehending stare.

Still, she tried to talk to the patients and offer some small comfort. But she choked on her own words. What could she possibly say to young men obviously dying? In her head she kept repeating, "They were never allowed to live." Did Julian die this way? She couldn't get that terrible question out of her mind. She hoped that somebody, somewhere, had at one time loved these dying men, but so many of them were ending their lives in total anonymity, piled up in the most brutal way.

In the school auditorium, lumpy straw mattresses had been laid in four rows. Many of the men were moaning, but no drugs were available to kill their pain. The rest of the soldiers were patient, even humble, as their feverish bodies took in the tepid water Marika gave them.

Throughout the day Brigitte remained above the human suffering, her uniform spotlessly white, in contrast to the doctors in trousers so bloody they looked like pig butchers. She carried a perfumed handkerchief close to her aristocratic nose, and whenever a bad odor drifted her way, she almost unconsciously turned her nose to the scent coming from the handkerchief.

As the long day at the hospital wore on, the sights and smells seemed to grow worse. By twilight Marika could not stand the hospital another moment. Slipping out the back way, she crossed a cobblestoned courtyard to an old, partially moss-covered fountain at the rear where the forest began, and leaning over the edge, she vomited into the fountain's stagnant water.

Still bent over, she felt a hand touch her back. It was gentle, even caressing. Straightening up, she found herself staring into the wide brown eyes of a young girl. "It is always this way in the beginning," the strange girl said. "My first day at the hospital I became very sick. In fact, I was sick for a whole month. But you can get used to a lot of things, even the sight of men dying."

Marika reached for a handkerchief to wipe her mouth. "You're French!" she said, the words sounding more like an accusation than she'd meant. "I can tell by your accent."

"Yes," the girl said. "But I've learned German as best I can. Mother Superior told me you must always learn the language of your conqueror."

"Were you studying to be a nun?" Marika asked tentatively.

"I still am," the girl answered. "At first I did not want to help the Germans at the hospital. They killed my Mama and Papa in Alsace-Lorraine. But the Mother Superior said I must. Germans are as much children of God as we are," she said, "although they don't always act it."

Marika stared hard at the girl. Even though what she said was critical of Germany, Marika didn't feel threatened by her. The girl was so thin she looked as if she had nothing to sit on but bones. Abruptly, a bell rang out with a loud and terrifying noise and they could hear the sound of booted feet.

"More of the wounded have arrived," the girl said. "I must go." She looked into Marika's eyes again. "Will you be all right?"

"Yes," Marika said. "Thank you."

"I'll see you at work," the girl said. "I come in in the late afternoon. My name's Christiane."

"That's a beautiful name. I'm Marika."

"That's pretty, too, but it doesn't sound very German."

"I don't think it is," Marika said. "Perhaps Hungarian. I don't know why my Papa named me that."

"Is your Papa still alive?" Christiane asked.

"Yes," she said. "He's here in Lille."

"A German soldier?"

"No," Marika answered quickly, "but he used to be a hussar."

The bell sounded again. "I really must go," Christiane said. "You'll be needed, too."

"I'll try to have a stronger stomach this time," Marika said. "You're very brave—I mean, helping the enemy soldiers after what they did to your parents. I don't think I would help the French if they killed Papa."

"It's the only way," Christiane said. "If we don't start treating each other like human beings again, this war will go on forever." The girl turned and ran across the cobblestones.

Marika sighed. "Or until all of us are dead," she added.

* * *

· 144 ·

That night at dinner the gloom of war settled over the table. Friedrich was in a rage. "God, my country can be stupid," he said. "It doesn't even know how to make decent propaganda. Do you know I confiscated English leaflets today, urging our men to surrender? And they were *good*. They hit the mark."

"Why shouldn't the men surrender?" Marika asked. "Why should they die, like the men I saw today."

A silence fell over the table.

"Defeatists," Brigitte charged. "They're all around us."

"Even my own daughter," Friedrich said sadly. He placed a knife on his plate. "You're a true Berliner. They'd rather have food in their guts than victory in their hearts."

"I don't know why we're fighting anymore," Marika said, almost near tears. "Nobody can offer an explanation. The only one I get is, it's 'for Germany.'"

"That should be reason enough," Friedrich said angrily. "But it isn't. Many Germans actually deliberately maimed themselves to avoid fighting. Germany deserves to lose the war, with men like that in the field."

"We even have Jewish officers out there," Brigitte said, eating her potatoes calmly, as if the subject were flowers. "They are traitors, of course. English spies. They even have the power to recommend that soldiers be awarded the Iron Cross."

Marika was adamant. "I still don't see why we are fighting. The battle lines aren't changing."

"You don't see," Friedrich said, almost threatening her, "because you're a silly, stupid schoolgirl."

Marika blushed in embarrassment.

"We had bad leaders in this war," Brigitte said.

"Yes," Friedrich replied, his eyes taking on a faraway gaze. "But in the next one, everything will be different. Everything!"

"What next war?" Marika asked, alarmed. "I don't want to go on living if it means war . . . always war."

"We'll have a great leader then," Friedrich said. "Not that idiot Kaiser. He allows the English and French to be caricatured in the newspapers. I've fought against them. I know. They only surrender when they're completely overwhelmed. It's wrong to give the German soldier the illusion the English and French can be beaten so easily."

"Papa," Marika said, trembling, getting up from the table, "there's something I've never asked you before, but I feel I must know now."

Friedrich raised an eyebrow. "What's that?"

"I fear I won't be happy with what you tell me," Marika said, folding up her napkin, "but what do you do in the war?"

Friedrich smiled grimly. "I deal with men whose lives are measured in hours—not days."

"Yes," Marika said. "I thought so. It seems to give you a kind of purpose I've never known you to have."

"To my dying day," Friedrich said, his steely eyes boring into Marika's, "I'll work for only one goal—the triumph of Germany."

"The triumph of Germany!" Brigitte echoed.

Marika turned and left the room.

* * *

Three weeks later Marika returned home early from the hospital to find her Papa in the kitchen, drinking. A German newspaper lay crumpled and limp on the floor, as if Friedrich had bled it of its news. He looked up at her. "I see you're home while Brigitte is still there slaving, I suppose. I worry so much about her."

Without answering, Marika sat down in a chair opposite him and looked deeply into his taut, bitter face. The man was a stranger to her. "Are you in pain?" she asked abruptly.

He glared at her, then softened his facial muscles, as if realizing she weren't the enemy, and sipped his drink. "I have a mission. There will be no peace for me, no peace at all, until Germany's enemies are destroyed." His hand reached out for his wooden leg, his fingers hovering over it, though not actually touching it. "*They* must pay for doing this to me."

"I'm sorry, Papa," she said forlornly.

"I don't want your sympathy," he said. "Sympathy I've never needed."

Feeling there was no way to break through to him, she got up. "I'm going to my room."

"Just a minute, young lady," he said. "I have something important to discuss with you."

Resigned, she sank back into her chair.

"Brigitte informs me you're spending a great deal of time in the company of a young French girl," he said. "I find this surprising.

The French are the enemies of Germany. They try to harm us in whatever way they can."

"Christiane spends every day of the week caring for the sick and wounded of Germany," Marika said curtly.

"Who in hell do you think wounded them? The goddamn French and British."

"What do you think we're doing to their young men?" The room was cold and gloomy, as she waited for his reply. She couldn't stand the kitchen. If only she could go back to a happier time. She wanted the Friedrich she'd known as a girl to come riding in on his white horse. It was all she could do now to look into the twisted face of the man across from her. At this moment—in all honesty —she felt nothing for him.

"I see your time in Poland has irrevocably, hopelessly, soiled you," he said, finally.

She jumped up so quickly she knocked over her chair. "Damn it!" she cried, raising her voice. The shock of her act made her tremble, yet she persisted. "Foreigners are filthy and dirty. I hear that all the time now. The French are barbarians. Yet in Baden-Baden, you knew French girls before meeting the Contessa. You saw a lot of French girls, in fact."

"They were prostitutes," he said, angrily, defensively. "A man has certain needs. I'd rather turn to cheap Parisian prostitutes than soil German womanhood."

"Oh, Papa, I can't believe you're so narrow in your prejudice. You've changed. After all, you married an *Italian* countess."

"Italians are inferior."

"Still, you married her."

"Only for your sake, my dear," he said. "Because I needed to provide you with money for support, and I thought the Contessa had it. That was the only reason."

Turning her back to him, Marika ran down a long corridor to the parlor. For one brief moment, she found comfort in the trappings left by the old French woman who'd owned the house: the Spanish shawl over the piano, the satin lampshades, the antimacassars over the worn sofa. But in seconds she heard the limping steps of her Papa, trailing her up the corridor.

"Don't ever walk out on me until I dismiss you!" he thundered.

"Stop treating me like a little girl," she screamed at him.

"Someone to order around. I'm a woman now!"

"You're just as defiant as your mother was."

Marika breathed deeply, the confrontation with Friedrich making her dizzy. But then, having men die in her arms made her even dizzier. It forced her to see everything—the world, her Papa, herself—in a different light. "I suppose you're going to tell me you married Lotte for her money. To provide for me. The only thing wrong with that story is I didn't exist at the time."

"Shut your mouth, before I knock it shut!"

"Once again," she went on, "you married someone of an 'inferior race.' Why's that? Are you attracted to women of the 'inferior races'?"

The palm of his open hand sent her reeling back onto the sofa. But after the suffering she'd seen at the hospital—men with their guts hanging out—she didn't think a bash in the face was worth a tear.

"You know!" he said.

"Yes," she said, rubbing her cheek. "I'm a Jewess."

"You were a mistake," he said, his whole body shaking. "I never wanted a child by that bitch." He sat down on the piano stool, reaching this time for his wooden leg. "I'm going to tell you something I never told anybody, not even Brigitte. I don't even know why I'm going to tell you. But I *must.*"

"Tell me!" she said, sitting up. "I want to hear."

"The day Lotte was giving birth to you, I prayed you'd die with her."

The long stillness that followed was broken only by the sound of a clock striking in the upstairs hallway.

* * *

At two o'clock that morning, Marika awoke, hearing Lotte's voice calling her, musical and magnificently dramatic, as if over a long distance. It was beseeching Marika to come and join her. From where her mother stood, war, pain, and rejection didn't exist. Suddenly, the walls of her narrow room seemed to close in on her. They were pea-green, the same color used at the Red Cross hospital. The walls never changed, only the bodies were different. Just yesterday she'd seen blood flow from an open mouth as if the corpse were drowning himself, and then the dead man was hauled off in a van. When he was thrown into the cab, his hand dangled out of the truck, a macabre good-bye.

Marika realized she was thirsty, and got up to go to the kitchen. Opening her door, she was just in time to see the tail of Brigitte's nightgown disappear into her Papa's room. Was he sick? Marika really didn't care at this point. Why should she? He cared nothing for her.

In the kitchen the water failed to satisfy her thirst. It tasted bitter. Had the blood of the winter's dead thawed and mixed with the water supply? Choking, she slammed down her glass.

She wandered into the parlor and sank into the pillows, caressingly running her fingers across the dead Frenchwoman's antimacassars. It seemed an invasion to be in her home, to use her furniture and possessions. On the piano stood a photograph of a smiling young boy. Her son? Her grandson? Was he dead now?

Squeezing the pillow to her, Marika said softly to herself, "Try not to think about Papa. Keep him out of your mind."

The clock struck three as Marika slowly climbed the stairs and found that the door to Brigitte's bedroom had come open. Her bed was empty. Surely she wasn't still in Friedrich's bedroom, yet there was no other place she could be. Was Brigitte sleeping with her Papa?

That was another question Marika would struggle to put out of her mind. Sometimes, it was best not to think. In the near-darkness, she stumbled to her own room.

She drifted into sleep, but by five o'clock a loud outcry woke her up. It sounded like a man screaming! Reaching for her robe, she rushed to the edge of the hallway, and from there she could see the entire parlor below. Seated in the center of the room was a young man, his face leaden and haggard, a face she would never forget. His eyes were closed. Behind him stood two German gendarmes. And sitting on the sofa, as prim as if she were at a ladies' tea, was Brigitte. There, too, was Papa.

"Allow me to introduce myself," Friedrich said, walking over to the prisoner. "I am Inspector Kreisler. If my reputation has not preceded me, then you'll have less to fear—at least for the moment."

The prisoner opened his eyes wide with fear.

"Normally I interview couriers in my office," Friedrich said. "But you were brought to my home as soon as you were caught. Too many Frenchmen would see you at headquarters. Nearly all Frenchmen are spies, but I'm sure you're as aware of that as I am. Who is your contact in Lille?"

"I'm not a courier," the young man said. "I'm a Belgian student."

One of the gendarmes struck the man sharply behind the ear with a truncheon and Marika covered her mouth to keep from crying out. The young man's face instantly reflected the pain shooting through his body.

"Let's dispense with such idiotic drivel," Friedrich said. "I never allow a prisoner to leave an interview with me without getting the truth out of him. That is, I never allow him to leave alive. After a few 'caresses' from my men, you'll beg for death."

The prisoner licked his dried lips.

"If you confess now," Friedrich said, "I'll consider sparing your life. Otherwise we'll spend the rest of the morning seeing just how much punishment you can take. I'm an expert at bringing a man close to the point of death, then reviving him . . . for a while." He dabbed at his mouth with a white handkerchief.

The prisoner licked his parched lips again. His look at Friedrich was dazed. "I'm not a courier," he said again, in a hollow voice.

Friedrich lowered his handkerchief like a signal. Pouncing on the prisoner, the gendarmes crushed their fists into his face and body. At the sound of a crunch, Marika screamed, "You're killing him!" and ran down the stairs, nearly stumbling.

"Get her out of here!" Friedrich shouted at Brigitte savagely. In moments Brigitte was behind Marika, dragging her back up the stairs. "Get into your room!" Brigitte shouted, digging her fingers into Marika's neck and pushing her violently. Marika heard the click of the lock in the door, and stumbling into her room, flung herself on the bed. Was she now a prisoner herself?

The screams continued from the parlor below. After an hour, they stopped.

* * *

The long summer of 1917 seemed without end. America had entered the war now, and it was clear the sun was setting over Imperial Europe.

In Lille, Marika went on night duty at the hospital with Christiane. That way, she could sleep at the house during the day and avoid Friedrich and Brigitte. She suspected they preferred to spend their nights without her anyway. Thanks to Christiane, Marika's French had improved dramatically and by September she'd actually become competent in it.

Food supplies had grown very scarce, however, and Christiane in particular seemed to be suffering. Once she dropped a tray, she was so weak, and, alarmed, Marika started slipping provisions from Friedrich's kitchen to help her. But regardless of how much she stole for her, Christiane remained dangerously thin.

One day Marika brought her a small loaf of bread, and, kissing her on the cheek in gratitude, the French girl started to slip it inside her dress.

"No," Marika said, reaching for the bread. She directed Christiane to the fountain in the rear courtyard where she'd first met her. Breaking off a piece of the stale bread, Marika handed it to the girl and commanded, "Chew it! Chew it slowly in front of me so I can see you eat."

"But why?" Christiane asked.

"I think you're giving the food I steal for you to somebody else."

Christiane said nothing, taking the bread and chewing it slowly as instructed. But her heart didn't seem in it.

* * *

Transported to Russia in a sealed rail car, Lenin preached, "Peace, land, and bread." On November 7, 1917, the Provisional Government at Petrograd had been arrested and the Bolsheviks proclaimed a socialist state under a banner of world revolution. From the new capital of world Communism came the announcement that Russia was pulling out of the war.

Friedrich met the news with gloom and despair. "Germany will regret the day it ever transported that swine Lenin back to Russia. Germany has bought only a momentary peace. The Russian hordes will move toward us again."

"But it's no longer necessary to fight a two-front war," Brigitte said optimistically.

"Not now," Friedrich answered sadly. "But one day it'll be more necessary than ever."

"But there will be no more war," Marika said.

· 151 ·

"That's drivel," Friedrich said angrily. "We'll fight and we'll fight again, until Germany has gained its proper place in the world."

"What is that place?" Marika asked, not bothering to disguise the hostility in her voice.

"The domination of the world," Friedrich said without apology or embarrassment. "We are superior—therefore, destined to rule."

"That's not what I hear," Marika said. Even though hungry, she didn't touch the food on her plate. "At the hospital, I heard America will rule in Europe. I understand Wilson isn't evil, the way he appears in the German press. I'm told he's for democracy."

"Oh, my God!" Friedrich said. "Such words spoken in my own home." He glared at Marika, then in one sudden move slapped her hard across the face.

* * *

Soon after, Friedrich returned to Berlin for two months without even saying good-bye to Marika. She welcomed his going. Lately, she'd become terrified of encountering him on the stairs.

On her way to the hospital that night, rain clouds loomed on the horizon and fog was everywhere. Feeling weak, she stopped on a bridge and saw, across the way, the silhouette of the hospital rising out of the mist. She stared at it for a long time, not really wanting to go in, but she was late. Hurrying through the big iron gate, she was startled to find standing menacingly in front of her, two German gendarmes restraining Christiane and Fräulein Kruse, Brigitte's night replacement, Fräulein Kruse's bulky Red Cross uniform seemed even more like a tent tonight, and her flat watery eyes brimmed with hate, as she waved some small printed papers in front of Christiane's terrified face.

Marika ran up to one of the guards. "Let her go. She's my friend."

"Your *friend* is with the underground," Fräulein Kruse charged. "She's been slipping these propaganda sheets to the French workers at the hospital. She's trying to destroy morale. They're filled with nothing but lies about Germany!"

Marika stared into Christiane's large brown eyes. The girl was frail, but those eyes were filled with a passionate strength, the passion of a martyr. Memories of the Belgian student who'd sacrificed himself caused Marika panic. She suddenly realized she had to protect Christiane from herself. She had to take responsibility for the sheets. As the daughter of Friedrich Kreisler, she'd get a lesser sentence, but if Christiane were taken away and found guilty, the girl might be shot!

"Those are mine," Marika said, forcefully taking the papers from Fräuline Kruse. "I discovered them in my father's secret papers. They were confiscated from a courier."

"Yours!" Fräulein Kruse rasped. "But why would you read such horrible lies?"

"I wanted to learn the news from the other side," Marika said. "I think the French people have a right to know, too. Besides, no one believes the official *Bulletin de Lille*—it does nothing but claim victories for Germany."

Fräuline Kruse stood thunderstruck, then slowly narrowed her eyes at Marika and hissed, "Take her away."

"No," Christiane cried out. "Those are my papers. Marika had nothing to do with them."

"We can't take her," one of the gendarmes said. "She's Herr Kreisler's daughter."

"She's also a traitor to Germany," Fräulein Kruse said. "If you don't arrest her, I'll call the police and have you arrested."

At that, the gendarmes gripped Marika's arms and forcefully escorted her down the long corridor. She turned and looked back.

Christiane's arms were reaching out. She was crying.

* * *

Locked in the Citadelle, Marika spent a sleepless night. In the first light of morning, she tried to adjust to the contents of her prison cell: a chair attached to the stone wall by a rusty chain, a rough board serving as a table, a yellowing porcelain basin attached to the wall just below a tiny window. Two hooks held up her iron camp-bed and its blanket-covered straw mattress, and a small hole had been bored above the lock in the door. Was that so prison guards could spy on her?

A sudden movement, and her door was being unlocked from the outside. It was the wardress, a bulky woman with matted gray hair damp with sweat and a head too small for her body. "Stand

· 153 ·

by the door with your bowl," she commanded Marika in German.

An attendant made his way down the corridor, ladling coffee from a tin bucket into the outstretched bowls of the waiting prisoners. Its taste was like black mud to Marika, but still she drank it. At least it was something to take the chill off her body, numb with cold.

Armed with buckets and mops, other tired, motherly-looking women appeared. One gave Marika a mop and a pail of dank water. "Scrub your cell," she ordered.

At noon a soldier brought Marika lunch: soup poured from a large pail into the same bowl that had held the coffee. She nearly vomited at the sight of dead maggots floating on top of the broth, but instead she carefully lifted them out with her spoon. She knew it would be the same kind of soup tomorrow. It would not get better. If she didn't force it down, she'd die of starvation. The soldier returned after she'd finished and handed her a tin cup of water. Then he was gone, and she was left alone for the rest of the afternoon.

As the shadows lengthened in her cell, the wardress reappeared at five o'clock and handed Marika two pieces of stale bread. That was dinner.

The routine was the same the next day and the day after that, and Marika's future loomed like an open grave. She was frightened, yet determined to hold herself together. Surviving was her act of defiance.

On the fourth day she finally learned she'd been given a sentence: two months, the minimum. She was filled with relief. At least she knew she would eventually be released. What had been hard was not knowing what was going to happen to her.

After coffee the next morning, the wardress told her she could go to the prison chapel for mass, but she was warned not to talk to the other prisoners, not even to make a gesture. Anyone violating the rules would get their ears boxed. The little chapel was bare except for a tablecloth, two white candles, and a silver cross, but before they could enter, the women prisoners, most of them French, had to undergo inspection. Marika was told if she didn't keep her hair tidier, she wouldn't be allowed into mass the next time.

Marika kneeled, and then the male prisoners were escorted in and segregated on the right, followed by a group of nine young German soldiers who were marched into the center of the chapel. They, too, were prisoners. Marika wondered what offenses they had committed. The soldiers looked neither to the right nor the left, but fell to their knees in front of the altar and prayed with their heads bowed low. They seemed almost too embarrassed to look at the other prisoners.

On her second Sunday at mass, Marika caught sight of a tall man with a mass of curly brown hair, heavy-set, with broad shoulders. His hazel eyes had a mischievous sparkle. "He's the new British prisoner," the girl beside Marika whispered.

The prisoner said "Amen! Amen!" at the wrong time—it appeared he'd never attended a Catholic mass before—and, for some reason, kept trying to attract Marika's attention. Filing out, the girl behind Marika whispered, "Give me your hand," and she slipped a piece of folded paper into it. "It's from him." The girl gestured with her head toward the British prisoner.

For one brief moment, Marika's eyes met his. He smiled. Alone in her cell, she read the note:

> I was caught yesterday. I had no papers and was arrested. I'm a friend of Christiane. Is there any way you could slip me a piece of bread?
>
> Charles.

She was quite willing to share her rations with him. He was such a big man, and she knew how hungry he must be. But what was his connection with Christiane? She suspected he might be a soldier captured by the Germans, maybe even a downed aviator.

That night she woke up in a cold sweat, listening to the tramping feet of soldiers and the clanging of a cell door. Once a piercing shriek echoed down the long corridor. The next night it was the booming of guns and the crackling of rifle fire that kept her awake all night. She soon lost count of her days in prison. Was it three weeks and two days or two weeks and three days?

Through another prisoner she managed to slip Charles half of her bread rations, and one day at mass she received another note. Again she read it in her cell:

DEAR MARIKA,

Thanks for helping me keep alive. Merry Christmas.

Charles.

P.S. Happy New Year!!!

She wept. The tears tasted bitter running into her mouth.

* * *

One dreary gray afternoon, Marika began to fantasize that she was Joan of Arc. At the Citadelle, Marika's hair had been cut short like a soldier's, like Joan's, and now she saw other similarities as well. The saint had been almost indifferent to pain, and Marika was convinced that if she could live through her present horror, she could endure anything. Joan of Arc was ready to take any risk for what she believed in, and it was principle, too, that had led to Marika's jailing. Her sacrifice had been made not only for Christiane, but for France, as well. She didn't fully understand why she should want to help the enemy, but somehow France didn't seem to be the enemy anymore. The French—and the Americans and British—had become symbols of freedom to her, nothing at all like the evil, militaristic spirit that Germany and Friedrich seemed to represent.

She removed a small wooden cross from the cell wall and gently kissed it. Soldiers, it seemed, were chaining her to the stake. She could hear the rattle. Yes, now a hooded man was coming forward with a torch and setting fire to the wood. As the smoke billowed up, she looked at the ceiling of her prison cell, dreaming it was a celestial doorway. "Jesus!" she cried out loud.

Only once did she look down at the earth. She did so just in time to see the torch carrier remove his black hood.

It was Friedrich!

* * *

Finally, on a cold day in January, the wardress came for Marika. "You're free to go," she said. "If you'd been one of the enemy, you would have been dealt with more severely, but fortunately for you, your father is highly placed." Marika stumbled into the corridor, unprepared for her sudden freedom. Coming after such a long time, it made her head reel.

In a cold, bare office, an Alsatian gave back her identity card, admonishing, "I hope this is the last time we'll be seeing you here,

· 156 ·

Fräulein Kreisler. I've worked for your father. He's a fine gentleman." She didn't answer. Escorted by military police, she joined other prisoners herded onto a tramway to go back to the city.

Waiting at the Porte de Loos was Brigitte, a tall, serene, autumnal beauty draped in a gray cape. Her handsome nose was white and pinched. She stared at Marika as if she were an enemy.

"Where's Papa?" Marika asked, looking around. "Why isn't he here?"

"He's returned from Berlin," Brigitte said coldly. "You should be grateful to him for arranging for your release a few days early."

Marika dreaded the confrontation that was sure to come, but she'd determined to get it over with as soon as possible. "Let's go home now," she said.

But Brigitte reached out, firmly placing her hand on Marika's shoulder. "I'm afraid not," she said. "He doesn't want you at his house anymore. Can you blame him for feeling betrayed by his own daughter?"

Stunned, Marika took a few steps back. Then, suddenly, all the privations of the past two months erupted in her with scalding anger. "I've not betrayed him! I was the one betrayed in that damn jail all this time. Not having visits, not knowing anything, not even able to remember the day of the week. How dare he? How dare you?"

"You're responsible for your own isolation," Brigitte said, seeming to enjoy herself. "However, because I'm familiar with the circumstances of your birth, I knew you'd start to display certain weaknesses of character as you grew older. You really can't help it, my dear. It's inherent in your race. I fear the worst is yet to come."

Marika fell silent for a moment, aghast at what she was hearing. Her voice barely under control, she bit out, "If I'm no longer welcome at home, why are you meeting me?"

"Simply to inform you of that fact."

Suddenly, Marika's anger collapsed, and a tremendous weariness came over her. "I want to go to the hospital," she said. "I want to see Christiane."

"She's not there," Brigitte said. "I dismissed her. You also have been dismissed from the Red Cross. With the sick and the dying, we have enough trouble."

· 157 ·

Marika's blue eyes flashed through her tears and, as if in a dream, she looked around the deserted tram station. All the other released prisoners and their families had gone. "But where can I go?"

"You're a woman now," Brigitte said. "Where you go is not my concern."

"I can't believe this is Papa's wish."

"You have my assurance," Brigitte said. Smiling maliciously, she leaned to kiss Marika on her cheek. The January sky over Lille was pale and lonely, and a heavy mist filled the morning air.

* * *

In the tiny parlor, Christiane's grandmother cried softly but concentrated on her knitting, murmuring something Marika didn't understand. "She doesn't know what is happening," Christiane said to Marika in German. "Just that something is wrong, and I'm in plenty of trouble. Come, we'll talk in the kitchen."

Once there, Marika hugged the girl. "It's so good to be on the outside," she said warmly. Now she knew what the other prisoners must have felt like when they greeted their families at the Porte.

Christiane bit her lip. "I would have been shot if you hadn't gone to prison for me." She paused. "How do you thank someone for giving up two months for you?"

"You don't," Marika said. "It's over with. But Charles . . . your lover?"

"He's not my lover," Christiane replied matter-of-factly. "When he was arrested without an identity card, we had to think of something to say. He's a downed airman. A Tommy!"

"But if that can be proved," Marika said, growing more alarmed by the minute, "Charles will be shot, or sent to Germany."

"I know," Christiane said. "So does he." She took Marika's hand and looked into her eyes. "Charles was shot down over Belgium," she continued. "A friend smuggled him to my house and I burned his uniform, but because I had no other boots for him, he kept his own. He was wearing them when a German soldier arrested him. Unfortunately, those boots have a serial number on them."

"But you've got to run away," Marika told her. "You're too much involved."

"I'm going to," Christiane said. "With Charles. He's going to escape with a British sailor tonight. When they finish their garden-

· 158 ·

ing today at dusk, they plan to knock out the guard, scale the walls of the Citadelle, and swim the canal!"

"Others have tried that," Marika said. "Some have been shot."

"But some have survived," Christiane replied. "Charles wants a fighting chance." She touched her breast pocket. "I have a map in here. It's very detailed, showing us how we can reach a farmhouse about twenty miles from here. A French farmer and his wife have agreed to let us stay there until we can figure out how to escape and make our way to Holland. I'm meeting the men at that old fountain where we first met." She walked over to a kitchen cabinet and reaching behind a large china platter, pulled out a gun.

Instinctively Marika backed away.

"What are *you* going to do now?" Christiane asked. "You told me your father won't have you back."

"I don't know," Marika said sadly. "Maybe go to Vienna. I have a grandmother there I've never seen."

Without warning, a loud banging sounded at the door. Quickly Christiane thrust the gun into Marika's hand. It felt strange and cold.

"Another friend was due back today," Christiane said. "He's in the underground, too, but he knows nothing about Charles. I'll get rid of him. I have no more time for propaganda." She motioned to Marika. "Hide in the pantry."

Marika crouched in the dark closet, momentarily startled to think she heard a rat inside. If she did, she thought, he was probably as hungry as she was. After what seemed an interminable time, she heard shouting in German. "Oh, my God," she said softly to herself. Her Papa had sent German gendarmes to arrest Christiane! The sound of gunfire made Marika want to cry out, but instead she stood trembling in the pantry, nervously clutching the gun. The old woman screamed as another shot rang out, and suddenly Marika heard booted feet racing back to the kitchen. She stared at the door of the pantry, her fingers tightening on the trigger. With a crash, a soldier threw open the pantry door. His eyes met Marika's for one brief instant and in that time she saw that he was no older than she was, his eyes filled with the same fear as hers.

Unconsciously, as if it were some other girl standing there holding a gun, her fingers pulled the trigger. The bullet blasted the man's face, parts of his nose flying into the air, like splintering glass in the bombardment of Warsaw. Blood spurted onto Marika before the soldier collapsed at her feet.

The other soldier was rushing down the hallway now, and Marika stepped back, concealing herself behind a screened-off sink. Wildly, the soldier scanned the room, his rifle pointing, but he didn't see her. He bent over his dead comrade, and it was then that Marika fired her gun once more, the bullet going into his back. A dark patch of blood formed on his uniform, and the soldier dropped across his partner, making a sound like a falling sack of potatoes. "At least I didn't have to see his eyes," she said out loud.

She ran to the parlor. Christiane was lying dead in the center of the room, her eyes wide open, staring, accusing. Her life had been taken from her, and she had wanted to live. Reaching out, weeping, Marika closed her friend's eyes, the way she'd been taught to do at the Red Cross hospital.

The old woman was dead, too. Blood covered her white moustache and in her hand was a small gun that must have been concealed under her knitting.

At any moment Marika expected more soldiers to descend on the house. There was no time for her to think of the dead—she'd have the rest of her life for that. Instead, she bent over Christiane, reaching into her breast pocket to remove the map. Then, gun in hand, she rushed back to the kitchen. The soldiers on the floor were like corpses at the hospital and she felt almost no responsibility for their deaths. The war had killed them, not she.

It was already dusk, time for Christiane's rendezvous with Charles, and Marika knew she would have to move as quickly as possible to the old fountain behind the hospital. Reaching for Christiane's coat, Marika slipped it on, concealing the gun and the map in its pocket. Only then did she realize that her dress was covered with the dead soldier's blood.

By the time she reached the fountain, Charles was waiting, ripping his shirt to bandage a wound on his leg. "Oh, it's you, he said, surprised. "Where's Christiane?"

Without her answering, he seemed to know. "She's dead," she said with outward calm.

"Goddamm it," he said. "They got George, too, the poor

bloke. The bastards killed him in the canal."

"We must not think about them," she said, handing the map to Charles. "We've got to escape. But I don't see how with your wounded leg."

"That won't stop me," Charles said. "I came very near the pearly gates just an hour ago. I'm not ready to die." In the darkening twilight, he carefully studied the map.

With him as her guide, she set out. Somehow it seemed right for her to take her orders from this soft-spoken stranger from a foreign land. War had created these mysteries, so hard for her to understand. In a matter of hours, the so-called enemy could become not only your friend, but your main hope for survival.

The harder their trip through the pitch-dark forest became, the easier it was for her to take her mind off the massacre at Christiane's house. Sometimes when she'd lag behind Charles, she'd whisper to herself, "It never happened." By midnight, she'd begun to lose confidence in Charles, feeling he was just as lost as she was. But he kept following the small canal, as outlined on the map, and gradually her doubts faded. She became totally passive, following him blindly. Her life was in his hands now, and she could only trust him.

As the trip grew harder, her whole body seemed to cry out in pain, but she tried to remember it was even harder for him. Her boots were caked with mud and, as they walked, the heavy rain turned the canal bank into a pathway of slush. Still, he churned through it. Even with a bad leg, he advanced swiftly, but each new twist of the canal caused her to stumble. Several times she lost her balance, almost falling into the water.

Finally, she cried out to him, "We've got to stop. The rain won't let up. We'll both die if we don't get some rest."

"We can thank this rain," he said, turning around to face her. "It will cover our tracks. We've got to reach the farm before the sun comes up."

At one point she had to urinate, and, too embarrassed to tell him, she let the liquid run down her legs. Her dress was completely wet anyway, and its warmth was momentarily welcome. She felt feverish. Even if he didn't get lost, she knew she'd die of pneumonia.

After what seemed hours, they finally stopped in a cave, and shivering she asked him, "How much more do we have to go?"

"I think we've come about halfway," he said.

At this news, she broke down in anger and frustration. "I can't go on," she said, choking back her tears. "You'll have to make it without me. I'd rather die."

He gripped her by the shoulders. Even in the darkness of the forest, she felt the penetration and intensity of his eyes. "We'll both make it . . . *together*." Tightening the makeshift bandage around his leg, he went on, and Marika followed him, her temper becoming increasingly irritable. She began to hate him, as she plodded along. It all seemed so hopeless. She suspected they would end up getting shot together. Why bother to escape?

After another mile, she felt him slowing down. He kept reaching for his leg, and she knew he must be in great pain. But she wouldn't feel right calling attention to his wound. She knew he didn't want sympathy.

Her ankles were swollen, and her boots were like tight bandages. Still, she continued to follow him along the trail, noticing him slowing down now, his leg obviously paining him. For this, she hated him less. Gradually, the rhythm and the monotony of the march took over her body. Her fatigue became replaced by a kind of demonic energy. She was determined to get out of this forest. It might be her last act on this earth, but she'd stick it out. It was the same feeling she'd had when giving birth to her dead son . . . to Julian's child.

The image of Julian flashed before her, giving her more strength and patience. He must have had to march through rain and mud, the way she was forced to now. The more she plodded along, the less painful it was for her. She was paying for having sent Julian to his death, for having killed those two young German soldiers. Someone might have loved them and been waiting for their return, the way she'd waited for Julian. She deserved to die. She was a murderess. Maybe she could throw herself in the dank canal and drown. What was the point in continuing?

Suddenly, Charles stopped. He turned back to her and reached for her hand, gripping it tightly. "I think we're almost there. It's nearly dawn."

Hope surged through her body. She couldn't believe it.

"I know how you feel," he said. "It hasn't been easy for me

either." The Tommy had a resolute calm about him. After what she'd been through, it was comforting to be with him.

Soon the clinging mire gave way to a harder surface. In the distance a light came from a small farmhouse, and smoke from its chimney curled in the brightening sky. She began to cry.

"Do that later," he said.

"But I'm so happy," she called to him. "I didn't think we'd make it."

He looked deeply into her eyes. "We're going to make it through one hell of a lot more before we come out of this bloody war."

* * *

Numbly, Marika stumbled through the next few months until spring came. The house and barn of the Alsace-Lorraine farmer who took them in was set back from the main road and could be reached only by a narrow, twisting pathway across a flat plain. Charles told her it was possible to see the approach of a person or vehicle for miles away, at least in daylight. But by May not one visitor had come to the farm and Marika had begun to feel it was a safe haven. At the beginning of each long day, Charles would predict the end of the war. "I bet the Hun won't be able to hold out till August." Then he'd head for the fields, the leg she'd nursed for him almost completely healed. He still walked with a slight limp, though.

The farmer had welcomed them, but it was obvious he wanted their free labor. He'd lost his wife the year before, and he was a gnarled old man, with skin the color of an overbaked apple. His body was so withered, his joints so twisted, he could no longer handle the work load. In addition, he could not see well, and he peered at Marika through slits under his bushy gray eyebrows. The stench of the man was like sour dough and the heavy woolen dress he'd given her, which had belonged to his wife, had the same smell. Nevertheless, she was able to wash it and managed to burn her blood-smeared frock before Charles could ask her about it. She didn't intend to tell Charles—or anyone—that she'd killed two German soldiers. He would have understood, she knew, but it was something she could not admit to anybody.

Regardless of how cold it was, the farmer always insisted that Marika and Charles sleep in the barn. The old man didn't want to get caught by the Germans harboring two fugitives. If they were ever discovered, the farmer told Marika he was going to say they were intruders. "They'd believe an old man," he predicted.

Nights were spent huddled under straw, wrapped in old blankets. As the weeks went by, Marika grew used to sleeping with the smell of the cows. The perfumed flowers of Baden-Baden seemed an unreal memory. She no longer concerned herself with her figure, her looks, or even her matted hair. She felt she'd truly become one of those peasant women she'd seen from train windows—or in Zakopane.

Sometimes Charles would press her with questions about Christiane's death, but she told him she couldn't speak of it. As May burst around them, Charles announced, "I'm going to take my first real bath in months," and she decided to join him, though at some good distance away. The water was still bitter cold, but it was cleansing and purifying, and seemed to remove all the harsh smells she'd reluctantly gotten used to.

In the distance she could clearly see the outlines of Charles's ghostly white body making a slightly awkward, ungraceful approach to the water. Nudity made him vulnerable, somehow. Without his clothes, he seemed reduced in stature. She remembered another day and Julian's manly stride to the water, the beauty and dignity with which he carried his body.

Rubbing her own body in the water, she was shocked at its angularity and the protruding bones. At first she'd been afraid that Charles might want intercourse with her, but in all the preceding months, he'd made no overture. Was it because she'd lost her beauty? Was she so ugly now? She longed for a mirror to see what had become of her, but the farmer said he'd never owned one in his life.

By summer, the baths had become more frequent, but Charles still kept his distance from Marika. One night, however, over a bottle of wine Marika had stolen from the cellar, he began to talk about his home in England.

"I'll never convert to French wine," he sighed, settling back in the straw. "In Somerset I got me this little farm. On it I grow the sweetest apples since Eve tempted Adam. I make the kind of cider that can get a man real drunk." Slightly drunk himself, he began telling her stories of the beauty of Somerset, and of the good times he had growing up there. Abruptly, he stopped. "Mary," he said, after a pause. He'd long ago stopped calling her Marika. He could never pronounce it properly anyway. "What are you going to do when this bloody war comes to an end?"

Stars shone in through the large windowed side of the barn as Marika sat silently, her blonde hair resting in the cup of her entwined palms. "I've never thought much about it," she said, breathing quietly. "I might go to Vienna. My grandmother is there. She's very rich, I understand."

He got up quickly and walked to the edge of the hayloft. "Yes, I guess she could do a lot for you. You're probably used to a lot of fancy, pretty things. I mean, being the daughter of a Prussian hussar and growing up in Berlin with the Kaiser and everything." His hands tightened. When he turned to her, his face was sad. "I don't suppose being the wife of a simple farmer in Somerset would interest you?"

"Are you asking me to marry you?" Marika said, sitting up in the straw in surprise. "The idea never occurred to me. It really hasn't."

"I guess it hasn't, at that," he said. He stood motionless in the strong night light that made his skin moon-pale. "You don't know how hard it's been lying next to you night after night and not being able to touch you."

A warmth came over her, flushing her skin and filling her body with a tenderness that she had not known for a long, long time. She got up slowly and walked toward him, listening to the rustle of her bare feet in the straw. She stood before him in the soft shadows, holding her breasts firmly and boldly in front of her. It had something to do with the barn, the strange light, the quiet, mysterious air, but she wanted to reach out to him. "If you had ever come to me," she said finally, "I wouldn't have turned you away."

That night, after he'd made love to her, he held her close and whispered in her ear, "I could tell I'm your first man. It means a lot for an old bloke like me to know I was the first."

* * *

Charles was wrong about the war. August came and went, but still the Germans fought on, the battles did not stop. As the first fall chill crept into the air, Marika wept. "I don't think I can go on like this," she told Charles. "We can't face another winter living on roots and being forced to sleep like animals. We can't!"

Rubbing her shoulders, caressing her hair, Charles tried to reassure her. "You're right," he said. "It's time to go. For all we know, the bloody war is over and that wretched farmer hasn't even told us. He needs us more than we need him and I bet he'd like to keep us here forever! We must make our plans now."

For the next few days, thoughts of escape filled the air, and their labor in the field and their love-making at night took on a renewed intensity. After feeding the cows and finishing the chores, Marika and Charles would retire to the barn and plot how they might get out of France and what provisions they'd have to take with them. "We'll hide out in barns along the way," she said.

One afternoon, as their plans were nearly complete, they spied a small band of people from some neighboring farms moving toward them across their field. Charles's first instinct was to hide and, grabbing Marika's arm, he urged, "We've got to make a run for it!"

"Wait," she said, "they're singing a French song." Almost paralyzed in her tracks, she waited until the freedom-marchers were near.

"The Germans are gone!" a young girl shouted at Marika. "English troops are in Lille."

"Charles," she cried out, "it's over!"

* * *

In Lille that night, Marika was overjoyed at her first sight of British uniforms. Laughing and smiling, she imitated the French girls and ran up and kissed the conquering army, but the soldiers were just boys, and seemed embarrassed at all the female attention they were getting.

The streets were packed with people and festive with bunting, like a carnival. French flags, hidden for so many years, came out of every attic and secret place in the liberated city to fly alongside the new symbol of freedom, the Union Jack. Everywhere, people danced and drank and sang and, caught up in the revelry, Marika turned and grabbed Charles by the hand, hugging him to her side. Usually he was so quiet and reserved, but tonight he, too, was shouting.

"Let's go to Christiane's house and see if anybody there knows anything," he yelled over the noise of the crowd.

"No," she said firmly. "There's nothing for us there." He seemed reluctant to let her dictate to him, but he weakened when she kissed him on the lips. "Let's not look back," she said. He seemed to understand.

At two o'clock shouts of joy still filled the street. As the town clock struck, Marika allowed herself to think of Brigitte and Friedrich. Had they escaped? She'd go to their house tomorrow and see if anything had been left behind.

With a yell of recognition, an airman Charles had trained with joined them, amidst much back-slapping and hand-shaking. He seemed to be from some place named Yorkshire, and she could barely understand what he said, but his round face glowed with good humor. He gave her a tin of meat and offered her some ginger.

"What is it?" she asked Charles.

"It's an English sweet, dear," he said. "I grew up chewing it."

She didn't like the taste at all, but still she was glad to get it and even more pleased that Charles had something good to eat for a change. "I love it, too," she lied.

By three o'clock she started to sob and couldn't stop.

"You're happy," he said. "It's all right to cry if you're happy— providing you're a woman."

* * *

With a groan, the train pulled out of Victoria Station. Her wedding in London had been cold and formal in a clerk's office, accompanied by none of the festivity or pomp of her first marriage in Zakopane to Count Dabrowsky. She wondered what Charles would think if he knew she was the Countess Dabrowsky. That he wasn't her first man, or even her second.

He'd never know, she told herself. The Count had probably died. What did it matter? Dabrowsky, too, belonged to a distant, different past.

On the train, Charles held her hand for a long moment and looked into her blue eyes. "You've been through a lot," he said. "But where we're going, it'll be peaceful again. No more harm will come to you, Mary Rankin."

The words came like a shock. Mary Rankin. How strange it sounded.

· 167 ·

In a little while, he left her to join some of his buddies in the rear of the compartment. Already the men bragged of their exploits in the war that was now safely behind them. They were the victors, Friedrich and Brigitte the vanquished. All Marika had left of her past life lay tucked into a small suitcase at her feet, rescued from her bedroom in the town house in Lille.

The towns and hamlets of England passed before Marika until, by nightfall, the landscape had changed to the rolling plains of the West Country. She sat silently, sometimes with her eyes closed. At first, the screech of the rails had seemed to grind out the words, "Countess Dabrowsky, Countess Dabrowsky," but now, as they penetrated deep into the country, the words sounded different. "Mary Rankin," the scream said, "Mary Rankin, Mary Rankin," with such precision it frightened her.

She closed her eyes and leaned back against her seat as the laughter of the men echoed through the compartment. They were drinking.

"Welcome to England," said a voice. An old woman with puffy eyes and a funny-looking hat too small for her had seated herself opposite Marika.

"Thank you," Marika replied in her German-accented English.

"I could tell you were a foreigner," the old woman said. "Had my eye on you, I did. Now that I hear you try to speak the King's English, I detect you're the daughter of a Hun."

"My husband's English," Marika said defensively.

"I guess a lot of our boys will be bringing back foreign girls," the old woman mused. "Frankly, I don't approve of it myself. There are plenty of English girls who need husbands, too. Take my family, for instance. I have two unmarried granddaughters your age."

"I'm sorry," Marika replied, looking out at the darkening plain.

"You did all right for yourself, duckie," the old woman said. "Getting him to marry you. Even though I don't approve, I wish you all the luck God sees fit to give you."

"That's very nice of you," Marika said.

The old woman sighed. "We can't fight a war like we fought and have everything remain the same, now can we?"

Book Two

1928–1936

Chapter 6

The year was 1928 and England was in the grip of the pleasure principle. Only two years earlier Loelia Ponsonby had invented the "bottle party," and everywhere, liquor and pink champagne flowed. Among the bright young things, women were boyish and men often effeminate, and Noel Coward went around London saying (about other people's work), "How awfully unfunny, my dear."

In Paris representatives from fifteen nations gathered to renounce war by signing the Kellogg-Briand Pact. Those in Europe who dreamed of a return to imperial glory, pre-1914 style, drifted into melancholy. Europe's preeminence was at an end. America had become the leading money center and industrial power in the world, and all through the country there, stock-buying had reached fever passion.

In Germany, the results of the general elections stunned a demagogue named Adolf Hitler. The National Socialists had received only 2.6 percent of the total. They had done better in 1924.

* * *

Once a rendezvous for smugglers, the Punch Bowl Inn attracted customers from as far as forty miles away on Saturday nights. On this particular night, three carloads of Cockneys descended on the pub from London, and, taking the best seats in the high-backed settles, created an atmosphere fragrant with beer suds and cigarette smoke.

Marika ran her hands down the simple print dress, unbuttoned at the top to reveal her ample breasts, and gulped down an extra shot of gin. It burned her throat but she needed the extra courage the liquor gave her. In front, the pub keeper was standing beside the piano player, both of them clad in Edwardian striped shirts. In one hand he held a mug of his own ale. "Now ladies and gentlemen," he said in a raspy voice, trying to get the rowdy audience to quiet down.

"Tell us about it, Guv," one of the Cockneys called out.

"Give me a chance," the emcee yelled back. "Tonight we give you that sweetheart of song, Mary Rankin. 'Ere she is!"

Dropping a flaming match on the stone floor, Marika took a deep puff from her freshly lit cigarette and boldly strode forth past the settles of Cockneys. She wiggled her large hips, smiling suggestively at the young men, and was pleased to hear her flirtatious march to the stage met with whistles.

In the harsh light, she glared under heavy-lidded eyes at the men, then, after a quick whisper to the piano player, launched into her number in a deep, throaty voice:

> Roll me over in the clover;
> Roll me over, lay me down, and do it again.

At the end of the song, she bowed daintily, hands clasped together, mocking a schoolgirl's recitation. A storm of bawdy catcalls greeted her, but she'd expected this response. Waiting for the noise to die down, she sucked in several puffs from her cigarette, then slowly raised the hem of her print dress, wishing she had the money to look like a real flapper.

"Listen, you blokes," she said. "Here's my 'lament' of the evening:

> 'If the skirts get any shorter,'
> said the flapper with a sob,
> 'I'll have two more cheeks to powder
> and a lot more hair to bob.' "

Loud applause and laughter greeted her, and Marika glowed. She liked that, and even more she liked the eyes of the men on her.

One pair of eyes she didn't want, however. Charles was standing nearby, at the bar, threatening her silently, his eyes, hazy with gin, demanding that she get off the platform. Ignoring him, she turned her rear to the young men. "Something for you to dream about tonight, boys."

Later, in the graveled forecourt of the pub, Charles confronted her. "You're nothing but a tart!" he accused her. "You think those drunks are attracted to you. That's a joke! They're making fun of you."

"You're just jealous," she yelled back at him. "You can't stand to have another man look at me."

He stopped and glared at her, angry enough to strike her, but he'd never resorted to violence, regardless of how she provoked him. "Take a look at yourself, a good long look in the mirror. Ask yourself if any man would want *that.* You're nothing but a tub of suet! That's why I don't come to your bed anymore."

She stood in the path listening to his steps fade away. At first she wanted to scream after him, but her vocal cords seemed paralyzed. Then she wished she could cry, as that would make it easier. But she had too much hate in her for tears. Instead, she walked silently along the dark road.

A tub of suet! Yes, Charles was right. What had happened to her in those ten long years? At first, she'd thought everything was going to be wonderful here in England, the first years particularly, when he'd still made love to her. After the pain of war, she'd wanted a refuge in the English countryside where nothing reminded her of Imperial Germany and the suffering she'd known there. It was enough just to walk along the narrow country lanes picking spring violets and listening for the sound of a meadowlark.

In her numbness, she'd found a healer in Charles, a man of simple tastes who presented her with no major challenges and demanded little more than the closely defined and regulated role of a housewife. With Julian and the Count, she'd had to chart new territory, but not with Charles, once the routine of their life together was established. At first her tasks around the house were like therapy, but in time and with endless repetition they had become petty and then increasingly deadly. A deep, pervasive discontent settled over her and each year added another layer.

She'd watched her weight closely at first, resisting Charles's favorite nightly meal of steak-and-kidney pie and two kinds of potatoes, but in time, as her sense of personal worth had dwindled, his diet became hers. The first few pounds went unnoticed, but before too long she'd gained a lot of weight and had found it impossible to shed it. She had no incentive, no one to look pretty for, no one to admire and compliment her beauty. Certainly not Charles.

Only once had he taken her on a vacation, and that was to Blackpool where he'd refused to wear beach attire, or let her. Instead they'd strolled along the boardwalk, where he'd tried his luck at various childish games of chance. He'd won a pink teddy bear and presented it to her as a souvenir of their holiday, and she'd given it to the first little girl she'd encountered.

Charles had no friends—"they're a waste of time"—and, a plumber, had no prospects for any advancement, preferring, even enjoying in a kind of proud, stubborn way, the boring country life his Somerset ancestors had known before him. The only time they went out was on Saturday nights, when they'd go to a pub together and drink a few ales in silence before returning to the house and retiring early.

Drowning in lethargy, she'd picked up a London tabloid one Saturday night at the pub and read it avidly, the way she used to devour the romantic novels of her youth. She yearned for a London life, dreaming of the excitement and glamour there, and loved to follow the exploits in the press of such idols as Tallulah Bankhead. She wanted to meet the actress, dress as she did, and say the clever lines attributed to her. But Charles gave her no money for such luxuries as clothes or trips to London. In fact, she barely had enough for such necessities as toothpaste.

That Sunday morning Charles was called to work in an emergency and, not mentioning their fight, turned to Marika. "I've got to have my papers from the service," he said. "I'll need them Monday morning. I think you stored them in the attic." Without a good-bye, he was gone.

Before lunch, when the sun was high, she scaled the ladder to the attic and squeezed through its narrow trapdoor. Brushing aside a cobweb, she stepped on the beams until she reached a small leaded-glass window, and, pushing hard, she was able to force it up for some fresh air. The rays of the noonday sun seemed to guide her eyes past the heavy boxes and trunks to a battered little brown suitcase. At first she didn't recognize it, but then a distant memory stirred. For nearly ten years she'd been successful in blotting out the past, but now it came back to her. The suitcase was hers. She'd rescued it from Friedrich's town house at the liberation of Lille.

Eagerly she untied the cord around it, and, opening it, discovered that moths had destroyed two of her white lace dresses from Berlin. In the bottom of the suitcase—wrapped in a piece of faded red velvet—lay the pedestal mirror, moldy spots peppering the glass.

In the harsh glare of the sun, Marika stared at the bloated face in the mirror. Her cheeks were puffy, her hair matted. She'd become like those overfed matrons she'd first seen at Baden-Baden. As hard as she could, she tried to conjure up the image of that eager-faced young girl who'd first stared into this same mirror, thinking she was the most beautiful creature in the entire world.

Marika knew she'd soon be thirty years old, a fact confirmed by the telltale lines under her shadowy eyes. She'd have to stop drinking as much. The more gin she consumed, the easier it was to forget what had gone before and to blur the dreams she'd had as a girl. Her face tightened, and she found herself crying. It'd been a long time since she'd done that. God*damn* it! In a rage, she picked up the mirror, and slung it toward the window, watching it fall against a stack of boxes and bounce back without breaking.

Slowly she went over and picked it up again carefully, handling it gently after her violence, even caressingly. Its velvet backing had come off in the fall, exposing a piece of yellowing paper, and, taking care not to rip it, she gingerly removed the paper. It was a letter, dated August 27, 1900, the day of her birth, the day Lotte had died. Marika read the German words, written in a weak hand:

> To my unborn child, whom I know will be a girl. If I'm not around, I've asked Lili to give you my favorite mirror. The mirror has little value other than a sentimental one. But

it was mine as a girl. I want you to have it now. Perhaps one day you'll give it to a little girl of your own. This advice I want you to have. Grow up to be beautiful, my darling daughter. It is the only defense a woman has in this God's world.

Lotte.

By six o'clock the sky over Somerset had begun to pale, but alone in the attic Marika still sat gazing with an air of reverence at the note. In the distance the bells of the old village church sounded across the fields.

For weeks, Marika was haunted by the message in the note. The more she thought about it, the more bitterly she hated her own body, until, finally, she determined to do something about it. She walked up the dirt road to a red telephone booth at the post office, and, after a long delay, reached an operator in Vienna. Then, her heart pounding, she asked for the telephone number of Gabrielle Schulz.

The operator gave it to her in German.

"That's the only such party listed?" Marika asked.

"Yes, Fräulein."

"Could you tell me the address?" Marika asked. "I want to make sure I have the right person." After the operator informed her, Marika said, "Thank you. That's the lady I want to speak to, but I'll place the call later."

Running back home, she ignored the preparation of Charles's supper and, instead, feverishly wrote Gabrielle, telling her of her experiences in the war and her lonely years of exile in England with a man she no longer loved. Just to make sure the woman was really her grandmother, and to ease any doubts Gabrielle might have about her, she reluctantly enclosed Lotte's note. Lotte's real mother would surely know of the pedestal mirror.

Before the post office closed, Marika mailed her letter. Sighing, she walked back home, wondering what her life would have been if she'd gone to Vienna ten years ago. Pushing open the wooden door to their thatched cottage, she slowly made her way across the bare planked floor.

Charles was already in the kitchen, frying eggs and bacon. "When a man comes home from a hard day's work," he said, "the least he can expect of the wifey is to have a hot meal on the table."

"I have a headache," she snapped. Turning, she went up to her own private bedroom, locking the door behind her. She stared at the brass bolt for a long moment, wondering why she bothered with it. Years ago, she had started sleeping in this room alone, and he had never come in.

Three weeks went by, and still no answer came to her letter. On some pretense, she always ran into the postman on the lane, but he never had any mail for her—until one morning, when she'd given up hope, the postman knocked on her door.

"You've got a letter here from Austria, it seems," he said. "Those foreigners can't even spell Mary right. You'd think they would at least know how to spell the name of the mother of Jesus."

The envelope was addressed to Frau Marika Rankin. Eagerly tearing it open and removing the letter, she was startled to see another piece of paper fall out of the envelope and flutter to the ground. It was a boat train ticket to Vienna.

She'd found the right Gabrielle Schulz.

After reading the friendly but cautious note, Marika checked the train schedules and found she could make a connection to London tomorrow afternoon. It seemed an eternity away. She quickly packed her one suitcase with a few personal possessions, carefully including Lotte's pedestal mirror—there were few items she wanted to take out of England—and then rushed to the bank, drawing out half of the ninety-two pounds she and Charles had managed to save in the last five years. "He owes it to me," she muttered to herself. "I threw away ten of the best years of my life. You *owe* it to me, Charles."

That night she fixed him a hot supper—his favorite steak-and-kidney pudding—but she couldn't bear to look into his face as he ate it. She knew it'd be the last time she'd ever see him. After washing the dishes, she excused herself and went up to bed.

Early the next morning, she heard him get up but she dared not go downstairs. It wasn't unusual for her to stay in bed and let him fix his own breakfast, so she was sure he wouldn't suspect anything, but if she did go down, she feared her rising excitement would easily be detected. It was almost impossible to conceal it. When the front door finally shut with a bang, she hurried down. All night long, she'd lain in bed trying to compose a note to him. After all, she didn't want him going to the police after her disappearance. After the war, he'd brought her security, but it had turned her into a cow. Finally she wrote:

CHARLES,

Bringing me to England did save my sanity. For that I'll always be grateful. But I'm leaving you. Our marriage is wrong for both of us. You deserve someone who will take care of you better, and I want another chance at life.

Marika.

She thought at first to cross out "Marika" and write in "Mary" instead, but she quickly decided against it. Marika had once been her name. Now it would be her name again.

Many hours later, the smokeless chimneys of outer London came into view and Marika settled back into her seat, her suitcase securely beside her. All the memories of all the train rides in all the different phases of her life came drifting back—the trip to Warsaw, to Lille, to exile in the West Country of England. But this one was going to be different. One thing she knew beyond a shadow of a doubt: from now on, the life she led would be the life *she* wanted to lead.

* * *

The weather had turned unexpectedly hot as Marika's train pulled into Vienna, but she was much too happy to care. On the outskirts of the city, she lowered the window in her compartment and, with a joyous gasp, sucked in the fragrant late-spring scents of the Vienna woods.

The city itself was filled with statues: standing regally in the heart of a cascading fountain, mounted on the back of a marble horse, preserving the illusion of imperial glory. Marika knew at once she'd found the mythical city of her girlhood dreams. Lotte had been born and had grown up here: she had walked and loved and whirled through these streets. Closing her eyes tightly, Marika tried to conjure up all the dashing hussars Lotte must have danced with in this special capital where the waltz was born.

To her disappointment, Gabrielle wasn't at the terminal to meet her, but a chauffeur in a mouse-brown uniform stood there, obviously scanning the crowds. An old man, he'd eaten too many pastries, but he had an air of quiet dignity about him. Marika heard him asking an elegantly dressed and beautiful young woman if she were Frau Rankin, and running up to him, she identified herself. His head tilted in surprise, as his discreet eyes traversed her body and his disappointment at her appearance fairly radiated, but his face remained as stonelike as one of the saints she'd seen in front of a church. He directed her to an ivory-colored Pierce Arrow convertible, and seated on its red leather cushions, she rode past elegant shops, theaters, museums, outdoor cafés—a constant stream of delights.

Arriving at Gabrielle's baroque town house, she was shown into the parlor. In the fading afternoon light, the room was dark, and it took a moment for her eyes to become accustomed to it. Everything was gilt and red velvet, set off effectively by crystal. The smell of a Turkish cigarette filled the room.

Gradually, Marika became aware of a woman lounging on a sofa in a pose that reminded Marika of Brigitte. Did all these elegant older women rehearse the same positions? She stared long and hard at Gabrielle, almost mystified by the experience of being in the presence of her grandmother after all these years. In her late sixties, the woman was a monument to self-preservation and good grooming. Her face was gorgeously bizarre. In its center was a pug nose, made shapely and perfect by the clever use of makeup. Her blonde hair lay in tight curls on her small head, and although she had large breasts, her waist was narrow, or at least tightly corseted. Moving closer to her, Marika met eyes wide and brown, although the right one was out of focus.

"You've just arrived," Gabrielle said, "and already you've discovered my right eye. I try to conceal the defect, but I'm not always successful. In Vienna my natural enemies call me 'old lazy eye.' "

"How unkind," Marika replied, slightly nervous. "I'm sure you ignore such criticisms. You're very beautiful. In fact," she blurted, "you're the most beautiful grandmother I've ever seen."

"I'm not beautiful at all," Gabrielle said, shifting her position. "It's an illusion I have carefully created." Slowly she rose from her nesting perch, staring intently into Marika's face with her left eye. "The left eye is the mirror of the unconscious," she said. "As you can see, I'm very much in tune with my left eye." She kissed Marika on both cheeks, then swiftly guided her to the window where golden light came in through the trees of a neighboring park. "Yes," she said softly, "behind the fat of your face, I see Lotte's daughter."

"I never knew her," Marika said, looking away from the window. Did Gabrielle really say "fat"?

Gabrielle turned around, holding her hand against her cheek as if to warm it. "You never knew her, my dear, because Friedrich killed her!"

The words seemed to stab the air. Marika looked first at Gabrielle's left eye, then at the old woman's tight mouth. The drawn lips told her more about Gabrielle's hatred and bitterness than anything else could. "I don't understand," Marika finally managed to say.

"The reason I'm telling you now," Gabrielle said, "is to explain why I've never gotten in touch with you, or even tried. It would have been too painful to me."

"You resent me for Lotte's dying?"

"No, my pet," Gabrielle said, taking her hand and squeezing it. "If Friedrich ever tried to lay guilt at your doorstep, you don't deserve it. Your birth was premature. Lili, your former wet nurse, came to work for me after Friedrich had dismissed her. She told me the whole story."

"What story?" Marika asked, her voice tinged with desperation. When would she learn the truth about her birth?

"You must know," Gabrielle said. "On the day you were born, Lotte was having lunch with Friedrich. I had sent her a dress I designed. It was pale blue and was embroidered with the skylark, her favorite bird." She paused momentarily. "Lotte always loved the skylark. It could fly so high in the air and sing such a clear note, all the things Lotte herself loved to do."

Gabrielle's hand in hers calmed Marika, but she still kept her head bowed.

"Friedrich resented me," Gabrielle said, "because he'd learned he wasn't going to tap in on my money. He screamed at her, 'I don't like color in a woman's dress. Color is for prostitutes, not for the wife of a gentleman and an officer. Larks are made for eating, not wearing.'"

Marika was amazed at how accurately Gabrielle captured the inflections in Friedrich's voice.

"Lotte's mistake was to protest," Gabrielle said. "Friedrich turned over the table in his fury with her. I can just see the cords in his bull neck swelling with anger. Then he asked her, 'How do I know it is my child you carry? After all, your mother is a common slut. For all I know, you take after her.'"

To brace herself, Marika walked across the Oriental carpet and sat down on a satin chair. Her arms fell down by her sides.

"Lotte screamed at Friedrich," Gabrielle said. "She said I was one of the most respected women in Vienna. But Friedrich wouldn't listen. He shouted at her, 'Your mother is one of the richest women in Vienna. But she buys respect, the only way she'll ever get it. She's nothing but a Jewess bitch in heat who's been tongued by all the mongrels in the gutter.'"

The echoes of her Papa's violence shook Marika's body. She prayed that Gabrielle would soon end her story.

"Lotte rose from her chair," Gabrielle said, her voice shattered. "She tried to strike Friedrich, but her fists could do nothing against his tough hide. She fell back in her chair. That's when he plowed his boot into her pregnant stomach."

"Please, *please*," Marika cried, standing up, almost shouting at Gabrielle.

Gabrielle ran over and held her in her arms. "Forgive me for subjecting you to such a horrible story, but I had to tell you, to clear the air between us. You must never feel guilty ever again about Lotte's death." She held Marika's puffy cheeks in her ringed fingers. "Your father, you see, was the murderer."

In the safety and security of her lavish bedroom, Marika stood before apricot muslin curtains. They seemed to be moving in the open window like whispering figures.

Ten years ago Gabrielle's story would have destroyed Marika, sending her into months of melancholy, but not anymore. She believed Gabrielle's accusation. In its special way, it was liberating for her to hear it.

"The bastard!" she said through clenched teeth. He was a murderer, of her own mother. The word "was" stuck in her mind. Gabrielle had spoken of Friedrich in the past tense. Was he dead?

She looked out the window at the gargoyles on the ledge of her balcony. Their ugly, grotesque, and distorted faces seemed to be mocking her. The memory of the two German soldiers came back to her. Those hideous little stone faces knew that she, too, was a murderess—just like her Papa.

* * *

At breakfast that morning, Marika was at first surprised, then disappointed, to discover that Gabrielle served only strong black coffee. No pastries were on the table, not even a pitcher of cream to go with the coffee. In a pink satin morning gown, Gabrielle slowly sipped from her cup. "The time has come," she said, "for us to discuss your weight problem."

Marika couldn't stand to have her weight talked about . . . ever. The mere mention of it made the thick, syrupy coffee settle even more heavily on her stomach.

Gabrielle stared intently at her granddaughter with her left eye. "Surely you know what it means to be overweight. Or do you?"

Sad-eyed, Marika didn't answer.

"You're ostracized, for one thing," Gabrielle said. "Who can know the lost opportunities? It can even lead to premature death, not to mention lost love. Ugliness, loneliness—who wants that?"

"I know all this," Marika said impatiently, an edge of bitterness in her voice. "It has already meant many of those things for me. But I can't do anything about it."

"That's ridiculous!" Gabrielle said. "I'm known in Vienna for resurrecting what were considered lost souls. It's my business, my dear. For example, take a friend I had many years ago, Madame von Meyerinck." The name seemed strangely familiar to Marika, then she remembered the Contessa introducing her to such a woman in Kraków.

"At one time she weighed three hundred and fifty pounds," Gabrielle went on. "I made her lose most of that—not enough. Still and all, she was able to marry a handsome young Italian." Sighing, she added, "My friend died a few years ago. Before her death, though, she had the good judgment to divorce Mario."

Mario! The name ran through Marika like an electric shock. He was the first man who'd ever kissed her. She remained silent however. She wasn't about to tell Gabrielle about the Contessa and her arranged marriage to Count Dabrowsky.

"In an indiscreet moment only last year," Gabrielle said, "I took Mario in. He's now my . . ." She paused, running her fingers through her dyed hair. "Friend in residence."

Marika squirmed in her chair and leaned on her elbow to steady herself.

"Which reminds me," Gabrielle said. "By no means should you tell Mario you're my granddaughter. I've lied to him about my age. Of course, the Latin beast knows my exact birth date, but we must keep up the pretense that I'm too young to be your grandmother."

"I understand," Marika said. Her eyes seemed to wander without purpose, but it was as if she were seeking a place to hide. So far, her life in Vienna wasn't going at all according to her fantasy.

"My dear girl," Gabrielle said, looking her up and down, "I simply can't introduce you into Viennese society until I've slimmed you down, restyled your appearance, and dressed you properly. It would be wrong, even cruel, to have you make your debut too soon. I suspect that behind all that blubber is a pretty girl trying to get out."

Marika slowly got up and walked to the edge of the terrace. Some white birds were fluttering around a fountain. "I used to be pretty . . . once. I was the prettiest girl in Baden-Baden. Everybody said so."

Gabrielle gracefully rose from her seat and walked over to the edge of the terrace to join Marika. "You will be again, except you'll be more stunning than ever."

"Do you really think so?"

"Look at me," Gabrielle commanded. "Touch my skin." She took Marika's chubby fingers and rubbed them along her smooth, peach-colored complexion. "As a little girl in Budapest, I developed history's worst case of bad skin. A disaster! I was even ashamed to go out on the street. When I thought that all was lost, I met this cosmetician."

The blood surged hard in Marika's veins; the conversation was painfully personal to her. At any minute she dreaded the appearance of Mario on the patio.

"He was a doctor from Poland," Gabrielle continued. "He'd created the perfect beauty cream, just the thing for old, wind-burned, leathery faces. After many treatments from him, my skin cleared up and turned into what you see now. It's never lost this quality. Not bad for an old woman!"

"I'm afraid beauty cream won't help me," Marika said.

"Of course, it'll help," Gabrielle said, "but you'll need my special diet as well. Believe it or not, I was also fat. Then the doctor put me on a severe diet—black coffee at breakfast, black coffee at lunch, and one glass of dry white wine and a quarter of a pound of horsemeat tartar in the evening."

"Horsemeat!" Marika said. "That's disgusting."

Gabrielle gently caressed her hand. "You'll get used to it. I did. In fact, I married the good doctor, and he became Lotte's father. Your grandfather. He was far older than me. When he died, I took the formula for his beauty cream."

"Is that the same cream I saw in my bathroom?" Marika asked. "With your name on it?"

"One and the same," Gabrielle said. "I opened a beauty salon in Vienna. That silly face cream became the foundation of my little empire. Lately, however, I've acquired a different reputation. They call me 'The Nail Woman.' "

"What a strange label."

"It began quite recently," Gabrielle said, "when I took over a small nail varnish company. Its success has been amazing. Having given all my clients beautiful faces, I'm now determined to paint their claws blood-red."

At that moment, Mario entered the patio. He'd matured—light gray streaked his temples now and a certain sag was noticeable in his cheeks—but it was the same Mario who'd tried to seduce Marika in Kraków. Walking over, Mario bent and kissed Gabrielle's hand. "Good morning, my lovely," he said in a caressing voice.

Gabrielle gently touched the sleeve of his blue velvet jacket. "I want you to meet Marika Kreisler, a young friend from Germany."

Marika's face turned pale, but even though Mario put his wine-red lips to her hand, he gave no clue that he recognized her. But then, why should he? She was so different, so fat. His eyes did meet hers for a brief moment, but they were dark and vague. He seemed indolent, yet sensual.

"Marika," he finally said. "I like that." His voice was puzzled. "It sounds hot, like paprika, more Hungarian than German."

"It is Hungarian," Gabrielle interjected, linking her arm with Mario's. "You see, Marika's father was in love with a courtesan in

Budapest when he was a hussar. But the woman found someone richer."

"You mean . . ." Marika was hesitant, yet slightly angry at the same time. Everybody seemed to know more about her past than she did. "I'm named after a prostitute?"

"Don't worry about that," Gabrielle said reassuringly, smiling into Mario's eyes. "The original Marika—I knew her well—ended up very old and very rich, and not entirely without company."

"*Cara*," Mario said to Gabrielle. "If your paprika-hot lady friend was old and rich, it sounds to me she had just the right combination of spice."

* * *

Vienna had seemed like a mirage. Now it, too, was a memory. Marika was in oblivion again, immured at the incredibly elaborate Pupp Hotel in Carlsbad, Czechoslovakia. Against a backdrop of romance and glamour, she dined alone in her room. The maître d'hôtel was a good friend of Gabrielle's, and she'd given him explicit instructions as to what Marika was to be served.

The splendor of the hotel's décor held little intrigue for Marika; in fact, she avoided even walking into the Grand Salon. She looked in once, but everybody was so fashionably attired, it made her feel even more drab and dumpy. She couldn't stand other people at the spa looking at her, especially men.

Food no longer had any meaning. After the first four or five times, she found she could even eat raw horsemeat. Her only pleasure in the evening was to sip her glass of dry white wine. Fat and miserable, she soon fell under the rigid regime of the spa. Every week she sat in mud up to her neck, reliving the awful memories of her murky escape with Charles that rainy night through the forest of Lille. The chemical smell of the water at the spa was even worse than the odor of the dying men at the Red Cross hospital.

The sight of the other nude women sickened her. At the steamy hot baths, their bulging stomachs, their heavy thighs, their sagging breasts only made Marika feel deformed, too. The masseuse assigned to her was a gorilla-large Bohemian woman who mauled her body without mercy. At night, after a heavy session, Marika would herself massage the roll around her stomach. In despair, she'd stand sideways before her long, oval mirror, sucking the air into her stomach to make herself look pregnant. The treatment at the spa seemed hopeless. She'd never get thin.

But in a few weeks, her depression lifted somewhat. The weight slowly seemed to be disappearing from her frame. She couldn't be absolutely sure, since Gabrielle had strictly forbidden her to weigh herself, but could the impossible dream be coming true? Was she going to be slender again, her old self?

As the weeks drifted by, a renewed confidence came over her. She no longer felt forced to take dinner in her private chamber. Instead, she timidly walked into the dining room. As if anticipating her wish, the maître d'hôtel assigned her a table in a far and shadowy corner. She welcomed the anonymity. Her dress hung loosely and it made her unattractive, but it also secretly pleased her. It proved that Gabrielle's diet and the spartan regime at the hotel were working.

By late autumn she'd gotten enough courage to enroll in a dancing class. She had to do something with the new freedom her body was suddenly discovering. It was easier to bend over, to get up from a chair, but she had to test this agility, to make it do something for her.

Standing at the bar, she stared at her figure in a mirrored wall. It still bulged in the wrong places and the dance costume only emphasized how unshapely she was, but it was better than before. She tried to lift her leg to the bar. It was impossible. But she didn't give up. The next month she could lift her leg as high as any girl in the class and her costume was two sizes smaller than when she'd first joined.

Gabrielle had written that she was coming to Carlsbad to check up on Marika's progress—and bringing Mario. Marika dreaded the visit of her grandmother, but then one day her dance instructor told her, "You're nothing but skin and bones, too weak to dance. You've got to get some meat on that flesh." After that, Marika anticipated her grandmother's arrival with growing impatience.

Late one Sunday morning, Gabrielle made a spectacular appearance at the entrance to the hotel dressed in mink and chauffeured in her gleaming-white Pierce Arrow, an automobile unfamiliar to most of the habitués of the hotel. She marched into the lobby and immediately spotted Marika. "I can't believe my eyes. Let's go to your room immediately."

Marika was pleased at her reaction, but the attention from the other guests made her feel shy and even more awkward than usual. As she walked down the corridor, she felt as if she were with Brigitte again, her plain dress made ugly by the more flamboyant attire of the older woman.

In the privacy of Marika's bedroom, Gabrielle commanded her to strip. Self-consciously, Marika slipped off her dress. "A miracle!" Gabrielle exclaimed. "If anything, you're too thin."

Marika breathed a sigh of relief. All those stinking mud baths, the brutal massages, the sickening diet of raw horsemeat—everything suddenly seemed worth it. A glow of self-satisfaction enveloped her.

"Of course, you don't have much bosom," Gabrielle said. "Unlike me. But at least you're a true blonde." She laughed. "Again, unlike me."

Marika was allowed to slip into a thin silk Grecian robe Gabrielle had brought for her.

"Now I will transform you," Gabrielle said. "There is nothing more exciting that can happen to a woman than for her to create an entirely new image. Or have that image created for her." With consummate skill, she plucked Marika's eyebrows to a fine line, arching them in a high, sweeping curve, then penciled in above them, making them even higher. Looking at the results in Lotte's pedestal mirror, Marika saw that her brows no longer overpowered her luminous blue eyes.

"The crease of your eye is perfect," Gabrielle assured her. "We'll call more attention to it. Your lashes are the work of God. But we'll paint them to show everybody how clever God was." She reached into her makeup kit, and, rejecting three different tubes, settled on a fourth. "Now, your lipline. I want to get a balanced, refined look."

"Someone once told me my lips were too big," Marika said.

"Not true at all," Gabrielle countered. "I'll make them even more exciting." She drew the top lip straight, rounding the bow, then extended the corners with fine lines. "I'm going to paint your lips a deep, deep red. When I finish with you, your face will tell a story."

At the end of the long session, Marika stared at the results in the mirror. Gone was the little girl of Baden-Baden, faded was the emaciated countess of Warsaw, completely obliterated was the dumpy housewife of England. Staring back at her was a breathtakingly beautiful woman. "Is it really me?" she asked the mirror. She only wished her mother had lived to see the face of the daughter she'd created.

"Heavens," Gabrielle said. "Look what I've done. *I* feel like God now." Both of her hands reached out, gently touching Marika on the sides of her head. "But we can't rely totally on our judgment. Tonight I'm dressing you for dinner." She opened a trunk of clothes she'd brought from Vienna. "Just as I told you what to eat for the rest of your life, I'll also tell you what to wear. To begin with, dress only in black and white—never a color. Your lips and your eyes will provide the only color you need."

At a loud knock at the door, Marika jumped in fright.

"It's just the hairdresser," Gabrielle said. "After such perfection of face, we can't ignore a woman's crowning glory." She paused before opening the door. "I must warn you, he's very effeminate, but he is the best hairdresser in Carlsbad. I figured you might as well get used to such flighty little creatures. They'll be dressing your hair for the rest of your life."

"But I've never had a man work on me before," Marika protested. "I'll feel funny. Besides, I hardly have on any clothes."

"Sweet child," Gabrielle said, "take my word for it. He won't be interested in your body."

"But I don't know what to say to him."

"Talk about boyfriends," Gabrielle said reassuringly.

Three hours later, dressed in a white sable over a white satin gown, Marika walked into the dining room. Gabrielle lagged behind. "I'll come in later," she'd said. "I wouldn't dare make an entrance side by side with you—not looking the way you do."

Immediately, Marika noticed a change in the attitude of the maître d'hôtel. Where before he had ignored her, now he bowed low and kissed her hand. "I don't think I have your name, madame," he said, "but welcome to our hotel."

It was then that Marika realized the man didn't even recognize her. She paused before giving her name, rejecting Marika Rankin in favor of Marika Kreisler. But that didn't seem appropriate either. "I am the Countess Dabrowsky," she said finally.

"For you, my Countess," he said, "we have ready the table of the house."

Marika trailed the maître d'hôtel across the crowded dining room floor. Her hair had been bobbed to her shoulders, then carefully burnished and smoothly brushed into a sensual, soft wave. She looked neither to the right nor to the left, but tried to maintain a petulant pout on her exquisitely shaped lips.

It began with a murmur from one of the tables, but soon a crescendo of whispers reached her ears. By the time she made it to the center of the floor, nearly every table buzzed with the news of the arrival of an enchantingly unique beauty. Everybody, it seemed, wanted to know who she was. She didn't need wine tonight. The very air was intoxicating to her.

She blinked her extraordinarily long lashes—carefully painted with Gabrielle's mascara. When she closed them, they seemed to cast long shadows against her prominent cheekbones. Instinctively she knew that the metamorphosis she'd undergone at Gabrielle's hands had created an enigmatic magic. She was determined not to break the spell . . . ever. For one brief second, she almost burst into tears at her own happiness, but she restrained herself, knowing that would ruin her makeup.

Where was Gabrielle? Scanning the room, Marika noted that all the other women sat with stiff backs, so she created a slight crouch in order to be in total contrast. In a moment of quiet hysteria, she realized she didn't know who this Marika Kreisler was any more than anybody else in the room. It was just as new to her as it was to the spectators. But how could she live up to this excitement day after day? "I'll find a way," she vowed to herself. Everything was going to be glorious from now on.

Just then, the maître d'hôtel arrived with a note. It was from Gabrielle. "I can't walk across that floor and join you now," the note said. "It would be the anticlimax of all time." She looked up to see a handsome young waiter standing before her with a bottle of champagne on ice. He smiled and bowed low in front of Marika.

"It's from His Majesty," the maître d'hôtel said. He nodded in the direction of a nearby table where a fat, bald man with jowls and elaborate whiskers dined with two military officers. Heavy medals decorated the little man's chest. He bowed his head slightly when his eye caught Marika's. She quickly looked away.

"His Majesty requests the pleasure of your company later tonight," the maître d'hôtel said.

"Tell him I'm already engaged," was her impulsive reply. She wanted to ask the maître d'hôtel what country the little man ruled, but she dared not display her ignorance.

On the way out, she overheard a woman at a table near the entrance whisper, "I was told she's the richest woman in America. *The* tobacco heiress."

Gabrielle caught up with Marika in the Grand Salon, taking her hand. "While I was waiting for you, one of the English lady guests informed me you were the mistress of Warren Harding. That you, and you alone, were responsible for his untimely death."

"What a silly rumor," Marika said. "I could have done much better than that."

Gabrielle gently touched her shoulder. "I see you have much to learn about the world. From now on, you must live with the most outlandish gossip spread about yourself. The only thing you must promise me is this: *some* of the rumors will have to be true!"

* * *

The next morning Gabrielle announced her return to Vienna. "Two of my workers have been injured in an explosion," she said. "I must get back at once." Marika kissed her on both cheeks. "For what you've done for me, I'll be eternally grateful."

"No, you won't," Gabrielle said, gently pushing her away. "You'll tell everybody you created your own image. But go ahead. I don't need the publicity. If anything, I'm too famous already."

At the terminal, Gabrielle took Marika's hand and held it tightly. "Mario is shooting some stupid film up in the mountains."

"A movie?" Marika asked, puzzled.

"This is his first one," Gabrielle said. "He knows he can't be a gigolo forever. So he's shooting trash and fantasizing about being a director. I'm paying for the thing."

"When will he be back?" Marika asked.

"In a few days," Gabrielle said, quickly checking off her luggage as a porter loaded it on the train. "He can drive you back in the Pierce Arrow."

Later, Marika sat alone in her hotel suite, but it wasn't the kind of depressing loneliness she'd known. It was, rather, a vibrant, lovely feeling. Every so often she made up some minor excuse to walk in front of the mirror. She still could not believe it.

Mario's return was delayed, although he telephoned the hotel twice announcing his imminent arrival. Both times he didn't make it, and it was not until one o'clock in the morning of the following day that he appeared, drenched with rain, pounding furiously on the door to Marika's suite. Sleepy-eyed, she cautiously opened the door. "My God," she said, "you're soaking wet."

Hardly noticing her, he rushed into the living room. "I've been shooting in the rain all day—fantastic scenes. But I fear I'm going to get the cold of my life. My little crew is very wet, too, and very mad at me."

"You've got to get out of those clothes at once," she said, searching for a light. Finding it, she turned it on, then moved quickly to her bedroom. "I'll get a robe for you."

"My God!" he shouted, seeming to see her for the first time tonight. She turned quickly, facing him squarely, her eyes meeting his. They were wide with anticipation, like a little boy's.

"Surely you're not the Marika I met in Vienna," he cried. He seemed to reach out to her, though he never actually touched her skin. Almost instinctively she assumed a seductive pose. She wondered if he could see her through her gown, but then relaxed, enjoying this moment of showing off her new figure to an appreciative male. She'd worked hard for the approving gaze of a man. "Yes," she said finally. "I am Marika. You mean you don't recognize me?" She wet her lips, deliberately teasing him. "I haven't changed *that* much, now have I?"

In one quick move, he ran to her, falling down in front of her. "I worship you," he said. He started to kiss her bare feet.

Startled, she backed away.

"Don't be alarmed," he said. "Mario is so happy, so enthusiastic to have made his discovery at last. You're going to be Venus in my film."

Her hands ran nervously along the hangers in her closet. "I didn't even know you were a filmmaker," she said, hardly able to digest what he was telling her. She could smell the wetness of the man. It was far from unpleasant, yet at the same time she was upset to be in such an enclosed area with him. After all, he was her grandmother's lover.

"I'm not a filmmaker," he said. "I'm a genius. With you playing Venus, the whole world will notice me."

She looked carefully at him, having never realized before what perfect teeth he had. The impact his dark red lips had had on her before the war came back. Her hand went to her own lips. She could remember exactly what his breath smelled like that night. No man had ever kissed her mouth before Mario.

He got up off the floor. After his outburst of excitement, he seemed shy. "Mario makes a fool of himself, I know. But you *are* the most beautiful . . . the most beautiful woman I've ever seen in my life." He paused, as if reading her thoughts. "You remind me of a girl I once met in Kraków. She was very much like you, but still a girl. I've never gotten the memory of her perfect face out of my mind. Seeing you tonight, I know what that girl looks like as a woman."

She said nothing. Indeed, she could hear nothing else but the pounding of her heart. "I've found that robe now."

* * *

The following day, Marika was the first to wake up. Mario lay sleeping by her side in a fetal position, his curly hair luminously black against the soft white pillow. She eased out of bed, reached for her robe, and tiptoed into the parlor of her suite, shutting the bedroom door gently behind her. Pulling back the brocaded draperies, she welcomed the bright morning sun. She noticed the day was cold, however, the wind blowing through the trees. Only the most diehard leaves clung to the barren branches. Winter was near.

Before Mario woke up, she needed some time to sort out events in her mind. Surprisingly, she felt no guilt for having gone to bed with Gabrielle's lover. Mario wasn't a real lover, anyway, merely someone available for a price to any woman of wealth. Or, in Marika's case, of enough beauty.

All her husbands and lovers had been different. Count Dabrowsky she couldn't even think about. Julian had been a serious lovemaker, intent on his own pleasure. And Charles had approached the marital bed as if performing an act of duty as a responsible husband—though, in time, that pretense had been dropped.

But last night Mario had made a game of sex. He laughed, he joked. "How hard your nipples are," he'd told her. "What lovely little breasts. I will make love to them." Stroking her breasts, he had caressed her body with his tongue. Every part of it. As he was nibbling at her toes, she had burst into giggles. He'd laughed, too, until his hand moved to her pelvic area, massaging her with his long fingers. "You are moist with love for me." He'd guided her hand to his throbbing penis. "I'm the same way for you."

He'd moved back up her body, kissing her neck, nibbling her ear. When he'd slipped his tongue into her ear, a new sensation surged through her body. She'd found herself reaching out to pull him closer. His tongue had forced her lips apart, and he'd sucked her tongue greedily. He'd been suddenly violent, then gentle again as he'd stroked her hair. "You are beautiful," he'd said, "the most beautiful woman in the world. No statue in Rome can compare to you."

At that point he'd lain in bed, smiling with pride at his erection. It'd taken her a long time to realize that he, too, wanted to be complimented. She hadn't been able to say anything.

"I'm beautiful there," he'd said. Was it a question or a statement of fact? "Gabrielle makes me take off my underwear and parade around in front of her." At the mention of Gabrielle, Marika had withdrawn from his penis. At a time like that, she hadn't wanted to be reminded of her grandmother.

Realizing belatedly what he'd done, Mario had held her close. The rock hardness of his body, as it lay on top of her, had made her forget Gabrielle. Again, his hands had explored between her legs. She'd welcomed his attempt to pull her apart. As he'd stabbed into her, her sharp fingernails had traced patterns across his back, damp with perspiration.

After a minute of intense penetration, she'd found herself meeting his rhythm. Awkward at first, her thrusts had challenged his, stroke for stroke. Even though he'd seemed to rip her apart, she'd enjoyed the feeling. Finding his earlobe at her lips, she'd begun to chew it wildly.

"I'm the best," he said through heavy breathing.

She couldn't answer.

"Answer me," he'd demanded, his white teeth clenched before her eyes.

"You're . . ."

He'd withdrawn slightly from her.

"No!" she'd protested, reaching to pull him back. "Not now."

"Then say it," he'd shouted, hovering over her. He'd completely pulled out of her.

"You're the best . . . ever," she muttered, almost in a whisper to herself. It was true. She'd reached for him again.

"What do you want me to do with this?" he'd asked, waving his wet penis in front of her.

"Come back to me," she'd said. Tears had filled her eyes.

"Say what you want me to do to you." His voice had been angry. Apparently, verbal confirmation was an important ritual in his lovemaking.

"Fuck me!" she'd screamed in a voice she'd never known before. Was it her own? Or a sound deep within her that Mario had summoned from its hiding place?

At that command, he'd plunged into her again. Her scream had been all the incentive he'd needed. He wasn't gentle, caressing, anymore. Instead, he'd bitten her breasts and cried out: "Bitch! Slut!" But she hadn't minded the words. He'd taken her where no man ever had before.

In the morning light of the parlor, Marika trembled. Almost instinctively, she found herself reaching for her groin, recalling the sensation Mario had aroused there. She was almost tempted to go back to his bed and demand that he make love to her again. After all, gigolos were like prostitutes. They were used to the demands of women.

Steadying herself, she sat down on a sofa. The little girl who'd lived so long in her had seemingly faded into the past. Her burial, she reasoned, was long overdue. After all, Marika Kreisler was twenty-eight years old.

But Lotte's mirror assured her she was far younger. On a whim, she rose from the sofa. Her step was light. "If anyone asks my age," she said to herself, "I'll say I'm nineteen." She opened the French doors and sucked in the late autumn air. It was easy to wipe out her past lonely decade of exile in England. It had never really counted, anyway.

* * *

Mario was like a rooster prancing through her suite. "It's the dream of every artist to paint his mistress in the nude. For me, my greatest triumph would be to photograph you. How can you deny me this?"

Marika sat silently, smoking a cigarette. Even though she had refused Mario, she was flattered and pleased that he wanted to capture her nude body on film. Only a few months ago, her body had been something to be ashamed of. Now a film director, and a handsome one at that, wanted to immortalize it.

"*Please,*" Mario beseeched her.

"To begin with," Marika said finally, "I'm not your mistress. You belong to Gabrielle, or soon will when we return to Vienna." She inhaled again from her cigarette. "And second, I can agree to nothing in which I am required to take my clothes off."

He raced across the carpet, practically collapsing at her feet. "But, *cara,* it is a beautiful scene, it is *art!* Ah, if you really understood the scene, you wouldn't turn me down. Besides, you'll have a veil covering you."

"I know," she said, slightly sarcastically, "a see-through veil."

His hands waved in the air as if he were fanning a fire. "No, no, no, it'll be out of focus. You'll appear as in a mist. The audience will know it's a woman—*my* Venus—but that's all. No one will see anything, I promise."

"If that's the case," Marika said, "I'll consider it. Only you must let me approve the film before anybody sees it. You're sure now I won't be recognized?"

"I give my word," he said, kissing her hand.

During the next three days, he asked her at least fifteen more times, and at least fifteen more times, she turned him down. But at last, on the fourth day, she relented. After all, what harm could it do? The fifth day found her at a château outside Prague. It was cold and damp, and she was glad she'd worn her white sable. Underneath the coat, however, she was completely nude.

A friend of Gabrielle's owned the château and had granted Mario permission to use it as a background for his film. Marika was stunned at its opulence, but most particularly at a hall of mirrors designed to simulate the Palace of Versailles. Fascinated, she watched her own image—encased in white fur—reflected endlessly down the corridor. Around her, servants had lit candles in large brass chandeliers, and then, at Mario's request, discreetly disappeared.

Mario thought her final acceptance of the nude scene was because of his devotion to him, but nothing could be farther from the truth. In fact, she was getting bored with him. Although skilled at lovemaking, his vanity made him almost impossible to live with. He constantly wanted praise, and she preferred a man who'd lavish attention on *her*. She found it embarrassing to give a man compliments, especially about his physical beauty.

There was also the gnawing awareness that she'd have to surrender Mario to Gabrielle the moment she arrived back in Vienna, and so she was reluctant to get more deeply involved with him. She found herself looking for flaws in the man, knowing he wasn't hers for much longer. It was her way of freeing herself from him.

To tell the truth, ever since he'd suggested the nude scene, the idea had begun to take hold in her mind. After hiding her body from the world for so many years, she was becoming increasingly intrigued with the prospect of exposing it. Many times she tried to visualize what the scene would look like on film. She saw herself flashing before the camera in a blur of white blondeness. Nothing clear, nothing sharply defined—but every man in the dark audience would know that a goddess had passed by in the night. Closing her eyes, she tried to conjure up the erotic fantasies she would inspire, in men she'd never seen, in countries she'd never visited.

Last night, she'd read the script of Mario's film and it was terrible. In the picture, a man not unlike Mario searches the world for the one perfect woman, always unsuccessfully, until in the final sequences, Venus appears to him in a dream. He wakes up in a panic when he realizes he has only dreamed her, but the very next day, he meets a real-life Venus in the form of a servant girl. Happy ending. Marika thought she'd keep her comments on the script to herself.

Mario came up to kiss her and she realized she was shivering. "I'd feel one hell of a lot better about doing this in summer," she said.

He opened her coat to make doubly sure she was nude. "It won't take long, *cara*. Now this is what you do. Hold the veil in front of you," he instructed her, "then run slowly down the entire length of the hall toward the camera. As you get right near the lens, hold out your arms and pretend it is a man you want to make love to."

"I think I understand," she said hesitantly. "Let's get going. I'm losing my courage."

He quickly hurried to the other end of the hall, stationing himself behind his camera. Looking around anxiously to see if any servants were about, she slipped off her sable and reached for the veil, holding it up against her. It concealed nothing. Goosepimples formed on her body.

At his signal, she started running toward the camera. Suddenly, all her tension faded away. She felt magically beautiful, a fact the mirrors constantly confirmed, as her nude image flashed before her eyes. Bathed in soft shadows, her body seemed to take on exciting forms and contours. She tried to think of herself as a real goddess, to be lyrically remote, the type of woman every man would desire, but never could possess. As she moved closer to the camera, it seemed to reach out and envelop her. Her moistened lips and dewy blue eyes loved the capture.

Then it was over. A sense of overwhelming disappointment consumed her. It was as if something very precious had been taken from her, and she burst into tears. Mario held her, kissing her cheeks, and putting his coat around her. He whispered in her ear, "Men will dream about you for years." Walking her back across the long hall, he told her, "When I was a little boy growing up in Italy, I prayed one day I'd come north and meet *the* blonde Venus. But I never had the chance. I had to eat, and to do that I had to make love to flabby old women whose skin and false teeth repulsed me." He turned and smiled at her. "With the money I'm going to make on this film, I'll never have to take orders from a woman ever again. Women will vie for the chance to take orders from me."

The next morning, he shot the final sequence in the film. In the close quarters of a well-lit bedroom in the château, he outlined the scene. Marika would be the servant girl, this time in clear focus. She had descended from Mount Olympus and was a woman of flesh and blood, not the shadowy mirage of the young man's dreams.

Hovering over her on the bed, Mario said, "I want to show the look on a woman's face at the exact moment she knows a man for the first time."

For hours, the shooting dragged on. He captured her face in a multitude of moods—from the first wide-eyed searching look to the final ecstasy of orgasm—but he couldn't get the one moment he wanted. "I was wrong," he shouted at her with impatience. "You'll never be an actress. Show pain!"

Minute after agonizing minute passed. She even tried to conjure up the terror of her rape in Warsaw, but none of her grimaces pleased Mario. "It's not real," he said.

Suddenly, in the middle of what must have been the twentieth retake, she felt a sharp jab in the bottom of her bare foot and shuddering in pain, she screamed out. Looking up, she saw he'd pricked her with a pocket knife and her reaction had been recorded.

"Perfect!" he cried, putting down his camera. Jumping on the bed, he kissed her.

"You bastard!" she said, slapping his face. Her foot was bleeding.

"You call me that now," he said, "but one day you'll thank me for making a star of you."

* * *

Back in Vienna, Marika launched into a round of party-and opera-going with Gabrielle. As she got used to her new look, her new body, and the new clothes that Gabrielle bought for her, Marika began to see herself as the quintessential woman. Maybe it was the champagne, which she drank with increasing frequency, maybe it was the heady night air, but she found herself taking on an effervescent, often quixotic, quality.

As the noonday sun poured into her bedroom suite, Marika fingered the invitations, more than she could possibly accept. One from a Hungarian countess was easy to turn down, because she was such an obvious bore, but an invitation to a dinner party given by the Turkish ambassador intrigued her. Turks sounded so mysterious.

At the last minute, Gabrielle bowed out. Hand at her head, she said she felt a migraine attack coming on. "You'll have to go to the dinner without me. I've just been on the telephone to Mario in Prague. He claims he needs more money for that damn film. I told him he's bled the last schilling from me that he'll ever get."

"How did he handle that?" Marika asked calmly, though she found it distressing to discuss Mario with Gabrielle.

"Darling," Gabrielle said, "I can't repeat what that dirty, rotten Italian male-whore said to me, forgetting completely he was talking to a lady. Besides, my friend in Prague, the one who owns the château, said Mario is keeping company these days with a notorious German banker."

"Why is he notorious?"

"Only because he's the most decadent homosexual in all of Germany," Gabrielle said. "And that's saying a lot!" She sighed. "In a few weeks, Mario will be but a memory, like all the others, and I'll be on to my next adventure."

Alone in the back seat of the Pierce Arrow, Marika inspected her makeup. She'd learned to do her face even better than Gabrielle could. Each day she discovered new subtlety in what had become her facial mask. Actually, she was glad Mario wasn't returning to Vienna. His presence in the household could only be an embarrassment to her. Her only regret was she wouldn't get to see right away what she looked like in the film.

Instead of lamenting, she soon found herself swept up in her arrival at the party. Ahead of her, a stream of elegant black sedans arrived in front of the embassy, and she could see gardens ablaze with light. A footman escorted her to the door, then, standing in a large entrance hall, waiting to be announced, she was approached by a servant. The woman bowed low in front of her, and slipping off Marika's satin shoes, replaced them with intricately embroidered slippers.

It was all very fine, but Marika was disappointed when she was presented to the Turkish ambassador. Far from being mysterious, he was simply an old man with too many medals weighing him down, like the king in the hotel in Carlsbad. His eyes were forbidding, however, and they flashed somewhat when he was close enough to smell her. She sensed a faint glow of the fire that must have burned in the man in the days when he was reported to have had five wives.

The women guests clearly envied the diamond diadem around Marika's neck. Gabrielle had been planning to wear it herself. "I need it more than you do, my dear," she'd told Marika, but at the last minute, she'd given it to her. "Just the touch to set off perfect beauty."

The dinner service was pure gold. Marika found herself between a young maharajah from India, who spent the evening talking about polo, and his mistress, newly arrived from Paris and dressed much too flashily. She was clearly bored with her lover, as revealed by her languorous smiles to a dapper figure at the far end of the table. Desperate for someone interesting to talk to, Marika's attention was caught by the man sitting opposite her. All evening, his eyes had been boring in on her, though she'd avoided looking directly into them when introduced. Try as she could, it was impossible not to be aware of him. He seemed to be peeling her skin off with his stare. Almost instinctively, she found herself looking down at her bosom to satisfy herself that everything was safely in place; then, slowly, she raised her eyes to meet his. They were battleship-gray and so devoid of expression they were almost like those of a blind man, yet somehow they conveyed the power of the man. A diagonal scar streaking his face, he was like a blond Visigoth, tall, slender, and impeccably dressed in black tie.

In the middle of one of the Indian prince's polo stories, Marika suddenly realized who the mysterious man was. It was Franz Hauptmann, the Austrian munitions giant. Of course! Gabrielle had told her so many stories about him—he was almost legendary by this time. Rich, powerful, the most sought-after bachelor in Austria—a Viennese actress was reputed to have killed herself because Franz wouldn't marry her. His entire life had been spent in intrigue and espionage, and it was said he was well known and often hated in all the major capitals of Europe. He was also said to be financing the Nazi Party in Germany.

As the stories had it, Franz Hauptmann had many mistresses, which he discarded with as little concern as if he were rejecting a bottle of bad wine. Whatever he did, it was on an epic scale.

Marika was enchanted and fascinated by the man, but also frightened. What special quality did he have that made her so attracted to him?

After dinner, she had a chance to find out. As she was dancing with the Indian prince in a small ballroom lit by crystal chandeliers, Franz cut in. "It would be my honor," he said to Marika. The Indian prince bowed gracefully and went to join his mistress. At the edge of the swirling group, Marika moved into Franz's arms. She felt a throbbing sensuality penetrate through her.

"You have turned what I thought was going to be another boring dinner into an event in my life," he whispered in her ear.

"Thank you," she said nervously, almost embarrassed at her high-pitched, little-girl voice. The more he whirled her, the more bubbly and intoxicated she became from the champagne. Engulfed in the music, she pressed closer against his shoulder, her head spinning, as the Venetian chandeliers cast flickering shadows on Franz's face and picked up deep highlights in his steel-gray eyes. He was a skilled dancer, even though slightly reserved, and Marika found it hard to keep up with his lead. The prince's hands had been clammy, but not those of Franz. They were perfectly dry.

"You are German?" he asked her.

"Yes," she said. "How did you know?"

"I wasn't quite sure," he said. "You have the grace and sensitivity of an Austrian. But your eyes are too cold and too brutal to be an Austrian's. Those are Prussian eyes." He smiled at her shock. "I can only say that about you because I have the same eyes."

At the end of the music, he still held her close. Some of the other guests looked at her, but she didn't know what to do. Then she realized why he didn't want to break from her. Pressing tightly against her, he unmistakably had an erection.

"Do you mind if we withdraw quickly to the study?" he asked. Turning his back to the group, he led the way, and once inside, he quickly sat down. By the light of a blazing fire, he reached into his breast pocket and pulled out a handsome gold cigarette case. "May I light you one?"

"Yes," she said demurely.

He withdrew two cigarettes, tapping them gently against the case, then, lighting both at the same time, he wet the tip of her cigarette. When she put it against her mouth, the wetness thrilled her. She knew he'd done it deliberately. Holding it for a long moment, she let the moisture evaporate against her own lips.

"We have a slight problem," he said.

"Yes?"

"I don't want to do something as obvious as leave the room with you," he said. "Our stay in the study is already stretching out much too long." He blew out smoke. "Leave in your vehicle. My driver will follow and meet you at the square beyond. Of course, all the other guests will know, but it's important to maintain appearances."

She rose quickly from the sofa. "What makes you think I'll rendezvous with a strange man I just met?"

He got up quickly, tossing his cigarette into the roaring fireplace. "Fräulein Kreisler," he said, "I've had to make decisions and move quickly in this world. To do that, I have never been able to indulge in the pretenses of which women are fond. The moment I took you in my arms, I knew you were going with me. You knew it, too. Let's not begin our relationship by telling lies to one another."

She stood looking uncertainly at him, knowing she was losing control, but unable to leave. Words of protest came to her lips, but they were silenced by his mouth on hers, pressing tightly, drinking from her lips.

"I need you right now," he whispered, holding her so close her breath seemed to be crushed away. "But, first, we must murmur an adieu to our host."

* * *

Before she fully knew what was happening, Marika found herself seated in a long black limousine, driving through a dense forest covered with snow, Franz holding her close in the back seat. She'd lost track of time, but they seemed to have been on the road for hours, and as the night mist began to blow against the windows, she felt the automobile climbing a steep mountain.

What had she done? The effects of the champagne were wearing off now and she began to feel uneasy. She wasn't sure it had been a good idea to run off with this strange man. But Franz had made the choice for her. He didn't believe in consultation.

The road writhed and twisted, and Marika grew alarmed, as the vehicle careened and once veered dangerously near the edge. The driver seemed skilled, however, and at last he came to a stop in front of a guardhouse with a large iron grill gate. An old man emerged, blinking his eyes, and let them through. The car sped to the entrance of a small château.

In the parlor, servants offered more champagne in copper ice buckets, but Marika protested, "I'm quite tired. I'd like to be shown to my room."

The bedroom suite in which she subsequently found herself proved to be even more elegantly decorated than the one at Gabrielle's. Decorated in crimson and gold, filled with fresh flowers, it looked as if Franz had expected her visit. She noticed a wide assortment of women's dresses and gowns in a closet. Did Franz bring women to his private château often? He was certainly well prepared to receive them.

Peeking into the adjoining parlor, she was startled to find Franz sitting in an armchair in front of a roaring fire. The light picked up the ridge of the scar that coursed across his cheek, but it also bathed him in a mellow glow. The quick flush on her own face made her skin tingle.

"If you're tired," he said, "you should turn in. I was born in that bed."

Turning back to the bedroom, she gazed at the canopied four-poster that stood there in the middle of the room like a giant throne. Quickly removing her clothes, she slipped into a light gown and climbed the three steps at the side of the high bed. Its fleur-de-lis spread had been turned back and the sheets were warm as if someone had seen to her comfort only moments before. She looked apprehensively around the room, almost expecting to see a silent servant standing in the corner.

Lying quietly, she stared up at the brightly colored, intricately embroidered tapestry of the canopy: a unicorn, with one foot poised delicately in the air, trapped by a pack of fang-toothed hounds. In the distance a hunter, shrouded in black and mounted on a white stallion, had drawn his bow, ready to plunge an arrow into the heart of the unicorn.

Marika closed her eyes in fright and lay on the bed for a long time while the fire dimmed and slowly faded. She felt like a bride on her wedding night. When was Franz coming to join her? Another hour went by before she became aware of a presence in her room. Franz stood at the far side of the fireplace, his nude figure framed in a doorway. If anything, he seemed taller than ever. He turned and looked back into the room he'd just left as if he'd forgotten something, and, just for a moment, his large genitals were clearly visible. They were just like Papa's. Without their clothes, Franz and Friedrich could have been twins.

"You're still not asleep?" Franz asked. "I thought you were tired and didn't want to be disturbed."

"I was waiting for you," she replied.

Slowly Franz climbed up to the bed, and slipping under the sheet, he carefully reached over and touched her skin. His fingers were educated in the art of arousal. They seemed to have the skill and precision of musical instruments as they patted and smoothed her flesh. Occasionally they would pause when they found a place which would make her moan softly, and Marika felt her willing body come alive.

"The skin . . . so soft," he said. "You're to be adored." Fingertips gave way to lips even more tender, and the movement of his mouth was like a trail of fire. With a soft nibble, he explored her budlike nipples and announced, seeming pleased, "They are hard." Tiny tongue-flicks traced circles, and she twitched and throbbed as his strong heavy breath came into contact with her stomach. She shuddered, but it was from a tingling pleasure slashing through her belly. Flashes of feeling flowed into a long, steady sensation. It rippled the entire length of her spine, striking across her stomach, ending in a flickering gulf between her legs.

He positioned himself over her and, his mouth again on her breasts, his hand caressing her, she welcomed him inside her. Gasping, she felt his steady pumping movement and his hands on her thighs, urging her legs upward and over his shoulders.

He battered into her, and she squirmed with pleasure. This was better than Mario and certainly better than Julian. This was Franz, the hussar of her girlhood dreams come alive. She wanted to submit to him totally. A star-fire began to burn within her. It roared, stronger and stronger, and finally burst in time to meet his. She screamed out as a shock wave swept over her entire body.

Later, in his arms in the early morning light, she realized she'd dozed. Someone, probably a servant, had discreetly entered the room and lit the fire again. In its glow, the black horseman in the tapestry over the bed looked more ominous than before.

"I've always owned it," he said, as if reading her thoughts.

"The horseman looks very cruel," she said. "My sympathy is with the unicorn."

"Nonsense," he said. "Unicorns don't belong to this world. They are only myths, like Santa Claus, beasts that never were." He touched her arm, his fingers tightening around it. "We must destroy the myths in our lives so that we can get on with the business of living in the real world." He turned over in bed, his back to her.

She lay silently staring into the fire until she, too, fell asleep.

* * *

Hours later, Marika opened her eyes to the unfamiliar room, to find Franz Hauptmann gone, but memories of last night flooding her memory. She rang for a servant, and in a few moments, the large oak door cracked open to admit a young girl carrying a tray. "Good afternoon, Fräulein Kreisler," she said. "We've been waiting for your call. I've brought your *Frühstück.*"

"That's very nice," Marika said. In the vastness of the room, her voice sounded weak, lacking distinction.

"Is there anything else I can get you now?" the girl asked.

"No," Marika said, "but you could tell me where Herr Hauptmann is."

"Early this morning he was called to Berlin on urgent business," she replied. "Herr Hauptmann is always being called away on urgent business."

"I see." A sense of disappointment came over her like a wave. She'd have to call Gabrielle at once.

"After you've tended to your toilet," the girl said, "you're to summon Herr Hauptmann's social secretary. He's been left with detailed instructions."

Just then, the telephone rang. It was Gabrielle. "My darling," she said, her voice triumphant. "Early this morning I received an unexpected social call from Franz Hauptmann. He stopped off before leaving for Berlin."

"He was there?" Marika asked in complete astonishment.

"He wanted to assure me you were fine," Gabrielle said. "To ask my permission for you to remain with him. I suspect he thinks you're underaged."

"What did you say?"

"I gave my permission, of course," Gabrielle said. "Franz

Hauptmann is only the most desirable man in Europe. Regrettably, he's not the marrying kind. Nevertheless, it's most prestigious to be his mistress."

"I take it, then, you approve."

"What an understatement!" Gabrielle said. "I view you as my greatest creation. But, please, have one of your servants return my diamond diadem. With Franz Hauptmann as your lover, you won't be needing that little trinket any more."

Bathed in scented water and her makeup carefully applied, Marika called for the social secretary and wandered out onto a large terrace. Although deep in winter, it was one of those surprising afternoons that occur in Austria when mists suddenly clear, and the sun shines brightly, even fiercely, on the land. For miles around, she could see nothing but trees and in the distance mountains topped with snow.

The social secretary came onto the patio and introduced himself as Peter Nebmaier. A handsome man, tall and slender, his long, blond hair fell over his forehead as if with a premeditated charm; he couldn't have been more than twenty-five years old. With a smile, he handed Marika a note from Franz.

MY DARLING,

For years I've searched for the one woman who could be my perfect companion in life, combining the perfect love-mate with the perfect hostess. At last I've found her! I'll be gone for one week (unfortunately, my next few days were planned before I was even aware of your existence). You are now the mistress of my household, second in command only to me. I count the long hours until my return. Please make your debut tonight as the hostess of a little dinner party I'd planned for friends and could not cancel at the last moment.

Your loving Franz.

That night marked the start of a long list of dinner parties she'd preside over in Franz's absence. As his hostess, she was startled, then delighted, to find that the guests included members of the theatrical and musical world: Sara Leander, Marta Eggerth, Willi Schmidt-Kentner, Greta Keller, and Richard Tauber. Marika stared in amazement at the monocle glittering in the great operatic tenor's eye. He bowed before her, kissing her hand. In a soft, caressing voice, he said, "It's a pleasure to gaze upon one so lovely."

She'd hardly recovered from the experience of meeting the matinee idol of Europe before Peter asked her to come quickly into the hallway. Another important guest had arrived. Emerging from a bulletproof limousine, Prince von Starhemberg stared into her eyes, then bowed much lower than Tauber as he kissed her hand. Her whole body tingled when his lips touched her skin.

As if in a dream, she drifted through the evening, adjusting to Franz's not being there, and amazed at how the other guests accepted her. Apparently, they were quite used to his mysterious arrivals and departures. Often she didn't know what the guests were talking about, but she learned that wasn't necessary. All that was expected of her was to listen and smile and be a mannikin for the evening.

When the men went into the study for brandy, Marika gravitated to Greta Keller, who looked stunning with her raven-dark hair and peach complexion. With great charm, Greta amused her with stories about her first big role on the Viennese stage, in an American play, *Broadway,* in which she'd appeared as a gun moll opposite Peter Lorre. Backstage, Marlene Dietrich, a young woman in the chorus, had introduced her to the music of Whispering Jack Smith and had taken some of the cast back to her hotel room, where she'd entertained them by playing a saw.

To Marika, it all sounded so glamorous and romantic. How she wished she could be a part of this glittering world. As the party gathered to end the evening, she announced impulsively, "Incidentally, a film I recently starred in will be released shortly. It's called *Birth of Venus.* All of you *must* see it." She hoped she sounded casual enough, as if this were something she was used to. Each guest assured her he or she would most definitely see the picture, and on leaving, Prince von Starhemberg told her, "I couldn't think of a more appropriate woman to play Venus."

"What inspired casting!" Tauber said.

She thanked each of them, blushing.

That night she fell asleep radiantly happy, even without Franz. The world was a fantasy after all. As a little girl, she hadn't been entirely wrong in thinking that one could grow up to lead an enchanted life. She wondered what Charles was doing or thinking tonight back in Somerset. He wouldn't know or even recognize his Mary Rankin.

* * *

The first two months with Franz were glorious fun, as Marika plunged into a round of parties, dances, theater-going, and weekend retreats at spas. All the excitement she should have had as Countess Dabrowsky was now hers as the mistress of Franz Hauptmann.

The dances she enjoyed most of all, as she whirled around the floor, her eyes out-sparkling the chandeliers. A hairdresser now visited twice a week, and her blonde waves shone with a luster— a fact that never went unnoticed by her dancing partners. Tossing her head with an animal vivacity, she danced from one man to another, looking deep into the eyes of her partner of the moment, always under her protector's steely gaze. As one set of hands parted and new ones touched hers, she seemed to come alive all over again. Sometimes she gazed into the eyes of brutality, especially among Franz's increasing roster of Nazi friends, but other times she looked into mature faces that told her they'd calmed their passions. These men she tried to arouse most of all.

Every time a piece of jewelry or a beautiful new gown arrived, Marika knew that Franz was leaving on another of his mysterious trips, trips that were increasing in frequency and length. The terms of their relationship had never been clearly defined, but without his telling her so, she'd come to understand that she was never to leave the château while he was away. To relieve her boredom, she would invite Gabrielle to come up from Vienna, and she would invariably arrive with some new face cream or dress to amuse her.

The more he left her, however, the more jealous Franz became. He accused her of having affairs with half the male guests he invited to his parties, and once when drunk he even claimed she was sleeping with Hans, his chauffeur. The innocent man was summarily dismissed the following morning without benefit of references. Strangely enough, Franz allowed her to spend all the time she wanted in the company of Peter. She could never understand it, since Peter was remarkably good-looking, but the secretary had never approached her, and sometimes she wondered if perhaps he hadn't been hired to spy on her. Nevertheless, she welcomed his company.

As the weeks went by, Franz's jealousy grew worse. Before a dinner party, he would elaborately inspect her makeup and gown, wanting to show her off to maximum advantage, yet at the same time resenting the men who looked too longingly at her. She'd finally begun to understand the contradiction. Franz didn't want people admiring the beauty of Marika Kreisler. Instead, he wanted them to say, "That Franz, he's so clever—only he could capture the most beautiful woman in all of Austria and Germany."

To her dismay, his interest in her as a real woman simply didn't exist. He wanted her to preside with him over a dinner, sitting demurely at the end of his favorite rosewood table, but she brought so little of herself to these gatherings, she felt virtually useless. If spoken to, Marika was expected to respond, but only with polite smiles. Usually Franz did all the talking.

One evening a terrible despair came over her. The night was cold, and a light rain fell, but, forgetting her wrap, she walked through the garden, letting the fresh drops fall against her lashes. How she longed for a lover walking beside her at this very moment. Franz was changing before her eyes, becoming more bigoted, more intolerant with every passing week. Marika blamed it on his Nazi coterie, but it was more than that. The man had other ambitions and dreams that no woman could satisfy.

Twice a week he demanded long nights of impersonal sex with her, and she responded passionately, because she truly desired his lovemaking, but she knew he was making love to a body and shutting her off. In time she began to feel she was his sexual convenience, even going so far as to yell at him in frustration one angry night, "It'd be a lot cheaper for you to ring up a harlot and have her sent here. You don't care about me." He slapped her face and became even more violent in his sex. Although she found it repulsive, violence seemed to whet his appetite.

More and more, Marika resented the fact that she'd become a puppet again. The men in her life, from the Count to Julian, to Charles to Franz, even to Mario, had always seemed to use her for whatever purposes they had in mind. She'd hoped at the restoration of her beauty in Carlsbad that she would lead a much more exciting life, a life she'd control. She wanted to captivate men, not have men dominate her, but she knew this would never be the case with Franz. A man like him would never allow any woman to assert herself. He didn't know what a woman was, other than someone to be his hostess, his unequal sexual partner, and his prisoner.

The idea of leaving Franz occurred to her again and again, and she even discussed it with Gabrielle, who strongly discouraged her. But when Marika found out she was pregnant, she no longer felt it possible to go. One day, with the sun streaming in the windows, she told him the news. He stood for a long time looking out at the grounds before saying anything. Finally, he spoke. "If it's a girl, I promise to let you bring it up." Abruptly, his expression changed, his eyes zeroing in on her. "But if it's a boy, he'll be my responsibility completely."

After the baby began to show in her figure, he refused to grant her permission to leave the château. "After all, we're not married. We can't flaunt our affair before society."

"But you let me preside with you at dinners," she protested.

"That's different," he said. "Now you look like a cow. I don't want my friends thinking the glamorous Marika Kreisler—or Countess Dabrowsky, depending on what you're calling yourself at the moment—is a mere *Hausfrau.*"

The accusation hurt her, but not as much as when Charles had called her a "tub of suet." Charles had been telling the truth, but Franz was wrong. Even though she was pregnant, she still felt as attractive as ever except for her stomach, and Lotte's mirror confirmed it. If anything, her skin was even more beautiful. It had a radiant glow, and in two short months from now she knew she'd regain her figure and be waltzing again.

One night Franz insisted she remain alone in her room, while he entertained friends from Germany, and she decided to defy him. It was October 29, 1929, the day known in America as "Black Tuesday." On New York's Wall Street, an avalanche of orders poured in, with the instructions, "Sell at any price," and before the day was out, millions of shares—and many lives—were lost.

Marika stood silently at the doorway to Franz's study, eavesdropping on the conversation.

"What happened on Wall Street," Franz was saying, "is just the harbinger. A great depression will come out of all this. It'll spread around the world."

"Anarchy will spread across Germany," one of his guests said with grim satisfaction. "There will be enormous poverty. That is the time to seize power."

"You seem to want Germany to have a catastrophe," Marika cried, throwing open the doors to the study. Startled, the men turned toward her, and she recognized the Baron von Schleicher, an unpleasant person resembling an overgrown ferret, and a shifty-eyed man known only as Baur.

Recovering first, the Baron bowed before her and kissed her hand. "Germany will be ready for a Messiah," he said.

Acknowledging him with a slight condescending tip of her head, but carefully avoiding Franz's harsh glower, she replied, "It is one thing for a man to promise he can cure all our headaches, but I've found trouble a constant condition of life. We merely trade one disaster for another."

"You don't seem to think our Hitler is the answer," Baur said, standing before her and kissing her hand in perfect imitation of the Baron.

"I'd rather trust the League of Nations," she replied.

"The League is stupid, weak, ineffectual," Franz interjected. "It'll never work."

"Are there too many Jews in Geneva?" Marika asked provocatively. She hadn't bothered to corset herself.

Franz was staring at her pregnant belly. "The Jews aren't our real enemy. The real enemy is the German people themselves. Their absolute blindness to the fact that Hitler can lead us to greatness."

Marika didn't bother to disguise the contempt she felt for his political ideology. With a grim smile, Franz turned to his guests. "As befits one so beautiful, Marika is naïve about international politics," he said, taking another puff from his cigar. "You must excuse her comments." But Marika wasn't going to let Franz dismiss her so easily. She turned to the Baron. "Do you really think destroying all Communists and Jews the answer?"

The Baron stuttered for a moment, then looked at Franz. "It will remove the sins of Germany—and her enemies, too."

"Our sins?" Marika asked, puzzled. "I've found that guilt always remains with us—never to be washed away."

"You're wrong!" Baur said, his beet-colored complexion turning even redder.

She faced him squarely, trying to make contact with his downcast eyes. "The trouble with people who preach death and destruction is this. They're never around to be held responsible for their crimes when proved wrong."

"We must be going," the Baron said nervously to Franz.

"Indeed!" Baur added.

"Gentlemen," Marika said. "I hope I haven't ended your little gathering."

Proffering apologies and good nights, the men eased their way out of the study, and soon Franz stormed back, slamming the door behind him. "How dare you intrude upon my business conferences!"

"Forgive me," she said calmly, "I'm so disappointed in your choice of allies. That Baron, for instance. So, he's a banker. I happen to know he took Gabrielle's boyfriend away from her. And that Baur. Peter told me he was a bouncer in a *bierstuben* in Munich before Hitler gave him a little more power to flaunt like a bully."

"In politics," Franz said reflectively, "one must keep strange bedfellows."

"I think all this National Socialism is merely a fraud on the public," she said. "Do you really want to see those beasts in power? Why are you backing them? So they'll make another war and keep your munitions factories going day and night?"

"I'm using them," Franz said, his face glaring into the fireplace, its flames casting a harsh glow over his features. "I don't care about their prejudices, their silly pretenses. I want to accumulate a vast fortune. Then I'll flee to South America."

He walked over to her and placed his hand on her stomach. "With my son," he added.

"What about me?" she asked, staring down at his hand and sipping her brandy. She recalled asking Friedrich almost the same question long ago in Berlin.

"You can come along, too," Franz said. His hand reached up, fingering the diamond necklace she wore. "I see you don't mind enjoying the profits of munitions yourself. Someone has to earn the money to pay for those Goddamn gems you wear."

Marika fingered her necklace. "Possessions exist," she said vacantly. "Does that mean we can't enjoy them? Just because there is a little human sweat and suffering involved?"

"You've had it easy," Franz charged. "You know nothing of human suffering!"

"You're a fool if you think that!" She turned and ran quickly from the study. For a moment she was tempted to flee the château altogether, but, reluctantly, she turned slowly and began the climb up the stairs to her bedroom where Franz no longer visited.

* * *

Marika was seven months pregnant when Mario announced the world premiere of *Birth of Venus* in Vienna. She was overjoyed, having long ago given up hope the film would ever be released. Her dreams of stardom had gone the way of her desires for a grand life with Franz.

On the night of the premiere, she begged Franz to let her go —she had even had a special gown designed that did everything possible to conceal her belly—but Franz adamantly refused. "I'm taking Gabrielle," Franz said, "but you must stay at home until my boy arrives." He patted her stomach. "I've ordered a print of the film for my collection. We'll have it shown privately for you."

The night was one long, agonizing wait for his return, and Marika felt cheated and furious. It was unfair that Franz and Gabrielle were getting to see the film before she'd had a chance! Mario had betrayed her. He'd promised to let her approve the film before its release. Why didn't anything work out right?

She opened the French doors and walked out onto the cold, dark terrace, momentarily tempted to jump over, crashing on the cobblestones below. But she quickly rejected such an absurd idea and didn't know why such a thought should have entered her mind. After all, she owed it to the baby to live. Why should she want to die anyway? The film might be a spectacular success, opening up the possibility of a screen career. She might become a famous star one day.

Of course, Franz wouldn't approve. Even before seeing *Birth of Venus*, he'd bitterly resented her appearance in the motion picture. "I share my mistress with no man, not even if it is only on the screen. Do you know what type of man goes to see films? The common, working-class type. He'll sit there and drool over you, wanting you for himself. But is that what you want? Could any *lady* want such a thing?"

Yes, a lady could want such a thing.

At two o'clock in the morning, she finally heard his touring car pull up in the driveway, and, running out to the terrace, she saw Franz storming into the main entrance, Peter trailing him. A half hour passed and still no one came to see her, then there came a light tap on her door. It surprised her. Franz never knocked, just barged right on in. But it was Peter.

The look on his face told her instantly that something was wrong. "It's Franz," he said, shaken. "He attacked that Mario creature in the theater lobby. The police were called."

"Why on earth?" she beseeched him.

"The film, Marika . . ." He seemed near tears. "It's obscene. You're completely unclothed, racing toward the camera. The camera zeroes in on you. It shows everything!"

Her screech echoed down the hallway. "That male whore lied to me! He said that part was going to be out of focus . . . like a mist."

"That's not all," he said. "The last scene shocked the audience most of all. Before the showing, this Mario had announced to the press that you were actually filmed in the act of sex. The reaction on your face dominates the whole screen."

"I could kill him," she said. "No wonder Franz attacked him!"

"Gabrielle practically had to be carried from the theater," Peter said. "She recovered, though, when she saw Mario in the lobby. He called her a broken-down old hag, and that's when Franz lunged at him."

"I must see Franz at once," she said. "Where is he?"

Peter reached to restrain her. "It's impossible."

"Why?" she demanded to know.

"He refuses to see you tonight," Peter said. "It's for your own good. You know what a violent temper he has. He would only turn on you. Right now he's on the telephone, trying to buy up every copy of that film in print, including the negative."

The door shut behind Peter, its click resounding across the bedroom. Marika stood stunned, barely able to digest Peter's words, and then she began to cry.

At eight the next morning a servant girl rapped on her door, carrying a breakfast tray and the morning newspaper. Marika's picture lay plastered across the front page, and the headline trumpeted: "VENUS GIVES BIRTH TO A RIOT!"

* * *

Two nights later, Franz invited her in for a private screening of *Birth of Venus*. He'd hardly spoken to her since returning from the premiere. Her chest ached, but she sat still through the man's boring search for his Venus, but as the film neared its final sequence, her heart began beating faster.

Franz remained in the background, the blue smoke of his cigarette drifting up in the light cast from the projector.

Briefly, she closed her eyes and when she opened them again, there she was, running nude in slow motion down the hall of mirrors. One thousand and one Marika Kreislers. The veil covered nothing. There was no mist. She was in brilliant focus, the light from the candles emitting a mellow glow that caressingly displayed her entire body.

Long before embarrassment set in, long before her fear of Franz started to overwhelm her, she basked in the perfection of her body, in viewing it as others might. Closing her eyes tightly, she tried to imagine those shining eyes that had looked upon her image at the premiere. Then the nude scene faded and the camera moved to her face for the final close-up. She gasped in astonishment at her own beauty. The screen version of herself possessed a dimension she never knew she'd owned. Her spun-silk hair fell softly against the pillow and she photographed so clean and fresh it was as if she could smell herself emerging from her own bath.

That face on the screen was like an icicle with a flame burning behind it. It was both mysterious and inscrutable, and because it had that essence of the indefinable, it was all the more alluring.

When her extravagantly long eyelashes closed sharply in a wince, she knew that was the scene where Mario had pricked her with the knife, but it was clearly, brilliantly suggestive of the first slicing pain, followed by ecstasy, of a woman giving up her virginity to the man she loves.

The film ended. Only the vacant white screen stood before her. She dared not turn around to face Franz. A dread suspicion crossed her mind now. It was that moment that comes in all dying

· 215 ·

relationships when you know you'll never be able to go back to what you had. Doors close and walls are built inside people.

Without his saying a word, she knew that Franz had assigned her to oblivion. She'd taken so many turnings, so many windings, and here was the blank wall, facing her again.

"I hope you enjoyed your moment of bliss," he said. "Apparently you did." The red glow from his cigarette was the only color in the blackness of the room. "You chose to let the world know how exciting it is to feel a man's cock tearing inside you."

She got up weakly from her chair, feeling her diamond earrings weigh on her ears. In an attempt to be alluring, she'd overdressed for the occasion. In the pale light still cast from the projector, she feared she looked grotesque standing in front of him with her big belly. "It's not what you're thinking," she protested. "Mario pricked the bottom of my foot with his knife." But he wouldn't hear a word.

In the adjoining parlor, a pair of shutters banged together in mournful concert. "You're to remain in this house," he said, with a frigid finality, "until the baby is delivered. If it's a boy, I'm to keep my son, and you're free to leave. If it's a girl, you're to go and take her with you."

He stood up and his very presence seemed overpowering. His arms and limbs were too mighty for her to fight against. He remained standing there for a brief moment in the darkness, and then suddenly he was gone, like a chilling draft. She could only imagine the coldness that must have lain in the gray eyes staring at her. Quickly she stepped away from the light of the projector. It exposed her, making her feel like a prisoner under interrogation.

Too restless to sleep, and with no place to go, she wandered alone through the château. Franz had disappeared, even Peter was gone, and no servant could be found. The more she walked through the endless rooms, the more a sense of fear began to overtake her. Would she always be building worlds to have them collapse around her?

In the study she poured herself a drink to steady her shaking hands. Only moments before she'd caught herself talking to the shadows in the empty rooms.

* * *

In her bedroom next day, the light had gone from Marika's eyes, and she only halfway paid attention to Peter.

"Listen to this," he said, holding a Viennese newspaper in front of him. "The U.S. marshal in New York has burned a copy of *Birth of Venus*. The Treasury Department said your appearance in the film was 'immoral, indecent, and an attempt to corrupt youth.' "

"Please, Peter," she said, "I don't want to hear it now."

Gabrielle would be arriving shortly and she knew she had some decisions to make. She'd had a dream last night of being adrift on the sea. She didn't know where she was going—only where she'd been—and none of it pleased her. She'd been a coward, allowing other people to make her decisions, determine her life. "I've got to put a stop to that," she said to herself.

As soon as she had her baby, she would be ready for freedom. Too many years had already gone by. Perhaps she didn't have all that many years left—but she planned to use the time remaining to its fullest.

The first hour with Gabrielle was strained, filled with polite conversation, but after she'd had a drink, Gabrielle settled back in her chair. "My darling," she said, "you've traveled far this past year. You've managed to turn yourself from a plain, fat woman into one of the most stunning creatures we've seen in this city— and we've known some beauties here. You've captured the most desirable man in Europe and are pregnant with his child. And in one film appearance, you've managed to become the most scandalous actress in all of Europe. Now, that's accomplishment!"

"Very dubious accomplishment if you ask me," Marika said. "At least some of it."

"Let's face the facts," Gabrielle replied. "It appears you've lost Franz—and your child, too—and you've tossed away any chance you'll ever have of being taken seriously as an actress."

"That's putting it bluntly."

"Of course," Gabrielle said, taking another sip from her drink. The conversation was obviously painful to her. "After seeing *Birth of Venus*, I know now why you and Mario lingered so long at Carlsbad. You were lovers."

Marika started to protest, and the blood rushed to her face.

"Don't!" Gabrielle said. "I know it. I'm an old lady, but not a stupid, senile one. I'm not shocked, really. The only problem is, I

· 217 ·

can't take you back in my house when Franz kicks you out."

"Why not?"

"In the four or five productive years remaining to me, I plan to take on four or five new lovers. Yes, it's true. But I don't want you around to remind them constantly of what they're missing. I don't want them making love to me while fantasizing about you."

"But . . ."

"No buts," Gabrielle said. "These days I'm settling for counterfeit love anyway, so things are bad enough."

"I think all love is counterfeit anyway."

"Perhaps you're right," Gabrielle said. "The only reason I take on new lovers is to conceal the fact that I *must* die someday—and that day is nearer than it is far away."

"In about twenty years," Marika said, "I'll be in the same position."

"It's inevitable," Gabrielle agreed. "I've been deluding myself, but I can't afford to abandon my delusion. I simply don't have anything to replace it with."

"What on earth do you mean?"

"I thought if I looked young, kept my shape, stayed well groomed, like I do, discovered some new skin cream, some new diet, found a lover a little younger and handsomer than the one before, one who could penetrate a little deeper, who could give me a more thrilling orgasm with more frequency, who could lie more skillfully about how much he loved me, that I could go on forever." She sighed. "Naturally, that's a ridiculous premise, but I'm caught up in it and must learn to live with it."

"I understand," Marika said, reaching for her hand. "I've found it easier to fantasize about love than experience it."

"We all do."

Marika opened a window because the air in the room was stifling. A smell of wet leaves, of something burning, assailed her nostrils. After the baby, could she put on a different body, another facial mask, lead another life?

"Peter has told me of Franz's demands about the child," Gabrielle said. "If it's a boy, you leave it here. But if it's a girl, I'll take care of it. I'll even pass it off as my own. I certainly will never admit to having a great-granddaughter."

"But where will I go?"

"Take the jewelry Franz has given you," she said. "He owes you that at least. Go to some new city, like Paris, even America. Start over again. Get your own apartment. Stop being a satellite to more powerful figures, such as Franz or me. To be your own person, you have to have your own place."

Even before Gabrielle had finished talking, Marika had made up her mind. She was going back to Berlin.

"You're beautiful," Gabrielle continued. "No one really knows how old you are, except me, and it's not likely I'll ever tell. You're even notorious at this point. But in a world where publicity is all, even notoriety is a start. You can build on that. Many rich, charming, and very captivating men are waiting out there to meet the nude star of *Birth of Venus.* At least they'll know what you look like without your clothes."

Marika's head was already spinning with thoughts of her new life. She'd find her Papa again, and perhaps forgive him. Friedrich was surely down and out at this point, that is, if he were still alive. Maybe she could buy back their old town house! The only difference now would be that *she* would be the mistress of the household. Friedrich would have to take his orders from her.

* * *

As her stomach grew larger, the days of pregnancy stretched out endlessly, and the nights became haunted with dreams of her stillbirth in Warsaw. She felt no love for the child stirring within her. She didn't dare to. She knew she would be separated from it as soon as it was born, and she was too beaten at this point to resist. The baby didn't belong to her, would never belong to her. After the baby was pulled from her womb, Franz would claim it like a piece of property.

"I can't imagine why Franz would even want to be a father," Peter said one day.

"Very simple," she replied with a wintry smile. "He knows he's going to die one day, and he wants to mold a copy of himself. It's not the child he's interested in. It's his own ego."

Once, when drinking heavily, she was seriously tempted to fall down the marble steps and hope for a miscarriage. It would save the boy from Franz's designs. By what act of irresponsibility could she bring a helpless boy into the world to become a victim of Franz's influence? The boy would never know love, compassion, understanding. He'd be taught to survive, to be ruthless, to be self-seeking in all his pursuits, like Franz himself.

But she never took that fall. The child moved and kicked intermittently inside her, and she felt she owed it to the boy to give him life. Maybe that life would turn out better than she feared—after all, Franz could give him many advantages that she could not. Perhaps he'd even be strong enough to resist Franz and become his own man one day. She felt totally inadequate to be a mother anyway.

"Stop being so morbid," Peter told her. "If you have a responsibility, it is to yourself. You must get on with the business of your own life. It is you, Marika Kreisler, who has lingered too long in the womb."

Her mind heavy with dreams she could barely fathom, she realized how much her actions were like those of her own mother. Lotte had abandoned her on the day of her birth, leaving her in the care of a severe father. Now, thirty years later, she was doing the same thing. But there was one important difference. Lotte had died giving birth. Marika was determined to live.

On the night of the delivery, she found herself in the room Franz had ordered prepared for his son, a room bold and masculine in design, spartan in every particular. The boy would not be spoiled by luxuries. The impending suffocation of her own child made her want to scream, but she could not find her voice.

The baby—she could never bring herself to call it "my baby" —came out of her shortly after midnight. The slippery mass that moved through her turned out to be a boy, as she'd known it would be, weighing only five pounds, its hair a bright red. It was an ugly, distorted little piece of humanity, so pathetic. How could such a small creature grow up to become a munitions king, to rule an empire, to make war?

The nurse assured her it was healthy in every respect and that relieved her, since she was certain Franz would tolerate no deformity, but now she knew her duty was at an end. When the nurse cooed about what a lovely baby it was, Marika cried out, all the pain of the last months finally finding full voice in her despair.

"It's not mine! Take it away!"

The baby was wheeled from the room, and she was left alone

to face the dead moonlight streaming in. In a far corner a nurse sat drowsing, a weak sentinel waiting for the new day.

* * *

With Peter at her side, Marika raced down the platform at the railway station. "You've got everything—you're sure?" she asked.

"Working for Franz these past few years has made me more than efficient," he said.

The conductor checked her tickets, then looked into her face. "You're the Venus woman, aren't you?"

Marika nodded in embarrassment.

Handing her a piece of paper, he asked, "Could you autograph this? For my wife, of course."

"Of course," she said, hastily scribbling her name. No one had ever asked for her autograph before.

In her private compartment, she turned to Peter. "This is good-bye," she said. "Thank you for all you've done for me. I'll miss you."

"No, you won't," he said, smiling. "I'm coming with you. Submitted my resignation just this morning."

"I don't believe it," she said, overjoyed, reaching for his hand and kissing him on the cheek. Maybe away from Franz, Peter would reveal his true feelings for her!

"This is a perfect opportunity for me," he continued enthusiastically. "I've been planning it for weeks. I can be with you, and, besides," he confided, "I have a lover in Berlin. Yes! It happened just in the past two months. That's why I've been away on so many long weekends."

Marika felt crestfallen, but managed to say, "I'm happy for you . . . for both of you."

Just then a knock on the door of her compartment made her turn around quickly. It was a boy with a large bouquet of flowers.

"How wonderful!" she said. "Who could have sent them? Surely not Franz."

"I sent them."

"But why?"

"*Liebchen,* you're a star!"

Chapter 7

Berlin—1930. The Wall Street crash had pulled out the props from German prosperity, and everywhere people jammed the banks. The greeting, *"Heil Hitler,"* was now heard among the party faithful, and in the streets of Berlin, Nazi storm troopers battled Communists. Blackmail and mayhem prevailed.

Early on the morning of February 8, the train carrying Marika and Peter pulled into its terminal in Berlin. Peter had fallen asleep, but one hand still tightly clasped the purse containing Marika's jewelry. As she got ready to wake him, Marika looked at the soft beauty of his face, then down at the handbag he held. In it was their survival.

As a taxi took them through the almost deserted streets, her mind drifted from her son, whom Franz had named Anton, to thoughts of Friedrich and Brigitte. Were they still living in Berlin? As lovers? Or were they beyond that at this point? Even dead?

There were too many questions for her fogged mind to explore at this hour. "Where are we going?" she asked Peter. "The Savoy, I assume. You never told me what arrangements you'd made."

"Wrong," Peter said. "My lover has a large apartment. We're staying there."

As the taxi drew up in front of a small town house, Peter paid the driver and jumped out into the snow, reaching back to help her. Marika pulled her white sable coat around her neck to fend off the chilling wind and stepped over the dirty snow, climbing the stoop to the door.

Peter had his own key. Inside the ground-floor apartment the small parlor was dark. "I'll light a fire," he said, flipping on a lamp. "Make yourself comfortable." When the fire was blazing, he disappeared down the hallway and into a bedroom, shutting the door quietly behind him.

Removing her coat, Marika warmed herself before the fire and started petting a large Siamese cat that had jumped up on her lap. Stroking it gently, she felt the cat's deep purring vibrate through her body, setting her at ease. Abruptly, a man in a satin dressing robe stood before her. "Good morning," he said. "I'm Wolfgang. Peter's told me so much about you. I just *loved* your film."

She gave him a startled look, then smiled with a good will she was too tired to feel. Who was this man? If anything, he was practically a copy of Peter. About the same age, he was built solidly, with broad shoulders. He, too, had long blond hair and light blue, playful eyes. The only departure from his perfect features was a tiny V-shaped scar on his forehead.

"I'm delighted to meet you," she said. "Only sorry that we woke you up. Is Peter with his friend?"

At this point Peter emerged from the kitchen carrying a tray with coffee and cups. He set it down on the table in front of her. "I certainly am with my friend, and I'm not going to let him out of my sight from now on." She stared in amazement, as Wolfgang winked and patted Peter affectionately on the cheek.

In her nervousness and embarrassment, Marika lifted the cat from her coat, placing him gently on the floor. The two men sat down on the carpet in front of her, the fire behind them. Peter poured the coffee, handing the first cup to Wolfgang.

"Now, now," Wolfgang said, sliding the cup over to Marika. "Peter, your manners are shocking. Don't you know you're supposed to serve the lady first?"

Peter reached for Wolfgang's ear, tugging at it lightly. "Not always, my darling man."

* * *

Three months passed before Peter secured the title of Friedrich's former town house for Marika. The house was in very bad condition, having served as a headquarters for processing refugees after the war, and then lying vacant for many years. As Marika wandered through the rooms she'd known as a girl, she found not one piece of the original furniture remaining. Even the fireplaces and mirrors had been damaged. Records of long-forgotten people —the displaced of the war—lay piled in every corner.

"I think I'm going to move in," she announced to Peter. "I'm beginning to feel like a third leg living with you and Wolfgang. You fellows really know how to make a woman feel useless."

"But the house has to be glamorous for you," he said. "I'll have to sell far more jewelry. If you're going to entertain producers, it's got to be in a setting of crystal and satin."

For a long time, Marika gazed at the study where Friedrich had confronted them with the news that he was penniless. "I want vibrant, happy colors—rose-pink, lemon-yellow. There are a lot of ghosts in this house that we've got to chase away."

"A center for displaced persons," Peter said. "From what little you've told me of your life, it sounds very appropriate."

Back at Wolfgang's apartment, Marika summoned her courage. She had to call Brigitte, an encounter she'd been postponing ever since she'd arrived in Berlin. It was hard to cross the bridge into her past, but she couldn't live another day not knowing if her Papa was alive or dead.

She heard the telephone ring at the other end, and then a woman's voice answered. "Miss Kreisler's residence."

It was the same apartment. Her aunt had never moved. Marika identified herself as Brigitte's niece, and after a long delay, Brigitte came to the phone. "Marika, is it really you?" she asked. "It's been a long time."

"Yes, I know."

"But I've read about you . . . only recently in the newspapers," Brigitte said.

Visions of her nudity flashed before Marika. "That was a misunderstanding," she said. "The producer tricked me."

"I'm sure he did, my dear."

Marika began pacing back and forth in front of the marble telephone table. Only a few seconds talking to her aunt, and already she was defending herself! Evening had silvered the windows, and Marika switched on a lamp, bathing the apartment in a moth-yellow light. Finally, she was able to ask the question she'd held inside for so long. "How's Papa?"

Brigitte's voice was cold and quick. "He's been dead for six years."

Marika's gasp was so small she hardly heard it herself, but the sound seemed to come from deep in her throat.

"After Lille," Brigitte said, "he was never himself again. His spirit died, and in his final years he was just a vegetable. *I* was the only one he had."

Her eyes glazed, unable to focus, Marika bent over the telephone table as if drunk. "I'm sorry," she managed to say. "Sorry he died. Sorry he sent me away as he did. Sorry everything went wrong."

"And *well* you should be."

Marika clutched the receiver, her eyes full of tears. "But I'm not to blame. All of us did the best we could, the best we knew at the time."

"I'm agreeable to comforting ourselves with that optimistic appraisal of our past," Brigitte said. "Perhaps we should meet for tea tomorrow at four."

"Perhaps," Marika answered vaguely.

* * *

When Marika arrived, Brigitte was lounging on the sofa in a black silk dress, a double strand of perfect pearls around her elegant, aging throat. She'd abandoned the wearing of makeup. Without her usual cosmetic mask, the strength and candor of her face lay clearly revealed and her magnetism seemed to fill the parlor.

"My acting career is no longer paramount to me," she announced to Marika. "Regardless of how bountiful our vitality, a younger, more sensation-seeking and, in your case, more dazzlingly attractive version of ourselves is always waiting to replace us."

With great discipline, Marika seated herself in a chair. She was determined not to allow her aunt to treat her like a little girl anymore, but staring at this monument to dogged determination, she found her carefully rehearsed speeches vanishing.

"I've had to fill these empty years with something," Brigitte said. "I live now for my political party and for Germany. One day my party will become Germany."

"That sounds pretty desolate to me," Marika said.

"I'm sure it does," Brigitte said, "but then you always were a weak-willed girl."

"I'm not weak-willed at all," Marika cried, rising defensively from her chair. "I cannot allow you to put me down anymore. Either you accept me as a fully grown person, or I'll leave."

"For heaven's sake," Brigitte said, "sit down. You've always been much too sensitive to the slightest criticism. That characteristic will only lead to heartbreak." She paused, opening her almond-shaped eyes all the wider. "If it hasn't already."

"It has!" Marika blurted out. "More times than I care to remember." Undecided, she returned to her chair.

"The major thing that has troubled me about you . . ." Brigitte said, her voice drifting off. "The Jewish question." After a brief silence, she resumed her natural voice. "I have finally resolved the issue in my own mind. For that reason, I think we can be friends."

With sarcasm, Marika asked, "And just how did you do that?"

"Very simply," Brigitte said. "As I look at you now, I see you're the finest example of Aryan woman, the almost perfect physical manifestation of those with whom we want one day to fill the entire country. The day will eventually come when all impurities have been eliminated."

"You talk about people as if they could be eliminated the way one does a bowel movement," Marika said, her face hardening.

"Please don't be foul-mouthed," Brigitte said. "What I mean is this: Friedrich's genes overpowered those of Lotte. The Jewish side of her was subjugated. That's why you became, in fact, the embodiment of Prussian femininity. Our power can absorb the weak and wipe it out. Lotte was merely a vessel that carried you —nothing else. You are Friedrich's child, completely, thoroughly, and forever."

"I find this completely unbelievable," Marika said. "Let me tell you this, Brigitte, I've come to live with my Jewish background, particularly after staying with Gabrielle. It no longer disturbs me. She's quite a lady."

"Because of my present political activity," Brigitte said, "I'm even more reluctant to call attention to even the slightest connection I might have had with a Jewish family. As you'll soon see."

"I won't embarrass you," Marika said.

"That's good." Brigitte rose from the sofa and stood rigidly. "In fact, imperative."

Marika appraised her figure. Although Brigitte's face was more heavily lined than before, her body appeared as lithe as though it were still Lille in 1916.

"I'm having a few young actresses over for tea," Brigitte said. "Also, a very special male guest whom I'm sure will be enthralled by your beauty. Stay around."

The young actresses arrived first, each one a copy of the one before. All wore creamy white dresses, the shade of their pale faces, and, like Marika, had white-yellow hair and blue eyes. Wide-brimmed hats were the fashion.

They put the same question endlessly to Marika: "How could you allow yourself to be filmed without your clothes on?" And before she could answer, always supplied the comment: "I would *never* do that myself." One woman actually used the word "nude," emphasizing it to reveal her condemnation.

Marika glanced anxiously at the clock on the mantel, desperate to leave, but awaiting the guest of honor. Finally he arrived, amid a flurry of activity in the foyer. Standing before Brigitte was a man full of nervous, crackling energy, his state one of tense excitement, as if he'd lost control of himself only moments before. His black hair lay across his forehead in the French fashion, above a moustache like those of many of the country farmers Marika had seen in Somerset. He bowed low, in the Austrian manner, kissing Brigitte's hand.

When he straightened up, Brigitte reached out, caressingly ruffling the forelock on the man's low, receding brow. *"Mein Wölfchen, mein Wölfchen,"* she said compassionately. The tense man handed her a bouquet of spring flowers and a box of chocolates, and she kissed him on both cheeks, her long fingers lovingly touching the back of his head as if it were a baby's.

Then the man stood before Marika. His nose was wide, with flaring nostrils, and she found herself staring into small magnetic eyes filled with the fire of fierce determination. It was hypnotic but repulsive at the same time. Franz's eyes had the same kind of intensity, but they were in a powerhouse of a human being. The man before her was a neuter. She didn't know what to make of him.

"This is my niece, Marika Kreisler," Brigitte said, turning with a gracious smile. "It is my pleasure to present Adolf Hitler."

Again, in his obsequious manner, he bowed and kissed her hand. Straightening up, he clicked his heels. For want of something to say, Marika was tempted to mention her friendship with Franz Hauptmann. But it seemed inappropriate to bring it up.

"Your reputation has preceded you to Berlin," Hitler said. "I was delighted that an Italian director had to turn to such a fine example of Nordic womanhood to play Botticelli's goddess of beauty." He smiled. "I'm certain that Mussolini will be very displeased."

She knew little about Hitler other than what Franz had told her, but she was shocked to realize he'd heard of her and amazed at how much notoriety the film had given her.

As Hitler moved through the room, Marika was intrigued at the reaction of the other women to this man. His manners were clumsy, and she could hardly believe the heel-clicking, yet that seemed to make him all the more appealing to these impressionable women.

Throughout the tea party, the actresses hung eagerly on Hitler's every word, but all his remarks were innocuous. He said he was enraptured at the beauty of the edelweiss at Obersalzberg. But the women listened with such passion, almost ecstasy, to this nature talk that it was as if Hitler were a visitor only recently returned from one of the lost cities of Atlantis. He did almost all of the talking, and only occasionally would Brigitte ask a discreet question if there was a lull in the conversation. Hitler seemed to treat women like adornments and paid absolutely no attention to their meek observations.

After a while, when an aide came in from the foyer and whispered something to Hitler, he rose quickly, bidding the actresses good-bye. Again, he kissed Marika's hand. "I wish you great success if you are in Berlin to continue your film career," he said. "I want Germany to turn out the world's finest motion pictures. I'm sure you'll be a shining star in our galaxy."

She thanked him, and even blushed. For some reason she found his attention embarrassing.

After the actresses had filed out, half an hour later, Marika turned to Brigitte. "I had no idea you knew this Bavarian rabble-rouser."

Brigitte's eyes instantly flared with anger. "How dare you speak of him in such a way! Whether or not you have the perception to realize it, you were in the presence of a great man."

Marika smiled condescendingly. In her opinion, a man had to be an artist like Richard Tauber to be great.

"He will save Germany," Brigitte went on, her eyes alive with the same fierce determination as Hitler's. "I was one of his early supporters, and he always acknowledges that. I still pay half of my yearly income to the cause. I'm devoted to the man." She seemed to utter a cry, but it was stifled in her throat. "Sometimes he calls me his 'Mummy.'" Her hands gripped her teacup. "Since I've known him, no birthday, no Christmas has ever passed that he didn't acknowledge. If he's in the city, he always comes to see me."

Marika looked at her quickly, dismissing Hitler with a shrug of her shoulders. "I'm sure he's devoted to you." She couldn't understand Brigitte's passion.

"The man is pure," Brigitte said.

Marika was struck by the odd use of the word. She'd never heard a man called that before.

"He can't give himself to one single woman," Brigitte continued. "He belongs to all of us. He is the husband of Germany, and we are his brides."

Marika's eyes widened. "That sounds like a group of nuns talking about Christ."

"Your comparison is apt," Brigitte said, placing her cup on the table with firmness and precision. "He's the coming Messiah."

Marika rose from her chair and stood defiantly, looking at Brigitte with a grim expression. "I'm not interested in your Hitler or your future Germany. I'm here to launch my film career. That is all that's important to me right now."

Brigitte got up stiffly. "I see I'm not going to convert you to our cause," she said. "You always were a selfish girl, totally blind to anything in the world that didn't affect you directly."

Marika's chest constricted with anger. "That is your opinion,

I'm sure." She made an attempt to control the harshness in her voice. "I choose to live my own life as I see fit. If what I do offends you, I'm sorry. But I don't plan to change."

"I see," Brigitte said, a nervous quiver appearing under her left eye. "When I received your call, I thought . . ." She paused, wetting her lips. "I thought you had grown as a person."

Rage gathered in Marika and she looked longingly at the foyer, wanting to leave.

"You're the same daydreaming girl you always were," Brigitte continued, "the same girl Friedrich rescued from Warsaw."

But now she was talking to Marika's back. "You're entitled to think what you wish of me," Marika said, checking her makeup in the mirror and reaching for her coat. "I really must go." She felt strangely disturbed, wanting to say more than she had. She'd come here for some specific reason, and it hadn't been fulfilled. "If you wish to get in touch with me, I'm at Friedrich's town house. It is mine now."

Brigitte gasped. When she spoke, she did so with barely contained violence. "You, mistress of his house?" Her words seemed an accusation. "You're not even worthy to be his daughter!"

A silence filled the foyer. Nothing had given Marika warning that such an attack was coming and she turned on Brigitte, her rage boiling over. Now she knew why she'd come to visit her aunt. She had wanted to confront her with some long overdue truths. "You sound as if Friedrich were a great man," she accused. "Nothing could be further from the truth. He was magnificent only in your eyes." She ran her hands through her hair, then held her head. It gave her courage to say what she was about to say. *"And that was because you were in love with him."*

Brigitte stepped back, as if trying to push Marika away from her, then, grasping one of her wrists tightly, seemed to fall against the banister.

"That's why you never married," Marika went on. She couldn't stop talking. "When Friedrich lost his leg, you moved in on him. Until then, he'd been able to resist your attentions, but you turned the relationship into an incestuous one." She thrust her hands into her pockets. She couldn't bear to look at the woman. "The guilt that followed what you did killed Friedrich more than any disappointment I ever caused him."

"You liar!" Brigitte shouted.

Marika looked into her aunt's face, a twisted, contorted mask temporarily covered with a veil of lunacy. She knew her words had destroyed Brigitte in front of her eyes, but it was too late to withdraw them. In blind fury, Brigitte was upon her, slapping Marika's face, the sound seeming to bounce off the walls. Quickly, Marika ducked Brigitte's blows and, throwing open the door, raced down the steps into the night. For one moment, she was tempted to look back at the apartment house where she'd spent so many unhappy months. But it was a temptation she knew instinctively to resist.

* * *

When Marika arrived home, Peter was at the door, waving a letter at her. "Listen to this! You're to report to UFA first thing tomorrow morning," he said. "You're going to be tested for the role of Flame in *Carnival!*"

Still flustered from her confrontation with Brigitte, Marika tried to bring herself under control. She knew the director, Walter von Menzel, had been conducting a widely publicized search for an actress to appear as the erotic dancer, the wicked tramp, in a novel that had swept postwar Berlin. And now he wanted to see her? "How did you arrange for the test?" she asked carefully, taking off her hat.

"It was easy," Peter said. "I got in touch with von Menzel's assistant and told him the star of *Birth of Venus* would possibly submit to a test if the conditions were favorable."

"Just like that?" she asked, removing her coat. She didn't dare hope for the part. She tried valiantly to hold back her enthusiasm; excitement at this point could only lead to disappointment. "I read only the other day," she said, "that Lucie Mannheim has practically been signed for the part. So why would UFA want to test me?"

"Could it be that von Menzel isn't completely satisfied with Mannheim?"

"Apparently, von Menzel is such a dilettante he isn't satisfied with anything." She waved Peter away. "Besides, I could never play a cheap woman like Flame."

Peter's face seemed to burn with anger, like a little boy who was not getting the approval he expected. "An *actress* can do anything," he said sarcastically, turning his back to her and walking away.

His words stung her. For a long moment she stood alone in the hall, not knowing what to do. She'd been unkind to Peter and was sorry for that. But the whole day—the meeting with Hitler, the confrontation with Brigitte—had been more than she could handle. Clenching her fists tightly in determination, she decided she'd make the test, for Peter's sake. But it all seemed so hopeless. Besides, she'd heard that von Menzel was a lunatic.

* * *

Alone in von Menzel's private office, Marika realized she was terrified. This man wasn't Mario. Von Menzel would be far more demanding—what if she couldn't deliver what he wanted?

The whole room was a gallery commemorating his past. A Hungarian saber hung over his desk, and an old army pistol seemed to have been converted into a cigarette lighter. Decorating the walls were photographs of von Menzel in some of his most memorable screen portrayals before he'd become a director. During World War I, von Menzel was cast again and again in American films in the role of a brutal Prussian commander, and patriotic audiences had grown to hate the Hun through the character he played with such devastating caricature. She noted one picture of him in particular, in which he was leering at an attractive Red Cross nurse through his monocle.

From every direction images of his dueling scar, his cropped head and bull neck confronted her. She could only conclude that the man was a beast.

When von Menzel himself entered the office, he wasn't at all what she had expected. A tall man in his late thirties, dressed in baggy jacket and trousers, he had long blond hair and limpid blue eyes. His large body seemed to convey a mixture of softness and massive strength. Although his face was rugged, she noticed that his mouth was surprisingly childlike. The only thing that seemed to fit her image of him was his posture, as rigid as a soldier's, and the cane he grasped firmly in his hand like a sword.

He reached to shake her hand after she'd introduced herself. The director had the most beautiful hands she'd ever seen—a masculine version of Brigitte's. His palms were broad and heavy, but his fingers were long and sensitive, the hands of an artist. He

· 232 ·

still wore the monocle he'd made famous in his pictures. It underscored his aloofness, but it was merely window dressing, like the scar, an attempt to disguise the fact that he was an elegantly handsome, almost pretty, man.

A vision of him flashed in front of her eyes. She saw him riding nude with her on a white horse across spring fields overrun with wild flowers. At the edge of a meadow, he lifted her from the horse and raced with her to the river for a swim. But then the scene vanished. Von Menzel would never do that. Any similarity to the free, soaring spirit she had just conjured up was carefully, almost ingeniously, concealed in a disguise of his own creation.

She realized with a blush that he was scrutinizing her, and only hoped he wasn't a mind reader. "Do you want me to walk around the room and show you my legs?" she asked in embarrassment at the prolonged silence.

"Fräulein Kreisler," he said in a well-modulated voice, "apparently your introduction to films has taught you that all an actress need do to be successful is to show flesh."

She resented his words, but she was getting used to insults about her appearance in *Birth of Venus.*

"With me," he said, "you are dealing with an entirely different director—not some Italian gigolo who doesn't know the first thing about films. I find clothes—not just any clothes, but a particular kind of dress—far more alluring on a woman than total nudity."

"That certainly tells me what you think of my film debut."

"Yes," he said. "Actually, I've never seen the picture and don't intend to. For the role of Flame, I plan to create a woman who's never existed in the cinema before."

"Could I play the part?" she asked tentatively. His eyes were as penetrating, as unmasking, as those of Count Dabrowsky and Franz Hauptmann. "I think I can act."

"Don't sell yourself to me," he said, fingering his pistol lighter. He lit a cigarette and continued to study her closely. "At this point I'm not interested in whether you can act or not. If you're the woman I'm seeking, and I'm not at all certain you are, I will create you. But I'm not God. I need some basic raw material for Flame. And, Fräulein Kreisler, it appears that God has given you an overabundance of basic raw material. The shaping of that material is the artist's job. *I* am the artist."

"You don't want an actress, then," she charged, slightly insulted at his remarks. "You want a mannequin."

He blew out smoke. "Exactly!"

* * *

The sound stage was a barn, like a huge, padded airplane hangar, but to Marika, its vastness was a comfort. Neither day nor night existed. You could create your own world. If you wanted sunshine, you could make it happen. If you wanted rain or spring flowers or the winter's snow, you could have that, too. For more than half an hour, she wandered alone in a maze of catwalks and girders, the sound of her heels creating echoes in the vast hall. Cowled lamps were brilliant white stars shining down on a make-believe world.

Suddenly the lights went on upon a single set far away, illuminating a huge white photographic backdrop. Walking toward it as to a medieval shrine, she felt like a wandering pilgrim, come to worship. As she neared the lighted set, a cameraman overhead turned a spot on her. She blinked at first, then opened her eyes wide, feeling her eyes sparkle in the glare.

"My God in heaven!" a man's voice cried from above. "It's not possible. Marika Kreisler, the most beautiful girl I've ever photographed. A woman now."

She stepped out of the spotlight and stared at the little man with the glistening bald head who was moving toward her on too short legs. He seemed vaguely familiar.

"I'm Hermann Goetz," he said. "Surely you remember me."

She remained silent.

"I've never been able to put your luminous quality out of my mind," he said.

"No . . . I'm sorry, I don't recall . . ." she answered hesitantly.

"Court photographer," he said. "Awards from ruling sovereigns and princes."

Abruptly, visions of sitting for her first photograph flashed through her mind. "Oh, now I *do* remember."

"Your Contessa friend ordered only two prints," he said. "One she had me send to Warsaw. The other she never picked up, and it remains one of my most treasured possessions."

"If I know the Contessa," she said, "you probably were never paid."

· 234 ·

"You're right," he replied, "but it was a labor of love."

"That photograph," she said, a sense of nervousness sweeping through her, "I must have it." She paused in embarrassment. "No one in Berlin, except my aunt, knows my exact age. But you have a very good idea."

"Your age is a secret that will never pass my lips," he said. "It's exciting to share a secret with Marika Kreisler. Besides, you're ageless."

"Thank you for reassuring me," she said. "I hope von Menzel agrees. I'm afraid to face all these lights. They're so revealing."

"Don't be afraid," he said, taking her hand. "Everything will work out. I'll be here to protect you. You see, I do lighting for von Menzel. He's a devout believer in lighting, as you'll soon see."

"I feel I can trust you," she said, squeezing his hand. It was as if she were entering into a conspiracy. "I must have that photograph. It is all that I have to remind me of my past." She smiled sardonically. "Except my memories."

At this point, von Menzel boldly strode into the studio, as if he were about to direct a crew filming an epic adventure. He positioned her like a dummy in front of the backdrop.

"The floor light," he called out to Hermann in a commanding voice, walking over to the lamp as it was switched on. He pushed it forward toward Marika. "Raise it a little higher."

They were both staring at her now, Hermann through his finder, von Menzel through his monocle. Their gazes were intent, powerful, they seemed to probe into her very soul, and suddenly all of Marika's doubts returned to her in a rush. But she had no time for them. "The back light now," von Menzel ordered.

Hermann climbed a ladder to an overhead structure and another lamp went on. Marika closed her eyes. "The baby spot," von Menzel called to Hermann. "Make that golden hair hot—real hot!" Standing in front of her, von Menzel adjusted her head. His long slender fingers made her tingle, but when she looked into his eyes, she stiffened at their harshness. "My dear Fräulein," he said, "the trick is not to veil your eyes as if giving birth to a calf. Bovine actresses don't interest me."

Her face turned red. Wouldn't anything please this man?

"We'll need a black gauze," he now called up to Hermann, turning his back to her momentarily, then going over to the viewfinder, "It's still not right. Raise the flag higher. No, no, stop! It's wrong. Forget the Goddamn flag. I told you to heat her head. I mean really hot. Don't you understand what I say?"

Hermann adjusted the back light and von Menzel walked up to Marika again, his voice patient but firm. "Lower your head ever so slightly. *Please,* relax."

For what seemed like forever, von Menzel continued to make adjustments. Some were so minor it seemed to her a waste of time. She didn't need to view the finished product to tell how she looked. When the filming began, he never took his eyes off her, not for one moment. He controlled every gesture, bellowing instructions, exerting some hypnotic power over her. No man—Franz Hauptmann, Papa—had ever controlled her with such complete authority. She was at peace now, as she moved deeper into this world of fantasy.

He pursed his lips, and she moved hers in imitation of him. He wanted her face cold, like marble, and her features instantly froze. He wanted animation, and she did everything he asked. "The forehead," he kept saying to Hermann. "We must not forget that." His hands gave signals to her that went far beyond the power of his voice. Those hands rose and fell. They hung dejectedly by his side when she failed him, but they sprang up again, full of power and beauty, when she reached the pinnacle of his dream. "The cheekbones," he said. "We'll photograph them like the finest pair ever made."

Hermann adjusted a light and von Menzel shot him a look, challenging him, then slowly released the tension in his face. "I know what you're doing," he said with a wry smile. "You're showing me you know more about lighting than I do. You've produced a short nose shadow—perfect! I bow to your superior ability. Now, put the hot light right on her chin—such a noble chin—and we'll try it again."

At the end of the shooting, when the lights had dimmed, a deafening silence filled the sound stage. Marika waited for a look, a sound, anything which meant approval, but she got nothing. Both men were staring at her intently, and she wanted to run and cry at her failure.

"But you didn't give me a chance to act," she protested. "I didn't get to do anything. Just stand and look like a dummy." Tears welled up in her eyes. "I thought you'd want me to say something, maybe sing a little song. I think we should have done *something.*"

"My darling," he finally said in a soothing yet slightly forlorn voice, "you do not realize what has happened." His eyes traveled up to Hermann, who sat in total silence. "Goetz knows."

"What do you mean?" she asked petulantly.

"We have just lived through an historic moment," he said. "If the oceans churned for a thousand years, they could create nothing more spectacular than what I've been able to do today." He extended his long fingers in the air. "I have just created a cinematic face that will beguile the world."

* * *

That night von Menzel invited her on a night crawl of Berlin. "You see," he said, taking her hand, "even though I call the picture *Carnival,* it's not a real carnival I'm after."

Marika gently withdrew her hand. It indicated a possessiveness that she wasn't at all certain she liked. She'd had enough of that with Franz Hauptmann.

"The carnival I seek is all around us in Berlin tonight," he said.

He then broke away from her and ran into the street, almost getting hit by a passing car. "Step right up, my good people," he yelled at the passersby. "See our star attraction, the tattooed lady." In a flamboyant gesture, he pointed to Marika. Two old women with shopping bags gave her a quick glance, then passed on their way in disdain.

"You're crazy," she yelled, running up to him. "You know that, don't you? People always say you're crazy, and now I believe it."

He laughed at her words, and his humor was contagious. "The snake charmers, the anatomical grotesques, the bearded breasts of the ladies, the crocodile men, the geeks, the fat Fräuleins—all are here in this mad Berlin. Even the Nazis will soon be making us swallow their swords."

Down a dark alley teeming with prostitutes and beggars, he took her to a dimly lit café, its doorway illuminated only by a red light bulb. She entered, passing a long, baroque bar with marble-topped tables, and was shocked to see a woman, no longer young, openly displaying her breasts to prospective customers. At another table, a woman removed a powder puff that Marika had mistaken for her breast. It turned out to be a young man. He powdered his nose and checked his makeup in a mirror.

Von Menzel was greeted by a man with bluish-black hair and six large rings on his fingers who ushered them into a circular room furnished with deep velvet ottomans, gazelle horns, Oriental carpets, and velours hangings. The cushions on the floor evoked an Arabian nights fantasy. Sprawled about were men and women in various states of undress.

Taking her hand again, von Menzel lowered Marika onto a large red cushion. Very well, she thought, if this was the style, she was determined to comply. Lowering her eyelids, she kept them languorous and perpetually half closed, as if she were drugged and bored.

At the adjoining booth a large Turk drew a cigarette from a gold case and a waiter hurried over, bowed low in front of him, and lit it. The Turk was surrounded by a bevy of pretty boys, some of whom had powdered their faces a pearly gray, who were hanging on their patron's every word.

"The man is addicted to pederasty," von Menzel said. "Because he's important in his own country, he cannot indulge his passions there. The filth of the world descends on Berlin. In this city, everything is possible."

The lights dimmed, indicating that the evening's performance was about to begin. Marika expected to witness an orgy, but when the overhead spot sprang on, she was surprised to see a short woman with large eyes and an aquiline nose standing before her. The performer had only a slit of a mouth, but she'd painted it turkey-red, extending it far beyond her lip line. Her orange-red hair was piled high above her wrinkled face, her drooping bare shoulders bore a greenish tinge, the same color as her eyeshadow, and she wore a feather boa around her neck to match her hair. Her worn, wrinkled dress looked as if it would fall from her shoulders at a moment's notice, its purple blackness radiating a funereal aura.

When she sang—of brandy, laughter, and green moons—Marika was shocked at her voice. Even though it had a slight Viennese lilt, it somehow seemed to embody the gaiety of Berlin, and also its squalor, waste, emptiness, and brutality. The voice was a soprano, but a tart one, like a bittersweet lemon—defiant and bold, a sound more for the back row of the darkest theater than for intimate cabaret. The diction, clear at all times, would suddenly become garishly daring, seeming to scream at and mock the people in the room. Marika caught a glimpse of a big-bellied man in the far corner seducing and nearly suffocating a tiny Oriental girl who supported his enormous bulk.

Marika found herself caught up in the spell cast by the chanteuse. It seemed that to live, one must sing. Somehow the performer's voice seemed to enter her own body. The witchlike figure sang of smoking cigars and blue seas, and Marika was completely carried away. She leaned her head closer and looked deeply into the face of the singer.

Between numbers, von Menzel whispered to Marika, "She's the greatest artist in Berlin. Unfortunately, she's an addict. It has destroyed her career and will soon destroy her."

Marika was disappointed at this news. She didn't want von Menzel to bring her back to reality; she wanted only the sweet illusions the woman created.

At the end of the performance, the singer came over to their table, and von Menzel introduced her as Hilde Harsch. "This is Marika Kreisler," he said. "She's going to sing two songs in my next picture."

Marika was stunned. This was the first time he'd told her she had the part.

Caressing Hilde's arm, von Menzel said, "I want Marika to sing those songs exactly like you do. You must teach her."

The old woman's eyes lit up as she took Marika's hand, and the red mouth clamped down on two of Marika's fingers. Her tongue shot out like a serpent's, licking the salt and oil from Marika's skin. Marika sat there stupefied. She didn't know what to do.

"For this beautiful creature," Hilde said, "there will be no fee."

Von Menzel rescued Marika's fingers. "Yes, there will," he said. "This is strictly a professional arrangement."

Marika swallowed hard. Hilde had stilled the air to make it ready to carry the waves of her songs, but when she spoke, when she became herself, the mood was gone. What emerged was a woman as corrupt and strident as the world she satirized.

"That is too bad," Hilde said, not taking her eyes off Marika. "I could take a woman like this where none of you silly men could ever take her." She raised her eyes. "To celestial delights."

Marika blushed and tried to cover her embarrassment. To be treated so openly like a piece of flesh was devastating to her.

"You've certainly had the experience," von Menzel said to Hilde. "But use your lips and tongue to teach your own special song—not to make depraved love."

"Ha!" Hilde said. "You call me depraved. Look around you."

As if to confirm Hilde's words, Marika stared at the Turk. He seemed to be sucking the tongue out of the head of one of his little boys.

After arrangements were made for voice lessons, Marika turned to von Menzel. The room seemed to be threatening her now, and her hands were shaking. "Everybody in this filthy place seems addicted to something. What is your passion?"

"You!" he said, to her surprise. "From this day forth, I'm determined to make a star out of you, and this will require all my creative juice, all my passion—and all my hours."

* * *

Peter attended the screening of her test the next morning, but Marika didn't go. In fact, she wasn't invited. She did everything possible to distract herself from what must be going on in that projection room, and finally, when she felt she could not stand it for one moment longer, she heard Peter enter the front door. The moment she looked into his sad eyes, she knew she'd lost the part. A sense of betrayal swept over her. Von Menzel had practically promised her the role!

"It's going to be Mannheim," he announced. "Everybody wants her. Everybody but von Menzel. Who knows what that sphinx thinks? He was silent while everyone raved about Mannheim's test."

"But what about me?" she asked angrily.

"You photographed fantastically," he said. "But you didn't do too much on camera. Mannheim had this big tearjerker that won everyone's heart."

In rage and disappointment, she rushed to her room and threw herself on her bed. She was starting to weep when the telephone rang beside her.

"You are going to burn as my Flame," von Menzel whispered as she put the receiver to her ear.

"But . . . Peter said . . . Mannheim."

· 240 ·

"Forget that. I can cast the role as I see fit," he said. "The announcement has already gone out. Your picture will appear on the front pages tomorrow morning. The year-long search for Flame is over."

"I don't believe it."

"Believe, Marika," he said, "and trust in me completely. Shooting begins in two weeks. You've got to learn Hilde's voice. You've got to dance. Between now and the time of shooting, you don't have one moment to spare."

"I can't thank you enough," she replied, her tears returning.

"Don't think about it," he said. "After the first day's shooting, you'll be denouncing me in tones as loud as any of my actors, anyway. By the way, Josef Bühle is your leading man. He saw your test today, too."

She'd heard that working with the temperamental actor was like a season in hell, and it made her all the more apprehensive. "Did he like me?" she asked hesitantly.

"Like you? Ha! That sausage-eater! Only minutes ago he informed me that if I made this film with Marika Kreisler, I'd be back pressing pants in New York City. Well, let me tell you, Marika, that is something I don't intend to do now—or ever!"

In the days ahead, Marika drove herself with a passionate fury she didn't know she possessed. Each morning at nine, a retired erotic circus dancer arrived and worked with her until noon, when Peter brought in some bouillon and gave her a massage. By two she was ready for a voice lesson from Hilde, and at the end of the day, all she could do was totter home and collapse. Three days before shooting was to begin, she arrived late at the house and Peter rushed to greet her. "Wolfgang is holding a big dinner, and he's already upset with me," he said. "Your horsemeat is ready. See you in the morning." Running out the door, he called back, "I almost forgot. A guest is waiting in the parlor—some old crone. Said she's a relative. I hope I did the right thing in letting her in."

In the unlit parlor, Marika could make out only the vague outline of a woman sitting in a wing chair. Walking over to a table, she flipped on a lamp. "I'll have to scold Peter for letting you sit here in the dark."

"I requested it," came an aging voice.

It was eerily familiar, an echo from her childhood. Standing before the woman, Marika stared into her face. The eyes that looked back at her were watery, the body emaciated. Her dress was faded and her thinning yellow-gray hair uncombed, her shoulders stooped. Yet beyond wrinkles wide enough to hold rivers lay a strong but bitter face. Though decayed, she seemed to cling tenaciously to a spirit both powerful and dominant. "You don't know me, Marika?" she asked in a tremulous voice.

Marika's vocal cords seemed momentarily paralyzed. "My God!" she said in a faint voice, almost like that of a girl. "In this very house—in Friedrich's house—*you* are back!"

"Could you believe the wreck you see now was once the glamorous, even the notorious, Contessa Villoresi de Loche?" The woman made a great effort and, reaching for her cane, stood up to greet her.

Marika stood uncertainly for a moment, then, walking over, embraced her. The Contessa had a musty smell. "You must know," she said, "Friedrich is dead." The old woman sighed, but it was not the sound of sorrow. Rather, despair. "All my lovers are dead!"

Marika began walking rapidly around the room, turning on more lamps. She couldn't stand being in darkness with the Contessa. For one agonizing moment, she regretted having bought Friedrich's town house. "What have you been doing all these years?" she asked.

The Contessa was a long time in answering. "Do you remember the morning of your wedding to Count Dabrowsky in Zakopane?"

"Of course," Marika said, shuddering. "How could I ever forget that dreadful time? I was so young, so innocent."

"Before you were 'kidnapped,'" the Contessa said, "an old charwoman passed by us, her head covered with a black kerchief. I reached for your hand and said, 'There but for the grace of God go I.'"

"I recall it perfectly," Marika said, growing more and more uncomfortable in the Contessa's presence.

"Ever since the war," the Contessa said, "I've been like that poor hag."

"What exactly do you mean?" Marika asked, not really wanting to hear.

"I've been a charwoman for Madame Dalecka at her school for blind children."

"Really?" Marika indicated astonishment, but somehow she felt she had known the answer all along. It would have been a perfect revenge for Madame Dalecka.

"The bitch resented my presence from the beginning," the Contessa continued. "But what could I do? You'd returned to Berlin with Friedrich, who had filed charges against me with the German occupation forces. It marked the longest, most humiliating experience of my life."

Marika was growing nervous. The old woman knew too many of her secrets. She feared she'd arrived in Berlin to stay.

"But I lost even that position," the Contessa said. "Madame Dalecka turned me out. The school was disbanded. I was out on the streets, in about the same plight as some of the blind children."

"How awful!"

"You don't know the half of it," the Contessa said.

"I can imagine," Marika countered. "When you finish, I'll tell you about my war years."

The Contessa didn't seem to hear her. "One morning, walking alone and penniless on the streets of Warsaw, I looked up and saw your picture on the front page of a newspaper. Marika Kreisler, a big motion-picture star living in elegance and luxury. There I was, the woman who'd launched you on your career in life with nothing but old age and emptiness facing me."

Marika lit a cigarette but stabbed it out into an ashtray after only two puffs. "Whatever happened to Count Dabrowsky?"

"Who knows?" the Contessa said. "No one ever heard of him after he fled Warsaw. I think we can safely assume he's dead. Even Madame Dalecka's son is dead."

"Yes," Marika said vacantly. Then she shook herself. "You've caught me at a bad time. I've been training for my next film. My schedule is completely exhausting. I come home every night and collapse in bed." Her forehead was dripping with perspiration. "Perhaps we could talk in a few days. I really must retire now. At what hotel are you staying in Berlin? I'll have my secretary get in touch with you and set up an appointment the first free time I have."

Slowly the old woman walked over to Marika, the sound of her cane ominously tapping the floor ringing loudly in her ears. "You don't seem to have listened—at least not understood. I've not even had a piece of bread for the past two days."

"I see . . ." An awkward stillness filled the room. Marika was trapped. Then, in the clear light from the lamps, she met the eyes of the Contessa and saw they were now as fierce and determined as those of Brigitte and Hitler.

"I hope you do see," the Contessa said. "I'm only the first of other visitors you're likely to have, depending on the life you've led since I've known you. My darling, when you become famous, figures from your past start coming out of the woodwork."

"What do you want?" Marika asked angrily, her whole body trembling.

"I'm going to face the newspapers tomorrow," the Contessa said. "You can't imagine how interested they were in interviewing Marika Kreisler's *mother*. One of them even offered to pay me." She stared hard at Marika. "I just happened to have with me a picture of you taken as a little girl in 1913. I don't think anybody in Berlin knows your age, except Brigitte if she's still alive. Most people seem to think you're twenty. The papers don't even realize that you, as a thirteen-year-old, married a Polish count for his money."

"That's a lie!" she shouted at the Contessa. "And you're *not* my mother!"

"Sweet child, I'm Frau Kreisler," she said. "I was mistress of this household." She paused. "At least for a while."

"You're blackmailing me!"

"Let's not put unattractive labels on things," the Contessa said. "You're my last chance." She weakly gripped Marika's wrist. "You owe it to me."

"I owe you nothing, Goddamn it," Marika cried, breaking away.

"Perhaps," the Contessa said, "though I'm sorry you feel that way. Sometimes life forces us to pay debts we don't even think we owe."

"I'm going to bed," Marika said. "I'm sure you'll find a bedroom somewhere. It's a big house."

"Yes," the Contessa said, taking off her shawl. "I remember it."

* * *

It took two ruby bracelets for Peter to settle the Contessa comfortably on the French Riviera's Cap Ferrat. An expatriate American couple had lost all their money in the Wall Street crash and were willing to sell their villa for very little. "The villa is sumptuous," Peter wired Marika "and the Contessa is busy restoring it and herself."

By then Marika was in front of the cameras. The first day's script called for her to plow through hawkers peddling salamis, knockwursts, and beer, and ended up in a mesh of Mother Nature's freaks—a 689-pound woman, a tattooed lady, a strong man, a snake charmer with a twelve-foot python, a sword-swallower, a three-eyed anatomical wonder, a two-nosed hermaphrodite, a crocodile man, a gorilla girl, and what was the most disgusting performer of all, a geek who was actually going to bite the head off a live chicken on camera! They were all real circus people, assembled from all over Europe, many from as far away as Roumania.

It didn't take her long to decide that a movie queen's life was not always glamorous. In her first scene, Josef Bühle was instructed to slap her as she stood in front of a spinning carousel, and on the first take he hit her so hard her earring flew across the sound stage. Stinging from the blow, she looked first at von Menzel, then at Bühle. When she took in the smug look on her co-star's puffy-cheeked face, she screamed, "You did that on purpose."

He walked up to her, his thick lips glistening wet. "Mannheim would have been concerned with bringing authenticity to the part. She wouldn't be rushing to the mirror every third minute to see how she looked. This is a brutal film. No place for cutesy-cute little girls."

His words made her so angry she wanted to stalk off the set. Von Menzel called to her, "I didn't like the first slap. We're going to shoot it again."

Now Marika was furious at her director as well, but she tried to control her temper. She stood firmly, almost defiantly in front of Bühle, a mountain of a man whose ego was as big as his bulk. "I'm warning you," she whispered to him, "if you slap me hard this time, you'll regret it."

As the cameras rolled, Bühle swung wide and the second slap was even fiercer than the first. Dazed, she fell back against one of the battered horses of the carousel, then, with blind determination, pushed herself forward again. The cameras were still on her, but she was hardly aware of them. With cold anger, she kicked

Bühle in the testicles. He collapsed on the ground, clutching his groin and screaming like a pig, his famous face contorted with pain. He was noted for depicting suffering in his films, she grinned to herself, but he'd never been able to act this well before! Knees up in the air, he bellowed and winced, in a veritable orgy of torment.

"Perfect!" von Menzel called over the shrieks, roars, and whistles of the carnival.

Marika stood looking at the director for a long moment, realizing he cared only for what the camera captured—not if his actors killed each other. Turning on her heel, she rushed to her dressing room, nearly trampling a woman only thirty inches tall. Gazing in the mirror, her face seemed to swim before her. She was so naïve, she thought, so ignorant of what making films meant. What other lessons would she be forced to learn?

In an hour von Menzel knocked gently on the door to her dressing room, then opened it. Marika was still in front of the mirror, watching her face turn black and blue. She was crying.

"I know why you kicked him," he said, "and Bühle deserved it, as he always does. Your improvisation made a great scene, a touch of realism. But Bühle is threatening to quit the picture. Right away he demanded an immediate apology."

"Look at me!" she wailed. "He deliberately tried to destroy my face, the swine. And he wants me to apologize?"

"Don't worry about it," von Menzel said. "I've taken the liberty of conveying your apologies to Bühle. Then I sent him away with my driver to sample all the pig's knuckles and sauerkraut his gut desires—at your expense."

"How generous of you," she said sarcastically.

"Do you always go for a man's most vulnerable spot?" he asked, provocatively raising an eyebrow.

"Never before," she said, reapplying her lipstick. "In fact, Bühle didn't look to me like a man who had any testicles. I was very surprised." All of a sudden, she wanted to be by herself. "If you'll excuse me."

Each day of shooting made the grotesquerie of carnival life more and more repugnant to her, but von Menzel seemed to revel in it as he staged spectacles such as an eight-foot giant wrestling a six-hundred-pound gorilla. Daily, he bathed her in a violent, erotic atmosphere, bringing out her own brutality, summoning forth an unknown personality from her deepest recesses. Without meaning to, she found herself walking and talking like Flame. "Remember," he kept telling her, "everything you do must be faintly cruel."

In one fantasy scene, he had her ride a horse on the carousel, dressed in black lace and black stockings, her white skin showing above her frilly garters. Up and down she rode the horse, waving her arms into the air with abandon, screaming obscenities at the men who crowded around to watch her. It was as if she were making love to the horse. At the end of the number, she kicked her legs into the air, as the camera moved lovingly and longingly up her calves, lingering at the white thighs. She seemed to invite every man in the audience to come and make love to her.

Behind the camera, von Menzel gloated, as he directed yet more smoky light upon her.

Back in her dressing room, Marika was surprised to see von Menzel already waiting for her. To her embarrassment, he knelt before her, removing her shoes. "Wear high heels always," he commanded her as he straightened up and regained control of himself. "Never be seen in public without them."

Through the remaining weeks of shooting, she wandered as if in a trance, the hypnotized victim of her director. She worried constantly that this film, on top of *Birth of Venus,* would destroy her career forever, but von Menzel was always around, assuring her, calming her. Sometimes he'd drive her into such rages she'd start crying, her makeup running, and the makeup man would have to rush to restore her face. After her fury died, von Menzel would be there to soothe her, almost as if he were stroking a cat.

One day when he'd warmed her spirit again, she turned to him. "Why don't you allow me to call you Walter? I feel I know you too well to keep addressing you as von Menzel. It sounds too harsh between friends."

A frown crossed his face. He looked at her strangely through his monocle, and seemed hurt, as if she'd penetrated one of the barriers of his posturing. "I'm not a Walter," he said in a faint voice. "That should be apparent by now."

For her final scene, the character, Flame, was to descend into Hell. By now a drug addict, Flame was no longer an exotic dancer in the carnival. Nightly and semi-nude, she had to enter a mud pit to wrestle a burly lesbian. The act was billed as "The Beauty and the Beast."

Hurled into the brown filth, Marika found herself engulfed in the mud. For one moment the lights from the set disappeared, and she felt near suffocation. Raising her arms, she struck madly at the woman wrestler. She hated the film, hated von Menzel, hated her decision to become an actress. This wasn't acting anyway. She'd become like one of Mother Nature's freaks, shamelessly on exhibit before the world. Momentarily catching a breath of air, she had it knocked out of her again as she fell back into the slime.

Springing from the mud, she tried desperately to make her way to the edge of the pit. "I can't take it anymore," she screamed at von Menzel, but a strong, rough hand on her thigh pulled her down again in the mire. Eyes covered with slime, she arched her nails and gouged at the face of the wrestler. The woman bellowed, falling back into the pit. With savage fury, Marika kicked her again and again.

"Cut! Cut! Cut!" von Menzel was shouting, as two grips rushed into the mud to haul her off the woman.

Shaking uncontrollably, Marika realized that she was no longer the beauty, but the beast.

* * *

At the completion of *Carnival*, von Menzel invited Marika out for a celebration, and, with Peter and Wolfgang, they set out to make a tour of Berlin's night life. By their fourth club, they were all reasonably drunk, and the walls seemed to be spinning around Marika.

"Look about you," von Menzel slurred. "Berlin is a limbo of mirror-images, a half-world. Soon even that will be gone."

"Don't get political," Wolfgang cautioned. "We're out for fun tonight—wicked, wonderful fun."

As colored lights lit the glass dance floor from underneath, von Menzel held Marika close. She knew before the night was over he was going to take her back to his apartment and make love to her —and she was going to let him. Until now, he had been a complete man of mystery to her, zealously guarding his private life. Although she had made herself available many times during the filming, he had never asked her out. Yet she felt he was attracted to her. At first she suspected he didn't want to get involved emotionally because of his business relationship with her, but finally she admitted she simply couldn't figure the man out.

Peter and Wolfgang cut in on their dance, Wolfgang taking Marika as a partner, and Peter going for von Menzel. Leading her to the edge of the dance floor, Wolfgang whispered in Marika's ear: "I've fallen in love."

"I know," Marika said, smiling, "although right now your divine Peter is in the arms of another man."

"No," Wolfgang said, a frown crossing his brow, "with someone other than Peter."

Marika backed away.

"I must tell Peter tonight," Wolfgang said. "I've postponed it for as long as I can."

"But Peter's absolutely mad for you," Marika said.

"Yes," he replied vacantly, "that's why it's important that you be with Peter at this time. You're the only friend he has, and I fear for him when he hears the news. He's so melodramatic he might do something utterly ridiculous like commit suicide."

Suicide! Marika broke away from Wolfgang and returned to her table, where a waiter poured champagne. Through the rest of the endless, unbearable night, she tried to conceal her desperation, but it was almost impossible, and von Menzel and Peter kept casting strange looks at her. She was on the verge of blurting it out, when at last it happened. Von Menzel invited her to his apartment. Finally, she was going to get a look into his private world. None of the camera crew had ever visited von Menzel's home—even his telephone number was unlisted. When he left the studio, he vanished for the day. Marika had heard speculation on the set that he was homosexual, but she didn't believe it, and furthermore neither did Peter, who could be trusted implicitly in such matters.

Standing before Peter, she kissed him tenderly, holding both his hands. For Wolfgang, she had only an icy good-bye.

Von Menzel's apartment surprised her. Unlike his office at the studio, there was not one clue in the place to tell her anything about the man. It was strictly utilitarian, totally devoid of personal mementos, but perhaps she could do something about that, she thought. As von Menzel excused himself, she removed her wrap, wishing she were fresher for her first time with him—surely he'd let her take a bath—and was surprised again this time to smell the wafting aroma of bacon. Perhaps von Menzel's cook was preparing breakfast. How nice!

A door at the back opened, and a statuesque, attractive woman emerged, her long black hair tied neatly in a bun. Suddenly, Marika had the sinking sensation that this was not a cook.

"Good morning," she said. "You're Marika Kreisler, aren't you? I didn't know Walter was bringing home a guest." Walking toward Marika, she stretched out her hand. "I'm Frau von Menzel."

Too stunned to reply, Marika stood looking at the woman, and before she had had a chance to fully register the impact of that announcement, two schoolboys emerged from the kitchen, wiping their mouths with white napkins. They looked like carbon copies of von Menzel. "Our sons, Hans and Rudolf."

"How do you do?" Marika asked weakly. A feeling of devastation swept over her. Without knowing it, had she fallen in love with von Menzel?

Just then the director came rushing into the room. "I've just talked to Pommer, the producer," he announced. "He's seen *Carnival*—and doesn't like it. He claims the picture isn't German. Isn't that ridiculous?"

"My option," Marika asked nervously. "Did he pick it up?"

"No, my dear," he answered softly.

She collapsed into a chair and found herself sobbing uncontrollably. All the tension of the past few weeks, her fear of failure, the revelation of von Menzel's marriage, Wolfgang leaving Peter—it was all too much. At her side, Frau von Menzel offered comfort with firm, kind hands that somehow seemed to give Marika strength. She couldn't resent the woman or blame her in any way for her pain. After all, it was Marika who was the aggressor, coveting the woman's husband.

Lifting her up from the chair, von Menzel led her into his private study. Taking her cheeks in his hands, he looked deeply into her eyes. "Do not cry, Marika," he said. "UFA may be blind, but Hollywood isn't. In my drawer are two contracts—one for me, one for you."

She paused, trying to form words, but no sound came at first.

Choking back her tears, she managed to blurt out, "What? I don't understand? We're going to Hollywood?"

"We're not just *going* to Hollywood," he said, his blue eyes sparkling, "we're going to conquer it!"

Chapter 8

On a chilly day in late September, a party of four—Marika Kreisler, Walter von Menzel, Hermann Goetz, and Peter Nebmaier—sailed on the *Bremen,* bound for New York and an uncertain future.

Marika spent the first two days almost entirely with a very distraught Peter, who threatened hourly to jump off the side of the ship. "I'll never love again," Peter declared. "I always get hurt. Why do we need to love? It causes such pain. I've been humiliated. Imagine Wolfgang leaving me for a *sixteen*-year old?"

She ran her fingers along his forehead and looked deeply into his eyes. "When I lost Julian, I thought life had ended. It had, I suppose, at least for the moment. But the next day I put one foot in front of the other and took one step forward. I was still breathing; the grass was growing; the sun was shining. I knew the world was going on without me whether I liked it or not."

"But I wake up in the middle of the night," Peter said, "and reach out for him. I take my pillow and try to suffocate myself, imagining it's Wolfgang."

"I know, my pet," she said. "I know only too well. I've been there myself." She bent over and kissed his cheek. "The worst thing for me to handle, the very worst, was to know I couldn't share secrets with Julian anymore. I still find myself holding imaginary talks with him."

"I don't want to talk to Wolfgang," Peter said. "I want to kill him."

"That, too, will pass," she said. "Wolfgang is a son of a bitch. In some ways, Julian was a bastard, too, using me, but somebody has to love all the bastards and sons of bitches in the world. When we do fall in love with them, let's not delude ourselves into thinking we're going to get anything but a kick in the mouth."

That night the moon was never fuller, and it seemed to rest right on the Atlantic, its huge orb casting pale, luminous shadows on the rippling water. Von Menzel stood by her side on deck, the first time he'd ventured out since the trip began. He'd been completely absorbed in their next film, *Istanbul,* and even his meals had been eaten in his cabin. "How is the lovesick puppy?"

"You wouldn't understand such things, my darling," she said, flicking his cheek. "You're the type who never gives his heart away —so how could anybody break it?"

"Love's in the mind," von Menzel said, gazing out at the dark waves. "If we control our minds, we don't go love-crazy. I don't need love from people. I need their assistance, their money, their appreciation, their ideas, their talent, and, yes, their sex. But I live too much in my own shell to love."

An American couple strolled by, and she fell silent for a moment. "Is that why you left your wife and children in Berlin?"

"I have no time for them," Von Menzel said. "When my wife married me, she knew her role would always be that of a supporting player. She accepted that right from the beginning. I'm wedded to my work. Right now I need all my strength—to make you the greatest star in the world."

* * *

As the *Bremen* sailed into New York harbor, reporters and photographers swarmed all over Marika. The ship's publicist had seen to that.

"How does it feel to land in New York where you're officially banned?" one reporter asked her.

"I'm not banned," she said with a smile. "Only my film is." She surveyed the skyline before her. "It looks like a dazzling city. I can see lines forming around the block to see my next film."

"How much skin are you going to show in your first American picture?" The reporter grinned.

She bristled at the remark, but managed to conceal her annoyance. "I realize now," she said, smiling provocatively at the other reporters, "that it isn't necessary to take off one's clothing. That man . . ." She pointed at the reporter who'd asked the question. "He's undressing me right now, the way he's looking at me."

"Show us your legs, Kreisler!" a reporter from the rear yelled at her.

"See *Birth of Venus,*" she shouted back. "You'll see more than my legs."

"We understand you're married," one woman reporter asked.

"That's right," Marika said firmly. "My husband, Count Dabrowsky, prefers to remain in Europe on our estate for the time being."

"Do you have a picture of him, *Countess?*" another reporter asked.

"He's never posed for a photograph," she answered curtly.

"Are you getting a divorce?" came another question.

"Definitely not!" she said, feigning anger. "We're very much in love. He's modern enough, though, to let me have my own career."

Grabbing her arm, von Menzel quickly steered her through the crowds and back to her stateroom. "Mayer won't like that interview. He's very touchy about your nude appearance. There was a big struggle at the studio to get him to sign the contract. No more talk about *Birth of Venus.* Play up *Carnival.* Now that's a film worth shouting about."

* * *

As Peter sat by the telephone, trying to book theater tickets for the night, Marika paced the floor of her hotel room, lighting one cigarette after another.

The pea-green walls of the room seemed to close in on her. At least MGM could have booked her into a suite at the Plaza, not this fleabag!

She now feared that her decision to go to Hollywood with von Menzel was a mistake. At least in Berlin she had been treated like a star, not some little second-rate bit player. Regardless of Pommer's reaction, she was sure the release of *Carnival* would have sparked bigger, better offers right there in Germany. Now what did she have? A lousy hotel room, and a director who was absolutely no help to her—he seemed to be spending all his days and most of his nights, too, visiting former cronies in New York. And she was confined to her room all day, waiting for a call from Louis B. Mayer. Mayer was at a deluxe hotel across town, and so far, not one word had come from him, other than that she was to "stand by." Stand by! Even if the man made himself free to receive her, she didn't have anything to wear except the dress she'd been photographed in on the deck of the ship. And even that was at the cleaners. The rest of her trunks had been shipped to Hollywood, where she had fully expected to be by now.

In addition, the New World had done little to lessen Peter's melancholy. If anything, New York, with its Great Depression, had only made him miss Berlin all the more, and she was getting bored trying to console him. It all seemed hopeless.

At three o'clock the telephone rang, and she jumped in fright. At last! As Peter took the call, she sped to her dressing table, where she rechecked her makeup for the ninth time today, but when Peter turned to her, she knew it was another disappointment. "Mayer had to go to the coast," he said. "An emergency. He's canceled all his appointments in New York. He left word, though, that you and von Menzel are to leave for Hollywood right away."

Marika swore under her breath. "Well, at last we're free to get out of this stinking hole," she said. "We can go out on the town. When von Menzel returns, let him wonder where we are for a change." A frown crossed her face. "But I have absolutely nothing to wear."

"Don't worry," Peter said, "you and I are about the same size. I've got plenty of clothes. Surely something will be appropriate."

"Dress up like a man?" she asked in astonishment. "I'm not exactly the type. You're mixing me up with some of your friends in Berlin."

"Darling," he said, "you'll be ultrafeminine in anything you wear, even a workingman's coveralls."

Marika looked dubious, but decided she had no choice. Later that afternoon, she could not stop looking at her reflection, as she walked in rapid strides down Fifth Avenue. Peter had been right. She did cut a dashing figure, and she didn't look anything at all like a man. Dressed in one of Peter's white shirts with a tie to match, a beige jacket and slacks, she felt the stares of everyone upon her, and it was very pleasant indeed. On an impulse, she decided to complete the outfit with a soft felt slouch hat designed in the style of a British trilby, and, gazing into a shop window, she decided she liked this style very much.

That night, she and Peter made the round of New York's nightclubs, drinking champagne at "21," eating sweet-potato pone with pork chops and green apples at the Red Rooster in Harlem. Pictures were being snapped all around her, and though she was sure some were of her, she didn't think any of the photographers knew who she was. After all, *Birth of Venus* was banned in America, and *Carnival* hadn't even played here yet.

The next morning, however, Peter woke her by thrusting a Hearst newspaper in front of her sleepy eyes. She was getting used to seeing her picture on the front page, but this was something special.

"KREISLER IN PANTS," screamed the headline.

The telephone was ringing, and even before Peter picked up the receiver she knew it was von Menzel. Without waiting for Peter to announce him, she took the receiver. "Don't lecture me," she said. "I've already seen the papers, and I'm sure Mayer has canceled my contract—that is, if anybody has gotten up in California at this hour."

"Quite the contrary," von Menzel said. "As an ex-tailor, I highly approve. Bernie, my old boss, woke me up this morning. After that picture ran, he said he's already received eleven calls from women wanting to be outfitted in slacks. You've caused a sensation!"

She reached for Peter's hand, clutching it. "You mean . . . you approve?"

"I not only approve," he said, "but I'm going to use it! Wait until we do *Istanbul*. One day Marika Kreisler will have all the women of America in pants."

* * *

Hollywood—the movies had found a voice. Daily, reigning stars lost their thrones because of thick, impenetrable accents or high, squeaky voices, and new ones arrived to take their places. On March 14, 1930, *Anna Christie* had opened at the Capitol Theater in New York, advertised by the magic words, GARBO TALKS:

"Gimme a visky, ginger ale on the side, and don't be stingy, baby."

With her deep, husky, throaty contralto, Marika did not fear the microphone. She knew she was as fluent in English now as in German, and her accent was hardly detectable—just enough to make whatever she said more mysterious. She was bone-tired, however. Von Menzel had booked a suite for Marika and Peter at the Château Marmont, on the outskirts of Hollywood, just above the Sunset Strip, and after crossing the empty vastness of America, she was in dire need of a rest before facing Mayer. The dark, heavy furniture and Gothic colonnades of the California feudal palace made her feel right at home.

The next morning was a different story, however. She found Culver City drab and intimidating, with its high walls and nondescript sound stages, and she wasn't the only one. "If some director wants to shoot a picture about a prison," von Menzel said, "he doesn't have to go on location." Nervously, she sat in Mayer's outer office. He had requested a private interview with her, and she kept cracking her knuckles in fear until she noticed she was irritating a secretary.

After an hour's wait, she was finally ushered into Mayer's office. A powerful, big fireplug of a man with deep-set brown eyes sat behind a huge white desk. "Miss Kreisler," he said, motioning for her to sit down, too, "we make good, clean family pictures at this studio." He studied her closely, too closely. She began to perspire, but she dared not reach into her purse for her handkerchief.

"We stand for the sanctity of motherhood and the home and also for love," he said, "providing it's blessed by marriage." A frown crossed his brow, and for a moment he looked like Lionel Barrymore. "We're against queers and political radicals."

Her breathing was heavy and she tried to control her voice. "I'm none of the latter."

He held up a newspaper. On the front page was the now famous photograph of her in Peter's pants. "Your personal life is your own affair," he said. "But if you become one of our stars, those affairs can threaten and destroy careers."

"Exactly what have I done that's threatening?" she asked. Her anxiety surprisingly had subsided a bit.

"I don't like to beat around the bush," he said, glancing at the newspaper picture again. "Are you a lesbian?"

"Definitely not!" she said, her anger rising at his rudeness. She almost wanted to get up and storm out of the office.

"That's good to know," he said, "because your contract contains a morality clause." His eyes traversed her body. "You're a very attractive woman. Your tits are bigger than I was told. Tits are important in this business."

She found herself blushing. No man had ever spoken to her like this before. "I'm glad you approve," she said sarcastically.

"A little fire in you," he said, smiling. "That's okay, too." He sighed. "Many of you *unknown* actresses are only too willing to give head to any two-bit producer in Hollywood who wants to put it on the desk."

She lit a cigarette and eyed him provocatively, almost tantalizing him. "You know I'm not willing," she said. "Very able, but not that cooperative!"

"Of course," he said, clearing his throat. She seemed to be embarrassing him now. "Personally, I don't mess around with members of my studio family. But I know such things go on."

"Have you seen *Carnival*?" she asked, trying to change the subject.

"Yes," he said vacantly. He paused. "We're booking *Carnival* across the country. I hope it will make a star out of you before von Menzel completes *Istanbul*."

"I certainly hope so, too."

"As far as that *Venus* filth goes," he said, "that's strictly for showing at smokers. Around here we don't like our ladies running bare-assed on camera, then getting humped by some stud."

She crushed out her cigarette and reached for another one. He was making her furious, but she had promised von Menzel to show no sign of temperament.

"You look like you've got class," Mayer said. "I don't know why you want to make dirty pictures. You'll have one hell of a time living it down."

"I didn't think I was making a *dirty picture*," she said defensively. "I still don't think I did."

"Bare-ass is bare-ass," Mayer said, "and a hump is a hump."

She got up from the sofa. "Everybody before was something," she said. "I understand you were an ex-ragpicker."

He bristled at her remark, but didn't say anything.

"Am I signed?" she asked.

He swatted a piece of paper on his desk. "At three hundred and fifty a week," he said. "I wanted you for two hundred and fifty, but von Menzel insisted on the higher figure. Since I wanted him, I agreed."

"I hope I'll be able to make that higher amount worthwhile," she said, her words voiced coldly and her face remaining stonily polite.

As she headed for the door, Mayer called to her, "I wanted Garbo for the part, but she turned it down."

Marika smiled. "Maybe I'll make her regret that decision."

Getting up hurriedly from behind his desk, Mayer trotted over to the door. Before opening it, he patted her on the rear.

* * *

Istanbul was a whole new brand of filmmaking for von Menzel. He was no longer interested in realism, as he'd been in *Carnival*, but in fantasy, poetry, spectacle. Daily, he draped Marika in feathers and furs to face the camera, with butterfly-wing eyebrows and gold dust sprinkled in her hair. Subtly, lovingly, Hermann bathed her in soft shadows, bringing out new contours, discovering disturbing new depths in her face. Marika wandered through the steamy film with moistened lips and dewy eyes, the image of the exotic, erotic goddess.

The press went crazy. Every day the newspapers were filled with reports of Marika Kreisler, "the new Garbo," and though Marika worked hard to achieve her own unique look, the comparisons kept cropping up. One day by accident Marika encountered Garbo herself in the commissary, dressed in slacks and a man's shirt, her face hidden behind dark glasses.

"Miss Garbo," Marika said, "please forgive me for coming over to you this way. I'm Marika Kreisler. I don't care what you read in the papers, you are—and will always be—the world's greatest actress. No one will ever replace you."

Garbo looked at her in utter astonishment. "Who in hell is Marika Kreisler?" she said, and left.

Marika stood stunned, bewildered as to what to make of the rebuff, then, turning, hurried out of the commissary, past the lavish dressing rooms of the stars, and to her own quarters. Compared to some of the other actresses at MGM, her own dressing room resembled a military barracks. Looking at herself in Lotte's pedestal mirror, she burst into tears at Garbo's words. "I'll show the bitch," she vowed.

That was how von Menzel found her on this Friday afternoon. Coaxing her out of her room, he drove with her to his beachhouse in Santa Monica. As the car sped along, her spirits began to return. She loved these weekends with Peter and Hermann and von Menzel, alone at the beach, just the four of them. It was like being back home again. None of them fitted into Hollywood, all of them hated parties, and somehow being together like this helped dull the sharp edge of loneliness that slipped like a keen blade into their hearts.

This weekend, however, everyone seemed to be in a blue mood. Hermann confided to Marika, "I've never had a woman I didn't pay for." Peter brooded, "I'll never meet a man in Hollywood. I just don't like cowboys." Von Menzel, as usual, revealed nothing of his inner feelings, but after tasting Marika's *Apfelstrudel*, he said, "You've just confirmed a lifelong conviction: behind every Nordic *femme fatale* is a little German *Hausfrau*." And then he sighed.

That Sunday, Marika wandered by herself on the beach, and sat for hours staring at the ocean. She didn't really know where her career was taking her. Even if she became successful, she instinctively knew that being a motion-picture star wasn't enough. She wanted somebody to love her, to feel she belonged to somebody else. One day the week before, she'd seen two child actors on the set and had burst into tears because her son, Anton, was growing up without her. He'd never known his mother, and it didn't seem fair that Franz should have taken him from her. Walking back to the house, she wrote Franz a long letter, not really expecting a reply, but feeling she had to do something.

To make her thoughts even darker that night, a cable arrived from Gabrielle, and Marika learned she'd been hospitalized, perhaps with cancer. That seemed to be the final straw. Marika lay down and began to weep.

About an hour later, a knock sounded at her door, and Hermann came in, concern written all over his face. She showed him the cable and he held her hand and kissed it. "Everything seems to be falling away," she said. "I'm so lonely. I need someone."

Suddenly, she became aware that Hermann was not just comforting her, but was actually fondling her hand. She pulled away. "Hermann, please," she urged.

"I'm sorry," he stammered. "But I fell in love with you the first time I photographed you. All day I spend lighting you and all night seeing your image on the screen. You're my life!"

She sat up, the most profound wave of sympathy and understanding sweeping over her. "It can never be," she said. "You know that."

"Yes," he said, avoiding her eyes, "but I can dream." He sighed. "Though many men die of unfilled dreams." He got up quietly and left her bedroom.

That morning, Marika grew increasingly impatient with von Menzel on the set. She had decided it was high time he noticed her as a woman, but though he was with her at all times, though he guided her through every interview, every scene, he seemed to regard her as a robot. Not since that day in Berlin when he'd knelt before her and fondled her shoes had he made her feel like a woman. On camera, she was a goddess, but off camera he treated her like one of his men friends! This lack of attention to her needs made her anger rise, and without meaning to, she grew testy. The next time von Menzel came up to her, she deliberately confronted him, trying to start an argument. "I've learned the French song for the café scene," she said. "It isn't right for me. I demand you have another one written."

"It's out of the question," von Menzel said, a faraway gaze in his eyes. "There isn't time."

"But the song as written should be sung by a man," she said indignantly. "Look, it even says here, the singer is dressed in white tie and tails, even a top hat!"

"That's right." He smiled at her. "You'll be the sexiest thing in pants on the screen. But about that song," he said, handing her a new script, "I'm glad you brought it up. There has been a slight change."

Quickly scanning it, she cried out, "No, now you've gone too far! This is ridiculous. You actually want me to sing a love song to a *woman* in the audience? You're trying to ruin my career!"

He glared at her. "I seem to have heard those words before. Now, look, Miss Kreisler, this is my movie, this is the part you are

to act in my movie, and I demand you act the part as written!"
Turning on his heel, he marched off the set with rapid strides,
obviously fighting to control his rage.

"My dear," came a voice from behind her, "I don't think anyone
has ever fully explained to you the enchantment of sexual ambiguity."

Marika turned around and found herself facing a woman
dressed in riding pants and with a skin so transparent it was almost
alabaster-white, in total contrast to her thick, almost blue-black
hair. Her head was small, and her brown eyes seemed too big for
their setting, but her finely chiseled nose was held high with all the
arrogance of aristocracy. After a moment, Marika recognized her
from her photographs as Rita de Alba, the screenwriter, a revolutionary woman who'd been famed in Spain for her beauty. Now
Rita's long arms and hands reached out to Marika, enclosing her
right wrist, then her hand.

"Our meeting has been long overdue," Rita said. "You know, I
wrote that part for you. Let's go back to your dressing room and
I'll rehearse you in how to do it."

Marika withdrew. "Von Menzel is my director," she protested.
"I take my orders from him—and only from him."

"It was von Menzel who suggested that I coach you in the part,"
Rita said. "You see, von Menzel doesn't know how two women
relate." She smiled provocatively. "On the other hand, I do!"

Rita de Alba turned out to be a woman of immense charm and
vitality, with a personality so strong that it was hard to resist her
demands. After two hours, she was able to convince Marika to do
the part as written, providing that she, Rita, would sit at one of the
café tables on the set and be the woman she sang to.

When Mayer viewed the shot the next day, he not only threatened to fire von Menzel, but also to replace Marika with Joan
Crawford. However, he grudgingly quieted down when Rita, who
was one of his particular favorites, took him aside and explained
to him how immensely the scene would add to the profits of the
picture.

She was right. *Istanbul* was wrapped up in five weeks—with
the scene of Marika in white tie and tails—and the critics and the
public alike loved it, one reviewer noting the Rita de Alba scene
added "just the right touch of languid decadence."

By the time *Istanbul* premiered in Hollywood, word had also reached Marika that "all of Europe is at the feet of Flame." The response to *Carnival* abroad was overwhelming and it was also enjoying a lesser but marked success in America.

As *Istanbul* flashed across the nation's screens, Marika moved into a strange new world. Von Menzel took her to an entire department at MGM assigned to answer her fan mail and send out photographs. At least ten letters arrived daily from men offering to give her their fortunes. One wealthy woman in Arizona posted a cashier's check for $35,000 "for one night of love with Marika Kreisler." Some men enclosed nude photographs of themselves with full erections, writing lengthy letters outlining in explicit detail the various sexual contortions they wished to put her through.

Even Greta Garbo learned who she was. Somebody told Marika that *Istanbul* had been especially screened for the elusive lady, and that Garbo's comment was: "I think Madame Kreisler looks like a female impersonator, and I'm not altogether sure that she isn't."

Again, Marika tried to break through the shell around von Menzel. "All the world adores me," she told him one day, "I'm everybody's sex fantasy, people long to touch me, but you still treat me like a slave. You humiliate me with your demands on the set. Why?"

"Measure the torture you endure at my hands," von Menzel said, "with the amount of adulation received for that labor. That is the only way to judge such matters."

* * *

Behind high sand-garden walls one Friday, Marika faced a lonely weekend at von Menzel's Santa Monica house. The director had just called to tell her he had to go to San Francisco on business. After Hermann had revealed his feelings for her, he'd seemed to avoid her except at work. It was too embarrassing for the little man. On the other hand, Peter had decided he wasn't entirely immune to the charms of American cowboys after all, and had run off with one to Las Vegas for the weekend.

A deep melancholy swept over Marika. She still had come no closer to finding someone to love her, and by Saturday night all she could do was sit and stare at the walls, listening to deep, soulful music that did little to break her mood. As the hours drifted by, she grew more empty, until, suddenly, she heard the sound of the key in the lock. It was von Menzel and she rushed into his arms. "You're back—a day ahead of time!"

"My, my," he said, holding her at arm's distance, "you've never been this glad to see me before."

"I don't think I've ever been this lonely before," she said, near tears. "I didn't think I could make it by myself through tomorrow."

He didn't seem to hear her and, excusing himself for being "completely exhausted," went to bed. Chagrined, she put on her most provocative nightgown and paced up and down outside his door, for one moment even tempted to throw it open and confront him. Here she was, one of the world's leading sex goddesses, and she didn't have the power to attract the love of just one man.

A sudden movement in his room made her rush down the hallway and into the study, like a frightened schoolgirl, she thought, but she couldn't help it. Shortly afterward, von Menzel joined her there, glancing briefly at her before heading for the liquor cabinet. "Can't sleep," he said. "Have too much on my mind."

She watched silently as he poured himself a scotch and soda. Finally, she asked, "What in hell's the matter with me?"

"Many things," he said without hesitation. He slowly sipped his scotch and eyed her intently, the way he did behind the camera. "For one thing, you're not self-sufficient. You never know from hour to hour what you're letting yourself in for. Whatever is immediately in front of you is what you're attracted to. You blindly enter into relationships without any regard for their outcome, or any thought as to how dangerous it is to love people who will only use you, then toss you aside."

His words stunned her. He'd never talked to her in such an intimate, personal way.

"Are you still in love with your wife?" she asked, lighting a cigarette and stabbing the air with it.

"What an idiotic question!" he said, slamming down his glass. "I've never been *in* love with my wife, not from the beginning, not now. She's my friend, a true companion in life, the mother of my children, an intelligent, sensitive human being who knows how to talk on subjects other than the movies, sex, and romance. Your brain cells can't conceive of a man and a woman being friends without a roll in the hay!" Then he turned and left her standing there.

* * *

In tears, Marika rushed out of the house and got into her car. She didn't know where she was going, only that she must get away from von Menzel. Speeding along the coastal road, she drove almost blindly, her lights out, her tears like a wet windshield. She almost wanted to hurt herself, to make von Menzel break down from his isolated perch and feel sorry for her. Maybe she'd even damage her precious face. What would he be without her beauty to capture on celluloid and splash across the screen?

The evening was chilly, but she didn't care if she caught cold. Why preserve and protect a body if there was no one to make love to it? She drove fast, recklessly, the power of the machine surging through her veins. She thrilled at controlling it, wishing only that she could control her life, her emotions as easily.

The sound of a motorcycle reached her ears, but it seemed far away, not really meant for her. When the policeman appeared in her rear-view mirror, she came out of her daze and pulled the car to the side of the road. But she was going too fast, the pavement was wet, and the brakes wouldn't grip. In panic she screamed out as the car lurched forward, and with a jarring, rattling crash, came to a sudden stop against the embankment. The last thing she remembered before she passed out was the steering wheel rushing so very, very fast toward her face.

* * *

When she came to, von Menzel was at her side. "Are you all right?" he asked. "A little the worse for wear?"

"Yes," she said lamely. "I think I'm okay. I don't remember what happened." She noticed she was in a hospital room.

"A little accident," he said. "Nothing serious. The worst problem is you'll make the front pages across the country. There are pictures."

She buried her face in the pillow, all the memories of that night flooding back to her, then raised herself up again, looking at him. "There are always pictures. Somewhere a camera is forever turning. I face it in my sleep."

· 265 ·

During the next few days it became fully, appallingly clear to her for the first time just how public her life had become. There were indeed front-page pictures—some enterprising photographer had been monitoring police calls and arrived just in time to snap a shot of her bloodied, unconscious face. It was the gossip columns that bothered her most, though, all those scurrilous, mean rumors—some not so far from the truth—about what had caused the accident. It made her realize she couldn't hide the events of her life anymore, or wipe out the past simply by getting on a train. She was now public property. Her face had become so well known she'd never be able to go anywhere for the rest of her life without someone observing her.

The day she was released from the hospital, Peter and von Menzel picked her up with secretive grins and drove her to a secluded house on Laurel Canyon. It was large, painted white, brick and frame with a gabled roof—and it was hers, they told her proudly, paid for by her new contract following the success of *Istanbul.*

"What, not even a swimming pool?" she asked, walking through the overgrown garden. The house was nice, but actually it was too close to the style of Friedrich's town house in Berlin to make her entirely comfortable. Everything was in a severe, masculine style, much more to von Menzel's taste than hers—even though she was paying for it. Didn't he trust her enough to let her select her own house? she thought, with a touch of resentment. "Peter and I are going to have to liven this place up," she said. "I'm not excited by antler chandeliers."

Secretly, though, she was pleased at von Menzel's attempt to make amends, and when she reported to MGM to begin filming on her second movie, *Reunion in Paris,* she found another surprise waiting for her. To her delight and amazement she'd been assigned a completely new dressing room, all mirrored, even the walls and ceiling. Pink marble and crystal were everywhere. She ran across the thick pink rugs, then hugged Peter. "Where's von Menzel?" she cried. "I've got to see him. We'll open a bottle of champagne."

"Yes, go get him," Peter beamed. Marika had come in a few days earlier than scheduled, and von Menzel was still doing preparatory work across the lot. "This is perfect! We can see you up there on the screen, but you're not a star until you have the dressing room to go with it!"

Marika ran from sound stage to sound stage looking for the one where von Menzel was shooting, and was rushing up to him with her news when a not altogether pleasant sight stopped her cold. There, being lit by Hermann, was an almost exact replica of herself, a pseudo-Marika Kreisler. The unknown actress had studiously copied Marika's blonde hair, her stylized clothing, her smoldering eyes, her crimson mouth, and her pale, oval, languid face. Hermann's lighting brought out the deep hollows in her cheeks, as he bathed her face in seductive shadows. Between her tapered fingers, she daintily held a cigarette, the exact way Marika did. Apparently, the stand-in had studied her every mannerism.

Shocked and astonished, Marika stood looking at the woman. Even though she knew she was only a stand-in, Marika felt robbed of something vital and precious that was uniquely her own. Was Marika Kreisler a real person? Or was she a manufactured item that could easily be duplicated on the assembly line?

Von Menzel turned quickly, aware of Marika's presence for the first time. "What are you doing here?" His voice sounded angry. "You weren't expected until Monday."

"So I see," she said icily.

He reached for the hand of the stand-in. "Here," he said, "I want you to meet Anna Berndt. She's from Berlin, too."

"Miss Kreisler," Anna said, her lips parting in a seductive smile, "I'm so honored to meet you. I'm such a fan of yours."

"So I see," Marika said, repeating herself. She turned and walked off the sound stage. Peter was standing outside her dressing room. "Take me home," she told him. "Only one movie in Hollywood, and already von Menzel's found the perfect look-alike."

"No one will ever replace you," Peter assured her.

Marika laughed bitterly. "That's the exact line I used on Garbo."

* * *

By the time her third film, *Blood on My Hands,* was released, von Menzel had convinced Marika that as long as they remained an artistic team, they could do no wrong. Despite the tension between them, she felt she was completely his creation, that she would be nothing without his direction. "He, and he alone, can bring out the *real* me," she told Peter. "Von can make me blossom in front of the camera."

In the film, Marika played a call girl, Clark Gable a small-time crook pursued by the police. Marika continued to be beautiful, erotic, but lyrically detached, and von Menzel grew ever more elaborate with her costumes, even going so far as to dress her up as a black-widow spider once, in a scene that had nothing to do with the cheap role she was playing.

The picture was reviewed, as were all of her pictures, with the line, "Marika Kreisler never looked more beautiful." Although she was nearing her thirty-third birthday, she seemed to remain eternally youthful. Rarely was she compared to Garbo these days. Now other actresses were compared to her. Anna Berndt was only the first of a legion of imitators who tried, but failed, to capture Marika's unique look. Even Joan Crawford made her face up like Marika's.

As the months in Hollywood passed, Marika grew increasingly temperamental, even imperious, in her behavior toward others. Peter often got the brunt of her anger, but when von Menzel came on the set, she was all submission again, as if he were a religion to which she was pledged. Von Menzel seemed to have less time than ever for her now, and Peter kept telling Marika that he must be having an affair with someone. But Marika refused to believe it. "I fear Von is either celibate or impotent. If not, why wouldn't he respond to me?"

After the premiere of *Blood on My Hands,* von Menzel disappeared for several weeks, with only some vague words about "going to the Colorado mountains," and when he returned it was to Marika's Laurel Canyon home late at night. Peter let him in, and Marika put on her robe and rushed downstairs to see him. The unshaven director faced her in his hunting clothes.

"You won't believe it," he told her in an eager voice he rarely used. "I've just written the script for our next film together. Rita's script was terrible. She keeps wanting to make you into Joan of Arc."

"Do you have it with you?" Marika asked. "I want to read it now."

"Of course I have it," he said, "but it's handwritten in German. There's been no time to have it typed."

"Dear Von, I know the language well," she said with a smile. "And I'll go over it while you shower. You smell like a bear."

From the moment she started the script of *The Dancer*, she knew this film would be von Menzel's ultimate erotic fantasy to date. It was the story of a spy posing as an exotic Middle-Eastern belly dancer, and the script described in detail the outfits she'd wear. They were to be alluring, even garish, flaunting her sexuality and suggesting a mysterious capacity to seduce. His favorite seemed to be a filmy voluminous silk skirt of pale mauve, held low on her hips by an encircling band of glittering violet amethysts. The world would see her navel uncovered. The same filmy material would be used to make a halter-brassiere, with a thin, tapering strap over her left shoulder, leaving her breasts semi-exposed. Clusters of jeweled bracelets on her wrists would hold a flowing cape, and she would whirl as she danced, barefoot, the cape billowing about her, cloudlike, her hair swinging loosely in the air, flowing with the rhythmic movements of her body. The description went on, breathlessly, ecstatically.

She was convinced he couldn't possibly write so enticingly about her body and her clothes without actually desiring her sexually. Tonight she was determined to have him. She'd waited long enough. He didn't have to live out his fantasies on the screen—he could turn them into reality in her arms. She'd even dress up for him, in whatever costume he wanted, if that was what was needed to excite him.

It affected her strangely to be the star in another man's erotic dreams. He'd selected her as his goddess to live out those dreams, at least on the screen, and the more she thought about making love to von Menzel, the more thrilling and compelling it became for her. He wouldn't take her as a real woman, no, he would elevate her to the role of Venus, he would worship her, adore her.

"Do you like it?" von Menzel asked, after he'd showered and put on Peter's robe.

"I love it," she breathed.

Two bottles of champagne later, they found themselves sitting before the fire in her living room. She'd never been this intimate with him before. Putting down her glass, she got up and walked over to him, easing down on the bear rug next to him. "I can't wait any longer," she whispered. "If you're not going to seduce me, I'll seduce you."

He seemed to ease away from her.

"Now what's wrong?" she purred. "I saw all those movies of you playing the Hun lusting after Red Cross nurses. I served in a French hospital once. Imagine I'm a Red Cross nurse, and you're a brutal Prussian commander."

He hesitated, then said, "It's precisely because you saw me in all those movies that I've never made love to you." He paused for a long moment, the flames of the burning wood lighting up his face. "Von Menzel the man is not as he was in those movies."

She huddled close to him, her hands reaching inside his robe and stroking his chest. "I please you on the screen," she said. "Why can't I please you off the screen?" She was kissing his cheek now, his neck, his chest. His body tightened suddenly, as her fingers dropped lower, and she discovered to her disappointment she wasn't arousing him. His penis was tiny, even smaller than Count Dabrowsky's and when she looked up into his face, his eyes were closed, a deep crease in his brow. It was obviously humiliating for him to have his lack of manhood exposed.

Her lips closed over his penis, and she began to bring it to life. Somehow, her loving caresses seemed to give him security. It was as if he'd been prepared to face rejection, but when it didn't happen, he started to assert himself. He reached for her head, guiding her. Slowly he assumed control, and as he began to mount her, he looked straight into her blue eyes. "Thank you."

Her body pressed against his, and she ran her fingers along his back. She tried everything she could to make him feel he was satisfying her, even though he wasn't. After all, she was an actress. She owed him a lot. What was one more deception? His climax was fast, and before she knew it he was pulling out of her. his face pathetic. All along he'd known he couldn't fulfill her, at least not that way.

Now he was kissing her breasts, his lips circling in long easy arcs. In some distant room of the house, Peter was playing music—too loudly. She half closed her eyes.

He moved between her legs, and she could feel his mouth on

her. Slowly she began to respond, stimulated into an animal demand. Though it wasn't the love she'd wanted from him, or even fantasized about, it was love, after all, and it could satisfy. The sensations going through her body proved that.

Upstairs the tempo of Peter's music seemed to quicken von Menzel's movements. She trembled and moaned, and the sounds coming from her throat served to stir him on. Mouth open, she felt her body growing tense. She was on the brink, her legs holding him in a viselike grip. Shuddering, she gave way.

* * *

On the last day of shooting on *The Dancer*, a cable came by special messenger to Marika's dressing room. Gabrielle was dead of cancer in Vienna. A needle-sharp pain pricked Marika and tears of despair welled in her eyes.

Peter held her hand and lightly touched her fingertips with his lips as she sat in silence with him, slowly sipping a glass of champagne. Her old fear of death was returning. All the important people in her life had died: Count Dabrowsky, Julian, Friedrich, Lotte, and now Gabrielle. Would she be next? Or perhaps von Menzel?

Only the Contessa seemed to survive forever, her letters from the Riviera more sparkling than ever. She wrote almost weekly, sounding more and more like a woman in love. How was that possible at her age?

Marika quietly fought against giving in to her pain, to her sense of loss over Gabrielle's death. After all, she had a film to complete, if she could only get through the last scene. Gabrielle was gone, but her life had been good and full. Apparently, she'd died without too much suffering.

Peter poured her another glass of champagne and she looked into his kind eyes. "I don't know what I'd do without you," she said. A sudden knock and the assistant director was in her dressing room, conveying von Menzel's request that she appear immediately on the set.

"He really is a brute," she protested, as a numbness descended upon her. "How can he expect me to work feeling like this?"

Peter excused himself, but returned shortly, a look of disdain on his face. "Von says it's all right. It's a crying scene. He thinks your pain will make it all the better."

* * *

The Dancer was not a success. The critics pointed out, rightfully, that von Menzel was repeating himself and that his entire career seemed increasingly based on a grab bag of tricks. Von Menzel grew sensitive to their comments, yet seemed trapped in his erotic fantasies. Again and again, he asked Marika to do scenes startlingly evocative of her earlier pictures, but ever more lavish, ever more decadent. On their new picture together, *Dishonored Empress,* he insisted that the court of the Empress be re-created in immense, painstaking detail, down to silk underwear for the Imperial Guards, even though it would never appear on the screen.

Throughout the film, Marika's lids stayed languorously half-closed, according to the legend she'd built up, as she moved among fantastically elaborate sets and costumes and bizarre court doings, but she'd begun to see quite clearly that she needed to break with von Menzel and work with another director.

Meanwhile, fueled by months of "Svengali and Trilby" reports, and the gossip that had circulated ever since Marika's car accident, Hollywood buzzed with rumors of an affair between Marika and von Menzel. Although she continued to refer to herself as Countess Dabrowsky, reporters were skeptical, and many speculated in print that there was no such person as Count Dabrowsky. One intrepid reporter in Warsaw managed to come up with a record of a Count Dabrowsky who had disappeared during World War I. The reporter wrote that the Count's birth date—sometime in the 1840's—hardly qualified him as a candidate for Marika Kreisler's husband.

Then, the final week of shooting on *Dishonored Empress,* a Berlin newspaper announced in front-page headlines that Frau von Menzel was divorcing her husband and suing Marika for a quarter of a million dollars in damages, alleging alienation of her husband's affections. Marika was stunned, then horrified, at what this would do to her life: the reporters, the publicity, the creeping, prying questions and sly grins. She felt naked, all her affairs soon to be paraded before the world.

And what about von Menzel? A life with him seemed totally out of the question, especially now, but she had nothing to replace him, either as a lover or a director. As inadequate as he was, both

· 272 ·

professionally and in bed, he was something to hold on to, she supposed.

She stood by the window, looking out onto the moonlit California landscape but longing for a winter scene. She remembered as a child walking in the Berlin streets when the snow was heavy and the limbs of the trees in the park were bowed down with their load of snow. She used to whisper a song to be carried by the wind to the river, and she tried to remember it now, but the sounds coming from her throat were mere moans. She placed her hand on her mouth to blot out her own strange-sounding voice, and it was then, with a start, that she noticed how sweat-soaked her palms were, even though they were cold as death.

With von Menzel at her side, Marika delivered a handwritten statement to the press the next morning. She refused to answer questions. Vowing to fight all lawsuits, she claimed she loved Count Dabrowsky and that he was standing by her.

"Our marriage might look unconventional," she admitted in a nervous voice, "but it works for us. He's opposed to my career in motion pictures, yet he grants me the freedom to have it. On the other hand, the Count prefers a life of seclusion." At the end of the conference, Marika dismissed Frau von Menzel's charges as "untrue and unsubstantiated."

The world press sharpened its pencils for what appeared to be the love-triangle battle of the thirties, but it was not to be. Von Menzel hurried to Berlin, and within hours of his arrival, was reunited with his wife, and announced that he had assumed complete financial responsibility for his family. The next day, Frau von Menzel's attorney reported that she was dropping all charges.

Back in Hollywood, Marika felt the loss of von Menzel, and found it hard to accept the fact that he was gone. She was sure he'd come back to her when world attention no longer focused so sharply on them, but she only wished he'd assured her of that fact before his departure. Instead, he'd kissed her on the cheek and predicted that *Dishonored Empress* would be their greatest hit to date. It wasn't much comfort.

With a deep feeling of uneasiness, Marika wandered alone in the garden, tense and impatient. She found herself dressed in black as if in mourning; her skin was almost too white against the cloth, and she noticed her weight was dropping. The situation was intolerable! She seemed to be a broken-off fragment of a woman. Upstairs she could often hear Peter and his lover of the evening wandering around in their suite, and once she was tempted to join them, but she held back.

And then everything changed. Her doctor informed her that she was pregnant again.

* * *

Disguised in a black wig and dark glasses, Marika took in the lush, blue-green Mediterranean coast of France with an eager eye. The Côte d'Azur was just what she needed. Free from the problems of Hollywood, she would have her baby at the villa occupied by the Contessa, and no one need know. Of course, the official story had been that she was going to meet Count Dabrowsky in a secret rendezvous.

As her taxi pulled up in front of a brightly colored villa, Marika took in the beauty of the fragrant garden, and, in the distance and over the water, the shimmer of Cannes and the mountains beyond. A housekeeper showed her through the parlor and out to a smaller garden in back, where a graveled walk led around to a pool with a sundial at the center of it.

There in a peacock chair sat the Contessa. The years had wrought a remarkable change in her. Her beauty had long ago faded, she was at least forty pounds overweight, and the two-piece beach-lounging outfit she wore, together with diamond earrings and high heels, was absolutely hideous. Her once-beautiful auburn hair had turned a flaming red, and she had become a chain-smoker, as attested to by the mountain of crushed butts at her side.

"Marika!" she called out, appearing owl-like behind huge pink-tinted sunglasses. Her voice had taken on a strident, aggressive tone. "Come over here at once!" Marika went over and embraced the old woman, although the act repulsed her a little.

The Contessa removed her sunglasses and stared at Marika through ancient eyes. "There have been changes in that face, my dear," she said. "I, of all people, know what they are." Raising a mottled hand, she traced the contour of Marika's face with autocratic precision. "Your face is everywhere. But I must confess I've never seen one of your films."

Anger flared in Marika, as she pulled back from the old crone, her eyes traveling around the trelliswork of the garden walls. "Those films pay for all this."

"I'm sure they do," the Contessa said, a capricious defiance coming over her face. "I was wondering how many minutes would pass before you'd remind me."

"I'm sorry," Marika replied, but the old woman's raised hand stopped her from continuing.

"It's all right," the Contessa said, after looking for a long moment into Marika's eyes. Then, softly, she went on, "We've gone through pregnancies before."

That afternoon, Marika began to unwind on her private terrace over a pitcher of martinis, and the Contessa, quite relaxed, began to confide in her. "You know," she told her, "you've restored my vitality by letting me live here. My unhappiness in Poland had drained me dry. I was ready to die."

Stabbing an olive, Marika said, "Nonsense! You'll live forever."

"It's one thing to possess vitality," the Contessa replied. "Quite another to use it."

As if signaled, two handsome young men appeared, an Italian, who introduced himself with a flashing grin as Gian-Carlo, and he in turn introduced his American companion, Steve. They bowed politely and kissed Marika's hand, before being dismissed like servants. "Marika and I must catch up on woman-talk."

After they were gone, the Contessa wrapped her shawl tighter around her. "Those escorts are my lovers. Of course, they're also each other's lovers."

Recovering quickly, Marika asked skeptically, "Why do you have two of them?"

"I'm making up for lost time," the Contessa said. "At my age, how much longer can I carry on?"

Later, Marika slipped into her bikini and went for a swim in the heart-shaped pool. Emerging from the water, she found Gian-Carlo waiting for her at poolside with a large white beach towel and, sitting beside her, he eagerly proceeded to pour out his life story, including his discovery at the age of thirteen in Capri by an English composer. "I have this young friend in Villefranche," he confided. "He's *very* interested in meeting the famous Marika Kreisler."

"I'm here for a rest," Marika said, shutting her eyes. "Not love."

"Okay, darling," Gian-Carlo said, "but you're missing out on something special. He's the best lover on the Riviera—and I should know!"

That night at dinner, as the second pitcher of martinis was passed around, the Contessa confessed, "Youth is a drug, and I'm hooked. It costs a lot, but I don't care!" Marika smiled sardonically. This was how the profits of her great erotic cinematic fantasies were being spent.

It was after midnight when Gian-Carlo and Steve came for the Contessa, and by that time, the two young men had to lift her out of her peacock chair and partially carry her to her upstairs bedroom.

Marika continued to sit by the pool, watching the reflection of light playing aimlessly on the water.

* * *

When the baby was born, it was a girl, painlessly delivered. How different from the throes of her first pregnancy, she thought, and, unlike her second, no Franz was waiting to take her child from her. It was hers, and hers alone. Von Menzel, she was sure, didn't want it. She named it Lotte in honor of her own mother.

After three weeks of recovery, she decided to fly back to Hollywood incognito, and have Peter return later with the baby. Von Menzel had already returned from Berlin, and Marika was anxious for a reunion—she hadn't dared write the director, or even speak to him on the telephone during their long separation.

On the flight back to New York, Marika discovered that *Dishonored Empress* had been released and, painfully, she read the reviews. The picture was a disaster, according to the critics, who were almost unanimous in their condemnation of the film, and the public was staying away in droves.

One reviewer wrote: "Marika Kreisler, never more beautiful, literally walked through the film in a dreamy trance, like a victim of shell shock. There is little or no action in *Dishonored Empress,* and what action there is is so vague and fleeting that this reviewer, for one, had not the slightest idea of what was going on. The film contains mostly elaborate, surrealist sets designed to show off Kreisler's unreal costumes, and that is hardly the rationale for a movie. Wake up, Marika Kreisler! If you keep on this way, you'll soon find yourself with a wrecked career."

Marika sank into gloom.

Back at her Laurel Canyon home, she found a new script and a letter from von Menzel waiting on her desk. Von Menzel's news was hardly more encouraging. Mayer had informed him he was assigned to one more picture and one picture only, and if that failed, he was through. Although European sales were still fairly high, von Menzel/Kreisler films were losing the American market. Something drastic had to be done, so to change both their images, von Menzel had decided to cast Marika in a Western. She would still play the role of a floozie, but at least the scenic backdrops would be different.

After reading the script, Marika decided she had to talk to von Menzel right away. Frustrated at the busy signal she kept getting from his house, she hopped into her car and drove down to Santa Monica, her heart pounding ridiculously, she thought, at the prospect of seeing him again. Outside the house, she stood for a moment in von Menzel's garden, a lovely, secluded, intimate place where he'd walked arm in arm with her, assuring her she was the most desirable woman on earth. Once he'd kissed her eyes and told her he worshipped her, though the next day on the set he'd been cold as an icicle.

She followed a moonlit trail of flagstones around to the side of the house, and took out her key from the secret hiding place where she always kept it. It seemed wrong to knock on his front door, as if she were a stranger. Inside the hallway, however, she froze at the sound of voices. Was she interrupting something? Perhaps she should turn back. It wasn't right to invade von Menzel's privacy this way. But then again, whatever he was involved in probably concerned her, too.

Slowly she opened the heavy oak door, and to her shock, there was von Menzel on the rug in front of his fireplace, making love to someone. Furiously, Marika quickly switched on an overhead chandelier. The woman screamed. It was Anna Berndt, her stand-in.

"Marika, what are you doing here?" von Menzel demanded, quickly dismounting Anna. To her horror, Marika saw he'd strapped a dildo around his hips like a harness. Tears of rage and anguish flowed down her cheeks as she watched him unstrap the dildo and reach for his dressing gown. She turned her back to him. She couldn't look at the shameful thing, at the way von Menzel was debasing himself. When he had regained his composure, he turned to Marika again. "I said, what are you doing here?"

"I'm asking myself that same question," Marika said shakily, reaching into her purse for a cigarette. "What a homecoming party!"

Anna defiantly continued to lie on the floor, not bothering to cover up her nakedness, flaunting her nudity in front of Marika. Sensing what she was up to, von Menzel reached for her dress and tossed it over her. "Get up!" he commanded.

Anna reluctantly rose from the floor. "Welcome home, Miss Kreisler. I heard the good news about your baby girl. Congratulations!"

"Thank you," Marika said in utter despair. She could hear her own heart beating.

"I've always wanted a little baby girl myself," Anna said. She slipped on her dress and headed for von Menzel's liquor cabinet. "Maybe Von will give me one to call my own one day—but not with the thing he was using tonight."

Swiftly, von Menzel was behind her, pulling her around, slapping her so hard one of her earrings went flying into a corner of the room. "Get out! You slut! How dare you say that?" Her face twisted with fear, Anna hurried from the room in tears.

"If she's a slut, what does that make you?" Marika asked quietly. "What does it make me?"

Von Menzel looked at her uncomfortably, then said, "A woman of your sophistication should never arrive unannounced at a gentleman's home."

Marika walked toward him, her hands limp by her side. "I was eager . . ." she said in a hesitant voice, ". . . to tell you about your daughter."

Von Menzel's face hardened. "I have no daughter," he said curtly. "I have two sons, both of whom are living in Berlin with *my wife*."

The sudden silence in the room was deafening. Marika stood bewildered, not wanting to be the usual jealous, unreasonable female. It seemed useless to appeal to von Menzel. "I see . . ." she said, finally. "I'm leaving."

His eyes flickered as he looked at her, and his face was dark, clouded over. The image was frightening. "No, don't go," he said in a straightforward, businesslike voice. "Now that you're here, we might as well discuss our next picture. Have you read the script?"

"Yes," she answered vacantly.

Von Menzel turned off the chandelier, and a stream of white moonlight filled the room. "What do you think of it?" he asked softly.

"I hate it!" she screamed. Crushing out her cigarette, she felt her courage flooding back as well as all of her earlier anger. "There will be no new picture with you. You and I are finished!"

The moonlight seemed to have disappeared and suddenly only the broken shadows and light from the fire filled the room. "I doubt that," he said in a low, creeping voice totally foreign to her. With a start, she realized it was his screen voice, used only when he played the loathsome Hun. He was at the liquor cabinet, pouring himself a brandy. "Did you read the terms of your contract? The new one we signed before you went off to your . . . rendezvous with Count Dabrowsky? I'm to be the director of all your American films for the next ten years. It says so. Of course, you have the right to go elsewhere if you wish. To London, for instance. Or," he added in a particularly nasty tone, "to Berlin if you want to go completely Nazi."

The realization stunned her. It was almost impossible to believe that this man talking to her was the father of her daughter. The lurid scene with the dildo came rushing back, and she started to say something, but only a bitter laugh escaped her. The laughter continued until choked off by sobs and blinding tears. She knew if the Western failed, von Menzel would be finished in Hollywood and she'd be rid of him forever, but the realization kept drumming inside her head that if she made another box-office disaster like *Dishonored Empress,* she'd be through in pictures herself. She'd already starred in too many bad movies. She had to make a success of that . . . *Western* even if it meant being stuck with von Menzel for years. It was all too much.

He moved toward her, but she didn't want him to touch her ever again. In a daze, she rushed to the door, pausing only briefly in the cool of the garden. It would be her last visit there.

* * *

In searing, 110-degree August weather, the filming of *Desert Flower* began in Reno, Nevada. The only ice-cold element on the set was the relationship between Marika and von Menzel, a condition made even worse by his refusal to speak to her, even to rehearse a scene. After the first day's shooting, the silent treatment got to her so badly she shouted in front of the cast and the crew, "Directors are supposed to direct! Tell me what to do!"

"Who am I," von Menzel asked, "to tell the great Marika Kreisler how to act?"

With tears of exasperation in her eyes, Marika hurried from the set, retreating to her dressing room. Her eyes were always bloodshot now, and she had taken to gobbling sleeping pills. She couldn't stand to watch the first rushes. Never before had Hermann photographed her so unattractively. For the first time in her career, she delayed appearing on the set in the morning, and instead sulked in her dressing room for hours, waiting for von Menzel to come and summon her personally. Instead, he sent a grip.

Marika knew her performance was terrible. She knew nothing of saloon life in the Old West, or of the women who had inhabited the bordellos there. The only backdrops she was at home with were the imperial courts of Europe or those of the years of postwar German decadence. Lacking a firm hold on the character she played, and getting no help from von Menzel, she portrayed Desert Flower as a Berlin cabaret entertainer in the tradition of Hilde, and as she watched the results of one week's shooting, she realized her acting was totally unrelated to the action in the rest of the picture. It was as if she'd been filmed in the clouds somewhere.

Joel McCrea, the leading man, played his role like a typical Western star, and, needless to say, their styles did not mesh in the slightest. Every day he threatened to walk off the picture, complaining, legitimately, that von Menzel directed the cowboy extras as if they were guards in the Imperial Court of Vienna. The situation got worse and worse, until one night von Menzel stormed into Marika's hotel suite, his steely reserve finally deteriorating. He found her huddled on the sofa in a ball, trembling with nervous exhaustion.

"Enough's enough!" he yelled. "This love you say you have for me. It's destroying me. It's ruining you. It's wrecking our careers. God save me from such love!"

"What conceit," she shouted back at him. "I never loved you. You were the most miserable lover of my whole life. And that includes a seventy-five-year-old count!"

"Shout louder!" von Menzel said, deliberately lowering his voice to a whisper. "Let the world in on our private business."

"Get out of my room!" Marika screamed.

The next morning she didn't appear on the set, and von Menzel stubbornly shot around her. When she did show up the next day, she had to be helped from her car by Peter. Von Menzel looked into her face and ordered Peter to drive her back to her suite at once. "Her eyes can't focus," he told his cameraman.

That night von Menzel announced to the press in Reno, "This is my last picture with Frau Kreisler. Creatively, we've gone as far together as we can." When Peter presented this item to her in the morning, she tossed the newspaper to the floor. "I'm the one leaving him," she retorted bitterly. But she was so confused now she barely knew what was the truth.

Soon the film began to run seriously over budget, and studio officials began calling von Menzel every hour on the hour to find out what was wrong. Naturally, he blamed the added costs on Marika, and soon he did something even worse.

In the final days of filming, he brought Anna Berndt onto the set. So as not to look like Marika, her appearance had been changed with heavy black eyebrows and a red wig, and von Menzel informed Marika that Anna was to play another tough, hot-tempered barroom entertainer in the fistfight sequence. At first Marika was determined to walk off the set altogether, but then another thought took over.

As the cameras rolled, Marika tore into Anna with a savage fury, as if she were plunging into a jungle. "She's killing me," Anna screamed, tugging at Marika's hair, but the voice of the struggling actress was blotted out by the catcalls of the barroom extras. Marika couldn't stop herself. Red fingernails arched for action, she raked Anna's face. Anna kicked her in the shins, but Marika was all over her, her fingers ripping off Anna's earrings, then gouging at her eyes.

Anna fell to the floor, and with her high heels Marika kicked her in the side. She was completely dizzy now, the world turning black around her, fighting blindly. It wasn't Anna she was attacking, but an awful caricature of herself, and as the fight intensified, she knew it wasn't even that anymore, but von Menzel she was striking out against. And then the hair-pulling grew bolder, and the final realization came to Marika. She was attacking herself, destroying—once and for all—von Menzel's creation of Marika Kreisler. "I want to be free," she kept muttering under her breath, as she hit Anna again and again.

Only when caught in a heap on the sawdust floor, only when staring into Anna's near-dead eyes, with their unseeing pupils, did Marika's sanity return. The stand-in lay slumped back, her head askew on the wooden floor.

"Cut! Cut!" von Menzel was screaming. Marika looked up into his face and saw there only utter glee at capturing such a scene on camera.

"Get a doctor!" Peter was shouting.

All energy seemed to drain from Marika, and she collapsed on the floor, falling on top of Anna.

* * *

Marika's picture didn't make the front page, but Anna's—all black and bruised—did, under the headline: ACTRESS CHARGES KREISLER WITH ASSAULT AND BATTERY. In desperation, Marika fled to London, leaving behind her a career in shambles.

Von Menzel had been fired immediately and another director called in to reshoot some of the location scenes in Nevada, but, except for the fight scene, *Desert Flower* was pronounced a catastrophe, even before its release. Critics everywhere were predicting the professional demise of Marika Kreisler.

Arriving in London with Peter and Lotte, Marika found herself front-page news there, too, at least in Lord Beaverbrook's *Daily Express*. One reporter wrote, "Marika Kreisler, in a desperate attempt to salvage a faltering career, has turned to England. But upon seeing her latest film shipped over here, *Dishonored Empress*, I can only concur with our American colleagues who 'branded' her box-office poison."

At least she wasn't the top scandal of the day, Marika thought with a grim humor. Her name might be in the headlines, but

England was far more interested in a story that nobody had even dared to print yet. Wherever she went, the subject of two lovers, the King of England and a twice-wed Baltimore divorcée, cropped up. The affair was rocking the Empire. At times, alone in her suite at the Savoy, Marika longed to trade positions with Mrs. Simpson. She was far more capable of being a suitable mistress for the King than the American woman!

The film offers Marika had hoped for in England were not forthcoming, except for some cheap roles as floozies. Typically, they wanted her to play women such as a Marseilles prostitute rescued from her way of life by a Cornish seaman. "But it's really a man's picture," Marika protested. "There's nothing in it for me, except to reform. I'm so *tired* of playing whores." Sometimes, when she couldn't sleep, she had Peter screen a print of *Carnival* for her in the early hours of the morning. "I've got to find another part like that," she said. "It's the best work I've ever done. I can't have peaked so soon!"

More than anything, she wanted to appear in a film version of Shaw's *Caesar and Cleopatra,* and she even went so far as to write the playwright requesting a meeting. In a few days he replied, on a postcard, respectfully but firmly turning down her request.

One gray morning, Marika asked Peter to order a small touring car sent around to their hotel.

"But you can't be seen in that," Peter objected.

"My whole purpose is not to be seen," Marika said mysteriously. "You and I are going to the West Country . . . incognito."

Attired in her black wig and glasses, Marika set out with Peter for Somerset, and finally, in response to his mystified looks, she confided, "Ever since I've been in England I've been worried about my husband suddenly appearing."

"Your husband!" The news hit Peter like a bombshell. "Count Dabrowsky?"

"No," she said calmly, "Charles Rankin." She glanced over at him. "Oh, it's a long story, Peter, and I don't want to bore you. Let's just say it's an unfortunate incident in my past. But it's *my* past. Somehow I feel I have to know what's happened to him."

Peter sat back as if all the air had been knocked out of him. Finally, about half a mile from her once-favorite pub, she braked the touring car. "I want you to walk to that pub from here," she said. "It's called the Punch Bowl. Everybody will know Charles. Find out what's happened to him. But be careful, he might even be there. After all, it's Saturday night."

An hour and a half later, Peter's footsteps could be heard slowly approaching. Climbing in next to her, he turned and said, "Rankin is dead. He died in 1930." A stillness came over the car. During Peter's absence, Marika had been looking at her wedding picture, snapped in 1918, and now her fingers slowly enclosed the photograph until it became a crumpled ball clenched in her fist.

"We'd better get back to London," Peter said finally.

* * *

At the hotel desk, a message awaited her, with most unexpected news. The German ambassador had called to say that an agent of Dr. Goebbels himself had flown in from Berlin with a very special request—a private meeting with Marika Kreisler, at which he intended to convey personal greetings from the Führer.

Marika was stunned. During her Hollywood years, she'd tried to erase all memories of Germany from her mind and had nearly succeeded. She'd kept away from foreign news, avoided gatherings of expatriates in Hollywood, and almost managed to close her eyes to the Nazis. Now all the memories of her past came flooding back: Brigitte, her son Anton, the lovely streets where she used to walk. Surely things could not be as bad as they said under the Nazis. She was suddenly homesick and anxious to return to Friedrich's town house in Berlin.

The next morning found her visibly nervous, as Peter escorted the Nazi propaganda official, Albrecht Eher, into the room. A large man with slicked-back hair, he bowed from the waist and kissed her hand. "The cinema does not even begin to convey your beauty."

Marika licked her lips and tried to smile seductively. "Thank you." She recognized Eher now. Before working for Dr. Goebbels, he had been an actor himself, known for his ferocious temper, which had inevitably led him to play heavies in films. Because of his red beard, he was nicknamed "The Red Boar."

Eher reached into his briefcase and handed her a letter and a photograph. Without his identifying it, she knew at once who it was. "Anton!" she cried out. "My Anton!" The boy in the picture was thin and delicate, a mass of white blondness, with pale, sunken eyes, in total contrast to the overpowering masculinity of Franz, his father.

"Your son has not been well," Eher said, coughing slightly. "He needs his mother with him." He sat straight and still in his chair, his eyes boring into Marika.

Hoping to control her shaking, Peter put a lit cigarette into Marika's mouth, and she drew on it deeply, picking at threads of tobacco that caught on the tip of her tongue. Brushing her hand across her blonde hair, she started to say something, but the sound came awkwardly from her throat. She got up slowly and walked to the window. The image of Franz kept appearing before her. In some way, she still loved him and wanted to be with him, even though he terrified her.

Peter took Anton's letter and began to read it slowly. It was a pathetic, touching, tender note from a brutalized little boy who was seeking the love of a mother he'd never known. Before Peter could finish reading it, Marika was crying. She excused herself quickly and headed for the bathroom, and stood there for a moment staring into the mirror. Drawing a deep breath, she patted her tears dry, checked her makeup carefully, and went back.

When she returned, Eher had another letter waiting for her— this one from the Führer himself. Marika was tremendously flattered, but frightened at the same time. Opening the letter, she read his message herself. Hitler recalled meeting her in Berlin, the introduction arranged by Brigitte: Brigitte was now the respected matriarch of the Nazi party. He urged her to come back, noting, "You will become the greatest cinema actress of all time, the pride of the German people."

"It's overwhelming," Marika said, carefully folding the letter.

"You're the Führer's favorite motion-picture star," Eher said enthusiastically. "But he feels you belong in Germany, making German films. Dr. Goebbels agrees, of course." He was reaching into his briefcase again. "I have a five-year contract here with UFA. We want you to read it carefully and seriously consider our offer."

Standing up, Eher again bowed from the waist, this time clicking his heels. "Heil Hitler!" he saluted. "We hope to have your decision tonight. I'm due back in Berlin tomorrow."

As soon as he was gone, Marika poured herself a drink. Following her debacle in Hollywood, she was pleased at the prospect of getting work. "Louis B. Mayer doesn't want me," she said. "Von Menzel is through with me. But Hitler thinks I'm great. Isn't that ironic?"

"It's incredible," Peter said, taking the drink from her. "You don't need this."

"At least I'll be working," she said. In the next room she could hear Lotte's crying and her English nurse comforting her. "After all, we do need the money."

Peter walked over and took her hand. "I was hoping for something in England. It seems safer somehow." His voice was forlorn, melancholy.

"Don't start this Nazi thing," Marika said impatiently. "I've heard nothing but Nazi atrocities from von Menzel. I'm an actress, not a politician." She paused, feeling defensive in front of Peter. "I'll have my choice of scripts and directors. I'll get to play some of the classical roles I've always wanted to. And if Berlin doesn't work out for us, we can always leave."

"Can we?" Peter asked pointedly.

"Why not?" she said. "Goebbels isn't a barbarian. He's not going to put me in prison." She went over and took the drink again that Peter had placed on her liquor cabinet. "I will leave if he asks me . . ."

"To make propaganda films for the Third Reich," Peter said, expressing the thought she didn't want to voice.

"Yes," she said firmly. "That I will not do. But anyway, it's inconceivable that he would ask me. If we can keep politics out of my pictures, then I see no reason why I shouldn't work in Germany."

"I hope it's that easy," Peter said. He picked up the contract from the coffee table and started to read it.

"You'll go with Lotte and me?" she asked tentatively.

"I'll go anywhere with you," he said, frowning, but not looking up at her.

She tightened her fingers to get a better grip on herself. "There is some risk," she said softly. "You must know."

His eyes met hers. "What risk?"

"I'm a Jew," she said flatly.

Book Three

1937–1939

Chapter 9

In Ethiopia, Italian forces entered Addis Ababa and the League of Nations proved totally ineffective against the invasion, while in Spain, Franco staged a military revolt. Bloody civil war broke out, and after Hitler agreed to give support to the Spanish rebellion, the Condor Legion proceeded to obliterate the Basque town of Guernica and its civilian inhabitants. Meanwhile, the Rome-Berlin Axis was being born. Count Galeazzo Ciano, Mussolini's son-in-law, made repeated trips to Berchtesgaden, and there Hitler assured him that "in three years Germany will be ready."

In Berlin, Goebbels had made a fateful decision. It was time the Nazi government took complete charge of all German motion-picture companies. Many of the leading members of the film colony had been leery of the long-range plans of "the little doctor," and now their worst fears had been confirmed. That is, the fears of those who had not already fled. By the time Marika arrived in Berlin, the cream of the German film industry had gone into exile, including Conrad Veidt. Although not a Jew, he'd written "Jude" across a racial questionnaire presented to him, and had fled in disgust to Hollywood.

On the train to Berlin, Eher told Marika, "With Elisabeth Bergner off the German screen, we're in need of a new queen.

Olga Tschechowa and Marianne Hoppe are completely inadequate to wear the crown. Your major competition will be Pola Negri, but with your great fame, talent, and beauty, you will be the film goddess of the Third Reich in a matter of months!"

As the train sped toward the city, Marika sat alone in her compartment, mulling over Eher's words. This was a new Germany she was entering, and she was in need of advice and strong support from somebody who could lead her through the maze. What she wanted was another von Menzel to guide her, but it was painfully clear that she was on her own now. The very air was filled with apprehension. Peter had warned her to keep her political opinions to herself. "Even the walls have ears," he told her.

In Bremen, Nazi banners and swastikas streamed from the buildings as the train pulled in. "Heil Hitler!" snapped from every mouth and the sharp clicks of marching black boots resounded in her ears. Seeing her face reflected in the railway car window, she stood up, her arm shooting out rigidly, her voice ringing with "Heil Hitler!" The image was so ludicrous it made her burst into laughter at herself, then into tears.

She could see the perversity and irony in her new career, and it both frightened and amused her. A Jewess becoming the film goddess of the Third Reich!

* * *

Her town house was waiting as if she'd never left it. Everything was in order, immaculately maintained by Brigitte, who'd been looking after the house while she'd been away. In her raspberry-red dressing room, she placed Lotte's mirror back on its familiar stand, noting that its gilt had become worn—as had her face. She looked tired, exhausted, and felt in dire need of a rest before facing the camera.

The house was lifeless without Peter. He would arrive next week with her little baby girl, but in the meantime, she had this time alone. Tomorrow, she decided, she would call on Brigitte. She wandered into her mother's private sitting room and noted a smell of lavender and expensive cigarettes. Had Brigitte ever entertained anyone here?

Suddenly, she was aware of a change in the room. Hidden eyes seemed to bore in on her. Glancing over the mantelpiece, where

Lotte's picture used to stand, she saw with distaste a rigid military portrait of Hitler.

Moments later, the stillness in the dimly lit room was broken by the sound of shuffling footsteps, and a man in a black suit entered from the hallway. He seemed unusually tall, but humped over, and she could see only one side of his face.

"Who are you?" she demanded.

"I'm Doctor von Schlabrendorff," he replied.

"Herr Doctor?" she asked, puzzled.

"Yes," he said. "I no longer practice. I'm your butler."

"Brigitte hired you?"

"That is correct," he stated. "I was once her personal physician. But my hands . . ."

She was aware of their tremulous quivering. Uneasily, she walked over to the French doors and opened them onto the garden where she'd romped as a child. The cool autumn air drove her back inside.

Doctor von Schlabrendorff seemed to be observing her too closely, and as he moved into the lamplight, she gasped as she saw his full face for the first time. The side he'd presented before had been sharply defined, almost an ascetic profile, but now she could see the crisscross of scar tissue that covered the other half, twisted and gnarled around a glass eye. His hair was sparse, just a few strands of gray which he used to cover up as much of his baldness as possible.

"The war," he said in explanation.

"I'm sorry," she replied, regaining control of herself. The damaged faces of the soldiers of Lille came rushing back to haunt her. "I didn't mean to stare."

"Good night," he said, turning his back to her. "If you need me, ring."

Though he had gone, his presence lingered in the room. She wondered if Brigitte had hired the man to spy on her.

* * *

At four the following afternoon, Brigitte arrived, accompanied by two immaculately groomed SS men, and, stepping out of the car, she motioned for the guards to wait outside. From behind her curtained window, Marika watched as the woman climbed the steps to the main hallway. Despite the hump in her back, she stood as tall as ever. Age hadn't diminished her stately walk—or made her less intimidating. Though Marika had earned the adoration of half the world, she still found that Brigitte's presence made her nervous.

"I didn't think you'd accept my invitation," Marika said, going over to greet Brigitte. Herr Doctor had ushered her into the parlor. Her aunt's face was heavily lined, though her skin looked radiantly healthy and her cheeks shone without makeup, as if she'd just scrubbed them with soap. Her long hair, completely gray now, hung down her back in a long braid, and she wore a colorful kerchief, a black velvet jacket, and a white silk apron over her skirt.

Brigitte stared long and hard at Marika. "I only agreed to see you," she said, "because you've broken with the Jew, von Menzel, and returned to the Fatherland."

Marika recalled their last meeting, and decided to ignore the remark about von Menzel.

As if reading her thoughts, Brigitte quickly interrupted. "Those demented accusations you made against me and your beloved Papa," she said, "I know now it wasn't you talking. It was the Jew who had you under his spell."

Marika bristled at Brigitte's appraisal. She hadn't even known von Menzel at the time! But still she kept quiet. A guilt still lingered in her mind for exposing Brigitte's love for Friedrich. The old woman was nearing the end of her life, and Marika didn't want to disturb her fantasies ever again.

She motioned for Brigitte to sit down on the sofa opposite her. "I appreciate your caring for the house while I was away," she said.

"I did it for Friedrich," Brigitte replied, speaking of her brother as if he were still alive.

"Herr Doctor seems very capable," Marika said. "He runs everything with an almost surgical precision." The light was already failing, and she went over to turn on a lamp.

"He was the same doctor who brought you into the world," Brigitte said.

Marika gasped in astonishment, and turned around to face Brigitte. Quickly she lit a cigarette to cover her reaction, the blue haze of its smoke drifting up. She offered her aunt one.

Waving her hand in disdain, Brigitte ostentatiously refused. "Germany has changed since you were last here. So have I. I've given up the filthy habit of smoking tobacco. No German woman worth her salt should be a slave to nicotine, or alcohol either, for that matter. The Führer is adamant on the subject."

Marika crushed out her cigarette. "I'm sorry," she said, "but smokes and drink are about the only pleasures left to me. I've certainly been hideously unlucky in love."

She got up and walked to the window. The SS guards were still posted outside, and that filled her with alarm. She remembered the jonquils that used to grow where Brigitte's car was now parked.

"Franz Hauptmann is the man you should have married," Brigitte said. "Even though he's Austrian, he's become very important to Germany."

Marika sighed, as if begging Brigitte not to press the subject.

But Brigitte ignored her. "Thank heavens you've been unlucky in love, if the object of your affection was the Jew, von Menzel."

"Must you keep referring to him that way?" Marika asked, not bothering to disguise the irritation in her voice. "I'm not even sure von Menzel is Jewish."

"I'm convinced of it!" Brigitte said, almost rising from her seat. "I've had the case investigated thoroughly. His wife and two sons have fled to Vienna. They wouldn't have abandoned all of von Menzel's business interests in Berlin if they weren't guilty."

Marika smiled, almost contemptuously. "You forget, I share in the guilt. I, too, carry the taint."

"I'm well aware of that," Brigitte said, "and will be until my dying day. In fact, I've gone to great lengths to keep you from being exposed."

"Thank you," Marika said vacantly. She sat down opposite Brigitte again. Running her fingers nervously through her hair, she said, "In a few days you'll get to meet my daughter. She's a lovely girl. I've named her Lotte."

"Another Jew-baby in the family," Brigitte said disgustedly. "The whole world knows it's von Menzel's child—though in my circles I maintain the Count Dabrowsky myth, of course."

"I think in your circles that's a very wise policy," Marika said. "For your own good." Her mouth was dry, and she needed a drink, but didn't dare take one in front of Brigitte. Even though Marika was thirty-six years old, Brigitte had succeeded in making her behave like a schoolgirl again.

Herr Doctor arrived with a tray. For a moment the room was still as he poured their tea, and then, when he was safely out of hearing distance, Brigitte quietly continued. "Eher, you know, frankly couldn't care less about your background. Can you imagine! He's still in love with the warped émigré Jew, Elisabeth Bergner. Keeps an autographed picture of her in his office so Goebbels can see it."

"I don't think that would amuse Goebbels."

"It doesn't," Brigitte said. "Eher detests Goebbels. Wants his job. Eher is sponsoring your entry into German films. That is going to make Goebbels your enemy. You must be careful. Watch your every step!"

In defiance of Brigitte, Marika reached for another cigarette, deliberately red-coating it with her lipstick. She knew how strongly Brigitte must disapprove of makeup now, even though she'd worn enough of it in her time.

"I'm an actress," Marika said. "I can't involve myself in National Socialism and political intrigue. I fully intend to make movies based only on the classics—nothing contemporary, nothing political."

"I see," Brigitte said, rising suddenly from the sofa. "What you're really saying is you're here to exploit us. A love for your Fatherland hasn't driven you back to Berlin at all. You're here for the totally selfish reason of earning our money!"

"Haven't you read the newspapers?" Marika asked. "In Hollywood, I'm considered 'box-office poison.' They actually use the term 'has-been' to describe me in print. If I am a big success in Berlin, Hollywood will be at my feet again."

"I can't believe it," Brigitte said. "You've grown worse. The whole Jewish materialistic side of you has taken over."

"I'm a painted woman!" Marika said mockingly. "A clothes-horse—everything a good German woman isn't."

"Parisian prostitutes are in league with Jewish clothing manufacturers," Brigitte charged. "Together they are trying to debase and degrade good German taste. It is the Jews who have paraded you on the screen to play and act the role of the whore. I can only feel sorry for you."

"Good-bye, Brigitte," Marika said. "I love my cosmetics, my furs, and my fancy clothes. So like you at my age."

"It's Gabrielle Schulz's influence," Brigitte spat out angrily. "She drained our women of their hard-earned marks for years. Our national resources were wasted on frivolous purchases."

"I'm not your good German milkmaid," Marika replied, "and I never will be!"

"You can't play a whore in German cinema," Brigitte said. "If you're here to revive the decadence of the twenties, you've come to the wrong place."

"We'll see," Marika answered quietly.

Without a good-bye, Brigitte turned and left.

* * *

Two weeks later, after leaving Lotte with her wet nurse, Peter drove Marika to the Tempelhof Studios where the filming of Emile Zola's *Nana* was to begin.

"At last I get to play a real role," Marika said. "Literature's most vivid courtesan—Brigitte will have a heart attack! She said I couldn't be a whore in German films." She lit a cigarette. "You know, Peter, it's very funny. As Nana, I'll rise to fame, I'll make conquests, then face a degenerate end." She sighed.

"I know what you're thinking, *Liebchen,*" Peter said. "Don't."

"You mean that my life parallels Nana's?"

"Exactly."

He drove past the guard at the gate, who meticulously checked their identification before giving them the Roman salute of the Third Reich. "But there is at least one very important difference. Unlike Nana, you'll end your life a very grand old lady—very rich, very well preserved, and with many young and handsome lovers in attendance." He smiled at her. "Who knows, we may even share some of those lovers?"

"It's a deal," she said, taking his hand and kissing it gently before pressing it against her cheek.

Later that day, as the cast broke for lunch, her director, Reinhard Ritter, called on Marika in her dressing room backstage. His face reflected his gloom. "We've heard from our Minister of People's Enlightenment and Propaganda," he said sarcastically. "I feared this."

"The little doctor?" Marika asked, hardly concerned. She was busy reapplying her makeup.

"Yes," he replied, handing her an official looking document. "Some anonymous person from your past has written Goebbels' ministry denouncing you as a Jew. You're being investigated by a special department for racial purity and genetics."

Trying not to show her alarm, Marika laughed nervously. "That sounds like an animal-breeding farm. Didn't you know? I'm contaminated!"

Ritter's eyes were cold and hard. "But the picture," he protested. "It may never be filmed."

"I was merely joking," Marika said gaily. "I'm more Prussian than anybody." But she kept her eyes shut. She was a skilled actress, but it was taking every ounce of her ability to keep her composure.

Ritter pointed to the document he'd placed on her dressing table. "You must complete the questionnaire before you can receive your *Reichsfachschaft Film* identification card."

"Very well."

"I'm going to start shooting *Nana* again this afternoon," he said. "Without you. Fortunately, we haven't shot too many of your scenes yet."

Marika rose defiantly. "You mean I'm out of the picture?"

"For the moment," Ritter said. Then, quietly, "Don't worry about it too much. These accusations are sometimes scandalous. Pola Negri had the same problem not long ago, but she was cleared of charges."

"Charges!" After he'd gone, Marika started to weep. How dare he? Charges! At first she was tempted to follow Conrad Veidt's example, to write "Jude" across the questionnaire and deliver it to Goebbels personally. But before she could pursue this thought farther, there was a quick knock at the door and Peter came in. "I heard," he said. "I've called the house." He began to pack her makeup kit. "We're taking a train to Vienna tomorrow morning. At least you'll get to see Anton before we head back . . ." He paused. His eyes met hers.

"Yes," she said, licking her lips, her voice almost an accusation. "But head back where?"

Peter remained silent, then slowly began to fold up her gown. "I'm taking you home."

That night was long, and as Marika lay awake in bed, she thought she heard her baby crying. What problems was she facing? Would she be persecuted one day as a Jewess? She rose and stared at her pale face in Lotte's mirror. She wanted to be brave, to be fierce. How she wished she had the courage, like a Joan of Arc, to assemble a crowd on Unter den Linden and denounce Hitler, Goebbels, and all the Nazis. What a golden opportunity it would be! She rehearsed the speech in her mind, hearing her ringing tones and the slowly gathering applause of the crowd, but she knew she'd never deliver it.

Even before dawn, however, Peter was in her room, jubilantly thrusting an early morning newspaper at her. "We're staying!" he cried.

"What on earth?" She quickly rushed over to turn on a lamp.

"It's there—right on the front page," Peter pronounced.

She read quickly: In an announcement from the Chancellery, the Führer himself had personally signed a document testifying that his investigators had determined that Marika Kreisler was of Aryan status. It also stated that her father was a distinguished Prussian hussar before his death, and that her mother was an aristocratic Polish Aryan before she died giving birth to Marika.

"It's amazing," Peter said. "Someone got to Hitler—and fast. Goebbels was forced to call off his bloodhounds."

Marika laid the paper aside and slowly sipped her morning coffee. She had mixed reactions about the announcement. It both thrilled and horrified her. "We know who that *someone* was, don't we?"

Peter joined her on the bed. "It had to be Brigitte."

"Of course," Marika said, slamming down her cup. She resented being under any obligation to Brigitte. "She had no intention of letting the world know that her darling brother married a Viennese Jewess for her money. The heiress to a cosmetic fortune, no less."

Walking into her wardrobe, Peter selected a dress for her to wear to the studio that day. "Your secret's safe with me."

"I know," Marika said, slipping out of her nightgown. "But we're treating my Jewishness like I'm a leper or something. It's nothing to be ashamed of."

Standing in front of her dressing room mirror, Peter held the garment up to his own body. "My being a homosexual is nothing to be ashamed of either," he said defensively.

"Of course, it isn't."

"But we don't go around telling everybody about it," he said. "Now, do we?"

She walked up and down the room, her hands snugged in her armpits, her steps like those of a predatory cat. "Naturally, we say nothing."

Peter tossed her dress onto the bed. "Then as long as we continue to inhabit a planet hostile to Jews and homosexuals, we'll keep our mouths shut, right? After all, we're not crusaders."

Minutes later, she lay in her bathtub, breathing heavily, as Peter soaped her breasts. His gentle strokes always relaxed her. "Later on," she said, "when Hollywood begs me to return, do you know what I'm going to do, Peter? I'm going to call a press conference and wave my document from Hitler in the air." She laughed. "Then I'll announce to the world that I'm a Jewess!"

* * *

Anxious to see her son, Marika decided to make the trip to Vienna anyway. The air was cold and dry as she got off the train. Back in Gabrielle's city, an air of quiet, contemplative melancholy swept over Marika. She felt the loss of Gabrielle now more then ever when she needed her grandmother to advise and guide her.

Outside the city, near the Vienna woods, she took a wreath, placing it on Gabrielle's grave. She held Peter's hand and stood silently for a moment, wondering what Gabrielle would tell her to do now if she were here. That night, as they drove past the glittering lights of the Imperial Hotel, Marika broke down and wept. "Everything Gabrielle knew and loved, everything, will be swept away soon."

The next day Marika was just as jumpy at meeting Franz again as she was excited at seeing Anton. Peter went through three complete changes of wardrobe with her before she finally settled on a white, form-fitting gown that amply showed her well-rounded breasts, and she spent hours making sure her makeup was just right.

In the chauffeur-driven limousine en route to Franz's château, she trembled so nervously Peter had to pour her another hefty drink from the car's bar, and, noting her uncontrollable smoking, warned, "This is only your second pack today."

"I can't help it!"

Rushing out to greet her, Franz was even handsomer than she'd remembered. His blond hair was graying at the temples now, but his figure was as tall, lean, and striking as ever, his presence as forceful. As he helped her out of the car, she kissed him lingeringly on the mouth, and the tightness with which he held her, the rock-hardness of his body, rekindled strong memories. She'd never known a lover as ardent as Franz.

"It's late," Franz said. "Anton's not feeling well. But he waited up just to see you."

"I'll make my visit brief," she replied. "What's the matter with him?"

Franz sighed in despair. "It's more mental than anything else. He's delicate. Just likes to be ill."

With a puzzled look, Marika entered the boy's suite, ushered in by a servant. She gasped. The room's walls were entirely covered with large photographs of herself in the most dazzling fantasy costumes from her films. At first she didn't see her son. Then, in the far corner of the room, she suddenly became aware of intense eyes staring at her. There sat a young boy.

"Anton!" she said hesitantly.

"It's sad you don't know me," he said in a forlorn voice. It was affected, high-pitched, and strangely decadent, not the voice of a child at all. "I'd know your face anywhere. I look at it all day."

"I'm your mother," she said, going toward him.

"No, you're not," he said, biting his upper lip. "You're Marika Kreisler, the movie goddess. You can't afford to have children."

As the boy's face moved into the dim light of the room, she saw him clearly for the first time. He was softly pretty, his alabaster skin so white his purple veins showed through, his face almost girlishly tender. Behind long lashes lay eyes which were blue, luminous, and extremely large. He was a young Marika!

She bent over and kissed him gently and he held her tightly. As

· 299 ·

she moved to break away, his fingers dug into the flesh of her back, holding her close a little longer.

"Franz wants to keep me here . . . a prisoner," Anton accused. "He's ashamed of me. I take after you. He wanted me to take after him. I hate guns!"

Marika grimaced as she paced the room. All these celluloid images were too much for her to handle, and Anton . . . "You are who you are. That's all that's important."

"But Franz doesn't want me to be myself," Anton said, the alarm increasing in his voice. He chewed his lip and was silent for a moment.

There were so many questions she wanted to ask him, but was afraid to, so she reached into her purse and fumbled for another cigarette. Not since meeting Louis B. Mayer had she been so nervous in front of another person. "Anton's my son," she kept repeating to herself. "Why am I afraid?" And then she knew.

His look was of such intensity that it denuded her, stripped her of all the props, devices, and facades she used to go forth into the world. He seemed to study her every mannerism, like Anna Berndt, and when her hand reached out to touch his face, it was cold. She noticed that chilly air seemed to be coming in through an open window, causing her to shiver in her flimsy gown.

"Do you always keep the room at this temperature?" she asked.

"Always," he said firmly. "I can't stand heat." He took her by the hand and led her over to a mirror. There he stood, looking at both of their full-length reflections, seeming to compare himself to her. "Do you think I'll grow up to be a big star, too?" he asked.

An unexpectedly pathetic expression came over her face, and turning from the mirror, she said, "I can't say. A lot has to do with luck." She fondled his head, her fingers resting in his silky blond hair. Seizing her hand, he touched her fingertips caressingly, obviously wanting to express some feeling but unable to get his voice to speak. She turned from the intensity of his wide and staring eyes, her breathing growing more labored.

When she looked back at him, an almost obscene smile was creeping across his face and his hands were moving down his body in the way a woman's does in outlining her curves. "I'm going to be an actress, too," he said, "when I grow up. As great—maybe *greater*—than Marika Kreisler!"

"You mean an actor." Drops of perspiration formed on her forehead, and her breath came in short, shallow gasps.

Making a dizzy turn in front of the mirror, he glared at her, his look one of both fascination and hostility. "I mean nothing of the sort, and you know it."

Moments later, in the safety of the hallway, Franz was at her side. "Now you see what we've created," he said. "An old hag in a young boy's body."

* * *

Later that evening, in the powder room, Marika looked forward to a dinner alone with Franz. Peter had conveniently excused himself and returned to Vienna. Hopefully, she'd be able to put Anton out of her mind for a while. She was getting good at that. Everything, it seemed, caused her pain—but only if she thought about it.

With heightened anticipation, Marika walked into Franz's study, where once they had enjoyed pre-dinner champagne cocktails in front of the fireplace, but she saw, with a start, that they were not to be alone after all. Sitting in the spot that had once been hers was one of the most beautiful women she'd ever seen. She was almost too beautiful. Under shining black wavy hair, the woman looked up at her with eyes that were dreamy and expressive, with a fleeting touch of purple. Her black lashes were heavy, almost dusky, in dramatic contrast to her soft, pale white skin.

"Hello," she said. "I'm Reatha." A long, slender hand reached out and took Marika's. Marika started to speak, but the woman interrupted. "Yes," she said, "you're Marika Kreisler, as if there were a man, woman, or child alive today who wasn't aware of that stunning fact."

"Thank you," Marika said, feeling her whole body tighten in the presence of this young beauty. "And who are you?"

"Didn't Franz tell you?" she asked, smiling. "No, I suppose not. I'm his mistress."

"I see . . ." Marika felt dizzy and quickly sat down, but instead of looking at Reatha again, she let herself be hypnotized by the flickering flames. She should have expected it, but it was still a shock.

"Yes," Reatha chattered on, "Franz and I have been lovers for three months now. I'm an American, you know—I've only recently come here. I was born in the New Mexican desert where I used to ride a big white horse."

"I had no idea . . ." Marika said.

"You've been away a long time," Reatha said. "Franz has hardly been celibate. In fact, that's the last word I'd use to describe him. I'm just one in a long line."

"I'm certainly glad Franz has found someone—someone so lovely," Marika said. The wind outside made sinister echoes, as cold as the dampness in her palms.

"It's not the furs," Reatha said, "nor the jewelry or even the seven cars he gives me." She didn't take her eyes off Marika. "I could have any man I want, rich or poor. But Franz is the best lover of them all, as you well know. I don't know how you could give him up. For von Menzel? I've been to bed with that one, too, only last year, when he promised to make me a bigger star than you. He's the world's worst!"

Marika got up and walked slowly to the window. It was beginning to snow. The soft white flakes sifted down, melting against the gray walls of Franz's château. From the cottage at the gate a dim light shone, a weak bit of brightness against the all-encompassing night. Reatha was saying something else, but Marika blotted out the sound of her voice. There was enough going on in the outside world to command her attention. She didn't need to concern herself with what she was hearing inside the study. What did it matter? Franz and von Menzel were yesterday.

"Are you ill?" Reatha was asking, standing beside her and reaching out.

At the touch of the woman's fingers, Marika instinctively pulled away. "It's been a long day," she said apologetically. "Seeing Anton has apparently upset me more than I thought."

"Of course," Reatha said, the corners of her mouth twisting into a small smile.

At that point, a servant entered. "Herr Hauptmann had to leave immediately for Munich while you ladies were getting ready for dinner. It was an emergency. He said to go on without him."

Marika sighed. "Nothing's changed here."

* * *

In Berlin, Hitler addressed the Reichstag, announcing the withdrawal of the German signature from the Treaty of Versailles.

After four years, Germany was booming, its unemployment low, its powerful military occupying the Rhineland. In the wake of a disastrous war, its confidence in the future had returned.

In the capital of a great and expanding world power, the premiere of *Nana* was held at Ufa-Palast-am-Zoo. As she stepped from a limousine, Marika heard a wave of cheers from a first-night audience of men in black tie and woman in elegant gowns, many the latest Parisian fashions, in spite of the Nazi disapproval of marks being spent "wastefully" outside the country. Guards protected her from milling autograph-seekers. Her white fur cuddled around her neck, Marika blew kisses at the waving crowd. Restrained by ropes, many of her more ardent admirers tried to touch her coat, one rotund male even falling on the ground and kissing the sidewalk which her golden slippers had touched.

Marika stopped briefly to pose for pictures at the entrance to the theater, but an SS guard quickly rushed her inside. New black limousines were arriving with guests even more important than she.

As she entered the theater, the audience stood up and gave her an ovation, and she smiled and waved, praying they'd be as enthusiastic after seeing *Nana*. From the balcony roses fell upon her, and, catching one, she kissed it passionately, then slung it madly in the air. Ushers rushed to restrain the crowd who would have overwhelmed her as they rushed forward from their seats to claim the rose.

In Marika's private box, Ritter, her director, bowed low and kissed her hand, and Peter eased her into her velvet-cushioned seat. As the applause mounted again, Marika stood up to acknowledge it, but then a hush came over the theater. Dr. Goebbels was walking down the aisle. The clapping started again, but this time polite, more restrained, as the stoop-shouldered, club-footed Goebbels made his way slowly to his seat.

Marika was surprised to see him and, leaning over, whispered to Ritter, "I didn't expect *him*."

"I'm sure he didn't want to come," Ritter said. "Hitler probably ordered him to attend. You'd be surprised how closely the Führer follows films. The little doctor, I understand, still isn't satisfied about your Aryan blood. But there isn't much he can do about it —at least for the moment."

Ritter's last words sounded ominous to Marika. Did she face more trouble from Goebbels? Who was the mysterious person from her past who had reported her in the first place? Goebbels briefly glanced up at Marika's box as he sat down, not bothering to acknowledge her presence, but chilling her with his penetrating look.

As the lights in the theater dimmed, *Nana* began, and before the cream of the Nazi hierarchy, Marika's image flashed across the screen. Sitting quietly, she was stunned by her performance. Without von Menzel's erotic fantasies to limit her, the actress she saw in the film was full of verve, humor, and depth. It was reassuring to know she could really act.

In the middle of the screening, Ritter leaned over to whisper, "You handle your body like Stradivarius with a violin. You should have been a dancer." Marika squeezed Peter's hand in her happiness as, tough, glamorous, and eloquent, the celluloid Nana floated through the Parisian demi-monde. She wanted to share this moment with a lover, but Peter was almost as good. She was so giddy with joy she was almost tempted to seduce him tonight.

At the end of the film, Marika was called down to make several curtain calls and the impact of a live audience affected her in a madly exhilarating way. Her face red, she felt reckless, extravagant, and somehow cheated that she had become a film actress and not a stage actress. Outside, a sudden burst of bells and sirens proclaimed a police emergency, but even a declaration of war could not have spoiled this moment for Marika. "I'm happy to be home again, my darlings," she said, as the entire audience, even Goebbels, rose to its feet. Swept away, she added, "It's where I belong!"

Backstage, Ritter took her over for an introduction to Dr. Goebbels, and upon actually seeing him close up, some of her fear diminished. Although widely known as a seducer of actresses, he appeared effeminate to her, a temperamental, emotional man, both vain and lecherous. He looked at her as if he were a man who loathed her and yet wanted to add her to his string of conquests. Clicking his heels, he bowed and kissed her hand obsequiously, his cold eyes meeting hers.

"Dr. Goebbels," she said, "our meeting has been long overdue, but well worth waiting for." She smiled coquettishly.

"You have a great talent and an artistic genius," he said. "But I fear it's been wasted."

"What do you mean?" she asked, suddenly puzzled and alarmed.

"The Führer told me tonight," he said, "that he doesn't want 'the glory of German womanhood' impersonating a French whore. We must find more suitable vehicles for you."

* * *

Buoyed by near-unanimous praise from European critics, even French ones, the international success of *Nana* was assured. Many newspapers claimed Marika's performance was the greatest since her debut in *Carnival,* and audiences all over the Continent rushed to see it.

Each day Marika waited for a signal from Hollywood, inviting her to return to make another picture, but neither the telephone nor the mail brought any response. American exhibitors, she was told, simply weren't interested in *Nana,* in spite of its success abroad. The 1934 Anna Sten version of *Nana* for United Artists had flopped, and exhibitors weren't easily enticed into taking another chance on the French courtesan. Besides, Marika's last American film, *Desert Flower,* had been such a financial disaster that the studios were still wary of her.

Nevertheless, news came one morning that Marika's former boss, Louis B. Mayer, had acquired the American rights to the UFA production—as a vehicle for Norma Shearer. Marika broke down and wept for two days at the news, even refusing to eat. Her beloved *Nana* would never reach an American audience. It seemed as if the entire American motion-picture establishment was locked in a conspiracy to deny her a chance to remove the "box-office poison" label. She would be stuck in Germany forever.

Deep in melancholy, Marika was awakened one night by a call from Ritter. "The little doctor is pleased by *Nana* after all," he said.

"What does that mean?"

"So much foreign currency is pouring into Germany as a result of the film," Ritter said, "that he wants us to do another picture together."

"Yes, it's plain. He doesn't want our art," Marika commented witheringly. "He just wants our money for armaments."

"Nevertheless, I'll send over your new script," Ritter said. "Goebbels himself is fond of this one."

The script was *The Broken Thread,* an absurdly sentimental story of a mother's sacrifice for her errant daughter. "I'm not going to play a mother," Marika screamed at Peter. "I absolutely refuse!"

"But the girl is only twelve," Peter said, "and you've already signed a contract for a second picture. You've got to do it. Besides, we need the two hundred thousand marks."

"No!" Marika yelled, but in the end she gave in, vowing to do the mother role only if she could play it strictly for glamor.

Ritter was very patient with her on the set. "But we've got to halfway follow the script," he said. "This role is not that of a sex goddess."

"I'm giving it my best," Marika shouted, storming off the set. "I'm embarrassed to deliver some of those lines written for me. I'll be laughed off the screen."

But Marika's prediction proved wrong. Although she refused to attend the premiere, the picture opened to great box-office success in Germany, and she became increasingly confident that she could do no wrong in German cinema. Everything she'd ever filmed in her own country had been a hit—but she still looked to America, and word from Hollywood.

Weeks later, Peter despondently held up a copy of *Variety.* "The film bombed in the States," he said. "It played only a few theaters, then was taken out of general release." Retreating to her bedroom, Marika refused to see anyone for days. She was sure now that her career as a film actress in America had been destroyed for all time. Only after repeated urgings from Peter did she decide to go out into the world again. "The invitations are arriving daily," Peter told her. "You can't go on ignoring them forever. You've got to think of your position."

Reluctantly, she dressed and went to a reception at the Polish Embassy, which seemed the most promising of the invitations available to her. Unhappily, she saw that Goebbels was there, too. After congratulating Marika on her two film successes, he called her aside in a confidential whisper. She suspected he was going to proposition her.

"I want to tell you something," he said. "The Führer has lately been suffering from bouts of chronic insomnia and in the small hours of the morning, he's ordered *The Broken Thread* screened for him a total of four times. He openly weeps at your performance."

At first flattered by the attention of one so highly placed, Marika later became uneasy at Hitler's increasing fascination with her. As if to confirm that fear, when Marika went shopping the next day on the Kurfürstendamm, and, finding a set of pearls she liked, inquired the price, the little shopkeeper smiled and said, "Frau Kreisler, take whatever you like from my humble shop. I will have your bill delivered to the Chancellery."

Marika turned away in shock and walked rapidly from the store. "It can't be," she said to Peter.

"You haven't been getting around much lately," Peter said. "Everybody in Berlin is whispering that you're the Führer's lady. In fact, one French newspaper has called you Hitler's Madame Du Barry."

* * *

At Horcher's that night, Marika and Peter were ushered to the finest table in the house by Otto himself, the owner of the restaurant. Every head turned to stare. In the middle of their meal, Hermann Göring, surrounded by a group of high-ranking Nazi officers, entered the restaurant, and Otto saw to it immediately that they were seated at the table next to Marika and Peter. Although they'd never been introduced, Göring nodded to Marika and, throughout the meal, couldn't seem to take his eyes off her.

She was afraid, but didn't dare to leave. How was it that she was occupying a better table than the Prime Minister of Prussia and the Minister of the Luftwaffe? Did he, too, think she was Hitler's mistress?

Finally, hoisting his heavy body up and excusing himself to his men, Göring walked to Marika's side, bowing and kissing her hand. He asked politely if he could join her table for a moment.

"By all means," she said, attempting to appear undisturbed.

"Your performance as Nana was superb," he said, easing himself in opposite her and staring at her with eyes that Marika found frightening, despite his jovial, cherubic face. He looked like an overstuffed Sybarite.

"I'm delighted you liked it," she said, unsure of how to handle the situation. Why was this man talking to her? She knew Göring was capable of great ruthlessness, but she had also heard he was a man of impulsive generosity. Was he just being friendly? Nervously, she sipped at the champagne that had arrived miraculously at their table.

"Actually," Göring said with a smile, looking now not at her, but at the expensive loden coat on her chair, "there are two reasons why I dared intrude on your privacy." He paused. "I wanted to congratulate you for your fine performance in German films . . . but I was also curious as to the name of the tailor who made that coat."

Startled and shaking with relief, Marika quickly asked Peter to give him the tailor's name. "You're welcome to have the coat, too," she stammered. "I have so many." With a roar, Göring threw back his head and laughed so loudly his officers looked over at Marika's table. "I fear we're not the same size," he said, choking, and as he continued to laugh, Marika joined him, but for some reason her shaking became uncontrollable. Her nerves were completely shattered. Peter quickly lit another cigarette for her, as Göring looked intently at her trembling hands. She tried to be still but such intense concentration was more than she could handle. "You've been so nice to me," he said at last, "I think I can help you."

"I've done nothing really," she protested.

"Forgive me, but I couldn't help but notice you're shaking," he said.

"Yes," and, not wanting him to think he was the cause of her anxiety, added quickly, "I've not been able to sleep lately. The pressures of my career . . . they're very strong."

"I understand completely," he said. "I have the same problem. But I know a cure. You gave me the name of your tailor, now I'll supply the name of an outstanding doctor for you. He prescribes something for me which I'm sure will be helpful."

"I'm extremely grateful," she said, genuinely meaning it.

He scribbled a name on a piece of paper and handed it to Peter. Then, after a quick toast to her, he slowly got up, bowing low again and kissing her hand, and returned to his own table. But not before he'd caressed her coat.

After a discreet interval, Marika told Peter she wanted to leave.

He called for the check, but the waiter assured him there was no bill.

* * *

The tablets, Peter learned, were paracodeine, a weak morphine derivative. When Marika could no longer cope with her anxiety, which was every day now, she swallowed those pills, and by the end of the first week, she was up to twenty-five tablets a day. The world began to appear to her through a slight blue haze, and at night unreal sounds blended together in her head to form a discordant symphony. At times, her bedroom became strangely still, and she could feel the presence of some unknown menace.

Her suspicions about Doctor von Schlabrendorff grew stronger by the day. Once she caught him at her bedside table examining the tablets from Göring's doctor that she'd carefully hidden in a little silver box, and she'd ordered him immediately from her room, instructing Peter to give him two weeks' notice. He left, but somehow his absence did not make her feel any easier.

Then at three o'clock one morning, she was awakened by an urgent voice on the telephone. It was von Menzel. He'd flown to Vienna and even now was at Badgastein, the nineteenth-century spa. "Meet me," he insisted. "It's most important. And it must be in *complete secrecy.*" Clearing the cobwebs from her brain, Marika decided to accept his curious invitation, but not without some reluctance. She did want to see him again, but she didn't know what to make of this air of mystery. She was also disappointed that he hadn't even asked about his daughter.

Leaving Lotte with a nursemaid, Marika drove to the spa with Peter. Memories of Baden-Baden and a younger day came back to her as her limousine passed the great hotels and shops arranged in a horseshoe curve on the flanks of a wooden amphitheater. In its heyday, Franz-Josef and his entourage had descended on Badgastein, as had Wilhelm I, King of Prussia, who used to visit to take "the cure."

Marika's suite was ready at the Hotel Grüner Baum, and even before she'd checked in, her telephone was ringing. Von Menzel wanted to come up to her parlor right away. "All right," she agreed, "but let me check my makeup first. After all," she added, flirting slightly, "you're a movie director."

· 309 ·

Waiting for him, Marika felt herself becoming more and more nervous, and it annoyed her. Did she still care for von Menzel? The bell rang, and she jumped. Walking as steadily as she could to the door, she opened it and there he was. Dressed in a simple business suit, his skin pulled taut over clearly defined muscles, his face smooth and nut-brown from the California sun, von Menzel possessed as imposing a presence as ever. Marika felt a quick burst of emotion within her, but she suppressed it as he entered, kissing her neither passionately nor perfunctorily, more like a loved member of her family.

After the briefest of small talk, he reached into his attaché case and removed a sheaf of newspaper clippings. Dramatically, he tossed them onto her coffee table, selecting one and holding it up. "It's Winchell, and he's very blunt. Not Nazi sympathizer—just plain Nazi!"

"What are you talking about?" she asked.

"You, Marika," he announced. "You're infamous now!"

Getting up quickly, she excused herself and headed for the bathroom, where she took from her purse and then hurriedly swallowed five paracodeine tablets. Walking back into the parlor, she shakily confronted von Menzel. "What about the stories that I'm the Führer's lady?" she asked sarcastically, trying to make light of it.

"They're there, too," he said angrily. "Are they true?"

"How dare you!" she cried, his words searing her like a hot branding iron. "Of course they're not true! I've *never* slept with the creature. I don't know why I'm even bothering to defend myself to you."

"Because you need to."

The light in the room was turning a somber gray. "What does that mean?"

"Whether you've slept with Hitler or not doesn't matter," he said. "What matters is that your films are making money. That money is being used to buy armaments, as you well know. By making movies for the Reich, you are contributing to the destruction of your own people!"

She felt a sudden catch in her throat, as if some object were lodged there. At first she couldn't speak. Finally, she managed to say, "Yes? And just who are my people? The Jews despise me.

America has rejected me. The German people—not the Nazis, but the people themselves—are the only ones who want what I have to offer. I'm a German woman doing the only thing she knows how to do, and that is to act. What right have you to try to take that from me?" The tightness in her throat was developing into a stranglehold. She felt she could no longer be in the same room as von Menzel.

* * *

At breakfast the next morning, von Menzel smoked a cigar, and its smell made Marika so giddy she couldn't eat her shirred eggs. Eyes smarting, she reached to rub them. Her head was on fire, her skin ice-cold. And her supply of paracodeine tablets was running low.

Last night, von Menzel had finally revealed his secret mission to her. Tomorrow at the old Hotel Imperial in Vienna, he said, he was going to announce to the world press his plans for his next motion picture. "The Austrian government personally invited me here," he told her. "The resources of the entire country, its wealth of artists, have been placed at my disposal. I am going to show the world that the German language is a tongue of art and culture—not just an instrument of verbal violence and intimidation."

"But why would you want me to star in such a film?" Marika asked. "I'm German, not Austrian. I think Austrians speak German with far more charm. Your movie should have an Austrian as the star."

"No!" von Menzel protested, crushing out his cigar in his eggs. "You've got to play the part. First, it'll show that you're independent of Goebbels and we'll win a lot of sympathy for you from people who now feel you're a Nazi. The second reason is to help me live with my own guilt."

The opening of the door brought two servants in to remove the breakfast table. Just as Marika was about to respond, von Menzel signaled her to keep quiet. Everybody, it seemed, was a spy these days. When they had gone, she turned to von Menzel. "What guilt?"

"*Carnival* is the most widely hailed and circulated German film of all time," he said.

"I know that."

"By making it," he said, "I glorified and made a goddess out of you, the representative of German womanhood! In every country sympathetic to the Axis right now—including the Arab nations—the film is a big hit. Don't you see? Indirectly, I've contributed to spreading good will for the Nazis!"

Such talk made her impatient. Picking up her coffee and pacing the floor, she said, "I think your point is far-fetched."

"Not in the slightest," von Menzel said. "I demand you play this part. I can win back America for you."

Her anger flared up. "Demand! You have no right to make demands on me, or pressure me in any way. As for winning back America, it's *you* you're worried about, not me. When's your press conference?"

"At ten in the morning."

"Very well," she said, putting down her cup. "I want to think about it and discuss it with Peter. I'll telephone you my decision at eight o'clock. If you don't hear from me by then, you'll know I've turned you down." Agitatedly picking up a cushion, she threw it back down again on the chair.

Von Menzel stood on the balcony overlooking the garden, watching a fat gray cat creeping along toward the hotel. Marika joined him. "You're frightened?" he asked her.

"Yes," she said softly. "So are you."

He said nothing, but picked up his coat and hat and looked back at her lingeringly.

"I'm having Peter drive me today to see Anton," she said. For a moment both of them stood silently looking at each other. *"My other child."*

Von Menzel's face suddenly turned cold. "He's with Franz Hauptmann?"

"Of course," she said.

"Hauptmann knows a war is coming," he said bitterly. "How can you be friendly with such a bloodthirsty killer?"

The brief moment of peace between them faded in a cloud of darkness. "He was my lover. That is over now. But I have a responsibility for my child."

"Hauptmann makes guns for whichever side will pay him," von Menzel charged. "I bet he'd make armaments for the Russians if the deal were good enough. He has no loyalties other than to his own empire."

"Nevertheless," Marika said, turning from the sight of him, "Franz is the father of my son. Just as you're the father of my daughter, whether you want to face that fact or not." She left hurriedly, sneaking away to the privacy of her bedroom and her remaining tablets.

* * *

In the back seat of a shiny black Mercedes-Benz, Marika and Peter sat watching the road to Franz's château. The prospect of seeing his beautiful, young Reatha again disquieted her, as did the thought of facing her own strange child.

She kept examining her reflection in her mirror. Her hair was still soft and blonde, though she'd been losing some of it lately, and though she was, unfortunately, becoming a little heavy around her hips, her waist remained that of a girl's. She noticed that the soft part of her jaw was beginning to show age slightly, too.

"Did you bring the tablets?"

Peter remained silent.

"Peter!" she shouted. "I said, did you bring the tablets?"

"Damn it!" he said. "Yes! But enough's enough. I didn't want to interfere with the doctor, but look at you, Marika. He's turning you into an addict."

The horror of the label made her cringe. It wasn't true. She didn't take that many—and besides, Peter wasn't in her position. He couldn't understand what it was like to be locked up in her own private dungeon—with no way out. "You don't know what it is to have your nerves collapse," she said aloud, almost pathetically.

His look was at once tender and compassionate. "I'm sorry," he said. "It's just that I love you so much. I don't want anything bad happening to you."

She took his hand and kissed him lingeringly on the lips, looking deep into his eyes. "I need them," she said softly. "If you love me as much as you say you do, you won't question it anymore. Just keep a supply of those tablets always."

Peter silently gazed out the window, as the afternoon shadows deepened. Marika leaned back, an awful burning in her brain. Fatigued, depressed, she tried to make a decision about whether to appear in von Menzel's film. What were the risks? Fear stabbed at her, whirling around. She was suspicious of everyone these days —even the driver in front. He wasn't the chauffeur Franz had sent before. Franz always had his limousines painted elephant-brown, and this one was black and didn't have a bar in it.

Sighing, she decided she was too weary and drained of emotion to know what to do about the film. Tomorrow morning she'd wake up early. Maybe she'd be able to decide then.

Peter put his arm around her, his firm hand enclosing her shoulder. "I know what you're thinking," he said. "You must do the film. It's true. I was keeping most of those newspaper articles from you. But in the outside world, you've become a Nazi. You've got to change that image."

"I guess you're right," she said. "After all, I'm not under exclusive contract to UFA. I can seek work in some other country."

In the distance she could see a fog rising and lights coming on in hillside-clinging farmhouses. The deeper the limousine penetrated into the mountains, the denser the fog became, rolling in like a ghostly sea. The chauffeur had not let up his speed.

"Tell him to slow down," Marika told Peter.

The driver only grunted at Peter's request. "Franz usually picks them better than this old goat," Peter whispered to Marika. "I'm going to report him."

As they hurried through a village, Marika noticed a graveyard near the side of the road, and in the distance a little chapel. A few crosses and granite headstones stood out as bleak sentinels against the night.

"I've often wondered," she said, a touch of melancholy in her voice, "what would happen if I were to die a sudden and violent death." She paused. "Like tonight."

"Don't think like that," he cautioned her. "You can make awful things happen with such thoughts. It's like asking for trouble."

"I wonder how I'd be remembered," she said reflectively.

"My dear, that's very easy," he replied, smiling. "You'd go down in history as one of the great cinema actresses of the thirties."

She braced her arms behind her head and leaned back in the comfortably upholstered seat. Outside, the moon made the fog even more mysterious. "I'm not so sure. I know I've reached millions of people throughout the world. I've affected women vitally in most countries, influenced their ideas about fashion, sex. But they were stirred by my beauty, not my artistry. As an artist, I've failed." She lit a cigarette. The driver seemed to be eyeing her in his rear-view mirror. "I can *still* do it, Peter. I know somewhere within me I still can give the most moving, inspired performance of my career. But I may have to wait a very long time for that role to come to me." She sat for a moment in silence.

Suddenly, Peter sat up in the limousine, peering ahead at the foggy road. "I think the chauffeur's lost. We seem to be nearing the frontier." He tapped on the window. But the driver ignored him. Instead, he stepped on the accelerator and hurled the limousine past the lone Austrian border guard and into Germany.

Impervious to Marika's screams, the Mercedes sped into the night until, a few miles inside German territory, it gradually slowed and came to a stop. Marika looked out to see SS guards on motorcycles surrounding the vehicle and another Mercedes-Benz pulling out of the shadows ahead. An officer got out of the car and approached Marika's window. She lowered it, trembling with fear and shivering in the night air. "I demand to know what's happening," she said.

"Welcome to Germany, Frau Kreisler," the officer said, peering into her car. "My men will escort you from now on."

"Escort us where?" Peter asked.

"You'll see," he said.

Her face tight, Marika settled back in stunned silence. Two motorcycles positioned themselves in front of the car, two in back, with the other Mercedes in the vanguard. A hoarse voice called out into the night, and the strange convoy began its journey.

"We're being kidnapped," Peter said, looking backward, his voice trembling.

Tears were in her eyes now, and her face twisted with rage and fear. "God help me," she whispered.

* * *

The car pulled up at the approach to a large compound, ringed by an imposing fence dotted by guards at strategic spots. After being checked by security, the limousine drove slowly into a large garage. Her brain working at top speed, Marika gripped Peter's hand. The Gestapo dragnet was closing in on her, she knew that now. The Nazis must have learned of her meeting with von Menzel and his plans for an anti-Hitler film. Frantically, she looked for a way to escape, as, ahead of her, huge doors swung open and the car descended a ramp descending deep into the base of a mountain. When it came to a stop, Marika saw a large fleet of touring cars.

The SS officer in the other Mercedes came around and opened the car door and, taking her by the arm, led her over to an elevator. At the door, he kept patting his uniform as if removing dust spots.

Peter was at her side, but as the elevator door opened, an SS guard detained him. Marika reacted sharply, reaching for him, but it was too late. The doors shut quickly. She closed her eyes and bit her lip, seeing only the stunned look of helplessness on his face.

On the third floor the elevator came to a stop, and Marika found herself being ushered into a reception area, where a large picture of Hitler stared down at her from the wall. For more than an hour, she waited, pacing the floor restlessly, her senses becoming dull. She was almost ready for anything now, just so long as they stopped this damnable *waiting*.

Finally, a guard came and took her into an office, leaving her there standing beside a desk of polished mahogany. Moments later, a young SS officer, blond and extraordinarily good-looking, entered the room. His uniform was meticulously tailored to show off his height and attractively masculine figure, but his body movements were ungainly, as if he were still very new at his task. At first he seemed more intimidated to be in the presence of Marika Kreisler than she was in front of him, and she wondered why. Then she realized that, of course, he thought she was Hitler's mistress. The young officer clearly feared and resented the task he'd been given.

"Frau Kreisler," he said, "we apologize profusely for the way you were delivered to Obersalzberg." Marika listened in stunned silence. For the first time she realized where she was. "But under the circumstances," the young officer continued, "we had no choice."

She decided to stare intently at him, concealing her nervousness and playing on his already mounting anxiety. "Who's responsible for this, and why am I here?"

He stammered, "Dr. Goebbels has found some irregularity in your *Reichsfachschaft Film* identification card."

"What irregularity?" she asked. At last the purpose of the interview was clear.

He offered her a brandy.

"I beg you to understand," he said. "But I don't think you answered your questionnaire properly concerning the racial identity of your mother." He reached into his desk and pulled out a paper. "Born Lotte Schulz, Jewess, January 16, 1876, daughter of Isaac and Gabrielle Schulz, both Jews."

"How did you come by this information?"

"The doctor who brought you into the world, Herr von Schlabrendorff, has kindly provided us with all the details."

"The son of a bitch," she said bitterly. "I should have known."

"At the moment," he said, "Brigitte Kreisler has been awarded temporary custody of your daughter."

She cast him a look of savage fury. "What! How dare Goebbels! First, he kidnaps me. Then he kidnaps my daughter. I demand to be set free at once!"

His face contorted. "I fear you have no choice but to cooperate. You see, Frau Kreisler, we hold not only your life in our hands, but the life of your daughter. Only Dr. Goebbels, Herr von Schlabrendorff, and I know of your contamination." He looked at her and smiled charmingly. But it was calculated to fill her with fear. "Eventually the Jews will be exterminated. It is the Führer's wish."

"Then kill me!" She got up, heading again for the cabinet to pour herself another brandy.

"What a foolhardy response," he said. He seemed to be growing into his role now, enjoying it, as his tone became more insolent. "Our surveys have found that you're the most popular film star with the German public, not to mention a valuable national resource to help us raise much-needed foreign currency for armaments. Therefore, Dr. Goebbels has concluded that we will overlook the Jewish question for the time being so that you can star in some films he feels it imperative to make."

She held her glass with trembling hands and looked searchingly at the officer. Her voice was choked and desperate. "I've always refused to make propaganda films. I will not give in to such blackmail. I'll leave Germany and take my daughter with me."

The officer's face was livid with rage. "You're not a stupid woman. You know that's impossible. And *we* know you left Germany only to meet with von Menzel and form a plan to stab the

Fatherland in the back. For your information, that Jew's hate film will never be made. Before it can be shot, there will be no Austria!"

"Frankly, I'm not surprised," she said. "When you bastards are through, there will be no Europe."

"As for me," he said reflectively, "I think Dr. Goebbels is being more than generous with you. If I had been in his position, I wouldn't have taken such a lenient attitude." His flashing looks of hatred seemed almost those of a man who had been personally betrayed. "You see . . ." He paused. "I despise Jews . . . *all* Jews."

She downed another brandy. "What's my alternative? I could kill myself. Not a bad possibility, perhaps."

"In time," he said, "in time." He returned her top-secret file to his desk drawer. "I wanted to get the unpleasantness out of the way before you were sent in to have an interview with Dr. Goebbels. He wants to discuss only art with you—not 'arrangements' about your daughter's custody, kidnapping, the Jewish question. Just cinematic art."

Two Gestapo men entered the room. "Dr. Goebbels is ready now," one of the men said.

Marika closed her eyes and listened to the accelerated beat of her own heart.

Standing at the door, the young officer clicked his heels and bowed mockingly in front of her. "Until I read your file, you were always my favorite film star."

* * *

Behind his desk, Goebbels looked like a timber wolf, fat from the kill but still hungry. He leaned over his desk to look closely at Marika, drilling her with hateful eyes. He did not bother to get up, but flicked his hand limply toward a chair, indicating for her to take a seat. Except for his eyes, the rest of his face was expressionless, almost gnome-like.

"Thank you for inviting me here," she said sarcastically. "But with most invitations, I prefer to retain the right to refuse."

He ignored her remark. "I've seen all of your American films, Frau Kreisler," he said. "I find them deplorable. Each one has been a little more lavish and a great deal more stupid than the one which preceded it. The Jew, von Menzel, has turned you into a screen slut."

Marika bristled at the remark, feeling the excessive heat of the room. Around her, statues and paintings gazed down at her with accusing stares. She needed her tablets badly.

"Now that I know your true age," he went on, "it's best that you appear on the screen no longer floridly vulgar, but in vehicles more to your taste."

"I've noticed," she said bitingly, "that you've abolished film critics, but that you don't seem above indulging in the 'decadent" form yourself."

Again, he failed to respond to her remarks, and instead looked vacantly at some papers on his desk. "You're German," he said finally. "As such, and as an artist, you must draw your inspiration from the Fatherland. Not from some Turkish harem. The degenerate, von Menzel, presented you wandering in a dreamland of fantasy. He completely ignored present-day problems."

In her weakened state, it was difficult to keep pace with the staccato rhythm of his speech and ideas. She knew he was leading her to some sort of submission. "But films must present the whole of life. Our dreamy fantasies reach another truth, maybe even a higher one. I'm not qualified to say. I'm an actress—not a philosopher of the cinema."

"Exactly," he said, rising and pacing the floor. "As such, you should do what you're directed to do. Films must educate the public, even if it means taking a financial loss. We must portray the natural life. We must accomplish the effect of truth. Therefore, all films must contain a National Socialist idea."

"No," she said, *"no,"* and paused to draw her breath. Suddenly she felt pathetically small and dependent before this powerful man, and in a flutter of helplessness, she began to feel faint.

Goebbels walked to his desk and removed from a drawer a bottle containing some tablets. "Oh, yes," he said, "your doctor sent these down for you."

She drew another quick breath and reached for the bottle. Hurriedly, she removed some capsules and swallowed them without water. "I've not been well lately."

"Yes," he said softly, "I know." At the window he threw open the shutters and a gust of cool air filled his office, restoring her. Had he deliberately overheated the room?

"Tonight you've been invited to a reception at the Berghof,"

Goebbels said then. "The Führer has expressed a desire to meet you. He's unaware of your activities in Austria. I prefer we keep that detail private between us."

"I don't want to go," she said.

"I suggest you change your mind," Goebbels said, raising his voice. "I think it would be unwise to turn down an invitation from the Führer."

She understood his point with chilling clarity. He flipped his hand in dismissal, but at the door he called to her, "Perhaps before going to meet the Führer, you'll remove some of your makeup. It is a particularly strong point with him. He does not like 'war-paint.' "

* * *

Shaking, Marika reached for her tablets, and after swallowing more than she'd ever taken before, started to feel better. Peter was at her side. She kept reaching for him, almost clutching, as if to reassure herself that he'd been given back to her. As she stood in the guarded bungalow to which she'd been assigned, applying only a very light makeup of eyebrow pencil and powder, she began to feel guilty.

"I know what you're thinking," he said. More and more he seemed to be reading her thoughts. "You think you brought all these troubles on yourself by returning to Germany in the first place."

"Of course, I did," she said. Looking into the mirror, she sighed. "Sometimes I think I care less about how the world might remember me than that it might forget me."

An hour later, to the sounds of Wagner, she made her entrance at the Berghof. All the top Nazis were there, not only Goebbels, but his wife, Magda, Göring, Werner von Blomberg, the Minister of War. Among them circulated waiters dressed in white vests and black trousers—SS guards out of uniform—carrying trays of drinks and canapés. Above the mantel a bronze eagle on a large clock looked formidably down upon the room, as on one wall, a bare-bosomed Bardone portrait surveyed the crowd, and on another, one of Titian's boudoir nudes reclined.

Seeing her standing at the doorway, Frau Goebbels walked over and introduced herself to Marika, then led her over to Hitler, who stood in front of a large plate-glass window overlooking the Kehlstein.

The man in front of her was completely different from the rattled figure she'd first met at Brigitte's apartment. Hitler wasn't frantic at all, but moved with complete assurance, almost a quiet dignity, now. His hair completely black, with not one trace of gray, his face well-tanned, his figure trim, he looked younger than his years, and she felt the news films caricatured him—as she feared von Menzel's movies had done for her.

He peered at her through eyes as clear and as blue as her own, then bowed from the waist and kissed her hand. "We get to meet again," he said, his voice almost soothing, in total contrast to his ranting speeches at Nürnberg. Was that voice of harangue used only to intimidate the foreign press?

"Thank you for inviting me," she said. "Brigitte's told me so much about the place."

"How's your wonderful aunt?" he asked.

"In excellent health," Marika answered nervously. She wasn't sure how much Hitler knew about her background.

"I saw her a few months ago," he said, "and thought she appeared like a woman of fifty. Brigitte, I said, you're a timeless wonder. You strengthen our belief in our own immortality."

She turned from his intense look to gaze at the view. He turned, too, looking out at the mountain peaks as he folded his arms across his chest.

"I used to rent a little place here," he said. "Haus Wachenfeld, it was called. An old cleaning woman who worked for me told me the legend of Untersberg. She claimed Barbarossa and all his knights lay sleeping in the limestone caves there, but that one day they'd wake up and usher in Germany's golden age."

Before she could reply, a commotion sounded in another part of the room, and framed in the doorway with two barking dogs on a leash was a woman whom Marika recognized from her pictures as Eva Braun. Hitler excused himself and went over to her, kissing her hands. *"Gnädige Fräulein."*

Excited, the dogs jumped up on him, barking, their tongues hanging out, and Hitler hastily pulled back his hands and, whipping a handkerchief from his breast pocket, wiped them carefully.

Turning to Frau Goebbels, he laughed nervously and said, "These dogs are the biggest lickers I've ever seen. One of my relatives in Austria used to have a cow that did the same thing. No one could milk her. She kept licking all the time."

Frau Goebbels laughed too, as did everyone else around them.

As Eva walked around the room, Marika observed her closely, and noticed, to her surprise, that she was wearing a deep shade of red lipstick, in violation of Hitler's rules. She was immaculately groomed, well poised, had a good figure, and her blonde hair seemed to be tinted. Two diamond-studded clips accentuated her décolleté.

At the dinner table, Marika found herself seated near Hitler, and eating off Meissen china with the initials "A.H." engraved in gold in the center, beside a swastika glazed in red. Opposite her, Eva Braun gave her a frosty nod.

"I know what most people believe," Hitler told his guests. "That I'm a vegetarian and abhor alcohol. Actually, I'm fond of *weisswürste*. I had a favorite little stall I used to go to in Munich very early in the morning. That's the only time to eat them. Of course, I'd have a mug of beer as well." He turned and looked toward Goebbels, his face enigmatic. Marika couldn't tell whether he was amused or angry. "You make me too ascetic," he told his propaganda chief. "I'm actually very German."

After dinner, Marika again sat by Hitler's side at the fireplace, with a whispered warning from Frau Goebbels not to speak to the Führer until he addressed her first. An eerie feeling swept over her. It was as if she were in an historical tableau in which she was one of the wax-dummy figures, but that feeling was soon replaced by an unmistakable excitement at being in the presence of a man whose thought and action could influence the entire world.

She kept trying to forget his image and concentrate solely on the man who surely lurked behind the imposing facade, but it was impossible. She felt lost in front of him, his personality so overpowering that she could only sit in silence and confusion. But then an intense, revealing look in his eyes gave him away. She realized that just as she had a set image of him, he, too, conceived of her only in terms of a movie star, as reel after reel of her film fantasies ran through his head.

As if to confirm that suspicion, he leaned over and said, "You know, I've seen all your films—and in their English-language versions at that."

"They never satisfied me," she said candidly. "I was always striving for some higher plateau that I never reached."

The Führer looked into the fire for a moment. "I understand that. I once did a watercolor of the Karlskirche in Vienna. I was very disappointed with it. The original, the real thing, was far better. I had merely reproduced it badly, without my own interpretation. I went back and did it again, and this time I captured it in a golden pink light. I transcended my subject matter. I enlightened it!" He looked at her and sighed. "Unfortunately, I had very little money in those days. I did such a good job that my landlady took it from me for nonpayment of rent."

Surprisingly, she found herself being put at ease. It seemed the man didn't want to relate to her as a sex goddess at all, but rather as an artist. Somehow, his menace was temporarily removed.

As after-dinner cordials were served, a tapestry was suddenly pulled back to reveal a motion-picture projector, and another tapestry, on the opposite wall—this one depicting a hunt—was moved aside to unveil a screen. Marika's own name and face flashed across the screen. The film was *The Broken Thread.*

In the dim light of the room, Marika watched not the screen, but the Führer's face. His blue-gray eyes searched the screen with a kind of intensity she'd never noticed in a viewer before. It was as if this sentimental story of mother love held some powerful, secret meaning for him that probably would never be known to anyone but himself.

* * *

Days later, Hitler accused Austria of "treason to the race" and the German army marched across the frontier. In Vienna dive-bombers flew low over the city, as young Austrian Nazis tore down their country's flag for the blood-red banner with the swastika of the Third Reich. SS forces arrived in Vienna by air. Immediately they set out making arrests from a list compiled by the secret police.

Near the top of that list appeared the name of Walter von Menzel. He'd stayed in Vienna too long, almost refusing to abandon his film and, as a result, had to escape in the middle of the night through the frontier at Bratislava. In a six-wheeled black

Mercedes driven by an aging countess—von Menzel's first love—the car crashed through the German barrier at top speed into Czechoslovakia. Von Menzel escaped. The countess died of bullet wounds. In Berlin, Marika anxiously followed the news of the escape, and only when Peter informed her that von Menzel was safe in London did she breathe easily.

By that time, she was already at work on her next picture, *A Question of Love*. When she first received the script, filled with green-ink markings from Goebbels, she had feared it would be the most blatant sort of propaganda, but to her great relief there was none. The story dealt with euthanasia and had her playing a concert pianist in love with a doctor who is unable to stand seeing her suffer from multiple sclerosis and so performs a mercy killing. The picture seemed free of political implications.

Near the end of the shooting, Peter arrived on the set with a message that Reatha was in Berlin and wanted to see her. Marika's heart leaped. Weeks ago, she had appealed to Franz to obtain Lotte's return, and now maybe his mistress had brought some word with her from Vienna. Eagerly, she rushed home and that evening received a startlingly different Reatha. Unglamorous, wearing no makeup, dressed in a simple suit, she seemed to be downplaying her great beauty, hoping to call as little attention to herself as possible. Wasting no time on preliminaries, she asked if there was some private place where they could talk. Marika, too, sensed their need for secrecy—even though he'd betrayed her, she had been forced to retain the services of Herr von Schlabrendorff again. She asked Peter to play a gramophone record as they talked.

"I'm sorry," Reatha said in a low voice near Marika's ear, "Franz can do nothing to get Lotte back at the moment. This is Goebbels' pet project, and with Brigitte's complete endorsement there is nothing Franz can do."

Marika burst into tears, but taking her own handkerchief, Reatha wiped Marika's face. "Don't cry," she said. "That's no way to get back at the bastards. There is another way, far more powerful."

Marika stopped crying and looked deeply into the woman's eyes. A fierce determination burned there.

"Before he fled Vienna, von Menzel told me to come to you.

That you'd be willing to entertain certain suggestions."

A chill swept over Marika. "What does that mean?"

"I'm risking my life coming here like this tonight," Reatha said nervously. "Only on von Menzel's orders would I ever consider such a thing."

"Von's orders?"

"Exactly," Reatha said, lighting a cigarette and puffing rapidly. "I'm not in love with Franz. In fact, I despise him."

"What!" Marika gasped, too stunned to react any further. Then, "Why are you telling me this?"

"I was assigned to Franz."

"Assigned? I . . . you simply aren't making sense."

Reatha crushed out her cigarette. "I'm a British agent. I'm an American, but my first husband, an Englishman, got me into it."

Marika walked to the window looking out over the garden and pulled the curtains as if that would keep the sounds more carefully within the room.

Reatha came up beside her. "A war is coming. The greatest war in history. You're in a position to supply London with very valuable information and it's vital that you help us. You'll be seeing a lot of these monsters of the Third Reich. They like you, they'll flirt with you, talk to you. The most trivial thing said to you at a party could have important significance in London. If you found out, for instance, that von Blomberg was spending a quiet weekend with his family in Bavaria, that would mean—at least in wartime—that a massive offensive would not be launched just then. Do you see how important that is?"

Marika turned and grabbed hold of Reatha's arm. "I'm afraid. I don't know what to say."

"You can't say no!" Reatha exclaimed.

"But if I get any deeper into this rotten Nazi world, I'll be labeled for life."

"No, you won't," Reatha promised. "At the end of the war, when the Allies win, we'll clear your name, I swear it."

"No," Marika said, "If there's a war, there's no hope for Britain. Hitler's too strong. He'll take it all."

"Don't concede defeat so quickly," Reatha urged, gripping her wrists. "I'm a fighter. I've already started my war against the Nazis."

"You mean you go to bed with Franz every night and let him make love to you, and you have no feeling for him at all?"

"That's right," she said coldly. "You see, I'm an actress, too."

"The whole idea sounds so cold-blooded," Marika murmured. Slowly she walked to her bedside table and reached for some tablets. "The fact I'm in Berlin right now, making films for Goebbels is insane. My daughter's been taken from me. My life's already in jeopardy. I probably won't live to see the end of a war. My reputation! The fact is I no longer have a reputation to protect. Winchell and all the others have taken care of that forever." She swallowed the pills. "I'll do my part!"

* * *

Neville Chamberlain, a man described as looking like a Victorian bootmaker, went to Munich to meet Hitler, and, home again, proclaimed to crowds in London that the peace of Europe was assured for another generation.

In Berlin, *Kristallnacht* marked a reign of terror, as pogroms were launched all over Germany. Synagogues burned before cheering Nazis. Jews were murdered. The next day Jewish shop windows were nothing more than gaping holes and smashed glass.

As Peter fed details to Marika, she felt waves of shock and terror flow over her. "I knew he was planning it," she said. She never identified who the "he" was, and even in her own mind wasn't certain. "But I didn't know it'd come like this. So fast and violent."

That night only gave her more determination to try to do her best for Reatha and Britain. Actually, she didn't think of herself as an agent at all, but more as a kind of reporter. That was enough, but even that was difficult. Her power of recall seemed to be fading these days.

Every night now in the cabaret world of Berlin she openly solicited the company of Nazi generals, even Italian ones who flew in from Rome. She traveled in their circles and attended their parties, and the pictures the newspaper photographers took on these occasions started appearing in the West with increasing frequency. Getting invitations was no problem for Marika. After all, she was the reigning star of German cinema.

No matter how trivial it sounded to her, Marika turned over the information she gleaned to Reatha, content to leave it to others to make an evaluation.

"But I fear I'm learning nothing," Marika said. "I've hardly discovered any big state secrets."

"You give us plenty," Reatha assured her. "Just keep on as you are."

She came away from the premiere of *A Question of Love* feeling sick to her stomach, suddenly all too aware of the political implications of the film. It was an attempt to indoctrinate the German public into accepting the idea of exterminating the physically incurable or the mentally ill. It was painful to face the truth that she was part of such a machinery. At night, she lay in bed wondering, "How did I get myself into this trap?"

The following evening she had to go to the Chancellery for yet another showing of *A Question of Love,* and she steeled herself with all the strength she had left. Standing in front of the Chancellery's large window looking out over the snow that had blanketed Berlin that day, she felt the icy darkness of the city clogging her brain and all the events of the past months running together in a whirl of confusion. She shook her head to clear it.

Several young and attractive women were at the screening, but throughout the evening Marika kept her eyes glued to Ribbentrop, Himmler, and Göring, hoping they'd drop something she could use. Actually, she thought ironically, she was grateful to Göring. His doctor had made it possible for her to get through many a night. Eva Braun was nowhere to be seen and neither was Goebbels, which surprised Marika, since he'd even written some of the dialogue in *A Question of Love.* Maybe the finished product didn't appeal to him.

Hitler arrived late, and obviously in a jubilant mood, smiling, making jokes. His walk tonight was that of a much younger man, and when he kissed her hand in greeting, his voice was low and caressing. He stood beside her and together they looked out at the glittering city. Tonight, in his formidable presence, Berlin indeed seemed to be the capital of the world. If it weren't, she felt the Führer was determined to make it so. The nearness of him caused her to tremble.

"I've already seen your film once," he said. "I approve heartily."

She noticed that Göring remained at a discreet distance from the Führer, but that he eyed both Hitler and herself intently.

"Thank you," she said. "But I felt pity for the artist I was playing. To be killed by the man you love."

"Perhaps that's the greatest act of love in these cases," Hitler replied, excusing himself.

After the screening, an attendant invited Marika to the private library of the Führer, where she expected to be part of a small group, but to her surprise, she was alone. The very room seemed filled with a satanic darkness. Fortunately, she'd fortified herself for the occasion with two pills.

Hitler appeared at the door, issuing some whispered instruction to an attendant, and then turned toward her, smiling. "I liked the film even more on the second viewing," he said, slamming the door behind him. "It was planned for some time. Before her defection, Pola Negri was considered for the part, but I told Goebbels she was too matronly. She has none of your beauty—your blue eyes, your blonde hair."

"I'm pleased that you liked it," Marika said.

"Goebbels is preparing your most spectacular vehicle to date," Hitler went on in a satisfied tone. "It will deal directly with the Jewish problem."

Marika decided to be daring, fearing that she was perhaps being too weak in front of the Führer. She suspected he was the kind of man who could lose interest in a woman quickly. "I thought Kristallnacht took care of that," she said provocatively.

He raised his eyebrows and at first didn't say anything. Then he replied curtly, "I knew nothing of that," as if to dismiss the subject. "To the civilized world, we must have looked like an elephant in a china shop."

"It was unfortunate," Marika dared to say. "As artists, we both know Germany isn't a barbarous nation. Yet I fear the international press is depicting it as such."

Hitler's face softened. He didn't appear to understand her point, but the reference to him as an artist seemed to please him immensely, as she'd hoped it would.

"That night has forced me to rethink my position on the Jews," he said. He sat down on the sofa, motioning for her to take a position in a nearby armchair. "From now on, I don't think we'll officially label the *Mischlinge* Jews."

"The *Mischlinge*?" she asked hesitantly.

"Those who have only one Jew as a grandparent—at the most two," Hitler said matter-of-factly. "But who don't practice the religion and who don't marry Jews."

Marika grew alarmed. Had Goebbels told him of her own background? Was this Hitler's way of discreetly signaling her that she wasn't going to be branded a Jew in Nazi Germany? Or was the Führer trying to protect his own background? She'd heard rumors that he, too, might have a Jewish grandfather.

For a moment Hitler seemed lost in his thoughts, as he gazed dejectedly at the fire, his mind seeming to wander. "I will soon be fifty," he said, after a long silence. "I fear that's a dangerous age for a man."

"For a woman it's disastrous," Marika said. "But I don't think so for a man." Her voice was reassuring, saying what she felt he wanted to hear. "At fifty, a man can be at the very prime and peak of his life. In full control. Not a boy, certainly, but a powerful figure, nevertheless. At the high point of his creative power."

He got up and nervously started to pace the room. "It's the time for a man to make his greatest mark on the world, if he's going to amount to anything at all. After all, old age sets in from then on. It's never the same." He clapped his hands with a kind of raging impatience. "My birthday's coming up. That means 1939 will be my year of decision."

An attendant knocked discreetly on the heavy oak door and Hitler opened it, accepting a communiqué. He read it carefully, then stuffed it into his pocket, slapping his thigh in glee. "What perfect timing!" he said in an excited voice. She looked at him questioningly, but he gave her no clue as to the nature of his good news. For the last few moments, he'd been unaware of Marika, but now he concentrated on her intensely, as if something in the communiqué had renewed his own sense of manhood. "You're a very beautiful woman," he said. "I would say the most beautiful woman in all of Germany."

She nodded in appreciation, her face flushing red. This surprised her, since she was used to accepting world tribute to her beauty. Even though Hitler filled her with fear and she loathed his policies, she was immensely flattered by his appraisal. Maybe Peter was right. Perhaps her sex appeal was ageless, her face forever fabulous.

"What I like about you is that you've dared to bring out your potential," he said. "Although I'm perfectly aware the role of women is very limited in this society." He sighed. "I, too, must realize myself. Otherwise, I will betray myself as a man. If I don't redeem my promise, it will be as if I'd never lived at all."

* * *

Two days later, the Chancellery called again, at one o'clock in the morning, and Marika found herself being shaken out of her chair by a suddenly wide-awake Peter. With alarm, he told her the complete contents of the telephone conversation. Her presence was requested at the Reich Chancellery within the hour. A limousine was on its way.

Quickly, nervously, she dressed, letting Peter tell her what to wear. But she could not leave before she'd swallowed more tablets. "This could mean serious trouble."

"No, no," Peter said, trying to reassure her. "I suspect the Führer can't sleep and he needs a little entertainment. He did say you were the most beautiful woman in Germany. Which you are, of course."

"Don't be flippant," she said, wiping off all traces of her lipstick.

"Darling," he said, brushing her hair caressingly. "I don't envy you. Hitler's not my idea of a stud. I can't imagine how I'd manage under any circumstances to go to bed with him. Really, though, I don't think you have to worry. He's a neuter, I'm sure."

A knock came at the door, and, clutching Peter's hand one more time, she left with two SS guards.

Hitler was in his private quarters, dressed very informally, wearing chocolate-brown satin pajamas with a matching brown silk robe on which a swastika had been embroidered in black against a scarlet background. "Forgive me for not dressing," he said politely. "But I knew that with a woman of your stature I didn't need to adhere to all those time-consuming bourgeois conventions."

She smiled provocatively, wetting her lips. "I've certainly been unconventional in dress. As you know, I became famous by wearing almost nothing at all. Giving birth to Venus."

He said nothing for a long moment, only stared at her intently. "I did acknowledge that fact when I first met you at Brigitte's. It's strange that you should mention the film. I've had it screened twice for me tonight. As a film, it has its unfortunate episodes. But your appearance is sheer perfection."

"I'm in your debt for that compliment," she said.

He reached for her hand and let her to a seat on a nearby sofa, leaving her only to put on a Wagner record. "I'm playing a section of *Die Walküre* especially for you. Once it was the music that said what I couldn't bring myself to say." The sounds were soft and by the time he'd joined her on the sofa, his robe had come undone.

Her pills were beginning to take effect now, and she was no longer nervous, but as he sat down half-naked next to her, the awareness of the power of the man beside her came over her body like a shock. She sat up abruptly, biting her lips hard, as if that would muffle the sound of her own heavy breathing.

A breath came out with a rush from Hitler's throat. He was reaching for her, and she was aware only of the smell of the oil in his hair. It was unpleasant, but an odor she couldn't identify. His fingers fumbling across her breast and touching her bare arm were moist and heated. His breath tasted of mouthwash, and his moustache was damp as he kissed her. It was an uninspired kiss, the way Peter kissed her, lacking passion.

Suddenly, he straightened up. "I want you to dance for me," he said abruptly. It was almost a command. "Wearing the veil you wore in that film."

"But I'm not a dancer," she protested mildly, her face flushing.

"It's most important that you grant me this favor," he said, getting up and walking over to a closet. From it, he removed a white veil, a duplicate of the one she'd worn in Mario's film. How long had he been planning such an evening with her?

"I've been sitting here all night pondering the future role of German woman," he said, handing her the veil. She let it rest on her lap, almost afraid to touch it. "I'm convinced that you represent the change that can occur in European women."

"What do you mean?" she asked, her hands reaching out finally to caress the veil.

"You became known for your roles as a superficial toy, a plaything for men, all decked out in furs, jewels, and finery. But it was like a glittering husk. Underneath, and I'm convinced of this, rests the pure soul of German womanhood waiting to break out from the artificial overlay."

Her mind was too fogged to follow his point, and she watched and waited, her fingernails tightening on the veil. Then she remembered that in the rush she hadn't bothered to remove her red nail polish.

"I want the German woman of the future to be healthy and attractive, even pretty," Hitler went on. "But that beauty must be discovered in the deep resources of a woman, the way an artist finds his subject. Deep in her soul, the way da Vinci found the enigmatic loveliness of Mona Lisa."

"I'm not sure I have such depths," she said hesitantly.

"Nonsense!" he said. "To me, you represent the very ideal of feminine refinement. You had it in your first picture before the Jew, von Menzel, distorted your pure qualities into the *Carnival* harlot." He sat down on the sofa, giving her a friendly pat on the knee. "Please understand, I am not a puritan. Many of my colleagues are, but not I. In fact, I think certain restraints should be removed." He paused, eyeing her carefully.

She raised her eyebrows. "Which ones, for example?"

"Nudity!" he said. "I favor the celebration of the healthy body. That's why I want you to dance for me. When a German woman dances now, she seems to be courting favor with men, but I'm against that. I want her to dance from her inner core—graceful, poised, genuine perfection, not with the flash and noise of a beer hall!"

"You mean . . . like Isadora Duncan?" she asked hesitantly.

Anger flashed in his eyes, terrifying her. "No, no, no, I'm not talking about Communists!" He rose and began pacing the floor angrily, then, quieting down, replied, "You say you can't dance. That is false. Every person can dance if he listens to the choreography of his own mind."

She decided it would be best to simply give in. "Very well," she said slowly, "I will try it for you."

He seemed pleased. "Wagner, who has forecast the eternal destiny of our people, can be your inspiration. Just give yourself to his music. Let him elevate. Lose yourself—no, find yourself—in him."

In the anteroom, Marika felt almost in a trance as she removed all her clothing and softly draped the voluminous veil Grecian-style around her. It hid nothing when she moved, and she kept telling herself she could get through this bizarre performance if only she could blot out the presence of that man on the sofa, if she pretended she was dancing on a stage in a deserted theater.

She entered to the sounds of Wagner's music, and slowly began to move. At first her steps were awkward, ungraceful, but soon she turned inward, trying to locate some seat of primitive emotions that would stimulate her movement. As her initial hesitancy wore off, she began to feel her steps quickening, flowing, rising from an inner compulsion. Gradually the power of the music seemed to take over, to penetrate to her solar plexus, and she began to be one with the swelling sounds. Her movements grew lighter, the music less oppressive. Freed of restrictive clothing, she suddenly saw herself as a woman of nature, denying artifice, a spirit casting a spell of enchantment, as Venus herself might do. Like a sculptured figure, she was self-contained, floating in her own space, a feminine symbol traveling the universe. She was a child again, moving in a harmonious line and form, pure once more, running and skipping. Even though her body was untrained, it instinctively knew the course of its direction, and the way to express the subtlest of emotional shadings. In ecstasy, she knew she had truly discovered her soul.

And then the music ended. Abruptly, she fell back to reality, her head spinning, her lungs reaching for air. She had no finish to her dance, she was in this strange, dark room . . . and then she gasped in astonishment.

His robe removed, wearing nothing but his pajama bottoms, Hitler writhed on the floor, moaning and panting. "Kick me!" he shouted at her. "In my ribs."

She hesitated, her mind too hazy to comprehend.

"I deserve it!" he shouted. "My thoughts, my thoughts. I must have purification. Kick me!"

She knew at that moment that he was temporarily mad, but that it was the insanity associated with greatness. She'd had it, too. At times, she'd started to drift into space where behavior became compulsive, and then anything was possible, all demands were reasonable. Mustering all her strength, she pictured him as the embodiment of all evil, a corrupter of men's souls. She was Salome again, and this was her enemy, supine before her, begging to be punished. With her bare right foot, she struck out at his rib cage.

· 333 ·

Her toes ached at the impact, but she continued to kick him, stronger now, fiercer, almost oblivious to what she was doing.

Excited, agitated, gritting his teeth, Hitler finally collapsed with a sigh. That seemed to be her signal to stop. Falling back into a chair, she closed her eyes, disbelieving what had just happened, no longer sure of anything.

When she opened her eyes, she was alone. He'd disappeared soundlessly.

Walking over to the large windows and drawing back the curtains, she looked out onto the city of Berlin. Dawn was about to break, and off in the east, the sky was ablaze with a startling red glow. It was the Northern Lights. She held up her hands in the eerie radiance and the crimson hue of the light made them look bloody.

* * *

Soon after, Marika reported to UFA to begin work on her new film, and was disappointed to learn that Ritter had not been assigned to direct her. In fact, very little seemed to be decided about the film—she knew nothing about the script, the subject matter of it, or even the title—and all she could do was sit around for days, while people ran around her, assuring her that everything was fine, that Goebbels was simply making some of his last-minute, green-ink markings on the screenplay.

On the fourth day she was finally introduced to her new director, and, to her great surprise, it was a woman—Lale Wessely— who was almost as strikingly beautiful as Marika, but much younger. Deeply tanned from an Alpine vacation, she walked onto the set with an athletically masculine stride that bespoke complete authority, dressed entirely in white, from the white hosiery that covered her perfectly shaped legs to the wide-brimmed white felt hat that perched on top of her brown-blonde hair. Part Swedish, part German, Wessely, like Marika, was rumored to be Hitler's mistress, but Marika doubted that. This woman looked as if she could be far too demanding in her sexual needs to have them satisfied by the Führer.

Marika had heard of Wessely, of course, but this was the first time they'd ever met face to face. Wessely was the chief propaganda film director for the Third Reich. A former Max Reinhardt player, she'd appeared on the Vienna stage with Elisabeth

Bergner before the latter's defection, and then gone into a number of military farces and the inevitable popular mystery thrillers before graduating to a series of movies glorifying the athletic prowess of German womanhood. It was these films that had made her a star, but, finding herself increasingly dissatisfied creatively with acting, she had decided to turn instead to producing and directing. She had lost out to Leni Riefenstahl on the coveted assignments of filming the party congress at Nürnberg and the 1936 Olympics, but, soon after, Hitler had honored her with two other important projects. Her film, *Triumph,* depicted the arrival of the Führer's cavalcade into Vienna after Austria's incorporation into the Third Reich, and became a particular favorite of Hitler's due to its scenes of his triumphant entry at the Hotel Imperial, where as a youth he'd waited outside with a cold nose, shoveling snow and watching the aristocrats emerge from their limousines.

Her second film, *Kristallnacht,* revealed the reign of terror as the pogrom against the Jews was launched, and was now considered the greatest propaganda film of all time. By now, Lale had edged out Riefenstahl as Hitler's favorite filmmaker, and all her cinema had now become devoted to creating the myth of Nazi supremacy.

The director was at the height of her prestige when she confronted Marika that day, and Marika took an instant dislike to her —a feeling she was sure was reciprocated. The woman's formidable personality intimidated her immensely, but boldly she decided to strike first. "I can't work without a script," Marika said.

"I do not work from scripts," Lale told her. She still spoke German with a slight Swedish accent. "The script is always being rewritten inside Lale's head. That is the only way Lale works. Lale improvises, listening to her creative impulses of the day."

Marika found herself trembling under Lale's keen gaze, which seemed to be searching for flaws in her face. "But at least you can explain the role to me."

Lale smiled, but there was no warmth in it. "Certainly, you'll be playing the madame of a bordello, an outrageous flirt who often sings."

Not that again! "But Hitler doesn't want to see me on the screen as a prostitute."

Lale's face grew stern, enigmatic. "Lale is more in a position to know the wishes of the Führer than you are." She turned and walked away to greet Julius Streicher, the bald, paunchy Jew-hater. Marika stood a few feet away watching the pair embrace. "My dear Lale," Streicher was saying, "I've just read the script. With the making of this movie, you'll be assured immortality in film history."

Marika felt cold all over. Why couldn't *she* read the script? What was this hate-mongering Amazon doing directing her film? Pale, she walked back to her dressing room and surveyed her blotched, puffy face in the mirror. It looked so unhealthy compared to the radiant good looks of Lale. Maybe it was the pill habit, but her world-famous beauty mask was collapsing, like a scarecrow in the rain.

Later that day, Marika met a handsome young actor named Rudi Seifert, and quickly became friends with him, but she could not understand his inordinate nervousness. Then, shaking, the smell of liquor on his breath, he drew her aside and confided, "Nobody of any repute, except Wessely, wants to have anything to do with this film. I know you were coerced into doing it." He stopped for a moment to look around. "I even volunteered for the Army to get out of it, but Goebbels has obtained a document from Hitler saying that anybody who tries to avoid this assignment will be shot!"

"I don't believe it," Marika said. "For heaven's sake, will someone please tell me what this film is about?"

"No one knows, really," Seifert said. "But with Streicher acting as technical advisor, we know it has to be very bad. Everyone's afraid, Marika. Everyone." He grabbed her hand and then quickly walked away.

That night Marika telephoned Reatha in desperation, even though she feared her line might be tapped. But Reatha only continued to give her assurances. "You must appear in the film," she said. "You're now a part of the inner social circle of the Third Reich. Your appearance in the film will be a testament to your belief in the Nazi principle."

Her tablets finally brought sleep to Marika, but she woke up the next morning as troubled as ever, and in spite of Reatha's warning and her own better judgment, she confronted Lale on the set.

"Although I still haven't read this mysterious script, which you claim doesn't even exist, it is common knowledge that you're planning to make an anti-Semitic film. I must tell you this, Wessely, I don't think the cinema is the proper forum to attack any race, even the Jews."

Lale's eyes blazed, but she kept her temper under control. "That's ridiculous," she purred. "Regardless of what you've heard, we're not attacking anyone. In fact, we're following such well established literary traditions as *The Merchant of Venice* and Marlowe's *The Jew of Malta.* Interesting character studies, that's all. Surely you're familiar with those dramas, my dear."

"But I will not appear on the screen in any scenes that are anti-Semitic," Marika said, even though she felt how weak the ground was upon which she was standing. It took all her courage to stand up to Lale. Perhaps it was the false courage of the pills, she didn't know.

"You won't have to," Lale assured her. "Rest easy, Marika, we'll keep a close watch out for you." Marika didn't like the way her eyes glittered. "By the way, you're going to sing in this picture. I have just been given the music. It's called 'Lili Marlene.'" She thrust the music at Marika.

As the days went by, Marika became increasingly nervous and insecure on the set, and although she couldn't detect any overt bias in her scenes other than that her fellow actors were dressed as Jewish caricature types, she decided it was time she saw what she was doing. She demanded to see the day's rushes, claiming, "It's in my contract," but Peter checked and found it wasn't.

Furiously, Lale pounced on her. "I won't allow you to see one single minute of the footage!" she shouted angrily. "No one sees a Lale Wessely film until I've finished with it in the editing room. That's where I do my greatest work."

Through Peter, Marika filed a protest with Goebbels, having heard that the little propaganda minister was growing increasingly jealous of Lale because of her influence over the Führer. Marika requested to be removed from the picture because of ill health, but Goebbels sent word back to her that same day through an agent. "As far as I'm concerned, you're a soldier of the Third Reich. Soldiers must obey orders, not question them."

The atmosphere on the set remained highly charged. Lale never seemed to sleep, working around the clock, as if the film had some impossible deadline to meet.

"Yes, it does," Rudi told Marika. "I don't know why, but Goebbels wants the German public to see this film right away. It has something to do with the 'final solution' to the Jewish problem, whatever that means."

Again, Marika filed a protest, asking to be removed from the picture. "I fear my health is deteriorating daily," she wrote. Goebbels sent word back to her immediately, hand-delivered by an SS guard. "The Führer approves of your role—he's read the script—and wants you to appear in the film as a personal favor to him."

When she arrived home that night, a white sable and a diamond necklace—compliments of "A. Hitler"—had arrived from the Reich Chancellery.

In the final weeks of shooting, Marika found herself growing more and more addicted to her pills, and unable to remember some of her lines, even after Lale screamed them at her. Many times, Lale had to shoot around her to save time and money, but nonetheless the filming dragged on. Only one scene stood as a complete triumph for Marika. When she sang "Lili Marlene," some members of the crew actually wept. The song seemed to cast a mystical spell. Even Lale paid her her first and only compliment. "It will be the most poignant and beautiful moment I've ever filmed."

All this time, Marika had continued to insist on seeing film footage, and Lale had continued to resist her demands, but finally Goebbels interceded. Peter felt he only agreed to let Marika see it because he wanted to cast her in yet another picture for UFA, which was scheduled for shooting in just two weeks, but, whatever the reason, a rough cut arrived at last at Marika's town house.

Peter got out the projector. At her first appearance on the screen, Marika gasped and held her hands to her mouth, as if to muffle a scream. Under Lale's harsh lighting and unflattering camera angles, Marika looked grotesque, like a woman deep into middle age. Every line and wrinkle stood out in stark relief, and Marika's eyes, photographed, at Lale's insistence, without makeup, looked like deep, hollow pits.

The second shock swept over her when she saw how Jews were

portrayed in the film. True, none of her scenes were openly anti-Semitic, but many of the others were so revolting as to be considered pornographic. Now the plot was known to her. The bordello she was running catered to perverted tastes. In one scene, bearded rabbis sodomized homeless blond German boys, in dark shadows. Jewish butchering practices in the Warsaw ghetto were presented as brutally repulsive. Scenes of Passover celebrations and Talmud classes were made to look disgusting.

Long before the film was over, Marika collapsed. Hurriedly, Peter switched off the projector and carried her to her room where he summoned her doctor.

In the coming weeks, Marika refused to leave her bedroom and wouldn't even accept Reatha's urgent calls. She became obsessed with the upcoming release of the film in which she'd starred. Goebbels had already announced the title to the world—*Judes of Sodom*—and had begun to drum up big pre-release publicity for the film.

After its premiere in Berlin, newspapers reported that Hitler youths roamed the streets, attacking old Jewish men, burning homes and looting shops. Everywhere throughout Germany, the film provoked violence—and became a box-office hit. For the SS, the police, even the military, it was compulsory viewing.

When the film opened in the West, French partisans bombed the theater, and street fighting broke out between partisans and French fascists. No theater in New York would show the motion picture, but it was immediately labeled "the hate film of all time."

"Rudi is dead," Peter told her one morning. "A car accident. Perhaps he was murdered. Maybe a suicide. Who knows these days?"

"I know how deeply troubled he was," Marika said. "He was a haunted man."

"His secret is known now," Peter said. "He was married to a Jewish girl."

Marika was haunted, too, but the pills helped dim the memory of her appearance in the film. Her mind was becoming deadened. At times, recall became almost impossible.

As her days in bed passed, one after another, she began to listen to ritual sounds around the house—the old doctor getting up in the morning to make coffee for Peter, the maid entering her room, the telephone that always began its insistent ringing at nine o'clock each morning. But it was the sounds at twilight, the late arrival of the afternoon paper boy, the delivery from the market of tomorrow's supply of horsemeat, that comforted her the most.

The newspapers she feared most of all, especially those items from the West that were always being mailed to her. Peter tried to keep them from her, but one day she accidentally found his secret hiding place when he'd gone to UFA studios on an errand. The first item she picked up struck at her heart. It was in French.

"By appearing in the now notorious *Judes of Sodom,* Marika Kreisler has lent her great reputation, her world-wide fame as a cinema personality, and her prodigious talent, to what can only be viewed as an attempt to revile and destroy—indeed, to advocate genocide of—a race of people. It is clear she has become a prostitute of the Third Reich and that the name Marika Kreisler is one that will live in villainy."

She burst into tears. At eight o'clock that evening, she entered her bathroom, broke a champagne glass, and in a deliberate, careful move, began to slice her wrist.

* * *

This was how it stood in Europe: The Germany Army was in Moravia and Bohemia. Czechoslovakia was dismembered. In Spain, the war-weary Republicans had capitulated to Generalissimo Franco. Italian forces had invaded Albania, giving Mussolini an easy victory. Poland was clearly threatened by Hitler. It took no great foresight to realize the world was on the brink of war.

At Franz Hauptmann's château, Marika lay in the bed where she had first made love to Franz, slowly recovering physically from her suicide attempt. Her mental recovery, however, was not so good. In fact, her condition was deteriorating at a rate that alarmed both Franz and Reatha. Marika knew it herself, and didn't care. If she couldn't destroy herself physically, she reasoned, she could let her mind go. Perhaps then, and only then, could she find the peace for which she was so desperately searching.

That morning when Peter came to her room, she sensed an uneasiness about him she'd never noticed before, and knew at once something was wrong. "It's Lotte!" she said in alarm, forcing herself to sit up in bed. "Something's happened to her."

"No," Peter said, avoiding her eyes. "I get to speak to Brigitte once a week. She assures me that Lotte is all right, even though she won't tell me where she's keeping her."

"Then what is it, Peter?" she asked, reaching for his hand. "Don't try to keep bad news from me."

"*Liebchen,*" he said softly, "I've been drafted. Hitler needs young men in uniform to train for the upcoming war."

The room grew ominously silent as she stared into his eyes, as if not comprehending his words, then let her attention drift to the window. In the early morning light, the garden was peaceful, the birch trees swaying in the wind. But a birdbath had been broken by the winter ice, and no one had repaired it.

"I . . . I always thought you'd be with me." As unfair as it was, she felt betrayed by him. "Somehow I always thought you'd be with me forever. I know it's wrong, but I took you for granted. I shouldn't have."

He began to sob loudly and she reached to comfort him, her fingers digging into his back. "I'll return," he said. "I promise."

The dim light in the room seemed to be growing fainter and she tried to smile, but she knew herself how ghostly she must look. A surge of bitterness swept through her. "No, you won't come back. None of us will survive this bloody war." She felt caught in a storm now, a tempest reeling around her head. Though she ran in all directions, she couldn't escape the fury, and she knew she had at last been caught by a despair so deep even the tablets would not be able to erase it.

Peter was kissing her tear-soaked eyelids now, and she was running her fingers through his soft blond hair. A fatal tenderness seemed to exist between them, but neither one dared to give in to it. An overpowering emotion flowed inside her body, threatening her like a cloudburst, and, gasping, she was aware that if he were going at all, he must leave her soon. Otherwise, she feared she'd be torn to pieces.

Then he was gone, leaving an unbearable emptiness in the room. Weakly, she stood and walked to the window to watch him go. Swallows were flying about among the trees, and the first of the sun's rays were breaking through. She prayed he would look back and wave to her before getting into his car. At least that would give her a chance to see his face once more. If he didn't look back, she knew she'd never see him again.

Without looking back, he stepped into one of Franz's limousines. She stood watching the brown Mercedes disappear down the road toward the main gate. It seemed like a hearse, taking her Peter away from her.

* * *

That evening, Franz stood by her bedside, hands on his hips, looking stern, but his voice was low and soothing. "You really wanted to kill yourself?" he asked. "You weren't just trying to attract attention?"

She hesitated a long moment before answering. "Yes," she said weakly. "I wanted it to happen. It would have if Peter hadn't returned when he did."

"Then make it count the next time!"

"What do you mean?"

He joined her on the bed. "A suicide who's really serious will try again."

"I have such awful guilt," she said, burying her face in her pillow. "I can't live with it. Everything's gone wrong, and it's getting worse."

He placed his hand gently on her arm, above her bandaged wrist, and she turned over to face him, looking up at him through tear-filled eyes. "I feel so small and alone. Now, with Peter's going . . ."

"I know."

He got up and walked to the window. A fierce electric energy seemed to be flowing through him, as he paced the room, pounding his hands together. They were hard with his strength. "I must tell you something. It's most confidential."

"What is it?"

"There are people in Germany planning to assassinate Hitler before he launches us into another insane world war."

A silence came over the room. "But war . . . isn't that what *you* want? After all, you're getting rich arming Germany."

"That's true," he said, almost under his breath. "I've been a stupid, foolish man, one who wants to have his cake and eat it, too." Louder, he went on. "I wanted a fully armed and united

Germany. A strong Germany. But now I know—Hitler is insane. Imagine anyone thinking he could settle for merely Czechoslovakia. Poland won't satisfy him either. He's dreaming of Russia. Even Persia and India, the ancestral home of the Aryans."

She sat up in bed. "He wants the world?"

"I think he always did," he said. "Except I was too blind to see that. Not just to conquer the world and its people, but to exterminate all those who aren't good Germans. To obliterate all cultures except our own."

"That's absurd!" she said. "There aren't that many Germans to go around."

"Hitler plans to breed them."

"Like cattle?"

"Exactly."

"It won't work," she said. "Germany may be strong, but hardly strong enough to conquer the world. What about America?"

He sighed. "Hitler doesn't seem to think America exists, except in cowboy movies. His ignorance of that country is beyond belief. Even though we'll win many victories, we'll ultimately lose. As a munitions maker, I'll end up facing a tribunal as a war criminal. So will you, my dear."

She raised her eyebrows, not believing what he was saying. "You're exaggerating."

"You think so? Do you have any idea how *Judes of Sodom* is being received by the rest of the world?"

Not answering, not wanting to know the answer, she remained silent. So did Franz. She felt he was sealing her doom somehow, and she was preparing herself to allow it.

With a life of their own, her fingertips traced the soft, delicate flesh inside her thighs, feeling the mysterious life-flow there that was going to be shut off. The flames from the fireplace seemed to be moving inside her, jumping, dancing, burning.

Suddenly, he strode to her bedside and, stooping down, kissed her tenderly, passionately, then with fury, biting her lips. "What a waste! My little sacrificial lamb!"

She rose from the bed, standing before him in only her thin gown and bare feet. "I know what you're going to ask me."

His eyes were searching. "Can you do it? Do you have the courage?"

The life-source continued to surge within her body. But it was best not to awaken any such feeling. She had to go on into her sleep of the dead, the way she'd been for these past few months.

With a voice that seemed to come from her darkest, deepest recesses, she said, "I'll do it!"

* * *

At the Reich Chancellery, the sound of her high heels clicking against the marble floor as she walked behind the two SS guards almost hypnotized Marika. Her request for a private meeting with Hitler had been granted in only three days. Knowing what she was about to do had numbed her entire nervous system, like the shock of a gunshot wound.

Reatha had worked many long hours making her beautiful for this occasion. Her face had been very subtly but lightly made up, and they had carefully chosen a long-sleeved, beaded dress with a matching purse. In that purse was a gold-plated revolver.

Franz's decision, and the decision of his allies, had been their own. He still didn't know that Reatha was a British agent—or that Marika was one, too. Both women felt it was for Franz's own protection that he not know.

At the door to Hitler's study, his private bodyguard stopped her. That had never happened before. "Good evening, Fräulein Kreisler," he said, his eyes focusing on her beaded purse. "Perhaps you'll be kind enough to let me safeguard this for you." He took the purse from her reluctant hand. "That is, until your interview is over."

Her protest died in her throat and she was ushered in to see the Führer. He stood near a window, drinking lime-blossom tea, and she could see his hands were shaking, and dark circles surrounded his eyes. Marika's thoughts were frantic. Was the SS examining her purse right now?

Setting down his cup and saucer, Hitler approached her, bowing low from the waist and kissing her hand. No acknowledgment was made of their last meeting. Marika felt a desperate air of unreality about the scene. If everything had gone according to plan, now was when she would have assassinated him, then taken her own life. She'd been so confident she would succeed, she hadn't prepared for anything else.

"*Judes of Sodom* is a masterpiece," he said. "It succeeded beyond my wildest dreams. Your performance in it pleased me greatly." He took her by the arm and led her to a nearby sofa.

She could not bear to thank him for this compliment. "It seems to be doing very well at the box office," she managed to say. "You know an actress is always concerned about that, too."

"I'm going to leave orders," he announced, with triumph in his voice, "orders I'll bury in a time capsule. On the one-thousandth anniversary of the Third Reich, I'll command that *Judes of Sodom* be shown."

She shuddered at the prospect. "I've never photographed so matronly. I don't think your friend, Fräulein Wessely, is too fond of me."

"Yes," he said, smiling. "The jealousies of women. Perfectly natural."

An aide entered the room and whispered a confidential message to Hitler. Was he being told of the revolver? The Führer frowned at hearing the news, then he barked, "I won't see him now. Don't interrupt me unless it's a real emergency, not a manufactured one." After the aide had gone, Hitler turned to Marika and said, "I must think for all of Germany, do everyone's thinking for them."

She did not respond. The room was so dark she could hardly see his face, and outside a light rain was falling. A few embers from a dying fire glowed in the hearth. She was vanquished. She hadn't succeeded in killing this man. She'd killed before, but that hardly mattered—this assassination would have possibly saved millions of lives. No difference now. She sat, waiting to be apprehended. Why hadn't someone told Hitler about the purse? Why was she allowed to remain?

Hitler was talking about her again. "I'll make you an even bigger star," he announced. "We'll name a studio after you. You can pioneer the films I want to see made in the future." What an awful promise, she thought. Abruptly, he stopped and looked at her shrewdly. "You know," he said, "at this point I'm indispensable to the Reich. That's why we're taking all these extra security precautions." A sudden powerful blue light seemed to pour from his eyes. "All of Germany right now depends on my existence. But a stupid idiot or someone criminally insane could eliminate me.

Only I, alone, have the complete confidence of the German people. Only my ideas can lead them to the greatness they so richly deserve."

Mercifully for her, he was summoned away then to an emergency meeting in the winter garden. As she watched him take his leave, she thought how unlucky both of them were to be alive.

On her way out of the study, she requested the return of her purse. She was told it would be delivered shortly to her town house.

Outside the Chancellery, a limousine was waiting for her. In the cold rain, it, too, resembled a hearse, like the one used to carry Peter away.

* * *

When she arrived home, a black Mercedes limousine and two Gestapo cars were parked in her driveway. She felt suddenly cold. What had gone wrong? Getting out of her own car, she rushed to the foyer of her house and was met there by Doctor von Schlabrendorff, standing with two Gestapo guards.

"Countess Dabrowsky," he said politely, "your dinner is ready."

She eyed him coldly. "I'm not dining tonight. Why are these men here?"

"I fear," the doctor said, ignoring her question, "Madame doesn't have much choice in the matter." The guards silently backed up his intimidation.

Numbly, she followed the doctor to her dining room. There at the head of a candle-lit table sat Dr. Goebbels. In his fingertips he held a bullet. "The whole history of the Third Reich," he said, "could have rested on this little piece of lead." Standing up abruptly, he barked at her, "Sit down!"

Beyond terror at this point, she obeyed his command. Resting before her was a Meissen plate with what appeared to be her regular horsemeat tartar, along with a tulip-shaped glass and a bottle of champagne.

"I fear you've become somewhat of a social embarrassment to me," Goebbels said. "The Führer would be very disappointed with me if he knew how I let this situation get out of hand."

She had kept her coat on. The room was extremely cold for this time of year. Behind Goebbels, through the window overlooking the garden, she could see a full, brilliant moon. She seemed to be waking from one nightmare only to descend rapidly into another. "Am I your prisoner?" she asked stiffly.

"Indeed!" he said. "You must eat what is prepared for you." The propaganda chief slowly sipped his champagne, not taking his eyes from her. Two guards stood at the door.

She knew she had no choice. The horsemeat was obviously poisoned. This was not a dinner but an execution. Her time had come, and she couldn't do anything about it. Her life force surged within her, but she tried to quiet it. She'd wanted to die and now was offered the chance.

"I knew what you'd want for your last supper," Goebbels said. "Your diet of horsemeat tartar and French champagne is famous. But somehow it never caught on with your many imitators."

Goebbels smiled. She'd remember that face forever—except forever was here. Carefully, she began to eat the meat, slowly at first, nearly choking on it, but then devouring it with intense relish. It was as if she wanted to grind every morsel to bits, to extract the very last drop of the deadly cyanide. Between each mouthful, she swallowed champagne.

Suddenly, her head began to spin, and she rose and stumbled dizzily, grabbing hold of the edge of the table for support. Once more she gazed into Goebbels' smiling face and into his steely eyes, then she collapsed into Doctor von Schlabrendorff's arms. The tired old man dragged her from the dining room and into the kitchen. The SS guards moved to aid him, but he arrogantly motioned them away.

Minutes later, Frau von Schlabrendorff appeared in the hallway where an aide was helping Goebbels with his coat. "She's dead!" the woman reported, dropping her eyes. "She will be cremated according to your instructions."

Goebbels nodded his approval, then turned to an aide. "Get my office on the telephone. I want it to appear that we're trying to keep her death a secret. We'll let my contact in London slip the news to the West."

* * *

In London the BBC interrupted its regular broadcasting to announce a bulletin to the world: "The Nazi cinema queen, Marika Kreisler, collapsed and died at her town house in Berlin tonight. The cause of death is said to be an overdose of drugs."

· 347 ·

Book Four

1945

The chances of being discovered were terribly risky, but Marika had to get out of the house. Disguised by her black wig and sunglasses and wearing no makeup, she strolled the labyrinthine streets of Barcelona, watching faces, enjoying the noise and bustle. She'd gained weight. Catching her reflection in a mirror, she wondered if anyone who spotted her would ever know that the dumpy middle-aged woman was the once-glamorous Marika Kreisler.

As always, she was accompanied by Rita de Alba, who'd flown —at Reatha's request—to Warsaw after Marika's drugged body had been smuggled there from Berlin in 1939. Rita had written some of Marika's screenplays in the thirties. Now she was writing her life. During the past six years, she had become Marika's sole link to the outside world.

Only today Marika's name had been splashed across the Spanish newspapers again, another one of those endless stories of speculation about her fate. By this time, probably more had been written about her mysterious death—or disappearance—than about anybody since Amelia Earhart. The years, it seemed, had only increased interest in the legend of Marika Kreisler. The most persistent reports claimed she was alive and living in exile in Argentina, but many writers discounted such a theory, comparing it to die-hard speculation that Hitler was still alive.

Since 1939, no less than five women—amazing look-alikes—had electrified the world with the news that they were the real Marika Kreisler. "Who'd want to be me anyway?" Marika had asked Rita. "I have no country. I'm in disgrace. The victim of the most lurid speculation, the worst lies and distortions." Marika shuddered as she passed a newsstand advertising the Spanish-language version of the latest bestseller, *Marika and Hitler, Their Love Story.*

That Marika was alive at all was a mystery even to herself. All she knew was that after that fateful dinner with Goebbels, a mysterious person had either pumped out her stomach, or forced her to vomit up the poison in time to save her life. It couldn't have been Doctor von Schlabrendorff—he was a spy for Goebbels—but she had never been able to find out who it was.

Reatha knew the answer but had refused to tell. "I must protect the man who saved Marika's life," Reatha had told Rita when she'd telephoned her instructions to go to Warsaw. "If Goebbels finds out he was tricked, the man would die a violent death."

Although an eternal source of wonder, Marika suspected she'd never learn the true story of how she had made it out of Berlin that night. She knew Reatha and Franz were behind the plot to smuggle her body out, but who else was involved, or how they did it, might never be revealed. The cast was no longer around to tell stories. Reatha was exposed by the Gestapo as an Allied agent in 1943. She had been shot. That same year, Franz was implicated in a plot to assassinate Hitler. Franz, too, had been killed. On such fates, Marika and Rita speculated endlessly.

What was known was that Franz had placed her drugged body —in a state of coma—in a casket with air holes, labeled "M. Dabrowsky," and shipped it from Berlin to Warsaw by night train. Once in Warsaw, the aging Madame Dalecka had claimed the body. A militant Polish partisan, Madame Dalecka had been informed by Reatha that Marika was a British agent. And when, a day later, Rita arrived from London, she found an unconscious Marika in her former room at the Dabrowsky household, no longer a school for blind children. A full two months went by before Marika regained consciousness.

Quickly, using fake passports, Rita drove the semi-restored

...ика to Barcelona, crossing Italy and France, and avoiding all German frontiers. A German attack on Poland seemed imminent and Rita wanted to make sure Marika was safely out of the country before the Nazi invasion.

When Marika fully came to, she was hidden away in a Spanish convent in the Navarre district. Disguised as a nun, Rita hovered over her. Reatha had known only too well of Rita's passionate love for Marika, and since Rita was desperate for any role she could play in Marika's life, she was only too glad to return to her native Spain to live with the fallen star. Rita was useful for another reason as well. She had grown up in the convent under the direction of the Mother Superior, Theresa. Theresa was aging now, but she'd gladly provided a safe haven for Rita and her mysterious companion.

High on a hilltop, Marika had gradually come to life again. Maybe it was the sound of the birds that had done it, or perhaps it was one morning when she'd looked up at the stark blue of the sky. She'd had to learn to walk again, slowly, and had suffered frequent dizzy spells, but for the first time in her life she'd felt no pressure from anyone. If she didn't want to get out of bed, she didn't have to. She'd begun to enjoy the scents of the garden and had asked Rita to sit there quietly with her on sunny afternoons. Sometimes a fly would land on her arm, but she wouldn't brush it away. It, too, had a right to live. Everybody in the world had a right to life, but thousands were being denied it. Whenever such thoughts troubled her, she'd close her eyes and smell the eucalyptus.

As the war years passed, Marika refused to learn about what was happening. She couldn't stand talk about war.

Sitting in a café with Rita now, Marika found herself surrounded by the whores, pimps, and beggars of the Barrio Chino, but she enjoyed their company. In such a society, no one condemned her, no one made judgments. Rita had bought her some fresh flowers on the Ramblas.

As she held the flowers, she let first one drop, then another. At first Rita moved to pick them up, but then she settled back, sipping her espresso. She seemed to understand she was not to interfere when Marika descended into one of her black moods. The flowers dropping one by one on the floor were like the people in her life.

All of them, falling away, ever so slowly. Her dear Peter, reported missing in action on the Russian front. Her baby, Lotte, dead of pneumonia. Brigitte, killed in an Allied air raid on Berlin.

Two friends were left. The Contessa—she could be called a friend now—still lived in her villa on the Riviera. Through Rita, Marika had sent her a letter, assuring her she was still alive, and the Contessa, too old now to journey to Barcelona to see Marika, had immediately returned a badly scribbled note. "You'll live to be as old as I am. You're indestructible."

The other friend, von Menzel, had retired to a bungalow in North Hollywood. He was poor, unable to find work, and one day Rita brought Marika a movie magazine in which von Menzel had been interviewed. He'd told the press he was convinced "my creation" was dead.

Each day the Spanish newspapers were filled with stories of the Nürnberg trials. Some investigators firmly believed that the story of Marika's death was a hoax, that she was not only alive, but should be ferreted out of her hiding place and brought to trial for "crimes against humanity." After all, she was the star of the notorious *Judes of Sodom*.

Returning to Rita's house, Marika walked past Anton's room. Before her death, Reatha had smuggled Anton out of Vienna to Barcelona to be with his mother. Marika had once thought her son would be some companionship to her, but he wasn't. When he wasn't feuding with Rita, he'd leave the house late at night to go God knows where, becoming more of a stranger every day. During the day and the early part of the evening, he'd remain alone in his bedroom, playing one record over and over again: "Lili Marlene." It was the Marika Kreisler version which had become the hit song of World War II, both in Germany and America. Marika never understood why GIs wanted to hear her sing "Lili Marlene," in German, no less.

In the parlor, Rita poured a trembling Marika a drink, trying to reassure her. "The war crimes thing will die down, you'll see. Besides, you're innocent. One day your role in Nazi Germany can be explained. But not now. It would be wrong for you to appear. There's too much hate in the air."

Marika suspected Rita's advice, fearing the woman wanted to keep her a personal prisoner for life. At times Marika felt she should simply go to Nürnberg to stand trial, hoping to clear her name. "I can't even remember the damn film," she said in disgust. "I was too drugged at the time. I wish Lale Wessely had lived to stand trial. She's the one responsible. If only I had a print, then I would know what horrible crime I've committed against my own people."

Rita lit a cigar and stared long and hard at Marika, as if not sure whether to reveal something. In a voice, almost as quiet as death, she announced, "We have a print."

A chill seemed to pervade the air and Marika rose from her chair, her face flashing her anxiety. "What?"

"I never told you this," Rita said, getting up to calm Marika. Soothingly, she ran her fingers down Marika's face and neck. "But Goebbels sent a print of a film to this house two years ago."

"Goebbels?" she asked. The very mention of his name stabbed her heart. "He knew? He found out I was still alive?"

"Obviously," Rita said. "Even our address."

"I must see the film," Marika said, clutching at Rita's arm.

Rita gently kissed Marika on the lips. "I don't think it's right. I've never seen it, myself. Only the handwritten note from Goebbels. It was in green ink."

"What did it say?" Marika asked, removing a handkerchief to wipe her forehead. The parlor had grown hot, as hot as the office in which Goebbels had interviewed her at Obersalzberg.

Rita walked over to a brass chest and, opening it, removed a note. "I have it here. It's not something you throw away." Putting on her glasses, she read, " 'To Marika Kreisler. With my compliments, Dr. Goebbels.' "

As the film flashed across Rita's private screen, Marika knew immediately that something was wrong. The film had no soundtrack and the opening shot was of an empty room. Two SS men were bringing in a prisoner. It was a large man, completely nude.

"Oh, my God!" Marika screamed.

It was Franz.

The men were strapping him to a stretcher. Broken and defeated, his puffy face bruised, it was obvious Franz had been tortured. Then a doctor entered the room. For some reason, he ran his fingers through Franz's hair, almost the way a lover does, then he fondled his large testicles, the way Marika had done when

Franz had made love to her in Vienna. Abruptly, the doctor's face changed, growing steely hard and bitter. With deliberate surgical skill, he began to castrate Franz, taking precaution to prolong the act and the pain as long as possible.

In horror, Marika turned from the screen, her glass falling on the floor. Stumbling toward a sofa, she tried to keep her balance, but the world was going black. She collapsed.

She came to in Rita's arms, but in her concern for Marika, Rita had not turned off the projector. At first Marika didn't comprehend what had happened. The room seemed bathed in eerie blue light, marked only by the sound of the flickering film and Marika's heavy breathing. Sitting up, Marika made one horrible mistake. She looked up at the screen once more.

The SS doctor was dissecting Franz like a carcass of meat.

The gurgle that escaped from Marika's throat almost sounded like a woman's scream.

1950–1951

Her weight at its lowest point since 1929, Marika spent more and more time in front of her dressing room mirror. It was about time. Frankly, she'd never looked more exciting, with her exquisite profile and luminous eyes, her high forehead and bright red lips slightly parted and moistened. An autumnal mask of beauty, her face showed a strength of character it had never before possessed. Far from disfiguring her, her pain had given her an inner beauty and depth. Almost daily Rita assured her of that. Even Anton.

Sometimes she stood nude in front of an oval full-length mirror and carefully examined her body. Her legs were still shapely and her hands seemed to move in new and subtle ways. She felt she could use her entire body to convey feeling and evoke emotion on the screen better than ever. Turning from the mirror, she sighed. "What a waste!"

That night, loud music and laughter came from downstairs, and Marika muttered to herself, "Thank God Rita's not here now." Rita had left for the Riviera to visit the ailing Contessa and take care of her needs, and Anton had brought home a group of people from the Barrio Chino to have a party. That would surely have provoked a fight with Rita.

Curiosity drove Marika to put on her robe and black wig to go downstairs. It had been years since guests had been entertained at Rita's house, and Marika found herself nervously anxious to get a look at them. She wanted to see what kind of friends Anton had, but when she peered between the curtains into the dining room, she got quite a surprise. The room was filled with Spanish sailors and *maricones* in heavy mascara from the bars. One transvestite was actually hanging onto a sailor's neck, rubbing his chest, and unbuttoning his trousers.

"Quiet down!" she heard Anton shout in Spanish from a far corner. The music of "Lili Marlene" filled the room and the parlor went dark, safely concealing Marika. Apparently Anton had rigged up a spotlight, because just then it went on, shining down on him, bathing him in pink light. There, to Marika's shock, was Flame! Anton in costume was the perfect re-creation of the *Carnival* harlot. Cringing in fright, Marika felt as if she were looking at her younger self. It was ghoulish, as if she'd been resurrected from the grave.

Motionless, Anton stared at the audience, then swallowed, his throat pulsating. Slowly he raised his black-stockinged leg onto a chair and contracted his nostrils, moistening his lips and sucking in the air gently between his teeth. It was erotic, just the way she used to do it. He lit a cigarette in her own special manner, then sensually, carefully, blew out the smoke. A sailor reached for him, but Anton pretended to kick the man back with his high black heels, and the sailor fell into a nest of giggling *maricones* on the sofa. Then the room fell quiet again.

Very softly, with tenderness and feeling, the words of "Lili Marlene" seemed to escape from Anton's throat. The song filled the room with a deep, nostalgic lament, speaking of all our lost loves, our unfulfilled nights, our unrequited passions. In spite of the grotesquerie of the moment, Marika could only be awed by so masterful a performance. Each word seemed to spring from Anton's gut to find new meaning in the minds and fantasies of the audience. Anton was beyond imitation. Through some strange transmigration, he seemed to have become Marika Kreisler. And he was better at it than she was.

Tears streaming down her face, she turned quickly and half-stumbled, half-crawled in the darkness to the sanctuary of her bedroom.

Rita came back from the Riviera with gloomy news. "The Contessa can't last much longer." Two weeks later, however, the news was very different. Running into Marika's room, Rita thrust the newspaper at her, laughing and breathless. Marika turned away, not wanting to read of the latest atrocity to which her name was attached, but Rita vigorously shook her head. "No, no, read it. The news is fantastic!"

Marika read in disbelief. The British Secret Service had finally released heretofore classified documents revealing Marika to have been an Allied agent. It seemed von Menzel had been working diligently for years to have Marika's name cleared. The London office now believed that Marika had been murdered by the Gestapo on the eve of the invasion of Poland. With a flourish, the articles dubbed Marika "the Mata Hari of World War II."

"At last!" Marika said, sitting up in bed. "I can come out of hiding."

Rita suddenly appeared less pleased. "Don't be too sure," she said, pouring herself a brandy. "Once the idea you were a Nazi has been implanted in the public brain, it won't be uprooted overnight by an announcement on the BBC."

Excitedly, Marika turned back to the newspapers and discovered an item she'd missed before. Buried deep in the news of Marika Kreisler's rehabilitation was the announcement that after not having worked since 1937, von Menzel was making a comeback in Hollywood. He'd been assigned to direct a low-budget motion picture insiders already considered "the sleeper of the year," and filming had begun, with Barbara Stanwyck cast in the lead. Marika could only feel jealousy and a sense of wanting to be there, back in front of the cameras, more radiant than ever.

Two weeks later, she read that Stanwyck had broken her ankle on the set and had been forced to withdraw from the picture. All night she walked the floor of her bedroom. She didn't want Rita's advice, because she knew Rita would say no. Rita wanted to keep her in Barcelona, and Marika was itching to get out in the real world again. This cloistered life was slowly suffocating her.

By morning she'd decided what to do. After endless delays on the telephone, and much shock and disbelief from the operators, her call was finally put through.

"Hello," von Menzel shouted into the telephone.

Marika almost wept at hearing his voice again.

"Which imposter are you?" von Menzel asked sarcastically. "I think the official count now stands at thirteen."

At first Marika couldn't speak. Then she held the earphone close and in a groggy voice said, "Von, darling, it's really me. *I'm alive.*"

* * *

When her plane landed at the Los Angeles airport, a sea of humanity waited for the return of Marika Kreisler from oblivion. It was a colossal spectacle staged by Metro-Goldwyn-Mayer for maximum publicity.

Marika was totally unprepared for the fanfare that greeted her appearance. After having been in hiding all these years, she feared she could no longer handle the emotional experience, the jolting reality of facing such a huge crowd. But as she stepped off the plane, the noise and the people exhilarated her beyond belief. Striding to the terminal, she felt a myriad of flashbulbs explode around her, and suddenly there was von Menzel running up to her and kissing her. "You're more fabulous than ever," he cried. Ahead of her, some of her more devoted fans were throwing flowers, as police cordons held them back. In her white sable, Marika waved at the cheering throng. "Thank God," she whispered. "They still care."

In the distance, however, she could see trouble. Angry chanting could be heard and swastikas and large caricatures nailed to poles bobbed up and down, depicting her as a tramp in black stockings in the arms of Hitler. "We have to get out of here fast," von Menzel told her. "Protests have been pouring in all day. The police fear the demonstrators will get violent."

In the background, members of the American Jewish Congress had hooked up a microphone, and the booming voice of its speaker resounded throughout the terminal. "The Nazi fanatic, Marika Kreisler, isn't welcome in the home of the free. That supporter of the Nazi war machine, Goebbels's pet propagandist for genocidal pogroms . . ." The voice died suddenly. The police must have located the microphone.

In the heavy-security area of the terminal, Marika shook violently, even with von Menzel's arms around her. "I shouldn't have come back," she said. "They hate me."

"They're wrong," he said. "They're so wrong about you. It's just some nuts. Look, the rest of them love you."

Pitched battles were breaking out between the group hailing Marika and that damning her. Suddenly, the police cordon broke, and they were all about her, surging in on her, the hostile and the friendly crowds alike. She was separated from von Menzel and she felt someone pulling at her coat, yanking her backward. In a dizzy rush, she closed her eyes and tried to move through the space in front of her, but they wouldn't let her. They kept clawing at her, wanting a piece of her. Wildly, she started to strike out at the people surrounding her, as the police fought to keep them back, but in another violent surge, she felt herself falling to the pavement. "Help me!" she screamed.

Churning feet stepped on one of her white-gloved hands, and a large, heavy-set policeman fell on her body, protecting her from the blows. Her arm felt as if it were being twisted off, but she couldn't free it. Gradually her attackers were clubbed back, and above the roar of the crowd, the scream of an ambulance siren could be heard. It seemed to have a soothing effect on the crowd, and slowly the mob calmed down, sanity now prevailing.

The policeman's face was bleeding, and the blood dripped onto her own face, but still she clung to him, her blanket of protection.

"Don't be afraid," he said. "We got it under control. Know what? *Dishonored Empress* is my favorite movie."

* * *

The mob scene again made headlines for Marika, and it also seemed to unleash all the hostilities still harbored against her. The next morning Hedda Hopper led the attack, writing that Marika Kreisler "should be run out of the country, or jailed as a war criminal." Fearing a backlash, Louis B. Mayer forced Marika to grant an in-depth interview to Sheilah Graham before he'd allow her to appear in von Menzel's new film *Best Performance,* explaining, "This girl's tough, but she'll give you a fair shake. Just give her the truth and we should be all right."

That afternoon, Marika attempted to explain her role in Nazi Germany and to amplify on how she had worked as an Allied agent. "I was never a Nazi, never Hitler's mistress," she emphasized to a somewhat skeptical Miss Graham. "In fact, I'm a Jew!"

That exclusive rocked the country, and the next morning, Miss Graham's column was sympathetic to Marika, but ultimately it satisfied only Marika's most diehard fans. The rest of the press continued to dredge up stories, many of them unsavory, from Marika's past, and protests poured in from all over the world. Despite them, the studio ordered von Menzel to begin shooting, closing the sound stages to the public and clamping down tight security.

As the filming began, Marika could plainly see that von Menzel had aged a great deal, but that he was valiantly trying to rally his energy to direct this film. She knew, and she suspected von Menzel did, too, that this would be his final statement in motion pictures. It was widely known that he was suffering from a heart condition.

On her first day at work, a telegram was presented to her, one of thousands that had arrived at the studio. Most of them were being kept from her, but this one they particularly wanted her to see. From Mary Pickford, it read: "I don't think a star is really a star until she or he has lived through two slumps. When everybody says they're through—finished—and they come back twice, then they are stars." Marika broke down in front of her dressing room mirror, openly weeping.

In *Best Performance,* Marika was to play an aging actress going blind, her career faltering, her lover—who was also her director—leaving her for a younger woman. After a life of adulation, she was to be painfully stripped of the props which she'd used to sustain herself, and find that, though she had been able to face life as a star, she was not prepared to cope with what came afterward. "This role I can play," she told von Menzel.

He just smiled and kissed her on the nose.

"You have resurrected me from the dead," she went on. "I'll always be grateful for that."

"We'll see," was all he said.

That first week was one of the most difficult Marika had ever put in on a set. Without a word between them on the subject, they worked urgently to avoid the mannerisms and over-stylized acting that had made both von Menzel and herself victims of caricature. She had to prove all over again that she was an actress. He had to

prove to Hollywood that he was a first-rank artist who didn't need
to re-create the courts of Imperial Russia or put a blonde Venus
in white tie and tails for sensation.

The reunion was not always harmonious. After the third gruel-
ing week, Marika broke down for the first time. "You forget," she
screamed, "it's me! Me! Marika Kreisler! I'm the one who has to
appear up there on the silver screen. I might as well be a forty-foot
donkey prick the way you're directing me!"

An hour later he came to her dressing room for a quiet glass of
champagne, and they made up, neither of them wanting to discuss
their fight. Such scenes were not common, however, and before
the film had finished, word had traveled through Hollywood that
a great motion picture was being made. For Marika it was a mem-
orably gratifying professional experience. She knew she was doing
her best work, and as for von Menzel, it was obvious he'd learned
and grown from his mistakes, and was all the better for it.

"You've known what you wanted," she told von Menzel near
the final day of shooting. "You've known how to ask for it, and I've
listened and tried to deliver. Goddamn, did I try!"

He put his arm around her. "We're not quite there yet, and I
won't be sure until after the editing, but I'm convinced that no
critic is going to call Marika Kreisler a donkey prick."

At the end of the shooting, von Menzel came to Marika's hidea-
way in Long Beach for a final dinner together. Marika was planning to return secretly the next day to Barcelona, fearing she'd be
the victim of more violence if she remained in the United States.
The content of their dinner conversation had already been agreed
upon. They would talk about anybody and anything, but not about
the past.

The evening went well, fading all too rapidly, and it was three
o'clock in the morning before either of them knew it. As he got
ready to leave, von Menzel held her for a long time at the door.
"I don't know why it is this way. It's taken a lifetime to learn how
to do it. But once you learn, it's too late. Here we are, mature
artists at the peak of our power and creativity, but our reputations
will ultimately rest on what we did when we were children
trapped in our fantasies and illusions."

"I'll probably never work again myself," Marika said. "There
will never be another part like that one—I fear they only come

around once as the merry-go-round rolls by." She smiled at her words. "But at least Marika Kreisler and Walter von Menzel gave the world one final black valentine."

He said nothing for a long moment, only looking deeply into her eyes. "Marika," he said softly, almost under his breath, "we've become legends in our own time. Had I to do it over again, I would have spent more time fulfilling you as a woman and less time on becoming a legend."

"Dear heart," she said, taking his hand, "that is the kind of hindsight one has after a long, wild weekend. Monday morning has finally come."

He looked deeply at her one more time, then kissed her softly on the lips. "I know what time it is." He turned and left, shutting the door gently behind him.

* * *

Back with Rita in Barcelona, Marika was informed that Metro-Goldwyn-Mayer didn't want her to go on tour to promote *Best Performance.* "You're too controversial," Mayer wired her. "There could be trouble. Let's see what happens with the film."

What happened with the film was extraordinary. On the day of its opening in New York, lines formed around the block, a coterie of Jewish groups denounced Marika and organized a boycott, and a distraught voice phoned in a bomb threat. The threat proved to be a hoax, but it led to panic and the clearing out of the theater, which produced even more publicity. The next day, the reviews were almost unanimous: "A tour de force! Marika Kreisler has delivered one of the screen's most memorable performances. The queen of cinema has come back in triumph!"

As *Best Performance* played around the country, it continued to get favorable reviews—but the poisonous attacks mounted, as well. On the day that Marika heard of her nomination for an Academy award, she was also informed that various members of the film colony, led by Hedda Hopper, had launched a campaign to deny her the award. Such petty acts were immaterial to her, however. She was simply happy to be nominated, and delighted that von Menzel had also been nominated as best director.

Two weeks later, *Best Performance* opened in Berlin, and, feeling Germany a safer climate, the studio asked her to fly there to attend the premiere. Rita was adamantly opposed to her going, but Marika longed to see the city of her birth. There had been so many changes, she'd heard. Clad in her trademark white sable, she arrived in Berlin late at night under heavy police guard and, as her limousine sped through the familiar streets she'd known, she was shocked at the sight of the ghostly city in the moonlight. Berlin was like a prehistoric skeleton, its deserts of rubble still piled high.

"We've been very cold," her chauffeur told her. "Very hungry."

Her arrival at the airport had been unannounced and so there had been no crowds, but at the widely publicized premiere the mob scene was a familiar one. Once more, police cordons had to hold back the cheering crowds, as all of Berlin, it seemed, turned out to welcome its most famous daughter. Unfortunately, just as her fans were there, so, too, were her enemies.

As she stepped from her limousine, she was immediately hit with a rotten egg, and then a rotten tomato. For an instant, she froze, as the juice ran down her carefully made-up face, and then, falling back into the car, she was shoved to the floorboard. The door slammed, a police siren sounded, and the limousine pulled out, while memories of Brigitte flodded Marika's mind. She, too, had had her sable splattered.

"Nothing ever changes," Marika said, almost under her breath. Her police escort didn't understand and thought she was asking a question.

"The Nazis are protesting against you," he said, "because they feel you were an Allied agent, a traitor to your country. The Communists are against you, because they think you were a Nazi. You can't win in this town."

The next morning the police told Marika that all of her appearances in West Germany had been abruptly canceled. "We cannot subject you to such personal danger—not for a mere film."

Before leaving Berlin, however, Marika was determined to make a sentimental journey to the eastern sector. She'd been told that Friedrich's former town house was still standing, although it had been converted into apartments. At first she feared the Russians wouldn't grant her a visa, but after two days the Soviet Embassy agreed. Marika was only too aware of why the visa had come through. She was certain the Russians would publicize her visit as that of an ex-Nazi cinema queen come to view her home and gardens left over from the heyday of Imperial Berlin. Nevertheless, she was determined to go. She'd never come this way again, and it was important to her. The changes in the house would mirror the changes that had taken place inside her.

Under Soviet escort, she arrived at the town house. The gardens had been destroyed long ago, the statuary carted off, and as she stood in front of it, she recalled that the last time she'd seen this house was the night Goebbels had forced her to eat poisoned horsemeat.

Each floor had been hastily divided into four apartments, but one of the tenants had agreed to let Marika come inside, into what had once been the Kreisler parlor on the ground floor. There, seated in a corner, was the widow of Doctor von Schlabrendorff.

"I don't believe it," Marika said, taking the old woman's hand. "You're still alive."

"The winters are colder," Frau von Schlabrendorff said, "the bones a little stiffer. But I'm still here. What's left of me." Supported by a cane, the old woman slowly rose from her chair. "Come into the kitchen. I'll give you some chicken soup. It's not very good. I only had two chicken wings. But it's all I have to offer."

Marika sensed the woman didn't want to give her soup at all, but rather to tell her something, and as soon as they were out of sight of Marika's escort, the widow grabbed her arm. "It was my husband who pumped your stomach out that night when Goebbels was here. Goebbels thought you'd died, but my husband wouldn't let you. He told me, 'I brought Marika Kreisler into this world. I won't be responsible for her death.' It's true! He always was in love with your movies, even though he worked for the Nazis. But Goebbels found out. My man was killed."

Marika shuddered. "I never knew." She kissed the old woman on the cheek. "But I'll be eternally grateful to him." The Soviet guard suddenly appeared in the narrow doorway to the kitchen.

On the way out through the living room, Marika spotted Lotte's pedestal mirror resting on the old woman's fireplace. She picked it up and examined it carefully, her fingers lovingly tracing the design along the gilt. "This was my mother's mirror. I'd know it anywhere. The only thing she ever left me. I had it with me ever since I was a little girl *until that night.* I thought it was lost forever." She turned to the widow, her eyes pleading. "I'll buy it from you. At any price."

"No, you won't," the old woman answered. She pressed Marika's fingers around the mirror. "It is yours anyway. I was merely its custodian, waiting for you to reclaim it."

Tears ran down Marika's face as she left Friedrich's town house. She turned and looked back once more as her car pulled away. In a way she wished she hadn't. The paint was peeling, and the facade had been riddled with gunfire.

* * *

Marika's performance had awed Hollywood, but opposition in the industry still remained strong against her, and on the night of the Academy Award presentations, von Menzel phoned to tell her she'd lost to a young newcomer. Marika had thought it wouldn't be important to her, but she was surprised to find out how much she really did care.

Weeping, she fired off a telegram to the winner. "This was my only chance. You'll have many more chances. But you took my only one."

Rita was horrified when she learned of the telegram. "She'll release it to the newspapers. Wait and see." And she was right. Hedda Hopper devoted an entire column to it, but Marika didn't care.

Meanwhile, the ordeal of the past few months had proved too much for von Menzel. He, too, had lost the Oscar as best director, and one morning the Associated Press carried the story that he'd collapsed and died at his North Hollywood home. As Marika heard the news, she felt the room begin to spin and that familiar void came over her, into which she used to slip when pain became unbearable in the real world. She hoped she could stay long enough in this semi-conscious state to wake up and find that it was only a bad dream, and during the next few weeks, she kept having a fantasy that if she had been with von Menzel, she could have breathed life back into his lungs.

"Von Menzel is gone," Rita kept telling her. "You must accept that. He'll never come back." But Marika's dreadful agony persisted. Sometimes she'd scream out in her sleep. Anton was never at home anymore. He always seemed to be with his strange young men, so, for comfort, there was only Rita and, in some distant way, the Contessa.

It was another blow, then, when exactly one month after the death of von Menzel, Rita told Marika that the Contessa too had passed away.

"Oh, no!" Marika said, sitting up in bed. "The poor old dear." She sank down again. "You know, after all we went through together, I think I'd grown to love her more than I ever hated her. I'd so hoped she'd reach her goal of one hundred years. She deserved it."

The Contessa had left instructions that she wanted to be buried in "my beloved Tuscany," and, with Rita's help, Marika felt she was strong enough to make the journey there by train. Upon arriving in the Italian village of the Contessa's birth, they found themselves besieged by the old woman's relatives. The Contessa, it seemed, hadn't been an aristocrat at all, but a peasant, a girl who'd tilled the fields when young, then run off to seek her fortune. All her relatives felt the Contessa had become a woman of great wealth, and they clamored around Marika, anxious to share in the riches they were sure were theirs.

As the sun beat down, a rickety black hearse carried the earthly remains of the Contessa Villoresi de Loche down a dusty country road, the mourners walking silently behind to a tiny church. In her last will and testament, the Contessa had requested that gypsy violinists play "The Blue Danube," a tune she'd loved all her life, and Rita had arranged for it over the vigorous objections of the local priest.

Marika sat numbly through the ceremony, remembering the way the Contessa's gnarled, lined face had looked in her coffin. In some way she imagined that was what her own face would look like in a few years, and she was relieved when the service was over and she could join the cortege as it began its slow, sad march to the graveyard. Cows were grazing in the fields and the scents of summer, of renewed life, filled the air.

As the men began lowering the coffin into the freshly dug grave, the sky suddenly started to turn threatening, with dark clouds moving in. Marika tossed a white rose into the open grave as her farewell. "The Contessa was a true survivor," she whispered to Rita. "If I didn't always love her, I always admired her guts."

Lightning flashed across the sky, followed by lashing rain, and the mourners, Marika among them, hastened their steps away from the graveyard, to return to their lives.

For Marika, it was back to Barcelona and an uncertain future.

1965

Rita was dead now, but she'd left a small annuity, plus a four-room apartment of cluttered elegance in New York. At first, Marika had welcomed the freedom that Rita's death brought to her, but she soon realized that it was a freedom to do absolutely nothing. There was no one in her life, and at the age of sixty-five she was reconciled to the fact that there would never be anyone ever again. Rita had represented strong, solid support, but no matter how Marika tried or pretended, she had never been able to feel affection for the woman. She certainly couldn't have returned or matched Rita's passion.

Marika had spent a lot of time studying her face and the subtle changes each year brought. A mass of tiny wrinkles now, that face could still re-create the illusion of youth if she worked hard enough on it.

A few months ago, an event had occurred about which she still had very ambivalent feelings. One night, Anton had come home with half a dozen drunken American sailors in port for the night, and in a fury she had kicked him out of the house. She had waited for him to return the next morning, but he never had. The police suspected he'd been murdered, because Anton's nighttime activities were well known to them, and there was much unwelcome newspaper publicity for Marika, but after it all died down, she was quick to reconcile herself to the loss. The prospect of sharing a home with Anton in her increasing old age had filled her with no pleasure at all. Unlike the police, she didn't believe for a moment that he was dead. Secretly, she hoped that he'd run off with a wealthy lover who would take care of him and check his wilder impulses.

When Rita's lawyers finished settling her confused business affairs, they reported to Marika that back taxes and final settlements with creditors had left a rapidly dwindling cash reserve and recommended that she seek work to supplement her meager income. The prospect frightened her, as few moments in her career

· 368 ·

ever had. What avenue was left open to her? "The queen of the glamorous grannies," as one reporter had dubbed her, had no intention of abandoning her image to play character roles—or worse, monsters—on the screen, and she doubted that mother roles were her style. What was still available for her?

The answer to her dilemma came in the shape of Richard Michaels, an entrepreneur from a New York theatrical agency, who had Indian black hair and olive skin. Behind his good looks and easy smile was an impenetrable spirit, a man of nerve and wit, a professional capable of pulling off miracles in show business. The agency assigned him only the impossible cases—he'd staged comebacks for at least three fallen actresses—and now he wanted to try Marika.

She agreed to see him at her Barcelona home, receiving him in the soft, kind light of late afternoon, the setting always preferred by the late Contessa. She suspected he'd found a suitable film property which could be developed and tailored for her. Instead, however, she was astounded when he arrived with an offer for, of all things, a personal appearance tour in Australia, provided she could piece together an act in three weeks.

That night, at Los Caracoles, she sat with him on a narrow, cobblestoned street in the old quarter, joyously breaking her diet, eating a spit-roasted chicken and snails with too much garlic. With excitement, and apprehension as well, she listened as he outlined a possible "act." He envisioned it as a part-talking, part-singing engagement, a journey into nostalgia, with clips from her early films shown in rear-screen projection.

"But that's not growing," she protested. "It's not creative. It's cannibalizing my past."

"Why not?" he asked. "You need money. After all, it's your past, you lived it. Why not exploit it? Besides, I've already lined up the back-up people you'll need."

By the second bottle of wine, she had agreed, ". . . providing none of the film clips from my movies in Nazi Germany are used."

"But *Nana*?" he asked, smiling and taking her hand. "Surely, you'll let me use *Nana.*"

"Perhaps that one," she said coquettishly. "But only that one."

"You were never lovelier," he said. He paid the check and overtipped. "Let's walk home. The exercise will help get you in shape. The next few weeks will be sheer hell, and you'll need all your strength."

* * *

As her plane landed in Sydney, Marika noticed the people and turned to Richard. "We seem to be landing in the middle of some protest demonstration." Everybody in the world seemed to be protesting these days. She was only sorry she was right in the middle of it, fearing it would distract from her arrival. To prevent her total embarrassment, she trusted that at least a few members of the press had been assigned to cover her arrival in Sydney.

"I fear I'm yesterday's news," she whispered to Richard. "You can't disappear for fifteen years and expect to be remembered."

"We'll see," was all he said.

As she stepped off the plane, the screaming of her name greeted her like a gust of wind. Her vision wasn't all that clear, her hearing wasn't at its best, and her step was wobbly, but she was convinced that her name was what everybody at the airport was shouting. Hundreds seemed to be waving autograph books at her.

"My God!" she said, desperately grabbing Richard's arm. "They're here to see *me*. Me!"

"Of course," he said. "All your American movies have been re-released here. The Aussies love you."

Before descending another step, she surveyed the mile of faces below. Unlike her 1950 arrival at the Los Angeles airport, she sensed no danger from these people. She turned back on the steps and looked up at Richard. "I had to travel to the other side of the world to discover I'm still big!"

Standing on the stage, facing the live audience, Marika felt terrified, but slowly the warmth and enthusiasm from the people started to put her at ease. She opened with "Waltzing Matilda," and after that she could do no wrong with the Aussies. The roar of adulation following each number was enormous. "I can only sing about love," she called out to her adoring fans. "Something most of us don't have much luck with." And she sang about that love, and as she sang, her voice reflected its despair and its anguish, but in that shattered sound was triumph as well, the triumph of a woman who'd managed to survive without it.

The Aussies admired courage, and they stormed the stage when she finished singing her mandatory number, "Lili Marlene." Pro-

· 370 ·

tected by ushers, she blew kisses at her newfound friends, as the hoarse cheering and feverish applause reached a crescendo.

In Melbourne, she stood tall and straight, looking strong, and sang from her heart. Outside, hundreds crowded the sidewalks, unable to obtain seats, but wanting to get at least a look at the legend. Onstage, dressed in her feathers, sequins, and furs, Marika felt beautiful again, young forever. She seemed to hold an extraordinary power over her audience. They kept asking for more—and she kept delivering. When she ended the show by singing "Auld Lang Syne," many members of the audience were crying.

So was she.

That night Melbourne fans summoned Marika Kreisler back for thirteen curtain calls, and on the plane back to Barcelona, Richard offered some bluntly candid explanations for her unprecedented success.

"The wheel of fashion has turned full circle. Your outrageous mannerisms and crazy thirties costumes—they're back again. The public's hungry for that kind of camp."

"Thanks very much," she said.

"Let's face it," he went on. "There's tremendous public fascination with you, an almost morbid interest in you as a period piece. A broad still radiantly glamorous who's survived beyond her time."

"Spare me," she said.

He ignored her objection. "Those young fans flocking to see you, they don't give a damn about your role in Nazi Germany."

But others did still care. At home she learned that the original negative of *Judes of Sodom* had been discovered in a film studio in Prague, and been widely reprinted and distributed throughout the Arab countries. There, it was a box-office hit and Marika's lawyers told her to anticipate the protests pouring in again. She'd begun to despair of it ever being ended, when Richard took over. "Forget it," he said. "We know why you made that stupid film. You have no more time for guilt about it."

With Richard's help, she began at once to prepare for her American performance debut. Her act had been booked into the Hollywood Bowl.

"Can I face Hollywood again?" she asked Richard one night, almost desperately.

He grabbed her and kissed her passionately on the mouth. "You'll knock 'em dead."

* * *

Outside the Hollywood Bowl, a group of twenty marchers paraded back and forth, one of them carrying a sign: MARIKA KREISLER WAR CRIMINAL, but backstage all was festive. Richard reassured her, "Give them your best. Remember, this is the big one. They'll love you out there."

As she dressed carefully for her appearance, she cast her mind back to other times, other performances. She remembered her dance of the veils before Hitler, and even before that, when she'd rushed down the corridor of mirrors, her nude body flashing in front of Mario's camera. In the flesh she'd dazzled the infamous, and on the screen she'd shocked the world. "I can still do it," she kept repeating to herself.

Slowly, she began the laborious task of slipping into a flesh-colored body stocking. Made of a secret supportive fabric that not only held up sagging skin but prevented wrinkles, it finally covered her from her feet to her neck, and then her dresser slipped ice-blue satin slippers onto her feet and wide, blue-jeweled bracelets to her wrists. Around her neck went a heavy choker and a cluster of blue stones the color of her eyes.

As the stage lights at the Bowl dimmed, then died, a hush came over the audience. Suddenly, a pink spot shot out, and for one breathtaking moment only the face of Marika, stage center, was visible in the stadium. The applause was tumultuous. One by one, more lights came on, in front, to the side, revealing Marika wrapped in a flowing silk Picasso-blue cape, standing like a goddess in front of her audience.

The orchestra commenced her first song, and just then the intense stage lights in back of her flashed on, and slowly, her body swaying, she lifted her arms, daring to reveal her secrets to the world. Under her thin cape, she appeared stark naked! Shouting, screaming, her fans rose to their feet as flashbulbs blinded her. Even before she'd finished her opening number, "La Vie en Rose," photographers were working feverishly to print pictures of her in *that* outfit. Before morning, copies would be wired around the world.

Every seat in the house was booked, most of them by young

men who had bought up their tickets the moment they went on sale. Many had driven or flown in from San Francisco, Denver, even New York and Miami, especially for this concert, and Marika sensed she could do no wrong in front of them. These elegantly dressed young men in their mod clothing and fashionably long hair styles had adopted her as one of them. She'd been told that posters of her as Flame in *Carnival* adorned their bars, even their bedroom walls.

Just that evening, before going on, she'd been shown a wire by Richard. It was from a young man who claimed, "THE ONLY WAY I EVER GET LAID IS TO THE SOUND OF YOU SINGING LILI MARLENE. IT'S THE PERFECT RHYTHM I NEED FOR THE ACT. MUCHO THANKS."

Although she tried to play her act straight, she failed. Her adoring audience was only too willing to read sexual innuendo into every word she said. At the end of the show, handsome young men lined up outside her door and, gazing at them, she whispered to Richard, "My dear Peter has come back to me thousands of times." Richard paid little attention, being busy pouring free champagne for the press. The debut of Marika Kreisler in Hollywood was considered a world news event.

Later, she sat with Richard drinking the champagne herself as he switched on the NBC news. A toothy announcer was saying, "Marika Kreisler is a woman of the ages. She walked onto the stage of the Hollywood Bowl tonight looking as if she had the figure of a twenty-year-old. Underneath her transparent cape, she was entirely nude. Not bad for a woman born sometime at the beginning of this century. Reliable estimates place her birth date at 1896. Miss Kreisler . . ."

Marika got up and rushed to the set, switching quickly to CBS in time to hear, "Marika Kreisler is the queen of camp, the ultimate caricature of woman, the darling of the gay world." She turned off the channel and faced Richard with an almost accusatory stare.

"Don't worry about it," he said, pouring her more champagne. "In an age of total publicity, publicity is all."

Her second night at the Bowl, Marika was astonished to receive a personal invitation to attend a surprise premiere attraction on the Strip. The attraction was Anton.

After all this time, he had reappeared, opening in an act billed as "The Other Kreisler." A professional female impersonator now, he'd had plastic surgery done to his face—to judge from the glossy photograph he'd enclosed with the invitation—and he looked astonishingly like her. The picture was autographed, "With love to my divine mother."

"Are you going?" Richard asked, with too much eagerness in his voice. "This is *great* publicity."

"No!" she said adamantly. "Anton wants me to go over there to see him. A cheap publicity stunt. If he wants to see me—after all this time without a word—he knows where to find me."

"There's going to be publicity whether you like it or not," he said.

"I know that," she answered, turning her back to him to attend to her makeup. "If Anton doesn't see to it, you will."

The next morning she turned on her television set and there was Anton being interviewed on a morning talk show. He was dressed as Flame. Unable to look at him, she quickly flipped off the set. "Oh, God!" she cried out. *"Please."*

Because of the embarrassment Anton was causing her, Marika grew increasingly anxious to leave Los Angeles, and Richard began negotiating a world tour for her to include England, Denmark, France, Canada, South Africa, Brazil, Russia, and even a farewell trip to Germany. "But not Berlin," she said. "I'll never go back."

"Very well," Richard said, "but it would be sensational. After the world tour, I'll come up with something equally as grand for you."

"Just a minute, Duke," she said. "After two years on the world tour, and with the money I've earned, I'm going to retire. For good!"

"But I know of other ways to exploit your reputation," he protested. "Beginning with your memoirs. We'll get a ghost writer. Then a tour to promote the book, and TV appearances."

"There will be no memoirs," she said. "No one will ever know my story. I'll take it to the grave with me."

"I believe you will."

"You're right," she said. "If I can last for another two years, I've earned my final adieu."

1972

The Waldorf-Astoria was ablaze with lights as the leading members of the film colony arrived in New York to honor Marika. The fête was erroneously billed as "the diamond jubilee" of Marika Kreisler, due to a certificate someone had dug up in Berlin giving her birth date as August 29, 1897, but at this point she didn't care what age people thought she was.

"Age! Age!" she'd shouted at Ann Richards, the committee chairwoman of her tribute. "Why is it the whole Goddamned world wants to know how old I am?"

After a lifetime of lies, she could barely remember how old she was herself. "Always lie by decades," the late Contessa had told her. "It's easier to remember that way." Marika had taken that advice, and in the heyday of her film career she'd pulled it off successfully, but now everybody seemed determined to make her antediluvian. "I'll reach the grave soon enough," she once told a reporter. "Don't rush me."

Twice, Marika had stubbornly refused to attend the jubilee, afraid of facing a press conference and the harsh television cameras. She suspected the jubilee would degenerate into a spectacle at her expense. "I have a feeling," she told Ann the first time, "that most people will attend not to honor me, but to dissect me. They want to exhume the body, raise the lid of the coffin, and see how I'm enduring in my decay."

The next time, however, Ann prevailed upon the Mayor himself to go with personal greetings, and Marika had been so charmed by his good looks and smooth personality that she'd reluctantly agreed to attend the tribute.

Later, Marika told her: "It's hard saying no to a beauty. I'm sure you know how susceptible I am to a good-looking man. One look at the Mayor and I wanted to ask him where he'd been hiding all my life."

The Mayor had told her that a member of the President's family would be at the Waldorf-Astoria representing the White House. The British consul had agreed to attend in recognition of the espionage work Marika had done for Britain at the dawn of World War II. Even some of the leading members of New York's Jewish community planned to pay tribute to her for risking her life as an

Allied agent. It was belated recognition that she was one of their own.

On the way to the hotel, Marika found her mind still preoccupied by her cousin Heidi's disappearance. After that encounter in the shower, she tried frantically to locate her, but with no success. She knew she'd frightened the poor girl beyond belief, but she hadn't meant to. Heidi had misunderstood her intentions. If only she'd remained long enough for Marika to explain why she'd lost control that way.

She talked to the Mayor, trying to blot Heidi out of her mind. The whole incident was too painful for her to think about now. Maybe tomorrow she would be able to sort it out. If Marika tried hard enough, she could blot thoughts from her mind. It was an ability that had helped her survive over the years.

As her limousine pulled up at the Waldorf, the Mayor got out first and reached back for Marika. On either side the familiar police cordons held back the mobs of amateur photographers and autograph-seekers, but amidst the cheers and shouts some of the screams were hostile. Marika looked only briefly into one old woman's bitter, angry face.

"Nazi! Nazi! Nazi!" the old woman yelled.

"I love you! I love you! Love! Love!" a young man shouted at Marika. "You're beautiful!"

Forgetting the old woman's angry face for a moment, Marika blew the young man a kiss. He pretended to faint, falling back into the surging crowd.

Inside, the lobby was decorated with huge blow-ups of Marika in some of her more flamboyant thirties costumes, including one twenty-five-foot cardboard blow-up of Flame, but with scarcely a glance, she walked past them to the hotel's conference room, where, trembling, she faced the loud-talking, voracious horde of cameramen. The intensity of the lights blinded her, and she feared they shone right through all her artificial beauty devices. They were penetrating, revealing, and she'd wanted to stay hidden. Her sight had been failing of late, and behind the constant cruel popping of flashbulbs she sensed the reporters poised for the attack.

The first questions were mild, though, and easy to handle. "How do you stay so young looking? Who was the most important man in your life?"

"These are decidedly old-fashioned questions," she told the press. "I've heard them all before."

"How old are you?" one reporter asked pointedly.

She dismissed him with, "Just write I'm ninety-two and let it go at that."

"Kiss the Mayor," one of the cameramen yelled at her.

"Why should I?" Marika asked, with a hint of tease in her voice. "Why, I hardly know the man."

"Show us how those million-dollar legs are holding up, Kreisler," one of the photographers yelled at her.

"My legs are my fortune," Marika shot back at him. "I'm not giving away my fortune for free."

Suddenly the questioning in the room changed and grew more intense, as the first hostile notes surfaced. Marika felt her face flushing.

"Why did you make *Judes of Sodom?*" a TV news reporter asked.

"The question is idiotic," Marika said. "All *that* has been explained."

"I don't think the question is idiotic at all," the reporter said, pressing her. "The film is playing right now in Cairo."

She ignored him, but the jungle of microphones protruding from the overloaded lectern seemed to be moving toward her. Each one was a trap, waiting for her to make one mistake, but she would *not* give them the satisfaction. She regretted again her decision to come here tonight. Was it her imagination, or were they all moving closer?

"You're so youthful looking," a chic television reporter said. "Have you ever had plastic surgery?"

Marika glared at her, scornfully lifting her fingers to her ears. "Would you like to come up here and examine my hair and ear lines?"

"That won't be necessary," the reporter replied coolly.

The Mayor reached for Marika's arm, as if quietly offering his moral support, then leaned over and whispered to her, "You should have been there when I've had to face some of these guys. They like red meat."

A fat, hairy man with an obnoxious leer was edging closer to the lectern. "Tell us, Fräulein," he said in a fake, thick German accent,

"How was Adolf in bed? Is it true he had only one testicle?"

At first Marika stared at him, unable to believe she'd heard the question right, as the camera bulbs flashed and the Mayor's fingers tightened on her arm. A silence fell over the crowded room, and Marika felt faint, shaken, unable to reply. She seemed to be perspiring more heavily than ever and she feared her makeup would run if she didn't escape the intense heat. She imagined her artificial face running down her white satin dress like a river. The mask gone, the old lady would be revealed to the world.

Quickly the Mayor announced the end of the press conference. "That's it for now, fellows," he said. "We've got to go inside."

But the man's questions had released the jackals.

As the Mayor hurriedly maneuvered her through the room, she heard all the questions she'd feared:

"Were you Hitler's mistress?"

"Are you anti-Semitic?"

"Did you advocate genocide?"

"Do you consider yourself a war criminal?"

"Was Goebbels your lover?"

"Are you a lesbian?"

When she turned her head and ran from the room, some of the younger reporters booed her.

"Take it easy, guys!" a more tolerant voice cautioned.

"I need some fresh air," she said breathlessly to the Mayor. She could feel her heart pounding. Head spinning, she half-walked, half-staggered through a congested hall where television sets were showing her old movies. On one channel she caught a quick glimpse of herself in *Dishonored Empress*. On another she lived again as Flame in *Carnival*.

"It's Marika Kreisler!" a middle-aged man in the lobby shouted.

Marika held tightly to the Mayor. "It'll be much easier when we get inside the ballroom," he said. "There, it'll be strictly love."

"I hope so," she said. A feeling of terrible apprehension had come over her and she felt she was losing control. It was as if she'd slipped back through a magic looking glass. She was no longer herself, but a kaleidoscopic image, dancing and whirling in little pieces on the nation's television screens.

She stopped in the lobby and breathed deeply, and a reporter rushed up to her. "Several people have walked out on your tribute, Miss Kreisler," he said. "They didn't like the way you handled —or didn't handle—those questions. Before people are going to accept you, you have a lot of explaining to do."

The man's arrogance seemed to sober her momentarily. "May I have a cigarette?" she asked provocatively, wetting her scarlet mouth and deliberately slipping into one of her screen slut roles. The reporter seemed to be taken aback, but slowly he took out a cigarette and lit it for her. She puffed on it a bit, in the way she'd made famous on the silver screen, then carefully, purposefully, blew smoke into his face. The Mayor looked away in embarrassment.

"Don't worry, little man," she said to the startled reporter. "They'll come back." She walked a few feet ahead, then turned and murmured over her furred shoulder, "They always do."

* * *

As Marika entered the ballroom, a brilliant follow-spot illuminated her progress and the audience rose to its feet with enthusiastic applause. Marika was visibly shaking, but she tried to conceal it. Occasionally a familiar face from the old days in Hollywood could be seen, but for the most part the people at the tables were strangers to her. Endeavoring to keep a slight, seductive smile on her face, she strode to her table, accepting the cheers of the people around her.

Moments after she sat down, the lights dimmed, and clips from some of her most memorable moments on film started flickering on a large screen behind her, ending with her spectacular role as the fading actress in *Best Performance*. Of all her German films, only *Carnival* was screened, and she was pleased. It was better that way.

After the films, the tributes began and they went on and on, endlessly. She didn't even know half the people up there praising her. As the night waned, she became curiously removed from her own jubilee, as if she were looking over her shoulder at someone else. The legend they were describing had little to do with reality. Most of it, she realized, had been created by others, not by herself —by studios, the press, the fantasies of the public.

"There is no doubt," the head of MGM was saying, "that Marika

Kreisler will be with us forever. She is, after all, immortal."

"I'm not at all!" Marika whispered into the Mayor's ear. "And neither is that man."

Suddenly the toastmaster of the jubilee stepped before the microphone. "Ladies and gentlemen, I give you our fabled attraction of the evening."

The lights dimmed again and Count Basie's orchestra began playing "Lili Marlene." In panic, Marika turned to Ann Richards on her right. "You want me to sing?"

"It's okay," Ann said reassuringly.

Marika held onto her icy glass, as the spotlight focused on the velvet curtain. She sat as rigid as steel, feeling all eyes turned on her. For a moment, she closed her lids and listened to the music, trying to make herself feel emotionally detached, a spectator to her own appearance.

"We've got to get you backstage," Ann whispered in her ear, nudging her arm.

The orchestra began "Lili Marlene" again and the toastmaster announced, "Here she is, the Queen of the World." Shaking, Marika nevertheless managed to stride convincingly onto the stage, as the applause burst about her, wave upon wave of approval. She could see nothing, only the blinding, glaring lights.

Finally, her hand went up to quiet the audience. "Good evening," she said in a voice so often imitated that it, too, sounded like the imitation. As if aware of that, she added, "Tonight I give you the *real* thing."

The music started, and Marika began to sing, at first falteringly, then more and more confidently, as the familiar sounds came back to her throat. Alone on the stage, she concentrated on the loneliness and sorrow of the words, the frustration and hunger of love. Tears glimmering in her eyes, she wanted the world to see her, to understand. Her body was supercharged, and her voice reflected that.

The lights were brilliant, sparkling. She felt like a wanderer in time and space, dazzling the world but also dazzled by it. The more she sang, the clearer her tone became, and the more the audience felt her passion. She wanted to reach up to the sky, into the world of the stars, and hang there forever.

"Give me a rose . . ." she sang, and suddenly a rose was tossed to her. In spite of the blinding glare, she managed to catch it.

She was marching now through "Lili Marlene." Her voice sang of the eternal sorrow of life, the enduring pain of the rejected lover, the blind hope for a tomorrow that may never be fulfilled. At the end, she kissed the rose gently and wept.

Pandemonium broke loose. People were laughing, crying, applauding. Even those who'd come to deride were caught up in the spell. Critics and fans jammed the aisles.

"More! More! More!" the audience shouted.

"There isn't any more," she called back through tears.

"Then just stand there!" someone shouted.

"Let us look at you," came another voice.

She wanted to reach out and touch everybody, friend and foe.

"I love you!" she cried out to her audience and really meant it. "God bless and keep you. Good night! Good night!"

The orchestra was marching through "Lili Marlene" again.

Marika had her rose. She had her fans. It was good. Everything she'd gone through was worth it tonight. She was back where she belonged.

Marika Kreisler was going over the top again.